She was an extraor... decided.

For many years, Hugh Marshall's life had been business. If he appeared socially with beautiful women, it was because his business life functioned more smoothly. If he went to bed with them, it was to relieve certain requirements of body and etiquette. But his passion was reserved for business; and he had never found a woman he felt was capable of understanding and sharing his passion. Until now. Until Tyger.

She stood before him, waiting. He found his voice. "You'll have to handle the Paris negotiations with a firm hand."

"But we will get what we want, won't we, Hugh?" Tyger asked.

His eyes met hers. "I usually do." There was a pause. "I imagine you do, too." His voice was husky now.

Then, without willing it, he took her in his arms and pressed his mouth down hard on hers. Tyger gave a startled moan of pleasure. Hugh wanted this woman as much as he had ever wanted anyone in his life, but . . .

BARE ESSENCE

Meredith Rich

FAWCETT GOLD MEDAL • NEW YORK

To Jonathan with love.
To the memory of Jude.
And to Maureen Baron
whose guidance and good ideas
made this book possible.

BARE ESSENCE

Copyright © 1981 Meredith Rich
All rights reserved

Published by Fawcett Gold Medal Books, a unit of CBS
Publications, the Consumer Publishing Division of CBS Inc.

All the characters in this book are fictitious, and any
resemblance to actual persons living or dead is purely
coincidental.

ISBN: 0-449-14386-4

Printed in the United States of America

First Fawcett Gold Medal printing: February 1981

10 9 8 7 6 5 4 3 2 1

CHAPTER ONE

LIKE a flock of prehistoric birds, they floated down through the orange Aegean sky. Their heavy rotary blades caught the last rays of the setting sun as they landed on the glittering strip of beach on the island that belonged to Stephanie Rhinehart Toscani. Onto this makeshift heliport stepped the tanned and expensively sandaled feet of the rich and beautiful to whom this part of the world, on this particular evening, was the place to be.

Greek boys in white silk tunics dispensed crystal goblets of Dom Pérignon to the arriving guests. Bikini-clad Greek girls presented handwoven bracelets of tiny white orchids to the women and placed crowns of white tuberoses on the men. It was Stephie Toscani's annual white party, and many of the guests had spent weeks with their couturiers devising this year's fantasy in white.

A funicular railway stood by to ferry the guests up the flower-bedecked slope to the Hellenic hilltop villa. Tyger Hayes sipped her champagne as she rode with her escort, Wesley Graham, up over the colorful banks of poppies, primroses and lilies.

"What extraordinary flowers. She must have a hell of a gardener," Wesley said. "All the other islands around here are practically barren."

"They've all been brought in, every last flower," Tyger answered. "Stephie has them replanted three or four times a year. Different varieties each time."

The cable car arrived at its destination, and their hostess greeted them. Blond, elegant and forty, Stephie Toscani was the daughter of an American electronics industrialist and widow of one of Italy's most astute financiers.

"Tyger, darling. Don't you look marvelous! Divorce seems to agree with you, although I am sorry . . ."

"Don't be, Stephie," Tyger interrupted. "Jeff and I are both better off. It was a mistake . . . fortunately a short one."

"Now, Wesley," Stephie said. "You take good care of Tyger. She's one of my favorite people."

"Oh, I will, I . . ."

"I'm so upset with your mother," Stephie continued, turning back to Tyger. "She and Jimmy were supposed to be here. She never misses my parties. But I got a cable yesterday from Bobbie with a cryptic regret. *What* is it all about, Tyger?"

Tyger laughed. "Your guess is as good as mine. I haven't heard from Mother in weeks."

Another cable car rolled up behind them. "Oh," Stephie exclaimed. "It's Prince Johannes, and Consuela and Rudi Crespi . . ." She kissed Tyger quickly on the cheek. "I'll talk to you later, darling."

Tyger and Wesley walked across the terrace—which had been furnished for the occasion with two hundred white wicker tables flown in from Bloomingdale's in New York—to the enormous, white-pillared living room with its picture windows overlooking the sea below. Lute and lyre players, strolling among the guests, played Greek folk ballads. Over a hundred servants passed trays of hors d'oeuvre. Here, at least, a lapse had been permitted in the color theme—dark-green *dolmas*, flaky triangles of golden-crusted *spanakopita*, feta-cheese-filled *tiropetes* and other Greek specialties, as well as caviar, batter-fried garlicky *escargots*, and other international favorites. The bar was stocked with roditys and retsina, the resinous Greek wines, as an alternative to the endless supply of chilled Dom Pérignon which stood in glistening bottles and bubbled from a Baccarat crystal fountain centerpiece.

"Fabulous party." Wesley beamed. "Now aren't you glad we came?" They sat on the marble rim of a shallow pool where tropical fish darted among miniature coral reefs and water lilies.

"Yes," Tyger said. "Thank you, Wes." In truth, she was not glad she had come. The party, which must have cost Stephanie

Toscani upward of $200,000, was no different from any other, except whiter.

"You're the most beautiful woman here, Tyger," Wesley said approvingly.

"And you're the biggest liar." Tyger laughed, although she knew she could hold her own in this crowd of sparkling sybarites. Tyger was wearing a long white satin adaptation of a Greek peasant dress, with tiny sequins and hand-stitched embroidery. She had happened upon it at a boutique on the Via Veneto in Rome before joining the house party on Wesley Graham's yacht which had brought them to the Greek isles. Tyger's thick shoulder-length auburn hair, curly from the seaside humidity, was pulled away from her face with delicate pearl hair clips which she had found in a little shop on the island of Spetsai.

"You look straight out of a Botticelli painting . . . Venus on a seashell," Wesley said.

Tyger smiled. "Unfortunately I couldn't bring my shell tonight. Wouldn't fit into the helicopter."

Wesley glanced at his gold Patek-Philippe. "Time for the fireworks. Shall we go poolside?"

Tyger accepted Wesley's hand and allowed herself to be pulled up. "Let's detour by the champagne fountain and refuel."

The Olympic-size swimming pool was filled with milk, in celebration of this special occasion.

"I heard it's powdered . . . Carnation instant," Wesley whispered.

"No, no, it can't be. We're in Greece. It has to be pure, genuine goat's milk." Tyger giggled. "I wonder how many goats it took. . . ."

There was a hissing sizzle and multicolored starbursts of light streaked through the Greek sky, soaring toward infinity before diving, extinguished, into the deep salty Aegean.

Wesley took Tyger's hand. "Let's sit over there. Away from the masses." He led Tyger over to a stack of white satin pillows, piled up next to the Athenian-temple-inspired pool house.

"Hmmm, good idea," Tyger said, lying back into the cushions so she could view the skyworks without bending her neck. "This is extremely comfortable."

Wesley turned his back to the spectacle and looked at Tyger. "I know you've said you've had it with marriage, but . . ."

Tyger's eyes were still fixed on the extravagant fiery display. "But what, Wes?"

"Marry me. You know, it could work out quite well. We like each other. Neither of us wants to be tied down. But for the sake of society, we could . . ."

Tyger looked into the young playboy's pale-blue eyes. "Wesley . . . why on earth do you want to get married?"

"Well, you know my parents would die if they knew I was gay. I might be disinherited. If we were married, we could each go our own way and compare notes by the fireside in our old age." He smiled. "I think you're terrific. It could really work. And, who knows? Maybe we could even have a child. . . ."

"What? Artificial insemination, or would we really do it?"

"Oh, Tyger, let's not be disgusting!" Wesley laughed.

Tyger ran the back of her hand along Wesley's smooth cheekbones. "Oh, Wes, you know I like you. But I don't want to get married again . . . for any reason."

"Look, Mother and Dad adore you. They'd be so happy."

Tyger sighed. "I know, Wes. But would we?"

A tunic-clad Greek waiter appeared before them. "Miss Hayes?"

"Yes?"

"There is a telephone call for you. From California. Follow me, please. You can take it in the library."

Douglas Turner, senior partner of Wilson, Turner and Stieglitz, and executor of the will of the late film director Harry Hayes, greeted the three women solemnly as they entered his office on South Beverly Drive in Beverly Hills, California. Sophisticated and experienced as he was, these particular three women made him feel ill at ease.

"Lady Rowan," he addressed the attractive fortyish blonde. "Will you please sit here?"

"Of course, Mr. Turner." Bobbie Hayes Rowan, wearing a simple black Geoffrey Beene suit, smiled warmly at the attorney and sat on the tawny glove-suede banquette.

"And Miss Hayes, why don't you sit next to your mother?"

Tyger Hayes, still feeling disoriented from the combined effect of her father's sudden death and jet lag, nodded and sat quietly.

"Ah, Mrs. Hayes . . ." Turner focused on Harry Hayes's widow. "I think you will be comfortable here." He indicated a tan leather tub chair across from his desk.

"Thanks, Doug." Sherry Hayes, wearing one of her more

subdued outfits, an above-the-knee Jean Muir brown crêpe de chine chemise, sat back and crossed her long tanned legs.

Turner took his seat and glanced at page one of the will before him. He paused for a moment.

"Let's get on with it, Doug," Sherry Hayes said. "I have a hair appointment at three." The former actress looked at him with humorless green eyes.

"Of course." Turner could ascertain no sign of grief in her demeanor, but he had been around long enough to know that one hundred people facing the same situation would react in one hundred different ways. Some women enjoyed displaying their sorrow, others prided themselves in camouflaging it, still others felt nothing at all. Turner put on his glasses and began reading.

" 'I, Harold Allen Hayes, of Los Angeles, California, hereby make, publish and declare this to be my Last Will and Testament and hereby revoke any and all other wills and codicils at any time heretofore made by me. Article One . . .' "

Turner read the will without interruption. Hayes's fortune was to be divided between his widow and his daughter. Sherry Hayes was to receive his estate, Tularosa, and its contents, including the art and antiques, " 'with one exception,' " Turner intoned, " 'to be specified below.' " Tyger inherited Hayes's private film library and his stock holdings.

" 'Finally,' " Turner read, " 'to my first wife, Bobbie, now the Lady Rowan, I bequeath the one item she neglected to obtain from me in our divorce settlement: the kitchen sink.' "

Lady Bobbie laughed. "Oh, Harry," she said. "You would drag me halfway across the world for one last joke." A tiny tear glistened in the corner of her right eye. "I always said, Tyger, your father was the most impossible man I ever knew."

"Well, that's that," Sherry Hayes said.

"Not quite, Mrs. Hayes," Turner said. "The financial matters are somewhat complicated. Mr. Hayes's accountant has informed me of some rather unsettling news. . . ." Turner cleared his throat. "It seems that Mr. Hayes had dipped heavily into his own resources to finance his latest picture. As you know, his recent films have not been commercially successful. . . ."

"What are you trying to say, Doug?" Sherry Hayes interrupted. "How bad is it?"

Turner looked at the papers in front of him. He sighed. "Very bad, I'm afraid. The bank holds a second mortgage on

Tularosa, and . . ." He looked at Tyger. "Your father's stock portfolio is almost totally depleted. Then there are estate taxes to pay." He glanced apologetically around the room. "It looks pretty bleak."

"The condemned ate a hearty lunch." Roberta, Lady Rowan, smiled, and gave her order to the waiter. She and Tyger were having lunch on the plant-filled terrace of the Polo Lounge at the Beverly Hills Hotel, alias the Pink Palace, as it is often called by celebrity regulars and aspirers to high chic who eat to be seen, and paged.

"Don't joke, Mother. I may have to pay for lunch with these." Tyger fingered the gold coins dangling from her Bulgari necklace.

"Don't be silly, darling. Besides, this is my treat." Lady Bobbie looked at her beautiful daughter. "Anyway, you can't be as hard up as all that. Don't you have a trust fund or something?"

Tyger shook her head solemnly. "Daddy never wanted to tie up such a large chunk of money. Instead, he gave me a big fat check every year for my birthday. Which, as you may recall," Tyger said, "is coming up again in two weeks."

"Of course I recall your birthday, darling." Bobbie pushed a wisp of blond hair away from her cheek, displaying a Harry Winston square-cut diamond ring nearly the size of an ice cube. "June twenty-sixth. I was there, after all. Out like a light, thank God, but there."

The waiter set their appetizers before them and poured more of the chilled 1976 Chevalier-Montrachet into their goblets.

"What am I going to do? I was really counting on this year's check, what with the divorce and all."

"Aren't you getting enough alimony?" Bobbie raised her glass and toasted her daughter automatically. "Tchin-tchin."

"I'm not getting any alimony." Bobbie's azure eyes widened, and Tyger went on to explain. "I didn't want any. Jeff and I didn't have children. There was no reason . . ."

"I never took you for a fool, Tyger," Bobbie said dryly. "Now I'm beginning to reevaluate my opinion."

"You may be right, Mother, but I thought I had plenty of money of my own."

Bobbie sighed. "A woman can *never* have enough money. Besides, alimony is what marriage is all about. It's how you keep score."

"Well, it's all water under the bridge. The big question is, what do I do now?"

"Try a bite of my salmon mousse," Bobbie said, "and then rush out and get yourself another man."

Tyger laughed. "I don't think so. That's not what I want."

"What then?"

Tyger sat back. "I want to take control of my own life, for a change."

"How, darling?"

Tyger sipped her wine. "Well, for starters, I guess I could get a job."

"Doing what? Oh, Tyger, there's no job in the world more challenging than a new husband. . . ."

"And the best way to get ahead is to change jobs often?" Tyger smiled at her mother.

"Now, darling, don't be catty. Anyway, I'll be more than happy to lend you some money."

"Thanks, Mother." Tyger cut into her smoked brook trout with capers. "But only until I can find a job."

Bobbie shook her head. "You've always been headstrong, Tyger. Just like your father. No one can tell you anything."

CHAPTER TWO

THE minute she saw him she knew she wanted him. But first, she had to get the job. The rest, she hoped, would follow; at least she assumed it would. Tyger Hayes had a history of getting what she wanted.

"Tyger's not your real name, is it?" Hugh Marshall leaned back in his chair. His teeth were outrageously white, his lips sensuous, even when he smiled. He was smiling now. Tyger Hayes temporarily distracted him from dwelling on tomorrow's board meeting, and the inevitable clash that would occur.

"Mary Hilliard, actually, said fast—as if it were hyphenated. My father nicknamed me when I was well into the terrible twos. He said I displayed a ferocious temper."

"Do you still?"

Tyger shook her head. "At least I don't throw my porridge on the floor any more. I've still got the temper, but it's pretty much under control."

"So—now you're looking for a job?" He displayed his white teeth again.

"Yes. Do you have anything for me?"

"Maybe." The intercom buzzed and his secretary came on. "Excuse me," he said. "I've been waiting for this call."

Tyger resisted the urge to play with her rings for fear of appearing nervous. She looked around.

Hugh Marshall's desk was splendid, intricately hand-carved oak, almost too cumbersome for the spacious penthouse office he inhabited as president of Kellerco Industries, the spiffy new name for the conglomerate which had started out seventy years ago as the Keller Copper Company. Like the desk, Hugh Marshall himself was splendid. He had recently turned forty at a highly publicized gala at his ranch in southern Colorado. The Continental Divide ran right through his 200,000 acres, and since he had flown in two hundred friends and business associates for the fiesta weekend that made a thousand acres of room for each person.

Marshall was tan, from Colorado, perhaps, although East Hampton or Rio or Acapulco or a yacht sailing benignly around the isles could have been responsible.

Hugh Marshall's skin was alive, resilient, tightly stretched over his large features. The eyes were smoldering blue; there was no other way to describe them. Marshall was a man who belonged completely to his surroundings. A man in his position, with his looks, would belong anywhere.

The one flaw in his perfection was the slight limp Tyger had noticed when he greeted her. She remembered hearing about the accident a few years back. Hugh Marshall had been driving; his wife had been killed. The limp was the only external scar that remained.

Hugh Marshall put down the telephone receiver abruptly. "Sorry. Now, where were we? Oh, yes." His face relaxed again. "You asked Andy Parrish to set up this interview. Why do you want a job?" Andy Parrish was an old friend of Tyger's who happened to own the thoroughbred farm adjoining Hugh Marshall's in Kentucky.

"I want to work. It's time I got involved with something. I'm dissatisfied with my life. The biggest decision I have to make these days is what to wear, where to go, you know." She smiled. "I guess I'm a society cliché. But I'm damned well not staying locked into this for the rest of my life. I'm ready for a change."

"Then why don't you take up photography? Or skydiving?" Marshall couldn't resist the dig. All his life he had been around women like Tyger. Even his wife had been like her.

Tyger chose to ignore his implications. "I have. I'm quite a good photographer, actually. I've sold some travel photos to magazines. Skydiving scares the shit out of me. I hate heights."

Tyger leaned forward and looked directly at Hugh Marshall. "I know I have the sort of dilettantish background that

(13)

employers are bound to mistrust. But I have positive points to offer. I had a good education and made top grades. I've traveled everywhere. I know a lot of people . . . I have excellent contacts. I can make small talk to strangers. So, somewhere there must be a job for me. Life experience has to count for something."

There was an edge to Tyger's voice now, and she tried to smooth it over. She didn't want to sound desperate. She didn't want Hugh Marshall to suspect how badly she needed this job—and the chance to prove herself.

Hugh Marshall studied the young woman for indications of feline unpredictability, as befitted her name. Tyger Hayes exhibited none that were evident. He knew from their mutual friend Parrish that in years past she had been prone to erratic, if not wild, behavior. That was probably because, as the daughter of two famous people, she was trying to cop some of the spotlight for herself. At the moment, she appeared to be haute couture out looking for a job. She was wearing a fitted Oscar de la Renta eggshell linen suit with the jacket open, casually exposing a soft pink-and-black printed silk blouse. The accessories all mirrored her status: Maud Frizon shoes, Fendi handbag, a gold and green enamel David Webb frog bracelet with cabochon ruby eyes. For a touch of whimsy, she wore a tiny hand-blown Venetian glass vial with a small coral sweetheart rose attached to a gold chain around her neck.

"How did you survive growing up in Hollywood?" Marshall asked unexpectedly.

Tyger laughed, bewildered. "Why do you ask that? Oh . . . because children of celebrities are usually screwed up? Well, I'm as normal as the next person, whatever that means. Or doesn't mean." Tyger was not about to dredge up stories about her childhood. If Marshall was trying to get a fix on her she refused to let herself by typecast.

She switched tone. "Did you know my father?"

Marshall shook his head. "Harry Hayes? No. I used to know your mother, a few years ago. But your father only by reputation."

"Then you knew him. He was his reputation . . . I'm not sure which came first. I often suspect that he was born with his persona." Tyger smiled wistfully. She and her father had had their ups and downs, but she had loved him fiercely.

"Anyway," she continued, "he wouldn't allow me to become self-indulgent. He adored Katharine Hepburn. She was one of his favorite actresses. One of the few he also considered a terrific person. He did a couple of movies with her when he was getting started, and they became great friends. He used to say, 'Take a good look at Kate. If you can turn out like that you'll be okay.' "

Hugh Marshall stared at her with interest. "And are you like her?"

Tyger looked straight at him, then issued the merest inflection of a smile. "Of course. Carbon copy," she said in her best Hepburn imitation. "Just grew up in California instead of New England."

Marshall began riffling through some papers. His desk was cluttered, unlike the desks of many high-ranking executives. Tyger knew that he took his business seriously. Some people said that he was head of Kellerco because his late wife's grandfather, Samuel Keller, founded the empire. Tyger could see before her the evidence to the contrary. He worked obsessively, she guessed. He was not a coffee-table volume, pretty packaging of stale ideas.

His packaging was pretty, though. In fact, he was startlingly good-looking. It wasn't just the perfection of his features. There was a special quality to his expression, a lot of action going on behind his eyes. Tyger knew a great deal about him, mostly from friends. It was odd that in all her twenty-six years their paths had never crossed. How could she have missed him? There weren't many splendid men whom she had missed.

Marshall came up with a manila folder and pushed it across the mammoth desk to her. "I suppose I'll have to hire you," he said, continuing the thread of suspended conversation. "Hepburn would have landed the job. . . ."

"And wound up president of the company."

Marshall nodded, amused. "Look through this while I make a call. Then tell me what I'm looking for. If you know, there may be a job in it for you."

He watched Tyger Hayes as she leafed through the folder. She was actively beautiful, radiating an aura of inner energy. The green flecks in her large hazel eyes injected them with a slightly inquisitive look. Even in repose, her full lips appeared poised and ready to smile. He guessed she was about five feet eight. She was slim, with just enough meat on her, in the places that counted. He still wasn't sure why she wanted a job. To play at it, he supposed. She obviously didn't need the money.

While Hugh Marshall discussed with a colleague the fate of a subsidiary, the name of which was never mentioned, Tyger tried to make sense out of the contents of the tan folder in front of her. It was full of newspaper clippings. Most of them were from *Women's Wear Daily*. Reports of American designers, perfume ads, an article with an asterisk in the column next to the paragraph: "Fragrance growth will outpace cosmetics and toiletries over the next ten years. Today, fragrances are thirty-two percent of the industry, but by 1985, fragrance will reach thirty-eight percent. Designer fragrances account for nearly fifty percent of all fragrance sales." Another quote leaped out from the following page: "Currently forty percent of all fragrance sales are to heavy users."

Tyger chuckled to herself. Heavy users. A lot of the people she knew were heavy users of one thing or another. She wondered how many would jot down perfume on their list of addictions.

"I'm glad you're not bored." Hugh Marshall put down the phone and looked back at Tyger.

"This is good reading." Tyger smiled engagingly. "Anyway, from what I gather here, Kellerco is interested in getting in on the big profits of the perfume industry. It must be one of the few areas you haven't tapped yet."

Hugh Marshall nodded. "Go on."

"You're also interested in the young American designers, so you must want one whose name will be marketable on a bottle of perfume." Tyger could see from a faint smile waiting on the outskirts of his mouth that she was on the right track. "I haven't figured out one thing yet. . . ."

"What's that? So far you're batting a thousand."

"Do you want to buy a perfume company, or start your own?"

"What do you think?"

Tyger was beginning to feel pressured. Up until this moment the drift had come easily.

"Well . . ." She gathered her inner forces of intuitive conviction. "I suppose you want to start from scratch. Your own designer, your own line. Perfume—and, perhaps, eventually cosmetics."

"Behind that lovely face is a good sharp brain."

"Sarah Lawrence . . . Class of '74."

"Have you ever worked?" Marshall asked.

"Sure. Summer jobs at the movie studio, mostly as a gofer.

Running errands, getting coffee. I also modeled for a couple of years, before I married Jeff Collins. Then . . ."

"Duke Collins's son? You were married to him?" Marshall snapped his fingers with sudden realization. "Now I remember. It was one of the most lavish shindigs in the history of Beverly Hills."

"The wedding . . . not the marriage." Tyger was surprised that the likes of Hugh Marshall followed events and gossip. "It was a disaster. Talk about your psychotic celebrity kids. Jeff was headed on a course of early oblivion. I thought I could change him because we had a lot in common. I fancied I could straighten him out, but . . ." She stopped short. She wasn't here to discuss why her marriage had fizzled.

She changed the subject. "What about a job? I'm a quick study. I'm quite presentable. I'm willing to work hard."

"You'll have to give up three-hour lunches," Hugh said.

"I'll bring yogurt in a paper bag from home." Tyger grinned.

"No more sleeping in. If you're out dancing till four in the morning you still have to be at the office by nine."

"That's understood. Four a.m. weekends only. Look . . . I know I have to change my life around. The point is, I *want* to."

"All right." He buzzed his secretary. "Annie, send in Tim, please."

Within seconds, a calm-looking young Englishman appeared. He was introduced as Tim Yates, Marshall's assistant.

"Tim will brief you on what's happened so far. You have a freelance assignment. Pick the designer you think we should use. Do some research. Interview your friends, but don't indicate why. Right now, this project is top-secret. Come back in two weeks. If I like your report, then you get the job."

"I still don't know what the job is," Tyger said.

"Well, I hope you'll find out," Hugh Marshall replied. Tyger Hayes had a lot to offer, he had decided, if she really had settled down and was ready for a career. She was a trend-setter. Exactly the kind of person he wanted for the job he had in mind.

In the elevator, Tyger breathed a sigh of relief. She had a good feeling about this job. The interview had gone well. Tyger had been job hunting for the past month, but nothing had clicked. Now she knew that Hugh Marshall was the person she wanted to work for. If she had to work for a living, Hugh Marshall would make the work—and the living—interesting.

But she had to get the job. Marshall had given her a deadline of two weeks, and she had her own personal time limit. Her bank account was frighteningly low. Besides, her mother was due to blow into town soon, and she wanted to move and be on her own before then.

CHAPTER THREE

"TYGER, where are you? Can I call you back? I'm in the middle of a shoot. . . ." Jake Danton realized that he sounded frayed around the edges. He never allowed himself to seem more frazzled than that, although his insides were generally in knots while he was working. He had a reputation for relaxing his models, and mollifying art directors, fashion editors and any other agency people who were clustered around the set at his photography studio on any given day. Appearing calm and relaxed under fire had contributed to his commercial success, a pleasant accompaniment to his professionally polished talent.

"I'm calling from a booth at Fifth Avenue and Fifty-fourth. I'm on my way down to see you," Tyger announced.

"Great . . . fine. You may have to wait a bit. If you want to do something else and come later . . ."

"No, Jake, I'm tired. I'll just flop down on your sofa and read."

"Okay, great. See you." Jake whistled to himself as he headed back to the set. Tyger Hayes was his favorite lady these days. They had been seeing each other only a month or so, but he liked her a lot. Her candor about herself relaxed him, although there was still something she chose to keep a mystery which made her exciting to him.

Jake Denton's enormous loft studio was divided into two main sections: one for sets built for specific jobs, the other for more intimate close-ups. Today's ad was for an all-purpose cleaner. An immaculate half-kitchen had been constructed, dazzlingly white and shiny. Everything had been painted with polyurethane to give a high gloss that the product itself could never have produced. It was the ad agency's vision of the typical American kitchen—after the homemaker had shined her floor, scrubbed her stove, wiped off the counters, destained the sink and polished the chrome, all with the wondrous Product. This particular heavy-duty miracle cleanser was called Challenge.

Jake's assistant, Ellie Baerwald, handed him his Nikon. "Everything's ready," she said. "The art director's just given his seal of approval on the floor. We don't have to hit it with another coat of polyurethane."

"Great. We're almost back on schedule. Okay . . . places, everybody."

Tyger decided to take the bus down Fifth Avenue. Ordinarily she would have grabbed a cab, but there was no rush. The July afternoon was quiet, almost as if it were a Sunday. Tyger had never spent a summer in New York before. There had been speedy shopping trips in from Amagansett, or interminable layovers at JFK in between planes from Europe to California. But never an entire summer in Manhattan.

When she reached Jake's she climbed the three flights of stairs to his studio rather than wait for the elevator. Something, anything, to keep her muscles from atrophying. Even though she tried to swim or play tennis several times a week it wasn't like being in California. In New York it was a hassle to exercise. In California, it just happened—courts and pools were everywhere.

Jake was busy setting up a shot, but waved to her and blew her a kiss. Tyger recognized three of the models standing around with Ellie. There was a fourth whom she had never seen before. Tyger called out a general hello and went into Jake's office. It was cool, done all in white. The late-afternoon sun filtered through plants hanging in baskets at different heights in front of the windows.

Tyger took off her jacket, kicked her shoes across the room and removed her panty hose so her legs could breathe again. She flopped down on the sofa and let her head sink deeply into a Marimekko throw pillow. She drifted off quickly into a hollow afternoon sleep.

She dreamed that she was swimming in the Pacific Ocean. The house on the beach was supposed to be her father's at

Malibu, but it was completely different from the way it had actually looked. Tyger's dog, Wichita, who had died when she was twenty, came swimming out to her. The dog bit down on her arm, firmly yet gently, not breaking the skin, and dragged her back to shore. Her father stood and shouted, "Cut! Print!" Her mother was there, looking young and very beautiful. "Darling, you're better than Kate Hepburn," she said.

Tyger spotted Hugh Marshall standing at the edge of the crowd, which by now had turned into a huge Hollywood party. Hugh Marshall's denim-blue eyes commanded her to come close to him. "I want you in New York," he said. He kissed her passionately. The dream became confused, chaotic.

Tyger awakened to feel Jake's kisses on her eyelids.

"Don't wake up. I'd love to take you while you're asleep. I could pretend you're dead." Jake laughed and pressed his nose into her hair.

"Jake, why don't you just go take pictures of yourself naked until you come. I'm still sleepy," Tyger grumbled. She loved naps, and was grumpy when anyone woke her up.

"Dirty talk will get you everywhere with me," Jake whispered, "in a coupla minutes. The women are still getting dressed." Jake always referred to models as "the women."

Tyger turned on her side, facing the back of the sofa, and closed her eyes. "Wake me when they're gone. Just a few more minutes. Please."

"Oh, no you don't," Jake bellowed. He leaned over and began tickling her.

"No . . . no . . . stop! I mean it, Jake. I'm serious. If you keep tickling me I'm going to be very mad. I'm *serious!*"

Tyger managed to break away from Jake's armlock. She loathed being tickled. But it was difficult to get convincingly angry while she was giggling from the tickling euphoria.

She stood up, barefoot on the white carpet. Her shoulder-length auburn hair was frizzing out in every possible direction. Her skin glistened with perspiration from the activity.

"God, you look fabulous! Come out here," Jake ordered, rushing into the studio, grabbing a camera and switching the lights back on.

"Jesus, Jake, I don't want my picture taken."

"Honey, I've got to have you in this moment. You're incredible. If you were still modeling this would be the key shot of your whole book."

Tyger followed Jake into the studio. Three of the models called out their goodbyes and stepped into the elevator. The one whom Tyger did not recognize hesitated. She remained in the studio, holding a present wrapped in antique wallpaper.

"Jake?" she said. Her voice was accented, Swiss-French with a top layer of London English. She was blond, with a wide open face. "Here . . . I brought you a little present from Zurich. I went back to see my son last week. It's a cuckoo clock. It's to thank you . . . about the pictures." The model laughed to camouflage her slight embarrassment.

Jake beamed. "Thank you, love. A cuckoo clock is perfect for this place. Fits right in." He gave her a big hug and a kiss on the lips.

"You are so sweet," he said, brushing his middle finger lightly over the tiny freckles on the bridge of her nose.

Tyger came over and introduced herself.

"Oh, Tyger, I'm sorry. I thought you two knew each other. This is Astrid Batault, or simply Astrid to her adoring public."

"Hello, Tyger. I've read about you . . . in the gossip columns. And Jake has told me a lot about you, too." Astrid smiled, and checked the antique gold watch hanging from a chain around her neck. "Oh, I've got to go. I'm really late." She vanished down the steps.

Jake tore into his present like a greedy child.

"Don't rip the paper, Jake," Tyger reproved. "It's old, and lovely."

"I don't want it. Do you? I didn't think you were the type to economize by hoarding wrapping paper."

"Sure, I'll take it. Underneath the diamonds there's a soul of thrift. It's a great clock. Do all your models shower you with gifts?"

"Whenever they can." Jake laughed. "No, Astrid is really a nice kid. She's going to be tremendous. I took some shots of her that Eileen Ford loved . . . and that helped her get started."

"Have you slept with her yet?"

"Of course." Jake looked at Tyger. An afterthought took him by surprise. "You aren't jealous, are you?"

"No. I don't think so. I liked her. And I certainly don't have claims on you."

Jake walked over and stood in front of her. His hands began playing with her shoulders. "You have the best shoulders in the business."

"What business?" Tyger smiled seductively.

"Any business." His fingers were sliding down the front of

(22)

her pink-and-black printed Matt Phillips blouse, leaving an unbuttoned trail of exposed flesh.

"What about the photos, Jake?"

"The moment is gone." He bent down. His lips followed along the trail, then detoured off to the right in search of a nipple.

"I've got a great idea, Jake."

Tyger broke away and ran across the left to the sterilized set, removing the rest of her clothes as she went. Naked, she grabbed a can of Challenge, threw herself down on the spotless floor, and spread her legs out wide.

"Challenge will get anything clean. Buy it today." She winked into an imaginary TV camera.

Jake stripped and kneeled down onto the floor between her legs. "So clean I can eat off it." He laughed.

Tyger groaned, first reacting to the bad joke, then to the shivery tingles shooting from the center of her body. Jake always turned Tyger on. She liked him very much, but she was pretty sure it wasn't love. First and foremost, he was a friend. She could talk to him about anything. In spite of his life, and the beauties that surrounded him, he was very down to earth. He dealt with a full deck. He always said what he thought, and did what he said he was going to do.

Jake smelled as if he had just stepped out of a shower. He tasted clean, too, although he had been working for eight hours straight, photographing under hot lights in a loft too large to air-condition satisfactorily.

"You are one sexy woman," Jake whispered, kissing her belly. His tongue was frantically trying to decide whether to move north or south of her bellybutton. The phone rang.

"The service'll pick it up." He headed south. He loved women's bodies. He almost wished his own were one sometimes, to add to the total of breasts and clitorises in any given bed. He fancied himself a secret lesbian. Jake wanted every woman he could get his hands or lips or tongue on. He could be faithful in spirit to the woman he loved, but never faithful in body. Tyger understood that and she made no demands on him. He loved her for that. Always ready to get into the action of the moment, Tyger didn't fret about the future. She was involved with now.

Jake's tongue was flicking madly now, and Tyger moaned. The friction built. She thrashed, writhed, unable to keep still. Finally, a chain reaction of rapid explosions flashed through her, like a string of live firecrackers on the Fourth of July. She shivered, and sighed one long sigh.

Jake slithered up Tyger's body and pressed his chest against hers, rubbing his nipples against her taut, distended ones. He smeared his lips over hers, teased her tongue with his. He liked to eat a woman and then kiss her so that she could taste the delectableness of her own juices. Tyger loved it too, and she kissed him back hungrily.

Jake's prick was throbbing. "Oh, baby, let's go now."

He invaded her with force. Tyger felt as if she were leaving her body. Part of her floated up to the ceiling to watch the scene of the bodies gyrating greedily down below. Then flashbulbs popped inside her head, and an invisible suction pulled her back down the tunnel into her body. Her muscles were contracting with orgasm. Little screams from deep within her burst their way out.

Jake wound down, still on top of her. "Sorry, baby, that was quicker than I'd planned. I was overwhelmed. Some days I am just ravaged by your beauty."

Tyger smiled and kissed his nose.

Jake was like a lean panda bear. All the edges and angles were rounded just enough for him to be cuddly. He was wonderful to sleep with. He hugged and kissed and stroked Tyger all night, even in his soundest sleep. She wished they could drift off right now, but an uncomfortable sensation forced its way through to her consciousness. The hard floor, which had been cold, was now sticky with sweat and felt even harder.

Jake shifted to his side. Tyger's back felt raw.

"I've had a rug burn before. Linoleum burn is a totally new experience. Ouch!" Her back was stuck to the floor.

"Poor baby. I bet you've never done it in a kitchen in your whole life. Cook always around?"

"No fair, Jake. Of course I've done it in a kitchen. But on an oriental rug, not bare tile."

Jake groaned. "Oh God. Who else would put an oriental rug in the kitchen? Anyway . . . there's a nice cold bottle of Soave in the fridge. Let's have a few sips and talk about dinner. Or are you off to a charity do?"

"I've told you. I'm not accepting many invites these days. In my old age I'm settling down."

"You mean you're ready to get married again?"

"Cool it, Jake. Remove the look of terror from your eyes. I

said settle down, not marry. I've decided to move out of Mother's place."

"Why? She's never there. The rent's free. Are the servants cramping your style? They never have in the past." Jake brought Tyger a large forest-green bath sheet. He pulled on his jeans, and went to find wineglasses.

Tyger called out after him. "You know, in my whole life I have never signed my own lease, picked out fabric for slipcovers, or even bought a bed. It's about time, don't you think?" Tyger had begun to build enthusiasm for the whole idea. "Hey, want to come look for an apartment with me this weekend?"

"We're supposed to visit your friends the Hatchers in East Hampton, remember?" Jake handed her some wine.

"Well, I'll cancel."

"Fine with me. They're your friends. We haven't spent a whole weekend together—alone—since I've known you." He burst into song. *"Hot damn, summer in the city . . ."*

CHAPTER FOUR

"MR. Bachrach's here." Tim Yates's face tightened with suppressed tension. He dreaded the days Nelson Bachrach, chairman of the board of Kellerco, flew into town to inspect firsthand the wheelings and dealings of his empire. "Annie is showing him into the conference room. Unless you'd rather see him in here?"

Hugh Marshall looked up from the eighty-five-page report on the fragrance industry Yates had prepared for him. "No, Tim. Conference room's fine ... I'll be right there. Have George serve lunch promptly at twelve. Before that, Bachrach will have his two bullshots. Double on the vodka. Iced coffee for me. Oh, give him a copy of this perfume report. He wants to read it before this afternoon's board meeting."

"Yes, sir. By the way, Mr. Bachrach doesn't seem in good spirits this morning."

"When is he ever?" Hugh Marshall rolled the sleeves of his shirt back down, inserted his Cartier gold-and-onyx cufflinks, and slipped on the jacket to his Georgio Armani beige linen suit. He stood, let his neck drop forward and massaged it quickly with one hand, to release some of the tension. Then he headed for his confrontation with the only man at Kellerco who wielded more power than he did.

Nelson Bachrach checked the time on the wall clock against his Rolex. Eleven thirty-three. He hated to be kept waiting, and Hugh Marshall was three minutes late. Bachrach took it as another subtle indication that Marshall was getting too big for his britches. In the old days, men had respect for their superiors. Bachrach would never have kept Sam Keller, Jr., waiting, and they had been friends and colleagues for over forty years. Hell, Hugh Marshall wouldn't be where he was today if he hadn't married Sam's daughter Sarah. Sam and Sarah were both dead now, but Hugh Marshall remained ensconced in the presidential suite, still flaunting his Newport polish and Harvard education.

"Good morning, Nelson." Marshall smiled and shook hands with Bachrach, who looked crustier than usual this morning.

Bachrach was in his seventies, and age had neither withered nor mellowed him. He was tan, fit, and towered four inches above Marshall's six feet. "Who the hell hired that new copilot? He's too short. Doesn't look competent to me. The flight from Phoenix took twenty-five minutes longer than usual."

"Could have been headwinds, or air traffic. You know how jammed up La Guardia gets these days."

"No headwinds. No air traffic either, at this time of day. I make the trip three times a month, you know. His name's MacDougall or McIntyre, something like that. Get rid of him."

Marshall tensed his jaw. "Jack hired him. I gave him authority to choose the man he wanted as copilot. After all, they have to work together. Also ... Jack says the Gulfstream'll have to go in for servicing the end of the month. You want the Twin Beach for the trip to Alaska?"

"Hell, no. Takes too long. Rent another jet if ours isn't available. Anyway, I'm not here to talk about transportation. I want to discuss this perfume scheme of yours."

Hugh Marshall pressed a buzzer, and Annie Johnson entered with the drinks, and her steno pad.

"Do you want this conversation on or off the record?" Marshall asked Bachrach.

"No need for formalities. We're just going to get some things straight."

"Okay, Annie, that'll be all."

Bachrach shoved the report Tim Yates had given him down the conference table. It glided smoothly along the highly polished ebony, stopping just short of the edge. "We've been over this before, and you know how I feel about it. You seem determined, however, to have your own way...."

"Most of the other board members agree with me that a

fragrance subsidiary will be enormously profitable. Look at the figures in that report. Designer perfumes are the rage of the industry . . . Halston's now a twenty-million-dollar company. Retail perfume sales are in the billions, and the expected growth rate over the next couple of years is fifteen percent in the women's market, slightly higher in the men's. And it's all over the world, too." Marshall leaned forward in his chair. "You know, Joy sells for two hundred and thirty-five dollars an ounce in Arabia. The profits are astronomical! Kellerco can afford to launch a new subsidiary this year. I don't understand your objections. Over the phone, you said . . ."

Nelson Bachrach pounded his fist on the table. "Over the phone I said that I absolutely oppose Kellerco's getting into ladies' perfume."

"And men's . . ."

"Hell, that's even worse. We're a goddam copper company. Sam Keller'd turn purple over this if he were still alive."

"I disagree. Sam was for progress, and profits. Perfume's a big moneymaker. You know what it costs to produce a bottle of perfume? After you've laid out the costs for the bottle and outer packaging, shipping, advertising, overhead . . . and the fragrance itself at the start, you can still clear, oh, from six to ten dollars on every ounce that's sold. More after the company's rolling."

Bachrach pounded his fist again, this time on the arm of his chair. "Yes, but we pride ourselves on making good honest products. Technologically sound tools, business machines, and scientific equipment. You take us into perfume and cosmetics, the next thing you know we'll be making candy bars and baby clothes. We're an industrial company. If you want glamour, then maybe you're wasting your time with us."

Hugh Marshall seldom lost his temper. He prided himself on keeping his cool in the most adverse situations. But Nelson Bachrach was a pain in the ass, and had been ever since Marshall had worked his way up into the top echelon of Kellerco. Bachrach had insinuated for years that the only reason he had made it was by kowtowing to Sam Keller and marrying his beautiful daughter.

It was a sensitive point with Hugh Marshall. He was the first to admit that marrying the youngest daughter of the son of the company's founder was an asset. He also knew that he had worked to get where he was. Sam Keller, Jr., was not the sort of man to give anything to anybody, including his son-in-law. People had to prove themselves to gain favor in Sam's eyes. That's why he had put his two other sons-in-law, Ed Knickerbocker and Mark Halligan, in charge of subsidiaries, out of the way, in Chicago and Los Angeles respectively.

Sam Keller had spotted Hugh Marshall's energy and ambition when he first came with the company. Sam had told Hugh that he recognized some of his own drive in the young man who was otherwise his total opposite when it came to background and polish. Keller had been a mountain boy who grew up in the West, but his astute business calculations had turned the copper mine his father had discovered into a multimillion-dollar company. With the help of his son-in-law's keen insight for acquiring other companies, Kellerco was now rated among *Fortune's* Five Hundred, and grossed just under a billion dollars a year.

"This is pure folly on your part," Bachrach continued. "There's an enormous initial investment involved, and it's chancy. If you get the board's approval to go ahead with this division, I don't mind saying that I'll fight you every step of the way. We don't belong in the damned perfume market. If the company's a bust it'll be *your* head that'll roll. I'll see to it personally. . . ."

"I get the drift, Nelson. However, I think you're letting your personal conception of Kellerco get in the way of your usually unfaulty judgment. Shall we have lunch now and go over the rest of the agenda for the board meeting?"

By four that afternoon, the Kellerco quarterly board meeting was in full swing. The eleven members had flown in from all over the globe. No one was absent, a rarity. They were all eager to see the sparks fly between Marshall and Bachrach over the proposed development of Keller Perfumes.

Hugh Marshall sat at one end of the long table, Bachrach at the other. Marshall sipped his coffee and studied the faces of the men who would be deciding the fate of his project.

His face was calm, and his fingers rested carelessly on the handle of the coffee cup, but beneath the table his right foot tapped silently against the thick-piled carpet. And for good reason. The known votes, as they added up before the discussion, put him at a disadvantage. Ken Blalock and Andrew Starling were old cronies of Bachrach's, allies and friends from the early days of the company. And three others, Paul Freund, Michael Triplett and Sloan Drysdale, were younger men with clear-cut obligations and loyalties to the old chairman. They almost always voted his line, and there was no reason to expect any departure on this highly charged issue. On the other side, Marshall could count on only four votes. Dave Thomas, Arthur Beech, Jim Richards and Stan Marcuse owed an allegiance to him, and he had their assurances already on this vote.

This left the predetermined count at five to four against. And it made the remaining two votes crucial. Marshall knew he would need them both, but he had been unable to pressure a commitment out of either man in advance. Still, as far as he knew, neither had Bachrach.

The complicating factor about these two swing votes was the family connection: Ed Knickerbocker and Mark Halligan were Hugh Marshall's brothers-in-law, husbands of the daughters of the late Sam Keller.

"You know I've been in favor of wider diversification for some time. But perfume—I just don't know. It's not really the ballpark we've been operating in. But you say it'll work, Hugh . . . all right. I think we'll have to toss you the ball and see how far you can run with it."

Ed Knickerbocker puffed on his cigar. His face was red and bloated. His wife, the former Marcia Keller, old Sam's first-born, would not allow him to smoke at home. She fretted about his blood pressure, and constantly fussed over his health. He had become, for her, the child they had never been able to conceive. Over the past few years Ed had grown to despise Marcia, as well as the whole Kellerco empire. Most of all, he resented his brother-in-law, Hugh Marshall. Knickerbocker was in favor of Marshall's perfume project because, just this once, Marshall's previously unerring perspicacity might prove to be fallible. Seeing Marshall fall on his face would give Ed great secret pleasure.

Mark Halligan, Sam Keller's other son-in-law, spoke up. "I agree that the proposal has sound profit potential. But isn't it a little risky, Hugh?"

"Look at the figures in front of you," Marshall said. "Every new business venture's a gamble. But if you study that dossier you have to like the odds."

Halligan, who had skimmed the prospectus but understood very little of it, quickly agreed. "I guess you've got a point, Hugh." He was married to the former Carol Keller, and he spoke for her. Carol would much rather be sitting in his seat on the board, and, except for her father's male-chauvinistic view of women in business, she would be. She agreed wholeheartedly with Hugh Marshall about the proposed subsidiary. She, too, felt that it was time for some glamour products to be added to Kellerco's solid industrial lineup. Carol Keller Halligan knew that the value of her stock holdings had nearly tripled since Marshall had taken the reins of the company. Whatever Carol thought, her husband voiced. In this case, Mark hoped she was right. Perfume could push the company's profits higher. That would mean, since Carol had put a chunk of stock in Mark's name, that he could afford to tell her and Kellerco all to go fuck themselves in another year or two. He was tired of his life, and ready for adventure. He had already picked out a playmate to share it with. He would back Hugh Marshall one hundred percent. But if the perfume division failed and the stock plummeted, he would never forgive his brother-in-law. Nor, in all probability, would Carol.

Bachrach and his cohorts pressed their argument for another twenty minutes, but the issue had been decided, and they knew it. When the vote was held, Keller Perfumes became a *fait accompli*, by a vote of six to five. Hugh Marshall was triumphant.

Nelson Bachrach looked as if he had swallowed a sack of rabbit pellets. He confronted Marshall again after the meeting was adjourned. "Well, you pulled it off, but I'm not going to let you run down the field alone. If we're in this, we're in it together. This is one division that I'm taking a very personal interest in. I'll be in touch with you next week with some suggestions, after I've studied the fragrance industry in depth."

Hugh Marshall's face was expressionless, except for a bulging vein above his left eye which gave a clue to his impatience with his superior. He forced himself to smile, and shook Bachrach's hand. "Glad to hear it, Nelson. The division can only thrive with your attention."

"And don't forget about that damned copilot. Hire someone taller," Bachrach grumbled.

"My assistant has already taken care of it. Jack and a temporary replacement are waiting at the airport for you now. And we've got a Falcon 50 to take you to Alaska next week. Hope the salmon are biting."

The smile had melted from Marshall's lips by the time he turned away from Bachrach. He had won the first victory, but he knew that Bachrach was out to see that battle was continuous. Keller Perfumes should be his easiest challenge to date, but it wouldn't be. There were too many barracudas in his wake, just biding their time until he made a mistake. Not that this was anything new to Hugh Marshall. All in all, he was pleased with the outcome of the day.

"Winner by a knockout," Tim Yates exulted as they walked back to Hugh Marshall's office.

"By a decision, Tim," Marshall cautioned. "And a damned split one at that. Besides, this was just round one. Nelson Bachrach isn't a man who knows how to lose."

"What do you mean, Mr. Marshall?"

"I don't know. But Bachrach's 'personal interest' is likely to mean problems for us. I've got a feeling that he plans to make things tough."

"Do you have any idea what he has in mind?"

"Could be any of a number of things: budget snafus, personnel shifts—we'll have to wait and see. And cope as things come up."

When Tim Yates left, Marshall poured himself a scotch and took a deep breath, as if to expel the drama of the past few hours. The photograph of Sarah with their two children, Angus and Leslie, smiled up at him from a silver frame on the desk. Sarah had died five years ago today. It was strange what time did to one's perceptions. Hugh Marshall remembered Sarah now more through Leslie, who was eight and the image of her mother in looks and personality.

Marshall sipped his drink and wondered what it would be like now if Sarah were alive. Would they be divorced? She had resented his ambition. He was cut from the same mold as her father, and that had both attracted and repelled her. Marshall couldn't help what he was, but he knew he had left her alone too much, and they had grown apart in the last two or three years before her death.

A few times Sarah had tried to take an interest in the business. She would ask Hugh what was going on and he would sit down and explain patiently all the intricacies behind the Keller corporate empire. At these moments he felt close to Sarah, as if they were on the verge of a breakthrough. Then he would see her eyes glaze over and she would silently begin arranging the objects on the coffee table.

As the years of their marriage went by, and the children were born, Sarah stopped asking Hugh anything at all about the business and his life. The children were all they shared in common.

Once the mourning period for Sarah was over, Hugh became in great demand as an escort to the world's rich, beautiful, desirable women. He knew there was much speculation about when he would remarry, to provide a mother for his children. Everyone said that it was because he loved Sarah so much that he couldn't marry again.

But it was the experience with Sarah that had soured him on marriage. Most of the women he took out were just like Sarah. He longed for a woman he could talk to, whose eyes wouldn't go blank when he brought up business. He wanted a woman who would understand his needs, and accept them, a woman who would share all the private moments of his life that he had grown used to keeping within himself.

Picking up Sarah's photograph, he dusted it off with his elbow. He remembered how he had felt about her when they first met, in 1963.

Sam Keller drove. The car was a two-toned 1953 Oldsmobile; Keller did not believe in "buying a new car every year just to show some goddam fool I can afford it. If anyone thinks I can't, he's a bigger fool than he's got any right to be." Hugh Marshall, sitting beside him, did not question that his employer could afford anything he wanted. What amazed him was that any car piloted by Sam Keller could survive one year, much less ten.

With a sudden lurch, the car dove across the opposite lane and plunged into the driveway that opened in a high stone wall, leaving behind it a squealing of brakes and the shocked cursing of the driver of an oncoming car. Keller gave no indication that he heard it. Marshall shrugged. The worst was over. They were still alive, and almost there.

Through an opening in the trees he saw the house. The castle, rather. It appeared to be one of those monstrous transplants of Bavarian Gothic, removed stone by stone and reassembled in Rye, New York, by some nineteenth-century robber baron. Marshall smiled. It was not the sort of place he would have pictured Sam Keller in. He guessed that Mrs. Keller had had something to do with it.

"My youngest daughter's here with a bunch of her college friends this weekend," Keller explained, as they careened onto the gravel oval at the end of the driveway in front of the main entrance, where a number of late-model sports cars were parked. "Oh, shit," he added, as the Olds came to rest with a tinkling crunch against the taillight of a shiny red MG. "Who the hell left that there?"

They got out and made a cursory examination of the damage, but Sam Keller seemed to have forgotten all about it as they walked up the wide stone stairs to the front door. From the back somewhere, Marshall could hear the steady thwack of tennis balls and the sound of laughter.

"We'll get the merger business sorted out first, Hugh. Then you can go cavort with the college crowd. I'll be with you in five minutes."

"Fine, Mr. Keller."

From the study window he could see the tennis court and the pool. Two young men were playing a very good game of tennis. Three girls sat or lounged in deck chairs by the pool. Hugh wondered which was Sam Keller's daughter.

A noise behind him made him turn. There in the doorway was a girl in a white maillot bathing suit which left no doubt that she had a breathtaking figure. Her black hair hung wet and straight well below her shoulders. Her eyes were large and mocking, and a smile twisted her mouth to the left side of her pleasantly angular face.

"So you're the earnest young executive," she said.

"I suppose I am," Hugh replied. "And you?"

"I'm the daughter. Sarah Keller."

"Hugh Marshall. How do you do?"

"Pretty well." She came into the room, not toward him to shake hands, but almost circling, until she stopped at her father's desk. Her body, moving within the white latex suit, was hypnotic. She sat on the edge of the desk and crossed her long perfect legs.

"So far you're doing very nicely," she said.

"What do you mean?"

"You're doing what's expected of you. Looking me over. That's what you're here for, you know. To look me over. I think you do it rather well."

Hugh grinned. "It's very easy to do."

She got up and circled again, this time ending up at a door that opened on the terrace outside. "You must be an up-and-coming earnest young executive, Hugh Marshall. We only get the blue-chip prospects out here for looking Sarah over." They could hear Sam Keller's footsteps descending the staircase through the hall door. "We can get back to this later. You're here for the weekend, aren't you? 'Bye." She skipped

(34)

through the door and disappeared as Sam Keller entered the study.

Hugh Marshall did spend that weekend looking Sarah over, and the rest of the fall as well. She was at Pine Manor Junior College just outside of Boston, and he caught the shuttle up from New York regularly. They went to Harvard football games, in the stadium where Hugh had won All-Ivy honors as a pass-catching end a few years earlier. They drove her sleek gray Mercedes 190SL out to the Cape, and dined on lobster and Pouilly-Fuissé in the romantic desertedness of the out-of-season resorts. They took a room in a guest house overlooking the dunes, registering as Mr. and Mrs. Earnest, and walked on the cold beach, and made love all night long. They were engaged at Christmastime, and married in June. Their two children had been born in quick succession.

And for the first few years, as Hugh Marshall remembered it, they had been happy.

Now, at forty, Hugh Marshall looked out across the polluted skyline of New York and over to a tugboat chugging down the East River. He realized that he hadn't felt young for a very long time. He wondered if he ever would again.

CHAPTER FIVE

ROBERTA Rowan stood beside her gray suede Botega Veneta luggage and tossed her hat and handbag on the marble hall table. She had just arrived from London, but she looked as fresh, in her gray Givenchy chemise and classic Hermès scarf, as if she had just emerged from her dressing room. The staff was assembled to greet her.

She smiled her famous smile. "Well, I must say, you all look well. And how's my daughter? Is she around?"

"Yes, ma'am," James Brannigan, the butler, said with his soft Irish brogue. "She's up in her room. On the telephone, I believe." He headed for the stairs. "I shall tell her that you've arrived."

"No, no . . . I'll go up myself. And James, I'd love a snack. Some melon, if you have it. The food on the Concorde's as vile as any other plane, in spite of what they say."

Tyger appeared on the staircase. "Mother! I thought I heard your voice. What on earth are you doing in New York? I wasn't expecting you for a couple of weeks." She ran down the steps and gave Lady Bobbie a quick hug and kiss.

"Well, it's a whirlwind visit. I'm going back tomorrow evening, but I was desperate to find something spectacular to wear. Jimmy's oldest daughter, Annabelle, is getting married next week." Bobbie looked at her watch. "James, forget the melon. Why don't we nip around to La Goulue for lunch, Tyger, and catch up on gossip?"

"Well, I'm terribly busy, Mother. I shouldn't take the time. . . ."

·"Nonsense. I have a fitting at Bill Blass's at four. We'll just have time for a quick bite." Bobbie never liked to take no for an answer.

The lunch crowd at La Goulue was beginning to thin out. Tyger, in a soft turquoise-and-beige Karl Lagerfeld crêpe de chine tunic, and Lady Bobbie, who had changed into a white Saint Laurent blazer with matching pants, white stockings and low-heeled Y.S.L. pumps, were greeted lavishly by the maître d'. He escorted them to a prime location, the center of one of the small Art Deco-inspired dining rooms, pulling out the snowy linen-clothed table so that the two beautiful women could wedge themselves gracefully onto the caramel leather banquette.

For a second, before sitting, Bobbie checked out her appearance in the large mirror set into the dark wood-paneled wall. She knew that all other eyes in the room were subtly evaluating her attire. She knew also that the eyes enviously approved. As she sat, she smiled, to no one in particular, then glanced around the room, nodding at acquaintances. She shifted her attention to her daughter.

"To start, how about splitting an order of melon and Bayonne ham with me?"

"If you'll share the steak au poivre with me. I'm not terribly hungry."

"Of course." Lady Bobbie lowered her voice. "Let's get right down to the nitty-gritty. What's this I hear about your turning down Wesley Graham's proposal?"

Tyger shrugged. "It would have been a marriage of convenience. Wesley wanted me as a cover. We'd go our separate ways while outwardly reflecting the aura of happily wedded bliss. . . ."

"*Tiens*! I had no idea Wesley was gay." Lady Bobbie sipped the Kir that the waiter had just brought her. "Still, he's charming and very rich. Not such a bad deal."

"Not for me, Mother. I don't need another marriage. I told you in California . . . I'm more interested in getting my life together. By myself."

Bobbie looked alarmed. "Really, Tyger, you're not still going on about getting a job! Surely this isn't going to be your latest kick."

"Mother, I need a job. . . ." Tyger took a quick breath, determined to keep her cool. Her mother had subtle ways of stirring her up. Bobbie could rile her like no one else, and

Tyger knew she had to keep the throttle on her emotions. Once Bobbie detected that she was getting her needle in a vein, she would launch into full attack.

"A beautiful young woman doesn't *need* to get a job. And, my dear, if I do say so myself, you are beautiful."

"Mother, we're in the Eighties! That sort of thinking is twenty years out of date. Everybody works now ... Jackie Onassis, Gloria Vanderbilt ..."

"Oh," Bobbie sniffed, "they have such a sense of *noblesse oblige*. Besides, you're too young to work."

Tyger sighed. "You keep getting younger, but *I'm* getting older. Remember? I'm twenty-six." Bobbie gave a sweep of her bejeweled left hand to dismiss the discussion of age. "Look, Mother, I want to work. There are thousands of women building careers or going back to work because they want to be in the mainstream. ..."

Now Bobbie waved both hands to silence her daughter. "Please. Let's not launch into a feminist diatribe. I'll accept the script: you want a job." She took a fork and jabbed it into the melon. "Do you have one yet?"

"No ... but I had a good interview with the president of Kellerco." The waiter brought their steak and divided it deftly onto two gleaming china plates. He set one before each woman.

"Hugh Marshall? Why didn't you *tell* me you were interested in Kellerco? I used to know Hugh ... and Nelson Bachrach, who's chairman of the board, and old Sam Keller, who's dead now, were both friends of your grandfather. I've held onto my Kellerco stock. Private offering ... they've never gone public. Grandfather bought a block of it, then gave it to me as a wedding present when I married ... your father, I think." Bobbie pushed the crisp thin *pommes frites* to the side of her plate. "Well, if you're determined to get a job, I'll call Hugh and tell him that he'd better hire my sweet daughter or else!"

"*No*, Mother! Please don't. Just leave it to me. I'll get the job on my own," Tyger said through clenched teeth.

"But, darling, you aren't *qualified* for anything. People with connections must use them. That's what it's all about."

"That's what *what* is all about?"

"Being one of the privileged class, Tyger." Lady Bobbie signaled for the waiter and produced her gold American Express card.

Outside the restaurant, on Seventieth Street, Bobbie kissed

her daughter's cheek. "I love you. Even if you are bullheaded, like your father. Of *course* I won't interfere with your job. Or your love life. When have I *ever* been one of those meddlesome mothers?" And she was off, her blond hair gleaming in the sunlight as she headed up the street toward Madison Avenue.

Tyger stood there for a couple of minutes, unwinding. *When have you not*, she thought wryly. Then she grabbed a cab for the Public Library, to research the perfume industry.

Many privileged people have something to overcome, even if it is just overcoming the fact that they are privileged. Tyger Hayes had been wallowing for years in the sticky syrup of inherited celebrity. The same was true for many of the friends she grew up with. They were second-generation Hollywood. Many of them were lost children with glittering names and too much money. They bought clothes and cars like candy; they latched onto alcohol and every kind of drug. Most of them rebelled, in one way or another, against having had too much given to them, and too little expected of them. Like many of her friends—the ones who had survived more or less intact—Tyger was sick of the life. Unlike most of them, she was determined to fight her way out of it. And the Kellerco job seemed like her best chance.

Harry Hayes had instilled in her his famous home-fashioned philosophy, his cinematic trademark: it's not what you're born with, good or bad, it's what you become. A good premise, and it had netted him several Academy Awards. The theme ran through his greatest movies. Sidney Poitier illustrated it in *Having a Wonderful Time*; Joanne Woodward fought her way against the odds in *Sensitive Encounter*. People flocked to the box office to see the latest entry with the "Hayes touch."

As kids, Tyger and her friends had mocked those movies. Such a homespun view of life seemed far removed from her father's Beverly Hills mansion. Tyger felt very sophisticated, sitting in the plush, private screening room, with famous family friends like Paul Newman and Elizabeth Taylor and Frank Sinatra. But some of that philosophy did sink in. Tyger, in the last analysis, became far more her father's daughter than her mother's.

Growing up mostly in Hollywood and at Eastern boarding schools, Tyger grew used to the billing "daughter of." There were even occasions when she chose to fall back on it. But although she was a celebrity, she had not always been a "beautiful person." In fact, from late childhood through early adolescence, she was an ugly duckling, a little too tall, and on the stocky side. As a result, she became an outsider. Physical beauty was a *sine qua non* with her crowd of Hollywood children, and, lacking it, Tyger developed a certain cynicism about it. And a certain distrust for the way of life that celebrated it. She spent much time by herself, writing poems about pain and heartache, even though she had not really experienced these emotions firsthand.

The summer she was sixteen, her mother stepped in and brought her to Lexington, Kentucky, where her latest husband, Cappy McNeeley, bred horses and distilled bourbon. As the teenaged Tyger stepped off the plane at Lexington Airport, Bobbie kissed her quickly, and started right in.

"My God, darling, don't they feed you anything but starches at that school? You're beginning to resemble the Goodyear blimp!"

"Gee, thanks, Mother. It's good to see you, too. *All* the kids gain weight . . . there's nothing to do besides study and eat." Tyger kissed her mother. "Did you get my report card? I made honor roll again."

"Yes . . . congratulations, dear, but we've got to do something about your figure before you start parading around the country club in a bathing suit. All of Cappy's friends have been so anxious to meet you and fix you up with their sons." She groaned. "Oh, Tyger, why didn't you *warn* me that you'd plumped up so?"

Tyger's eyes filled with tears, but she looked away so her mother couldn't see her. When she turned back, Cappy, her new stepfather, was there with the bags.

"Why Tyger, honey," he said. "You've grown so. We've all been lookin' forward to havin' you spend the summer with us. I hope you'll like Kentucky. There are a lot of folks for you to meet."

Tyger wanted to head back immediately to California, and the solace of her sunny bedroom at her father's house, but she knew she had to stick it out in Kentucky. Her father was on location in Africa.

Bobbie immediately enforced a strict regime of cottage cheese and calisthenics. Over the next month, Tyger grudgingly dropped every pound of her extra weight, and grew two additional inches, bringing her to a striking five feet eight inches. In addition, a bump on the bridge of her nose was rendered nonexistent by the city's leading plastic surgeon, and Bobbie spent hours teaching Tyger how to apply makeup as skillfully as Degas had used pastels. By the end of July, the young men at the Idle Hour Country Club were more interested in Tyger's ripening physical assets than the fact that she was a "ce-le-bruh-ty." The local girls were no longer anxious to fix her up with blind dates; nor did they have to. At dinner parties, Bobbie's and Cappy's friends could not help remarking that Tyger was becoming a real beauty.

Over those weeks, something began to happen between Tyger and her mother. As Tyger dieted and sweated into the image her mother wanted for her, Bobbie herself grew more distant with her daughter. It was as if, having created perfection, Bobbie suddenly regretted playing Pygmalion. The idea of her daughter as grown-up competition caught up with her, and she didn't like it. Bobbie resolved the situation by talking Cappy into taking her to South America, and shipping Tyger back to California a month early.

Once back in Hollywood, hailed as an "overnight" beauty, Tyger launched into a phase of being dazzled by her own attributes. She was seduced by the sudden sensation of being an insider at last, and enjoying it too much to evaluate the superficiality of the situation. She teased, flirted, sat in back seats at drive-ins and made out like crazy. But always only up to a point. She was in great demand. She could pick and choose. She consciously decided to keep her virginity intact until she fell in love.

By the time Tyger was eighteen and ensconced at Sarah Lawrence, she was beginning to wonder whether she would ever find the perfect male. She was getting horny, but not enough to back down on her original decision.

In southern California, in the summer of 1971, there were very few eighteen-year-old virgins. Tyger was greatly sought after; yet she remained as unattainable as ever.

That same summer, Tyger flew east to Charlottesville, Virginia, to be maid of honor at her best friend Julia Williamson's wedding. Julia and Tyger had survived four years as roommates at Miss Porter's: their bond was tied tightly forever. Yet, in spite of their many shared interests, Tyger loathed the boy Julia was marrying, Sparky Hatcher. She absolutely did not see what attracted Julia to him, although at first she couldn't quite pin down her own objections to Sparky. On the surface he was the perfect Virginia gentleman—well-to-do, nice-looking, polite to parents. His

(41)

wardrobe of slacks and sports jackets was a tribute to Jack Nicklaus and country clubs across the land. Sparky Hatcher drank too much, as did his whole crowd, and had "raised a lotta hell," by his own admission, at the University of Virginia, where he was currently in his second year of law. He was typical, and presentable.

A festive whirl of prenuptial parties given by local first families, such as the Van Deveners, the Randolphs, the Scotts and the Keiths, preceded the wedding. There were brunches, lunches, cocktail parties and buffets, climaxing with the rehearsal banquet at the Farmington Country Club. All the members of the wedding party and close kin assembled in the Olde Dining Room and saluted the happy couple with toast after toast of champagne.

By ten o'clock, Tyger, and everyone present, could tell that Julia was completely in her cups. Tyger dragged Julia upstairs to the powder room and held her head while she threw up. The powder-room attendant fetched a pot of black coffee, and after three cups Julia returned shakily to the party. Soon after, her parents whisked her off, to get "one last good night's sleep," her father winked.

The party dispersed into smaller groups, and Tyger, Sparky, and several of the bridesmaids and ushers weaved their way downstairs to the Tap Room, for more drinks and dancing. Throughout the week Tyger had been carrying on a flirtation with one of Sparky's fraternity mates from Kappa Alpha, Larry Babcock. Now Sparky wedged himself between Tyger and Larry, jovially feigning jealousy over her close friendship with Julia, and now Larry.

"I can see that you've got good taste, Tyger. We both like the same people," Sparky said, his words slurred a bit.

"I guess we do, Sparky. But all you Virginians are so charming." Tyger tried to be convivial, but was less than pleased at Sparky's horning in. She and Larry Babcock were getting along well, and she wanted him all to herself. She could see from Larry's impatient face that he was none too pleased with his old friend either.

Sparky leaned in to semi-whisper in Tyger's ear. "You watch out for ol' Babcock here. He's a regular snake in the grass."

Larry pretended to be amused. "I heard that, Hatcher. An' it looks to me like *you're* the snake around here. Why don't you go an' serenade Julia from under her window? Or do somethin' constructive. In other words, leave Tyger an' me alone."

"Well . . ." Sparky hesitated. His besotted brain raced to think up a good comeback.

"Beat it, Hatcher. You've got a woman," Larry persisted.

Sparky stood up. "Okay, okay. I'll take a hint." He moved to another table to chat with the other bridesmaids.

The party moved on to another sprawling house where several of the out-of-town guests were staying. They sat out on the terrace behind the white-columned brick Virginia mansion. A mixture of Jack Daniel's and magnolia blossoms mingled in the still night air. The conversation drunkenly drifted around to each of them, and what they would be doing five years from that night.

"Sparky'll still be tryin' to get it up for the first time with Julia," Larry offered. The rest of the crowd broke out in laughter.

"Hell, Larry, you'll still be tryin' to figure out what the hell it is that you're supposed to be gettin up," retorted Sparky.

After a while Patsy Flordon, whose house it was, aimed her guests toward the kitchen and cooked grilled cheese sandwiches. People began to sober up.

Larry put his arm around Tyger. "It's gettin' late. I'll drive you back to Julia's," he said, and then whispered in her ear, "There're two ways to get there. The high road, or the low."

Tyger giggled. "Definitely the high one."

"That's the long way. It may take hours." He kissed her hair.

"Okay with me," Tyger purred. "Let's go."

Sparky came over to them. "Did somebody say somethin' about goin'? It's too early. Besides, I wanted to talk to Tyger." He looked earnestly at her. "About Julia." He had sobered up somewhat, and seemed sincere in his request.

Larry answered for Tyger. "Y'all can talk tomorrow. We're leavin' now. . . ."

Sparky put his right hand on Larry's shoulder. "Look, Babcock . . . I'm serious. I'm committin' myself to a lifetime sentence tomorrow. Tyger is Julia's best friend. I've got to have a talk with her." His tone quieted, and he looked squarely at Larry. "It's really important."

"Well . . . okay. I'll wait an' drive you home, Tyger."

"No," said Sparky. "I'll drive her. I don't know how long we'll be."

Tyger wanted Larry to stick around, but she felt she owed

it to Julia to talk with Sparky. "Look, Larry, it's okay. Maybe it's better for me to stay and talk. Besides, I'll be seeing you all day tomorrow . . . and tomorrow night."

"All right." He turned to Sparky. "I want you to remember what a good friend I am, Hatcher." He gave Tyger a quick kiss on her cheek. "Goodnight, Tyger. Tomorrow we'll take the high road," he promised seductively.

Patsy led Sparky and Tyger into the library, where they would be uninterrupted, and discreetly left them alone.

"Let's make this brief, Sparky. I'm exhausted." Tyger flopped down on the sofa and put her feet up on the coffee table.

Sparky went over to the bar and filled his glass with bourbon and a splash of water. Then he came over and sat on the sofa next to her. "You know," he began in his soft Virginia drawl, "I don't think you're pleased that Julia and I are gettin' married."

"I want Julia to be happy, and she is with you. But just because Julia likes both of us doesn't mean that we have to like each other," Tyger answered candidly.

"I disagree." Sparky set his drink down on the end table. In the same move he edged close to Tyger and draped his arm casually around her shoulder. "Because we both love Julia, I think we've gotta work on liking each other. I'm really a nice guy."

Tyger realized what he was doing. She leaned forward to get up, to end the game at once, but Sparky's arm deterred her. He pulled her toward him. His wet lips attacked her face, but Tyger turned away so that he missed her lips and sloppily kissed her cheek.

"Cool it, Sparky. You're drunk. I'm going."

He tightened his grip on her shoulders and blew gently into her ear, whispering, "Did Julia tell you what a big cock I've got? Oh, Tyger, I want you . . . I love you." He had been a varsity wrestler at school, and with one quick motion he pinned her down. Tyger was defenseless. Sparky weighed close to two hundred pounds. With one hand he tore Tyger's blouse open, while the other unzipped his pants. Tyger stopped struggling for a second, to gather momentum for her escape. She planned to gather all her strength and spring up and out of the room in one swift move.

Just then there was a voice outside the door: Patsy's. Sparky put his hand over Tyger's mouth. She tried to pry it loose, but couldn't.

"Listen, y'all? I'm goin' to bed now. Turn off the lights before you leave, okay?"

While Patsy was speaking, Sparky ripped Tyger's bikini pants off and plunged himself into her forcefully. Then he called out to Patsy, in a carefully controlled voice, "Okay, Pat. Goodnight."

Tyger heard Patsy's heels click down the hall and up the stairs. Sparky bobbled up and down on her, moaning. As her pain went from sharp to dull, and the stench of liquor and sweat and bay rum aftershave engulfed her, Tyger began to feel as if she were going to be sick. She struggled again, with one last burst of energy, to get loose, but he was too strong for her. When Sparky finally removed his hand from her mouth she couldn't scream. He came quickly, and crumpled down on top of her, giving her neck a slobbering kiss.

"Oh, baby, that was great. Oh, I love you. You've always turned me on." He remained there, an exhausted lump pressing her into the sofa cushions, nearly suffocating her.

Slowly, Tyger returned to lucidity. Fury and disgust and hatred welled up in her. She wanted to kill Sparky. But when the emotion finally reached the surface, it manifested itself in tears. She began to heave hysterically. She couldn't talk. She couldn't hit Sparky. She couldn't move. Sparky pulled his wilted penis out of her.

"My God," he said, "there's blood. You gettin' your period?" He got up and grabbed a towel from the bar, and handed it to Tyger. He asked her repeatedly why she was crying, but she ignored him.

Her flood of tears diminished to a trickle. Slowly, she rubbed the blood away from her vagina and the sofa cushions. She felt numb, removed, as if she were far away and watching herself from a distance. Sparky had his pants back on, and was looking for a button that had popped off his shirt. It never occurred to him that Tyger had been a virgin. He was humming to himself. He construed her tears to be caused by some female quirkiness which allowed women to cry when they were happy.

"Hurry up and get dressed. I'll take you back to Julia's."

Tyger stood up, dazed, and began assembling her outfit. Sparky slapped her buttocks.

"You're a damned fine piece of ass."

The slap pulled her back into reality. "Get out of here, Sparky. I'll stay here tonight. And, so help me God . . . if you ever come near me again . . . I'll kill you. I mean it."

Sparky's face suddenly showed alarm. "Oh, Jesus, you're not gonna tell Julia about this, are you? I didn't think you'd take it this way. I thought you'd want it as much as me, once I got you turned on. . . ."

"Get out of here and leave me alone!"

Sparky retreated hastily, and Tyger sat alone in the library until dawn, chain-smoking cigarettes. She hated herself for having been so powerless against Sparky. She had waited all that time—and for this. Ironic. She finally fell asleep on the sofa, exhausted.

Tyger walked through the formalities of the next day. Once Julia and Sparky had left for the honeymoon, Tyger opted for the first plane out. Larry Babcock wanted her to stay. He tried to convince her all the way to the airport, but she held firm.

On the plane, Tyger still felt very detached. A "friendly" rape, she remembered once hearing it called, the sort of encounter she had had with Sparky. No matter what the name for it, it had happened. There was nothing she could do now. She dreaded seeing Julia again.

Tyger ordered a bloody Mary from the flight attendant, and tried to concentrate on the paperback she had bought at the airport.

"Hello?" A voice startled her. She looked up to see a blond, handsome soldier standing in the aisle next to her.

"Excuse me, miss. Nearly everybody else is asleep. Since you're drinking, and I'm drinking, I thought maybe we could drink together—and talk. My name's Ed Brown." He extended his hand and Tyger shook it.

"Sure. If you do most of the talking. I'm Jean Pearson." Tyger always gave a fake name to strangers. Ed Brown sat in the vacant seat next to her.

"Cheers," he said, and raised his glass to her. "I'm celebrating my discharge from the army. This is a day I thought would never come." He had been in Vietnam, as lowest-ranking member of a fact-finding team, and had just concluded testifying before a panel at the Pentagon. He hadn't been in combat, but he was glad to be back home. He had seen and heard a lot of terrible things in Vietnam. Things he was anxious to forget.

Ed Brown was also from California—Anaheim. His father was dead; his mother and brother both worked at Disneyland. As he chatted away, Tyger studied him. He had blond beachcomber good looks. Out of uniform, she supposed he would look at home on a surfboard.

"What now?" Tyger asked.

"First, I'm going to relax for a couple of weeks. Unwind. Then get some kind of job to support myself while I try to break into the movie business. . . ."

"What do you want to do in the business?" It didn't take psychic acuity for Tyger to know what his answer would be. Ed was too handsome to contemplate action behind the scenes.

"Act, of course," he said, smiling. "As soon as I get my teeth capped."

Tyger smiled. She knew a lot of actors and liked most of them, although she was also aware that her low tolerance of their vanity had been inherited from her father. Nevertheless, by the time the plane had touched down in Los Angeles, she liked Ed Brown. He was soft-spoken, unsophisticated. He projected an attractively vulnerable quality.

Ed's family had come to the airport to meet him, even though it was three in the morning. They offered to give Tyger a lift, but she declined with thanks. Ed insisted on getting her phone number. She surprised herself by giving him her real one, telling him to ask for Tyger, her nickname.

"Meeting you was the best homecoming present I could have had." He smiled down at her. "I'll call you tomorrow."

Over the next few weeks they saw each other often. In order to avoid having him know where she lived, Tyger always managed to meet Ed at a prearranged spot, mostly the beach. He didn't seem to mind the mystery with which she surrounded herself and he was confident that she would relax with him, sooner or later.

Tyger didn't set out to fall in love with Ed. She was comfortable with him, with her anonymity in the situation. Ed was like a salve. Even his family was nice. He allowed her to play the role of girl next door, right out of one of her father's movies, and she loved it.

Sexually, Ed could tell that Tyger was getting over a bad experience with someone, although she had only insinuated, and never supplied details. He didn't press her. Then one night he suggested that they spend the night together. His best friend was away on business, and Ed had the keys to his apartment.

"Well . . . okay," she said thoughtfully. She knew she had to exorcise the experience with Sparky from her consciousness.

"You will?" Ed broke into a delighted grin. "I don't believe it. I never thought you'd say yes when I asked you."

"Just don't rush me, Ed. And if I want to back down at the last minute, you have to try to understand."

Ed bent over and kissed her lips softly. "I love you, Tyger. I don't want to do anything to scare you away."

That night, they warmed up slowly by smoking a joint. Finally, they were naked together on the thick shag living-room carpet, and by the time Ed entered Tyger, she wanted him to make love to her as much as he wanted to. Ed was considerate of her, and he was also a good lover. They experienced each other over and over again, until late the next morning when Ed's friend Lewis arrived home.

Tyger was scrambling eggs for the three of them when Lew began his barrage of questions.

"Ed tells me you are one mysterious lady," he began.

"Oh? How so?" Tyger rescued the English muffins from burning under the broiler.

"Well, he's been goin' out with you for weeks now, and doesn't even know where you live."

Ed broke in, embarrassed by Lew's bluntness. "Don't mind Lew, honey. He's famous for his lack of tact."

Lewis agreed, sensing his own heavy-handedness. "Ed didn't put me up to it. He doesn't care where you're from. He's so happy with the present that he's not interested in your past. I'm the one who's a nosy bastard." Lew laughed, and his beard vibrated. Tyger decided she liked him.

She also decided to fill them both in on who she was. She felt guilty lying to Ed. And after last night it seemed fitting that Ed know who she was.

"My real name's Tyger Hayes. My father's Harry Hayes. I live on Doheny Drive in Beverly Hills." She set their breakfast down in front of them, and proceeded, amid Lew's "oohs" and "ahs" and Ed's silence, to tell them everything.

When she concluded, Ed remained quiet, but Lewis was unabashedly impressed.

"Hey, maybe your old man'll give Ed a job in one of his movies."

Ed blushed. "Don't pay attention to him, Tyger. You know I want to act. But I plan to make it on my own, like everyone else."

"Yeah," said Lewis. "But since when does it hurt to have connections?"

"Don't listen to him, honey," Ed said to Tyger. "I'm not interested in who your father is, or what he can do for me. Until fifteen minutes ago I didn't even know Harry Hayes was your father. I'm only interested in you. Believe me." And Tyger did.

Ed picked up a temporary job as a parking-lot attendant, and began taking classes at night: acting and writing. On his free evenings he and Tyger would meet after work, have dinner and go back to Lew's to make love. Lew was living with a girl in Venice, so it worked out fine. Ed never asked to see Tyger's house, or meet her father. Both of them, though they never said as much to each other, were afraid that if Ed saw Tyger's turf their dream would be spoiled by reality.

Tyger was content to spend her time either alone or with Ed. She avoided her old friends. She knew they would put Ed down. He was attractive enough to be admitted into the group, but he lacked their degree of sophistication. She realized that she was judging her friends as being shallower than they actually were. Nevertheless, she avoided all potential confrontations between her two lives.

In the meantime, Tyger slowly began to fall in love with Ed. Sex with him was terrific, and she was happier than she had ever been in her whole life. She decided that returning to Sarah Lawrence in September was the last thing she wanted to do.

And so she decided that she and Ed should get married. She had four thousand dollars in a savings account, and she devised a plan. They would elope to Mexico. She had a friend in San Miguel de Allende who would lend them his bungalow for a couple of weeks.

Tyger was sure that after the initial shock of her marriage, Harry, even Bobbie, would come around. After all, Ed exhibited all the old-fashioned values Harry's movies espoused. She was also positive that, with a little pressure, she could convince Harry to give Ed a part in his next film. Once Ed was a star, no one would care what his original background had been.

It took some convincing, but finally Ed came around to the idea. He loved Tyger. Why not marry her? He was flattered that she was more ambitious for him than he was for himself. Here was the girl of his dreams, offering herself and possibly a solid gold future. It was all happening fast, but why shouldn't it?

"Tyger Brown. Tyger Brown. Tyger Brown. Has a good sound to it." A judge had married them the night before. The hot Mexican sun streamed in on them through the screened window of the sleeping veranda in San Miguel.

Ed kissed Tyger, and handed her a slice of mango. "You're not tired of it already? I thought you Hollywood playgirls were extremely fickle."

"Not while we're still on our honeymoon . . . we're not *that* fickle!" Tyger leaned over and licked a drop of mango juice from Ed's chin.

"Well, then let's make it a long honeymoon."

"As long as you like, darling. Our whole marriage will be a honeymoon," Tyger purred. "I can hear Miss Rona now: 'Who says marriages in tinsel town don't last? Ed and Tyger Brown just celebrated their silver anniversary. I spoke with the former Tyger Hayes today, at their home in Mexico, and she says the secret's simple. They're still on their honeymoon. . . .' "

Ed laughed and pulled Tyger close to him. "Enough talk. Let's have some more action."

"All right . . . kiss me, you fool." Tyger giggled and Ed obeyed.

With their arms around each other they walked over to the edge of the veranda and looked through the wisteria vines to the clay-colored bungalow next door. Two dark-haired little girls, both singing a Spanish nursery ballad, were playing with rag dolls. Ed pulled Tyger closer to him.

"Just think. In a couple of years we'll look out into our back yard and watch our own little girls playing like that." He looked lovingly at Tyger.

She smiled. "Or little boys. I'd like to have boys so they can look just like you." She turned and hugged Ed tightly. "I'm so happy! We're going to have a wonderful life together, aren't we?"

Ed's full lips pressed against hers, and they kissed for a long time. When they broke away, he smiled, and said, "This is only the beginning. It'll get better . . ." He kissed her. "And better . . ." He kissed her again.

"How can it? It's already perfect."

"You just wait and see." And he led her back into the bedroom.

* * *

When Tyger left she had told her father that she was off to Mexico to visit a friend from school. After two weeks of bliss with Ed, when it was time for her to be heading back to college, she wired Harry that she was married and not returning just yet. The very next day Harry's secretary tracked them down and was standing at the doorstep of their honeymoon cottage before noon. His mission: to fetch them home. Harry was furious, Bill reported. And Bobbie had flown in from Kentucky. For the first time since they had faced the judge in their custody battle ten years before, Bobbie and Harry were allies.

Tyger pretended to acquiesce, but when Bill went out to get a bite to eat, Tyger began packing their bags. "We've got to get out of here fast, darling. I know a place where no one will find us. In Guatemala."

Ed put his foot down. "No, Tyger. Be realistic. We've got to face them sooner or later. I'd rather get it over with so we can go on from there. I'll talk to your father. He'll see that I didn't marry you for your money. Hell, I didn't even know who you were when I fell in love with you. We'll be okay. I'll get a better job. . . ."

Tyger sighed. "I suppose it's inevitable—you have to meet my parents. Just be prepared. Together, they can be dynamite." She dreaded the encounter.

Ed put his arms around her and kissed her lightly. "Don't worry. I know you think I'm out of my depth when it comes to your folks. But I'm a quick study. I can handle it. Jesus, I just came back from Vietnam."

They made love once more in the flower-studded garden. Then Bill came back, and it was time to go. As they piled into the taxi, Tyger looked back at the ugly pink bungalow, and her eyes filled with tears. She sensed that things would never be the same again, even if Ed did manage to win over Harry and Bobbie. She felt apprehensive about seeing her parents together again. Around them, she wasn't as tough as she liked to believe.

On the flight back to Los Angeles, sitting between Bill and Ed, Tyger downed three martinis in rapid succession, and passed out. Long before she was ready to face her parents, Harry's chauffeur pulled the Bentley into the winding driveway of Tularosa, her father's enormous Spanish hacienda.

Tyger squeezed Ed's hand and kissed him before they got out of the car. Her hair was limp and streaked from the Mexican sun. She tried to fluff it up. "How do I look?"

Ed kissed her forehead. "Beautiful, as always." He smiled. "Remember, there's nothing to worry about." But Tyger could see from a tightening behind Ed's jaw that he was scared stiff.

"Darling!" Bobbie appeared at the door, swathed in a Moroccan tunic and wearing a three-strand Zuni Indian fetish necklace. Turquoise-and-gold snake bracelets slithered up both arms. Her hair was blonder, the area around her eyes a little tighter than the last time Tyger had seen her. Bobbie was radiant. Combat excited her.

Tyger hugged her mother and kissed both cheeks. "Mother this is Ed . . . my husband."

Ed extended his hand, but Bobbie swept over and kissed him, also on both cheeks. She smiled and looked at him for the merest fragment of a second, but Tyger could see the calculation behind Bobbie's eyes. She was sizing up the enemy and revising her strategy. Tyger felt a knot in her stomach. The scene was going to be bad, worse than even she had anticipated.

"Where's Daddy?"

"At the studio, working with the editor. But he'll be here soon. I told him I'd ring when you arrived." She took hold of both Tyger's and Ed's hands. "You darlings must be exhausted from the trip. Why don't you go up and bathe? Then we'll have drinks in the study. Would you like a snack sent up? I'll bet neither of you ate dinner on the plane." Tyger wasn't sure whether Bobbie was referring to the airlines' cuisine or their nerves.

Up in Tyger's lilac-carpeted room, Ed paced around, restlessly inspecting mementos of Tyger's past, staring at the wall full of framed photographs behind her bed.

"Golly, you were a cute baby. It's amazing—your mother looks just the same. She's really beautiful. And," he added tentatively, "she seems nice."

"Yes, she oozes charm, always. The more upset she is, the more vivacious she becomes. She makes me nervous when she's like this. We've just got to be cool. It's not going to be great, but we'll get through it."

"That's the spirit." Ed put his arm around Tyger. He was reassuring and sincere, and totally innocent of what was in store for him. "Sure we will," he said.

Harry Hayes burst into the study about twenty minutes later. He kissed Tyger quickly and perfunctorily, and ignored Ed's outstretched hand. He poured himself a brandy snifter full of scotch, and sank down into his weathered leather chair. Tyger could sense ominous thunder rumbling around inside of her father. He drank. No one said anything. Tyger felt like vomiting. She got up to pour herself a club soda.

Bobbie, the diplomat, began a gush of chitchat to fill the silence, but Harry interrupted her. His voice was louder than it needed to be, which meant that he was either drunk or angry, probably both. "Tyger, sit down. I want to talk to you."

Tyger snapped, "I don't feel like sitting. And if you want to talk, you can address both Ed and me."

"Hell!" Harry stormed out of the room. It was obvious that he had been too busy at the studio to write his scenario for the confrontation. In those rare instances when Harry felt inarticulate he retreated, to drink alone in his suite.

Bobbie seemed surprised, and unprepared for the move. She stood up quickly. "Well, darlings, it is late. Perhaps we'd all better get a good night's sleep. We'll talk tomorrow."

Tyger and Ed both tossed restlessly in Tyger's canopied, white-ruffled bed. When they came down in the morning, Harry had gone to the studio, and Bobbie was out shopping. They spent the next day by the pool and tried to relax. Bill Sullivan called to tell Tyger that dinner was planned for eight o'clock, and to dress.

Tyger pulled a hand-painted chiffon by Holly Harp out of her closet. Ed had only a wardrobe of jeans and T-shirts, and one sports jacket that Tyger secretly hated. She phoned Bill Sullivan and asked him to lend Ed something for the evening, since they were about the same size.

At seven-thirty, when Ed was dressed, he looked smashing. Tyger could see his star potential more clearly than ever. Ed, of course, was uncomfortable in borrowed clothes. He and Tyger had their first argument on the subject, both of them wound tight with anxiety. Ed had finally relented, to a point. He wore Bill's dinner jacket with his own jeans.

Tyger and Ed and Bobbie had drinks alone on the terrace. The air was tense, and they all stuck with light subjects.

"Wasn't Mexico too hot this time of year?" Bobbie inquired.

"Not really. It was quite idyllic." Tyger was on edge. To think only yesterday morning she and Ed had been in paradise.

Reginald, the butler, appeared in the doorway. "Mr. Hayes has arrived. He has gone to his suite to change."

In less than ten minutes, Harry stood before them, a figure of enormous power, dashing and crusty at the same time. He didn't bother greeting any of them. "Let's eat," he said gruffly.

The scene at the dinner table had been done often, in many movies. Bobbie chatted endlessly about trivia. Harry said nothing. Ed fumbled awkwardly with his artichoke Hollandaise. He wasn't exactly sure what to do with it.

Bobbie glanced at Ed's plate. "Oh, look what Ed's doing!" she exclaimed. Ed turned four shades of magenta. Bobbie continued, "You're arranging your leaves so *artistically,* darling."

Wine flowed into the Baccarat goblets, poured by the nearly invisible Japanese houseboy. By dinner's end, Harry was drunk, and exuding mute belligerence. He had not spoken more than five sentences during the entire meal. Bobbie was in peak form, playing the ambassadress. Ed was by then lightheaded enough to feel relaxed, and, baited by Bobbie, was loosening up. Tyger drank much more than usual, and stayed sober, a witness at her own funeral. She saw Bobbie's game plan, saw that it was working. She knew what was going to happen, but she couldn't stop it.

Ed was so high by now that he was getting cocky, and asking Harry questions about the movie business. Harry answered him monosyllabically. Tyger could feel the dining-room table tremble. She felt as if they were all sitting over the San Andreas fault. Harry was just about to erupt.

"Okay," Harry bellowed suddenly, cutting off Ed in midsentence. "Let's get this damned thing over with. Bobbie, you talk to Tyger. Her young man here"—he refused to call Ed by name—"and I are going to have some brandy in the library."

Bobbie smiled at Tyger. "Let's bring the bottle of wine into the living room. It will be more comfortable to sit in there and talk."

"There's nothing to talk about."

"Don't be silly, Tyger. There's a great deal to discuss. Your entire future is at stake. Your father and I only want what's best for you . . . surely you can understand that. We love you."

"And I love Ed," Tyger said defiantly.

"It's okay, honey." Ed grinned at her bravely. "Your father and I are just going to talk."

Tyger squeezed Ed's hand and kissed him on the cheek. "Hang in there," she whispered. "It shouldn't be any worse than Vietnam." Then she picked up the bottle of wine and walked past her mother into the living room. A platform at one end of the large room housed a fully stocked eighteenth-century Régance bar. Tyger selected two Baccarat wine goblets and took one over to her mother, who had gracefully arranged her slim body—legs tucked underneath her brocaded harem pants—on the burgundy suede sofa. The walls of the room were covered with a lighter wine-colored suede, and the carpets—three large hand-knotted Isfahan rugs in the classic Persian medallion design—added additional red hues. The lighting was recessed, with the exception of four strategically placed spiderweb glass-and-bronze Tiffany floor lamps. Displayed on the square coffee table in front of Bobbie was a centuries-old, one-of-a-kind carved pewter chess set. The other sets in Harry Hayes's vast collection were housed in a custom glass-and-mahogany breakfront at the far end of the room.

Bobbie absentmindedly picked up the heavy pewter queen and examined it with her fingers, without looking at it. "I gave this set to your father on our first wedding anniversary. Just before you were born. . . ." Bobbie trailed off, replacing the queen in its resting spot on the board. She patted the sofa cushion next to her, for Tyger to sit. "Darling," she said quietly, "you're not pregnant, are you?"

"No, Mother, I'm not!" Tyger said feistily, dropping crosslegged onto a suede hassock, facing her mother with hostility.

Bobbie poured some wine into her glass. "Well, that's a relief! I'm sure Ed's a very nice boy . . ."

"He's *not* a boy!"

"Young man, then. But face it, darling. He's from a totally different background. I've spoken with some of your friends. None of them has ever met him. You can't give up your life, everything you've ever known, for him. . . ."

"I'm not giving up. . . ."

Bobbie held up her hand, as if she were a traffic cop waiting for the cars to stop. "Let me finish, please. Believe me, I'm more experienced than you. There are some facts that just don't change. You can't go against your background . . . and Ed just isn't part of it."

"You talk about *my* friends. You just don't want Ed to embarrass *yours*. Mother, you're a snob."

"Perhaps I am, Tyger. All right. Forget about now. Think about your life with Ed in . . . five years. Think where you'll be living, what you'll be doing, what *he'll* be doing . . ."

"I don't know what we'll be doing in five years. But we'll be happy . . . because we'll still love each other."

"And that's all that matters? Good Lord, Tyger, you sound like the script from a B movie." Bobbie decided the Renoir was crooked and went over to straighten it. "Tell me, why haven't you introduced Ed to your friends?" she asked casually, launching another offensive.

"We've preferred just being alone with each other. Besides . . ." Tyger trailed off. She wasn't about to be trapped.

"Besides what, dear?"

"Of course I plan to introduce Ed to everyone. I had thought that you or Daddy would throw some sort of bash for us when you announce our marriage. You don't think Ed will get along with them. But he will. You aren't even trying to give him a chance."

"Tyger, you've got to finish college . . ."

"That was never important to you before. If some eligible young prince had come courting, you'd have married me off in two seconds!"

Tears welled up in Bobbie's eyes. "I'm your *mother*. You are a part of me. Of *course* I want you to do well for yourself. You deserve love and money, and all the other things that go with it."

"Ed gives me love. And he'll make money. He's smart . . . he's ambitious . . ."

"Perhaps he is. Maybe he will make a success of himself, but how long will it take? He certainly can't afford to keep you in the manner you're used to. Charge accounts at every store on Rodeo Drive, a Porsche . . . and what if you have children?"

"Mother, it's not as if I didn't think of all those things before I got married. Besides, if you really loved me you'd understand. Ed is the only man I've ever wanted. He's the only one who has ever actually cared about *me*. He fell in love with me before he even knew who Daddy was. . . ."

Bobbie was prowling around, looking for another pack of cigarettes. She found a carton in the Chinese lacquered cabinet next to the bar. "That's all very romantic, dear . . ."

Tyger broke in. "Anyway, Mother, I have a solution. I know how Ed can make money right away, and become respectable in everyone's eyes. . . ."

Bobbie looked skeptical. "How, dear?"

"Talk Daddy into using Ed in his next movie. He has

tremendous screen potential. Other people have been made into movie stars, why not Ed?"

Bobbie Taylor Hayes Prather McNeeley looked at her lovely young daughter, and then laughed. "Oh, Tyger . . . sometimes I forget just how adorable you are."

The next few hours were filled with Tyger's tantrums and scenes, screaming, crying, vociferous arguing. Bobbie talked with Ed; Harry talked with his daughter. At no time were Ed and Tyger left alone to reassure themselves.

In the end, it was Ed who gave way. Outargued, awed, and beaten down by a gap in sophistication and power for which he was no match, he capitulated shortly after midnight. The agreement was smoothed with the sweet poison of a screen contract ("We'll see what you're made of, boy. But you're not going to ride in as Harry Hayes's son-in-law. You're going to have to make it on your own").

"I'm sorry, Tyger. Maybe it's better for us to wait. I just don't know. I'm too worn down to think. Your parents are something else." Ed smiled forlornly and tried to put his arms around Tyger.

"Don't touch me!" She turned away from him and ran upstairs to her room.

Ed Brown walked over to the window and looked at the full moon shining on the rose gardens of Tularosa. Tears trickled down his cheeks. He knew it was all over for them, forever.

Once it was over, Tyger despised them all. She was embarrassed, humiliated, defeated. She was deeply distressed that Ed had given in to being bought off. It took a long time for her to realize that the poor guy had never stood a chance. Their final farewell had been one of Tyger's anger and Ed's misery. As Ed stood by Harry's Bentley, just before he was to be driven home, the range of emotions in his face betrayed a boy who was totally wounded, but resigned to his fate. Tyger remained expressionless as she watched the Bentley disappear down the palm-lined driveway.

Tyger had expected Bobbie to act the way she had, but she felt deeply betrayed by Harry. After all, his films championed the underdog, and look what happened. It was all a sham. She had tried to live the plot of one of his movies, but she was no Jane Fonda, nor was Ed a young Steve McQueen. Her father's entire philosophy, she realized, was marked by sentimentalism and false idealism. And for the first time she had flashed onto one deep basic truth: her father never really believed in those things either.

After spending a week alone in her room, Tyger decided that life had to continue. It was up to her to retrench, grow up, and make her own way and her own philosophy. She returned to college, became a semi-recluse and made dean's list. She spent holidays with her roommates and refused to return to California, where Bobbie, separated from Cappy McNeeley, was reconciled with Harry.

Harry's picture, *Captives of Paradise* won him a fifth Oscar the following spring. Shortly after that, Bobbie left him and moved to England. Tyger saw Ed once on a television episode of *The Waltons*, but he was not very good.

After college, Tyger was once again ready to have fun. She ran around New York with an international clique of celebrities, and refused to allow herself to be affected by anything or anybody, her mother especially. Eventually, she married Jeff Collins, the son of one of Hollywood's most famous and venerable actors. That relationship didn't work out either, but she didn't care because she had never been in love with Jeff.

And now here she was, Tyger Hayes again, changing gears at twenty-six, trying to figure out how the hell she could get the information she needed for a report about American designers. She was determined to land the Kellerco job.

CHAPTER SIX

"GOOD morning, Miss Mary." Mary Rogers knocked and entered Tyger's bedroom in one swift motion, carrying a tray with a two-cup pot of *café-filtre* and a half of pink grapefruit. Mary Rogers had been working for Lady Rowan ever since she had been Bobbie Hayes. Mary Rogers had been the most consistent factor in Tyger's growing up. No matter where Tyger was living, Bobbie usually managed to see to it that Mary Rogers was somewhere nearby, to appear quietly whenever needed.

"Morning, Mary Rogers." Tyger sat up in bed and smiled at the skinny Englishwoman. Her hair was white now, but Tyger could remember when it had been a peculiar shade of bright orange. Mary Rogers had always called Tyger "Miss Mary." To retaliate, Tyger had always called her mother's maid by her first and last names. Mary Rogers was also a cook and had recently insisted on getting her chauffeur's license. She was a mixture of British propriety and eccentricity.

"There were a few calls for you last night. I put them on the tray next to your bed." She always did. Tyger always saw them the instant she got home, although she seldom bothered to read them. Mary Rogers always mentioned it the next morning.

"Your mother has gone to have coffee with Countess Poletti. After that, she's going shopping. She's heading for the airport around six, and hopes to see you to say goodbye."

"Well, I'll be out all day. I'll leave her a note. You and James have a nice holiday." Mary Rogers and James Brannigan, the butler, had been married the previous year, after a fifteen-year courtship. They were leaving today to go camping in Colorado for their two-week vacation, and the idea of the two of them pitted against the wilderness amused Tyger enormously.

"James is picking up our tent right now. We'll leave as soon as Lady Roberta gets off. Don't forget to call Mrs. Hatcher. She rang last night and wants you to bring some towels from Bloomingdale's when you go out for the weekend."

"Oh, Christ, I almost forgot. I have to call her and cancel."

Mary Rogers left to answer the door. Tyger looked over her messages and opened her appointment book. She had been thinking a lot about Hugh Marshall and her assignment. She would begin interviewing her friends, subtly, to find out their designer preferences. She jotted down a list of names. Many of them were away for the summer, but she would call around and set up as many people as she could for lunch or drinks.

First, she had to deal with Julia Hatcher. She looked up the East Hampton number and dialed. A child answered.

"Hi, Nell. It's your Auntie Tyger. Is your Mummy there?" The child put down the phone wordlessly and Julia got on.

"Listen, I've changed my mind about the towels. I want seafoam instead of celery. Six of everything."

"And good morning to you too, my darling," Tyger said.

In person, Julia could be the essence of charm. On the phone she was always hurried, abrupt. Bad phone manners, Tyger had told her more than once. They had been best friends since fifteen, and they could say anything to each other. Almost anything. On the subject of Julia's husband, Sparky, Tyger kept her mouth shut. She didn't want to lose an old friend.

"What? Oh, sorry. Good morning, Tyger," Julia enunciated slowly, for effect. "And how are you this bright sunny morning? Are you just getting up? I've been up since five."

Julia loved to make Tyger feel guilty about sleeping late. Julia liked to insinuate that it was the three kids who were the cause of it all, but Tyger knew better. Julia was a morning person and always had been. In school, after lights out, Tyger always wanted to stay up and talk. Julia usually dropped off within minutes, to Tyger's everlasting annoyance.

"Anyway, my dear . . ." Tyger hated canceling out on Julia. She was not a gracious loser. "I'll get the towels. Seafoam. But I wondered who else would be driving out to bring them. . . ."

Julia remained silent. Tyger could imagine her jaw setting into indignation.

"Something's come up. I can't leave town this weekend. Jake and I were looking forward to it. Really, it's been weeks since I've seen you, and I have so much to tell you . . ."

Julia broke in, "You can stop running on. I'm not insulted. As it turns out this weekend is getting unbelievably crowded. Sparky's partner and his wife are coming out. He invited them at the last minute. You've met them. . . ."

"Oh, God yes. Steve and Merrill. All she did was talk about the significance of experimental theater. No sense of humor."

"You've got it. Deliver the towels to Sparky's office, and if you promise, *promise* to come out weekend after next, I'll still be your best friend."

"Terrific. By the way, who's your favorite designer, currently?"

"Why do you want to know that?"

"I'll tell you when I see you. Who? Come on."

"Well . . . let's see. Most of my new things are Matt Phillips's. Yeah, I guess he's my current favorite."

"Last time we had lunch you had on that terrific Tasha Powers tunic."

"Hmmm, you're right. I like her too. Oops, I hear a big crash. Gotta go. 'Bye." She hung up.

Tyger went to her closet and started looking over her own wardrobe. Then she looked through the clothes by American designers in Bobbie's closet. Halston. Mary McFadden. Bill Blass. They already had their own perfumes on the market. So did Ralph Lauren, Geoffrey Beene, Oscar de la Renta, Galanos and Calvin Klein. Then there were Perry Ellis, Norma Kamali, Stephen Burrows, Scott Barrie, Cathy Hawthorne, Holly Harp, and on and on. All good candidates. And Matt Phillips and Tasha Powers. Any of them, she knew, would kill to have a company like Kellerco catapult his or her name into the big bucks of the cosmetic and perfume industry.

Tyger sat down with her address book and spent the next two hours interviewing friends over the phone or setting up appointments with them for the next week.

Her last call was to Elaine Talbert, an old friend of her

mother's. Elaine was the venerable and venerated *grande dame* of American fashion, and she could be very helpful, as long as Tyger camouflaged her reasons for needing information. Elaine was a notorious gossip. Tyger reached Marta Kellogg, Elaine's lover-secretary, and set up a date for tea that afternoon.

The telephone rang the moment she hung up after talking to Marta. It was Hugh Marshall's secretary, Annie. "Please hold for Mr. Marshall."

"Hello, Miss Hayes." Hugh Marshall's voice boomed convivially into Tyger's ear. "I've been thinking about you."

Tyger felt a blush creeping up the inside of her neck and behind her ears. Something about the man made her feel sixteen again.

"Well, I'm busy at work on my assignment. . . ."

"Good. That's what I'm calling about. I'm stepping up your deadline. I want your report by the middle of next week. Thursday at the latest."

Tyger laughed. "You don't ask too much of your unpaid employees, do you?"

Marshall continued, "If you can't get the report to me by then, our deal's off." Tyger was surprised by the sudden coldness in his voice. A friend had warned Tyger that Marshall was mercurial, friendly one minute, a son of a bitch the next. She was surprised to hear the unpleasant side, just the same.

"You'll have it." She was not going to make excuses or show annoyance. "On Wednesday afternoon."

"Good," Marshall approved. "I look forward to seeing it."

Tyger stuck her tongue out at the telephone receiver before she hung it up. The bastard. She was going to have to work her ass off to meet the new deadline. Once she had the job, she was sure things would settle down into a routine. What on earth would it be like working for Hugh Marshall? Tyger couldn't wait to find out.

The Palm Court was quiet. Thursdays in July it did not get crowded. Nonetheless there was a respectable smattering of patrons, regulars and out-of-towners, enjoying the violin serenade which accompanied teatime at the lovely palm-bedecked enclave on the main floor of the Plaza Hotel.

Tyger recognized a graying distinguished television anchorman with a slim young brunette she knew was not his wife. Tyger followed the maître d' to the table at the center of the court that Elaine had reserved for them, and tried to avoid looking at the temptingly elaborate cakes and pastries, openly displayed near the entrance.

"Hello, my pet." Elaine Talbert arrived, wearing an old Norell suit, oyster-colored with black braided trim around the jacket. Her wide-brimmed black felt hat was vintage Lilly Daché. Only her garnet-and-pearl amethyst-clasped necklace by Kristin Moore and the Charles Jourdan shoes and handbag were new. No one else would dare wear a thirty-year-old suit and hat to the Plaza. But Elaine Talbert was famous for walking the tightrope of fashion. Her tall lean figure had always looked smashing in clothes. Even now, somewhere in her late seventies, she could hold her own.

"Hello, Elaine." Tyger rose and greeted her. "You look simply marvelous."

"Well, you cannot match Norell for clean, sculptural lines and subtle workmanship. Oh, how I long for the old days. Ah, well ..." Elaine sighed, then leaned over to kiss Tyger's cheek. "What a joy to see you, my lamb."

Elaine Talbert had burst into New York from Corinth, Mississippi, back in the Twenties. She had worked under Frank Crowninshield at *Vanity Fair*, then on to *Vogue*, and for the last half of her life she had been a freelance fashion consultant, one of the most successful women of her era. She still worked part-time, even though she had stashed away a decent fortune. Over the years, Elaine had developed a considerable talent for freeloading off the super-rich. A subtle talent, for she and Marta, her constant companion for the past forty years, were still in great demand as houseguests. Elaine was likely to be invited anywhere in the world for a weekend. What's more, she and Marta would be fetched via private jet. People dreaded the repercussions involved with not inviting her. She was stylish and amusing, but she could also be venomous.

"George!" With a flick of the wrist. Elaine summoned her favorite waiter. "Bring us iced tea right away. I'm about to expire from the humidity."

"Will you have some Sacher torte, Miss Talbert?"

"Oh, George, how wicked of you to tempt me. What do you say, Tyger? Shall we split a tiny piece?" She didn't wait for Tyger's reply. "Yes, George, just a smidgen. Well, Tyger," she said breathlessly, "what are you up to these days? How's Bobbie?"

"The same. You know, as vivacious as ever."

Elaine smiled delightedly. "Don't be wicked, darling."

While Elaine devoured the chocolate cake, Tyger tried to plot her strategy. It would never do to be candid with Elaine about her assignment. Elaine would tell Marta, and Marta would have it all over town by dusk.

"Where are you off to this weekend?" Elaine licked the last bit of chocolate from her fork.

"Nowhere. I'm staying in town to go apartment hunting. I think it's time for me to get my own place."

"How lovely. There's a wonderful apartment coming up in our building. The Lodges—do you know them?—the Lucien Lodges." Tyger nodded. Lucien Lodge was a senior vice president of Chemical Bank. He had been an under secretary of the Treasury in the first Nixon administration. His wife, Margaret, chaired several of the larger charity balls each year, and drank too much. "They're moving to Scottsdale for his health."

"Actually, I was thinking about looking in the Village. I've always wanted to live there."

"Well, you just can't," Elaine stated emphatically. "It's much too dangerous. All those junkies and winos—it's a freak show. Your mother won't allow it." Elaine loved to be the last word on all subjects. It was pointless to argue with her. Besides, Tyger wanted her to remain in a good mood.

"Elaine, what's the perfume you're wearing? It's scrumptious." Tyger knew it was Mystère by Rochas, but what the hell.

"Mystère. Haven't you tried it yet?"

"Oh Elaine, I'm shocked. You, the greatest lady of American fashion, wearing a French perfume?"

"Well, I circulate my scents. I like Halston in the fall, Beene's Red at Christmas. But it's true, the Americans have been boring lately. All that mass-marketed fragrance—Charlie and Smitty and Maxi and God knows what else. I always thought one of those manufacturers should come to me. Elaine. Now that's a good name for a perfume."

Dead end. Another tack. "What's the latest word from Seventh Avenue?"

"You're asking me? You and your mother both have a knack for knowing what's in before it is. Anyway, now more than ever, quality is the word. Like this Norell I have on. You just can't go wrong with good fabrics and expert craftsmanship. Those things never change."

"Well, confidentially . . ." Tyger knew that Elaine expected her to drop some tidbits of gossip. "I've been seeing a lot of Jake Danton. You know, the photographer?" Elaine nodded. "My mind just hasn't been on clothes."

Elaine's eyes sparkled. "Oh, he is a doll. But let me give you a teensy word of advice. Don't ever neglect your appearance for anything, least of all a man." She laughed. Elaine Talbert hated men. Her wound was left over from the Twenties.

"Well, there are so many terrific American designers these days. Blass, Beene, Halston, Lauren . . ."

"Entre nous, my dear, a couple of the big ones are sliding dreadfully. " She looked piercingly at Tyger. "You know who I mean."

Tyger wasn't sure, but she nodded anyway.

"Besides," Elaine said, "they're making anybody a superstar these days, any riffraff. My God, look at the good press Matt Phillips is getting. And snippy Tasha Powers. You'd think they'd *invented* clothes. . . ." Elaine continued her attack, inadvertently telling Tyger exactly what she wanted to know. If Elaine hated them they would be just right for younger women; Elaine's taste ran toward the more conservative these days. She ranted on, cutting the young designers to shreds: one used inferior fabrics, another lacked an eye for color, a third merely copied the best of all the others, using his personality to dazzle his clientele, and so on.

"Oh, my dear! It's nearly five, and Marta and I are flying to Virginia for a long weekend. I hate to rush, but it's been divine seeing you." She proffered her cheeks to be kissed, and left Tyger to pay the check.

Tyger arrived home in time to see Bobbie off. Then she called Jake.

"Why don't you come over here? The apartment's empty, and right now I'm too tired to move."

"Sure, babe, I'm just finishing up. I'll bring some food and we can cook there." Jake loved Bobbie's apartment almost as much as Tyger hated it. He was like a little boy, goggling over the art collection and the antiques. So what if there was a Manet over Bobbie's bed, a Turner in the dining room, Matisse and Derain and Berthe Morrisot in the study? To Tyger, the place emanated uneasy vibrations, perhaps because of the subtle tensions that existed between her mother and herself. Even when her mother wasn't there, Bobbie's electricity remained in the air.

"Great. But keep it light. It's too hot to do a lot of cooking. There's plenty of wine here."

She blew a kiss into the phone. "I'm going to take a nap. Keep your elbow on the doorbell until I answer."

Tyger cooked mussels with fresh tomatoes, garlic and basil. Jake tossed up an arugula and mushroom salad. They dabbed French bread from Dumas into the rich mussel sauce, and drank lots of Frascati.

After dinner, Tyger and Jake sat out on the terrace and enjoyed the quiet of the city on a warm summer night.

Jake kissed Tyger's forehead. "This is a nice evening."

Tyger brushed her lips against his neck, but was temporarily preoccupied.

"You know, Hugh Marshall's already shown his true colors!"

"You saw him again today?" Jake was pleased by Tyger's late-bloomer enthusiasm over jobbing down and getting her own apartment. She had a lot going for her, too much to waste.

She was the first woman that he had actually considered marrying, at least since his ex-wife, Lizzie, who had been his campus love. And, unfortunately, the spark that was ignited in the Colorado mountains around Boulder was quickly extinguished when they arrived in New York, Jake to make his fortune as a photographer, Lizzie as a painter.

Lizzie had beginner's luck and hit the jackpot right away. Her bizarre, funny happenings—staged at SoHo lofts, in the Connecticut hills and on Long Island beaches—delighted the critics. Even when the Sixties zaniness faded away she was such a favorite that she could do no wrong. She had supported Jake then. He had resented it, even though he could not rationally justify the indignation. He loved her, but he was jealous. By the time Jake had built his own success, they had gone their separate ways.

Jake was still attracted to strong-willed, independent women. Tyger fit the bill partially. Born strong-willed, she was on her way to being independent, and Jake was more attracted than ever.

"I'm going to have to borrow your typewriter this weekend, and get started on this report. That bastard shortened my deadline. Marshall wants everything by Wednesday."

Jake put his arm around Tyger and licked the tiny mole on her left shoulder. "You can do it."

"Hmmm, I really think I can. I have a feeling . . . it's more than a feeling. If big business is like the movie business then it's all mostly illusion. Bluffing . . ."

"You've got it, kid. It's not what you say, but how you say it. Or whatever the hell the quote is."

"All right. I have to convince Hugh Marshall that I *know* what I'm talking about." Tyger began giggling. "Jake, have *you* ever had any idea of what I was talking about—at any time in our entire relationship?"

He took the last sip of wine from his glass. "I've never been aware that you even talked. When I think about you, I picture you in bed, with your legs spread apart, moaning loud." He grinned.

"Jake, you creep! You are a total nerd." Tyger grabbed one of Bobbie's needlepoint pillows and began hitting him in the lap.

"Okay. You asked for it. You're getting it right here, on Mom's terrace." Jake stretched his six feet over her in one lunge, and pinned down Tyger's arms into the goosedown cushions. Tyger struggled, still giggling, and almost kicked him in the groin.

"I'm sorry." She laughed.

"The hell you are! That's where you were aiming. You just missed. Now I'm going to have to rape you."

"Not out here on the terrace—people will see us."

Jake was nibbling on her ear now. "The only people who'll see us are people who have penthouses in even taller buildings than this. Those people are all out of town. No, my dear. No one will see you. No one will hear your screams," he whispered sadistically.

Tyger began to feel prickly all over. Visions of him tying her up, whipping her, swept over her. In the ninety-degree heat she felt chills creeping over her stomach. It was exciting, and a bit terrifying. Jake was ripping her clothes off at a frantic pace.

He thrust himself into her, and made love roughly. It lasted a long time. But his toughness was not brutal. The game was just a game after all. A good one, though. Tyger felt terrific when it was all over.

The two of them lay in a moist afterglow. Jake looked at his watch. Eleven o'clock.

"Well," he said, stretching. "Now that I've gotten my rocks off, what do you want to do?"

"Nothing that involves moving."

"No, really. The night's young." Jake came alive when it

got late. Tyger knew that he was anxious to go out and carouse.

"Let's take a shower first. Then I'll think about it. I refuse to be rushed."

They showered together. Tyger wrapped a gigantic towel around herself and sat down on the edge of the tub.

Jake snapped his wet fingers. "Shit, I almost forgot. We're invited to a party tonight. In honor of Page Cutler's new play."

"Oh Jake, I'm tired. Can't we just get in bed and watch the late show?"

"Those words are being brought to you by Tyger Hayes, former jet setter," Jake said, imitating Howard Cosell. "Page'll be furious if we don't show up. He just slipped us house seats for next Thursday. The play's already sold out through January. So . . . are you coming quietly, or do I have to pull a macho number and drag you?"

"Where is it?" Tyger asked reluctantly.

"Tasha Powers and Billy Youngblood's townhouse."

Tyger jumped up. "Why didn't you say so in the first place? I'll be ready in five minutes."

Page Cutler was Broadway's current songwriter *extraordinaire*. His latest musical, *Edith!*—based on the life of Edith Wharton—had just opened to rave reviews. Jake had photographed its star, Irene Worth, for a spread in *Harper's Bazaar,* and she blew Jake a kiss from across the room when he and Tyger arrived.

Despite the fact that it was vacation season, people were crowded into the barn-sized split-level living room and candlelit Japanese garden adjoining it. Page Cutler had friends from many worlds, and so actors mingled with bankers, sports celebrities, dancers from the chorus line, Seventh Avenue designers and a smattering of royalty. Jacques Cousteau and Robert Redford were off to the side of the room, deeply engrossed in conversation about windmill generators. Halston and Liza Minnelli stood by the piano chatting with Page.

Tyger caught sight of Hugh Marshall, talking with Jackie Onassis. He nodded to Tyger from across the room. Shortly afterward she saw him exit, before she could work her way over to his area of the enormous living room. Tyger helped herself to a glass of wine from the tray of one of the circulating waiters, and began to mix. She liked parties where she knew most of the guests.

Tyger milled around, greeting old friends and deftly avoiding her host, Billy Youngblood. She had gone out with Billy once, back in her modeling days before she had married Jeff Collins. It had been a disaster. Billy was loud, and he drank too much. He had attacked her in the back seat of his Rolls, and called her some nasty names when she had refused to participate. Since then, he had married the designer Tasha Powers, and they had become renowned party-givers. Although Tyger liked Tasha, she still loathed Billy Youngblood. In her estimation, he was nothing but a rich, overbearing, tactless jerk.

Tyger had just finished talking to Diane Von Fürstenberg about designer sheets and towels and was making her way over to Calvin Klein and Adolfo, to talk about their perfumes, when Tasha Powers came to greet her. She was wearing one of her own designs, a glittery fuchsia wrap dress with kimono sleeves.

"Haven't seen you for ages, Tyger. What've you been up to?" Tasha Powers Youngblood's throaty, New York-accented voice was completely at odds with her diminutive, black-eyed ethnic beauty.

"Oh . . . nothing much. Spending a lot of time on the Island," Tyger answered vaguely.

"In seclusion? We haven't run into you at any of the parties out there. . . ." She lowered her voice. "Are you involved with someone else besides Jake?" Tasha was known for her bluntness. She had grown up on the Lower East Side, and worked hard to get where she was. But there was a charm to the earthy feistiness, and a certain vulnerability underneath it all that smoothed the edges of her toughness.

Billy Youngblood suddenly came weaving drunkenly toward them, and dropped his arm leadenly around Tyger's shoulders. She wasn't sure whether he was faking affection or simply needed her support in order to stand erect.

Billy gave Tyger a wet cheek kiss. "And a good evenin' to ya!" he gushed his mock Texas friendliness, complete with down-home accent. "I hear you've been job huntin'." He turned to Tasha. "Did ya know, honey? Tyger may be goin' to work for Kellerco."

Tyger could barely conceal her astonishment. How could he possibly know about her interview with Hugh Marshall? She started to deny it, but his voice rolled over hers. He realized suddenly he was talking too loudly and lowered his volume. "I also hear that they're lookin' for a designer name to put on a bottle of perfume." He paused and looked accusingly at Tyger. The silly drunk was more dangerous than he looked, Tyger concluded. He must have spies everywhere.

Tyger kept a straight face and matched his stare. "Where'd you hear that, Billy? You seem to know a lot more than I do."

"Well . . . maybe I do, and maybe not. But just between you and me, the best designer in the entire country, hell, the whole world, is standin' right here." Tasha looked uncomfortable. She tried to change the subject.

"Sugar? Will you go check with the bartender and see if we need more . . ."

Youngblood ignored her. He kept his attention focused on Tyger, and pointed his finger at her. "I want you to see that it's *her* name Kellerco puts on all those perfume bottles."

Tasha flashed a bewildered, apologetic glance at Tyger, and tried to steer Billy away, but he wouldn't budge. He kept his finger pointed at Tyger. "Ya hear me? Tasha's the one to pick!"

Jake appeared. "Sorry to butt in, but there's someone I want Tyger to meet." He led her off in the direction of the garden. "You looked like a damsel who needed rescuing," he said, kissing her cheek. "What was that letch up to? He really had you cornered."

Tyger filled him in. "Where in hell does that drunken ass get his information? He's ridiculous, but I also think . . ."

Jake raised a cautionary eyebrow, and Tyger turned to see Tasha coming over to them. She looked distressed.

"Tyger . . . I'm sorry. I have no idea what Billy's talking about. But you know he can be less than charming when he's had a few too many."

Tyger put her arm around Tasha's tiny shoulders and gave her a hug. "Don't worry, Tasha. I've known Billy even longer than you."

Tasha smiled with relief. "I'm glad you understand. Now if you'll excuse me, I have to go check the kitchen."

"Yoohoo, Tyger, sweetie! Surprise, surprise." Tyger turned around at the sound of a familiar slightly high-pitched voice to see the cause of Tasha's hasty departure. Matt Phillips. Tyger had known him since her modeling days. He was wearing a black loose-weave suit of his own design, in a blend of linen, wool and silk. The jacket was softly shaped with a narrow lapel. With it he wore a white silk shirt, but the focal point of the outfit was his left arm, which was sheathed in a red satin sling.

"Matt!" Tyger said, her eyes resting on the cast, which was almost hidden by the sling.

Matt Phillips kissed Tyger on both cheeks. "*Don't* ask! It was a roller disco accident. Too boring to bother you with details."

"Okay. Next question—what on earth are you doing here? I can't believe it."

"Well, Page Cutler's one of my oldest friends in New York. Tasha *had* to invite us because Page insisted." The "us" referred to Matt and his boyfriend, Garry Gray, a sometime model who had been living with Matt for the past three years. "Anyway," Matt continued, "it's an absolute riot because Tasha refuses to acknowledge my presence. I must admit I was looking forward to a showdown. . . ."

Garry Gray joined them and handed Matt a glass of champagne. "The gossip columnists are about to chew up their pencils. Everybody's waiting for the fireworks."

Garry was blond and beautiful with the sort of carefree California look that can only be reproduced in Manhattan with hours of careful primping. His sand-colored hair gleamed with golden highlights. His skin glowed with Fire Island tan from his square-jawed face down along the open front of his epaulet shirt practically to his navel. He looked at Tyger. "Don't you just love it? Just the whisper of intrigue gives me a hard-on."

Matt brushed Garry's cheek with a kiss. "Just about anything gives you a hard-on. By the way, pal, who was that boy you were off in the corner with? He didn't look old enough to be out this late."

Garry flashed his blue eyes, innocently. "He's in the chorus of Page's show. But it turns out he's straight. I was only trying to line up a little threesome for later."

"Hmm." Matt smiled. "A delicious idea. Well, keep circulating. I'm sure you'll come up with someone good. Oh, there's Candy Bergen . . . I must have a few words with her. Lovely to see you, Tyger. Let's have drinks soon." He kissed her cheek, and was off.

As soon as Matt Phillips had crossed the room, Tasha Powers came back over to Tyger. "I'm being so good I can hardly stand myself. It's been three years and I still want to kill him. . . ." Tasha and Matt had once been a team, designing under the label Circus. More than that, they had been lovers. Now they were ardent rivals. And they hated each other.

During all the years that Matt and Tasha were living and

designing together, Matt had struggled, four times weekly with his analyst, to conquer his homosexual stirrings. Then he met Garry Gray, and fell madly in love. He didn't set out to hurt his old friend and lover, but the consequences were inevitable. Tasha, on the rebound, turned right around and wed Billy Youngblood, the fiftyish Texas cattle millionaire who financed and managed her new designing firm.

Tasha continued, "That little fag. Page made me invite him, but how fucking civilized does a person have to be?" She raised her empty glass. "After the next refill I may explode."

Tyger smiled sympathetically. "I can imagine how you feel, Tasha. But . . ."

"It's yesterday's new . . . I know, I know." Tasha sighed. "I guess I also feel a little sorry for him. His wimpy little friend cheats on him all over Seventh Avenue. . . ."

"Nasty, nasty, Tasha. That's not nice." The young designer Cathy Hawthorne poked her head in between Tasha's and Tyger's. "You know Matt's very touchy when it comes to Garry's . . . indiscretions."

"All right. Enough. I need another drink." Tasha blinked her eyes quickly, and Tyger could see that she was fighting to hold back a few uninvited tears. Tyger wondered how she would feel if someone she loved left her for another man.

Tyger found Jake and put her arm around him.

"Hey, babe," he said. "I was just coming to look for you. How about hitting a wonderful late-night spot I know, way downtown? Barnabus Rex will provide a little culture shock from here. Very seedy, *very* degenerate."

"Hmmm. Sounds interesting, but let's do it another night. I want to get up early in the morning to go apartment hunting, remember?"

"Okay, we'll pick up the *Times* real estate section on the way home."

Billy Youngblood stood at the bar in the library and poured another scotch. It was four in the morning, and he wasn't bothering any longer with Perrier or ice. He just wanted to relax in his favorite room, with its dark-brown lacquered walls, hunting prints, and the built-in steel cabinets that housed the sound equipment, television, video recorder, Advent video beam, and, of course, the bar. The only thing missing was books. Youngblood unbuttoned his Ralph Lauren Western shirt, took off his Lauren jacket and tossed it casually onto a leather chair. He lowered himself down onto the cowhide sofa and propped his cowboy-booted feet on the round chrome coffee table.

Page Cutler and the last of his well-wishers were gone, the ash trays were emptied, the glasses cleared, the caterers and bartenders had packed up and departed into the night. The five-story townhouse on East Sixty-first Street, recently purchased and renovated by the Youngbloods for just under a million dollars, was quiet until Billy broke the silence with a deep, rumbling belch.

"You pig," Tasha said, entering the room. Her voice dripped with contempt.

"Shucks, honey, I'm just a country boy." He smiled. He turned around, and was surprised to see her standing there, with her arms folded, gazing at him. He felt a little uneasy. He never knew what was going to rile her.

"Is it true that Kellerco's looking to market a designer perfume?" Her voice was sharp.

Youngblood took a couple of swallows of whiskey. "I've got it from one of my best sources . . ."

"And is it true that Tyger's going to be working there?"

"Did you hear her deny it, honey?"

Tasha started shrieking. "Then why the fuck did you act that way with her? Jesus! You are a stupid-assed moron. Don't you know that you just lost any chance I had to be the designer they choose?"

Billy yelled back, "Just one minute here, my little street urchin. You're the one I'm lookin' out for."

"Well, you sure as hell don't act that way!" She turned, and started to leave the room.

Billy jumped to his feet and grabbed her roughly. "Look, you were getting along fine with Hugh Marshall tonight. He's the one calling the shots around there. Don't worry about it."

Tasha pulled away from his grasp. "No telling what *you* said to Hugh Marshall. He left pretty early."

"C'mon, honey, gimme a kiss. We'll make up in bed."

"You're drunk, Billy. You disgust me when you act like this. You've probably loused up my chances, and I hate you for it! You can sleep alone, tonight and every other night you choose to stick around here."

Billy looked contrite. "Honey . . . I was just lookin' after your best interests."

"The hell you were!" Tasha huffed out of the room. Billy rushed after her.

"Look, sweetie . . . I promise you somethin'. On my word. If Kellerco doesn't pick you, then I'll market you a damned perfume. Hell, it's not so hard. Anybody can get themselves into the perfume business. In fact . . . it's a good moneymakin' idea."

Tasha's eyes narrowed. "Don't play around with me, Billy. If you're serious . . . I want your firm promise." Billy nodded. Tasha gave him a coquettish smile, and pecked him on the cheek.

"Okay, sugar," she cooed sweetly. "Come to bed. Just wait a few minutes till I get ready."

Tasha spent the next fifteen minutes in her enormous mirrored bathroom, smoking a cigarette and plucking her eyebrows. When she emerged, Billy Youngblood was asleep, as she knew he would be, passed out on the bed in his clothes. She left him there and went into one of the guest rooms, where she spent most nights.

By ten the next morning, Tyger had rented an apartment in the West Village, on Jane Street. It had a small terrace, sunken living room, highly polished parquet floors, one bedroom, and a woodburning fireplace. Charming, sunny, oozing with rustic charm, it was a schoolgirl's vision of the perfect New York apartment. At nine hundred dollars a month, no schoolgirl could have afforded it. Tyger, however, considered it a proper investment toward her new life as a working woman.

CHAPTER SEVEN

SHELDON Shaw got out of the air-conditioned taxi and hurried through the white Phoenix heat to the Kellerco building. It was 120 degrees that day, and though he reached the door in less than half a minute he was sweating as he walked across the stark lobby and gave his name to the receptionist. But it was more than the heat. Shaw had been summoned halfway across the continent by a cryptic phone call from Nelson Bachrach, chairman of the board of the company for which he had labored in executive obscurity for a quarter of a century. In that time, Shaw had seldom been singled out, and being ordered like that to a personal interview with Nelson Bachrach made him nervous.

"You may go up," the gray-haired receptionist said. "Mr. Bachrach is expecting you."

Bachrach's office was on the penthouse floor of the Kellerco Building, one of the first skyscrapers to be built in downtown Phoenix. Other buildings towered higher now, but Nelson Bachrach had resisted any suggestion that Kellerco try to compete by building splashier quarters. The Keller Copper Company ran effectively and economically from the building that he and the late Sam Keller had planned, and Bachrach was not the sort of man to spend money on window dressing when it wasn't necessary.

Bachrach's office was a model of luxurious austerity. Large modern Fritz Scholder Indian canvases faced each other on opposite walls, but Bachrach never noticed them, and would probably not have recognized them in another setting. The masculine interior was the recent work of a decorator from Dallas who had done what he could to make the office suitable for the chairman of the board of one of the country's larger conglomerates. But Bachrach's battered and chipped old redwood desk and his cracked leather swivel chair bore testimony to the old man's determination to keep in touch with the practical realities that he understood the best.

Bachrach did not rise from his chair when Sheldon Shaw entered. "Good day, Shaw. Have a seat." He nodded toward one of the red leather chairs across the desk, subtly lower than his own. "How was the trip?" He did not wait for an answer. "I called you here because I think you're the man I need for an important job."

Sheldon Shaw shifted uncomfortably in his seat and felt a trickle of sweat run down his side. The several martinis he had had on the plane had worn off. He wished desperately that Bachrach would offer him a drink.

"You wrote an article a couple of years ago for the company magazine. It caught my eye. 'The Importance of Listening,' wasn't that it?"

Shaw nodded. "That's right, sir." He remembered the article. It had been ghosted for him by his assistant, Dave Kirshenbaum.

"I need a man who can listen," Bachrach said. "As you may have heard, we're opening a new division."

"The perfume company?"

"Right."

"Yes . . . it's an interesting idea. . . ."

"It's a damned stupid idea . . . and that young radical Marshall is running with the bit between his teeth. I want someone in New York to keep an eye on things for me. Someone I can trust."

"Yes, sir."

"Shaw, I'll come to the point. I'm naming you president of Keller Perfumes."

Shaw looked stunned. He had come to Phoenix afraid he was about to be raked over the coals. Suddenly, he was the president of a major new venture. But instead of elation, he had an uneasy feeling he was being forced into a dangerous position, a pawn in a power struggle between Kellerco's two giants. Still, he had been chosen out of a sea of middle-echelon executives. It was a once-in-a-lifetime chance. "Thank you, Mr. Bachrach. I'll certainly do my best to justify your confidence in me."

Bachrach smiled. "You look all worn out from your trip, Shel. Or perhaps it's our Phoenix climate. Can I offer you a drink?"

By Wednesday morning, Tyger's head was swimming. She had been up nearly all night typing. The fact that she had not typed since college considerably impeded her progress. So did the fact that she did not really know what Marshall expected from her. She had spent the past three days solidly researching the fashion and perfume industry, and interviewing friends. Finally, she had reached the point where she had too many facts and opinions to be sorted through in the matter of a few hours. And that was all the time she had left to get everything together.

She called Hugh Marshall and arranged with his secretary to see him that afternoon. Then she forged ahead, hoping the report would somehow write itself by deadline.

She had narrowed the choice of designer down to Matt Phillips and Tasha Powers. Now it was time for a decision.

Tyger had an instinctive feeling that Marshall expected her to come up with one name and her reasons for choosing it. Not a list of possibilities, not two choices. Which would it be: Matt Phillips or Tasha Powers? Tyger closed her eyes and imagined two perfume bottles, one bearing Phillips's name, the other with a Powers label. Both looked fine. Both designers, she knew, were top sellers; both made clothes which were contemporary and comfortable, yet fancifully unique. Either one of them, she guessed, would kill to sell his or her name to Kellerco.

There was a lot of money to be made from the fragrance business, which accounted for well over a third of the high profits in the cosmetics industry. A great deal of prestige was attached to designer fragrances. After all, women who could never afford a Dior original for five thousand dollars could purchase a bottle of Diorissimo, and share the mystique of haute couture with the idle rich.

Tyger leaned back and stretched. Then she went into the bathroom to splash water on her face. Her mirror confirmed that she looked exhausted. Damn it, she had to finish the report so she could wash her hair and try to look terrific for Hugh Marshall. She went to her jewelry box and pulled out the lucky silver dollar her father had given her when she was ten years old. Heads: Matt Phillips. Tails: Tasha Powers. She flipped the coin.

Tim Yates escorted Tyger into his office, not Hugh Marshall's. Tim spoke softly, and was consummately polite, every bit the proper Englishman.

"Terribly sorry. Mr. Marshall was called off to a conference. An emergency. He instructed me to see you and look at your report."

Tyger felt her anxiety flatten out. Not getting to see the boss in person was a bad sign, but she quickly hid her disappointment. With her most engaging smile, she handed over the ten typewritten pages of her final draft. "Forgive the typos. My fingers are out of practice."

Yates nodded vaguely, and dove into the report. He read with the intensity of an Evelyn Wood speed reader, quickly turning from one page to the next. His face was devoid of any reaction. Tyger wished it were all over, and that she were back home taking a nap. Marshall had just been stringing her along. Obviously, Tim Yates had been assigned to the unpleasant task of letting her down tactfully. Yates finished the report, and set it neatly on his desk. Tyger held her breath.

"Your report is quite thorough. Mr. Marshall should be well pleased with it." He hesitated.

"I'm waiting for the 'But . . .' " Tyger smiled, resigned.

"Oh, I'm sorry. Do I sound grave? I was temporarily preoccupied with identifying the scent you're wearing." He laughed, a bit nervously. "I guess we're all caught up with fragrance these days. Let's see . . . is it Bal à Versailles?"

Tyger relaxed. "Yes . . . you have a good nose. But I'm wearing it only until Matt Phillips comes out with his fragrance," she added.

"Right. You seem to be very in tune, Miss Hayes. Your report confirms the recommendations of our people here. Mr. Marshall was most anxious to have your opinion on the matter, since you are a woman who is obviously in the thick of things."

Tyger smiled, relieved. "I'm flattered that Mr. Marshall thinks so."

"Oh, yes. It's one thing for our marketing staff to come up with Matt Phillips's name. But they don't buy the perfume. They don't follow the trends in the same way a woman such as you would. Mr. Marshall feels that you reflect our target market. . . ."

"What if my report had named someone other than Matt Phillips?"

Yates shrugged, but his smile was friendly. "Oh, I'm so glad it didn't. It would have complicated things considerably. Mr. Marshall would have probably put you in one corner and the marketing department in the other, and let you slug it out." He laughed, self-consciously. "But I'm only joking, Miss Hayes."

"Well . . . what's next? For me, that is."

"Mr. Marshall was quite impressed with you. But since you lacked solid business credentials, he gave you this assignment to see whether you would be right for this job. You've come through with flying colors, as they say." He smiled. "I have been authorized to offer you a starting salary of twenty-two thousand."

Tyger was flabbergasted. "To do *what?*"

"You will be the assistant to the president of Kellerco's newly organized subsidiary, Keller Perfumes—a man named Sheldon Shaw." Yates paused. "You'll be handling a wide assortment of details involved with the launching of the Matt Phillips perfume."

"Well, I still don't know what that means, but I'm willing to find out." Tyger tried hard to keep from showing her excitement. She was on her way to independence. And she had done it on her own, with no help from her mother. "When do I begin?"

Yates pulled a file out of his top drawer. "Mr. Shaw is in the midst of moving over from one of our business-machine companies. We have rented a floor in the Solow Building on West Fifty-seventh Street, and the decorators are in there this week. Let's see, can you begin on Monday?" Tyger nodded. Tim continued, "Shaw probably won't move in until mid-week, but you'll have a chance to get acquainted with the rest of the team. . . ."

"Team . . . ?" Tyger asked.

"Connie Larcada," Tim continued, "will be heading up the in-house advertising and promotion. We stole her from Benton and Bowles. Jess Leibowitz is head of marketing, and he comes from Estée Lauder. The staff will be small at first. New members will be added as needed." Tim looked up, and was pleased to see that Tyger was taking notes. "Mr. Marshall wants to keep this project under wraps, at least for a while.

Which reminds me . . . if anyone asks what your job is at Kellerco, tell them that you are working on a research project for the electronics division."

"The *electronics* division?"

Tim was sincere. "Oh, you can say the camera division, or rent-a-car division, tools, whatever. I'll give you a list of all our companies . . . just don't mention the word 'perfume' to anyone. Mr. Marshall is quite adamant about the secrecy of the project."

"Okay . . . mum's the word." Tyger closed her notepad.

Tim Yates stood. His gray herringbone three-piece suit was impeccably tailored. His sandy brown hair was cut English-style, slightly longer than the mode for American businessmen, but still short enough to look quite proper in the conference room. Yates's eyes were gray, and matched his suit. He was around thirty, Tyger guessed, and shy when the conversation moved from business and into small talk. He shook hands with Tyger. "Welcome to Kellerco, Miss Hayes." His eyes focused on a point in the vicinity of her left shoulder.

"Please call me Tyger. After all, we're going to be working together. Sort of, at any rate." Tyger thought Tim's face reddened ever so slightly.

"And you must call me Tim." He escorted her to the reception desk, bid her goodbye, and headed briskly down the long hallway to Hugh Marshall's office.

"How'd the meeting with Tyger Hayes go?" Marshall looked up from the financial reports he'd been studying.

"Just fine, Mr. Marshall. She chose Matt Phillips, just as you guessed she would. Her reasons were as sound as her instincts. The report is sharp. She accepted the job. Starting on Monday."

Marshall nodded, taking Tyger's report without glancing at it. "Good. I think Shaw can use an assistant with her contacts. After all, he's not entirely qualified to head up this division. . . ."

Tim Yates hesitated. "I have been rather wondering why you appointed Sheldon Shaw. Not that it's any of my business."

"Believe me, Shaw wasn't my choice. He was Nelson Bachrach's."

Tim nodded. "This is the shoe we've been waiting for him to drop, isn't it?"

"It looks like it," Marshall said. "One of them anyway." He

shrugged. "It's too early to engage in open wafare with him. I have to take his recommendations at this point."

"But why did Mr. Bachrach pick Shaw? Looking at his record, Shaw's not terribly impressive."

"Nelson wants an errand boy. Somebody who'll keep him posted on everything we're doing. Well . . . that's all right. I expected something like this. I think we can handle it."

"21" was crowded as usual, but Tyger and Jake Danton rated one of the "good" tables, in the front VIP section. Seated on the banquette, amid the restaurant's strongly masculine interior, Tyger looked radiantly feminine in her simple black silk Matt Phillips dinner dress, unadorned except for a diamond crescent-moon pendant, which Angela Cummings had designed for Tiffany's.

"Order champagne, Jake. Tonight's my treat."

"In that case, caviar, too," he teased. He was pleased that she had landed the job at Kellerco. When the Dom Pérignon arrived, he toasted her. "To the career woman . . . and her career."

"I wish I could tell you more about the job, Jake, but they've sworn me to secrecy. The truth is . . . I haven't the vaguest idea what I'll be doing." Tyger was as happy as a kid with her first two-wheeler.

"You know, Jake," Tyger said, as she downed her second glass of champagne, "I don't have anything to put into my apartment except clothes and a few knicknacks. Can you believe it? I own no furniture. Even when Jeff and I were married we lived at one of his father's extra homes. It was completely done in vintage MGM memorabilia."

Jake laughed. "And Bobbie's place is a mini-museum. Well, I guess you're going to have to work very hard to support yourself in the manner to which you've become accustomed. However, I happen to have an extra bed. You can have it if you want."

"You would. Jake the Romeo. No extra tables or chairs or pots and pans. Just leftover beds. It probably doesn't have any springs left after all the activity you've given it."

"It's a good bed. From my marriage. And, therefore, hardly used."

"Well, I do have to sleep. I'll take it." She smiled her thanks. "I've decided not to buy anything but the barest essentials. I want to have one of those dream apartments where everything is just acquired." Tyger pointed to an imaginary piece, and assumed her ritziest vocal tone. "Oh, that little Victorian chaise. Well, it simply *walked* over to me at this darling little shop in Amagansett, and said, 'Take me home.'"

Jake and Tyger were enjoying themselves immensely, giggling and gossiping, when Tyger saw Hugh Marshall making his entrance with a very beautiful, not-yet-divorced blond heiress on his arm.

Tyger leaned forward and lowered her voice. "Don't look now, but guess who just walked in?"

Jake looked around curiously. "All right," he said, "I'll bite. Who just walked in?"

"That's Hugh Marshall, you jerk!"

"Mmm. She's ravishing."

"Not her, wise guy. The one with the cane." Tyger was not sure whether she should go over and speak to Marshall. Because Tim Yates had emphasized secrecy about the Keller perfume project, she was almost afraid to be seen talking to Hugh Marshall in public.

Hugh Marshall, however, spotted Tyger and stopped by her table. His date was chatting with a group at the bar. "Tyger, my dear. Sorry I couldn't see you this afternoon. Tim informed me that you had a successful meeting." He smiled. "Welcome. Feel free to telephone me with any questions or ideas. Sheldon Shaw will, of course, be your direct superior, but I've taken a personal interest in the success of this division. I'm counting on you, Tyger."

"Thanks. I'll do my best."

When Marshall had rejoined his companion, Jake put his glass down with a skeptical look. "You're going to be working for him? I don't think I like it. He's very smooth. And too good-looking for the corporate world. In that slightly haunted way . . . like Laurence Olivier in *Wuthering Heights.*"

"Are you jealous, Jake?" Tyger teased, then went on, "He'll only be overseeing the project from a distance. I'll be working for a man named Sheldon Shaw. Tim Yates showed me *his* photograph from the Kellerco subsidiaries magazine. You don't have anything to worry about. He looks very fatherly . . ." She paused. "Getting back to Hugh Marshall. Don't you think he acted rather cool to me? Cordial, but . . ."

"No, Tyger. He was perfectly friendly. Don't tell me you have a schoolgirl crush on him."

"Of course not. But he has a reputation for blowing hot and cold on people. I just want to stay on his good side."

"I'll be watching you, Tyger. You're definitely interested in that man," Jake insisted. "But I'm not going to give you time to even think about him."

Jake and Tyger finished dinner. They spent the next few hours roller-discoing at Roxy, and the next few hours after that making love.

The following Monday morning, as Tyger walked toward the Solow Building—home of Avon Cosmetics and the brand-new Keller Perfumes—she was besieged by butterflies in her stomach. First-night nerves, she told herself; or rather, first-morning nerves. The streets were crowded at nine o'clock. Everyone else worked, she realized, but she had never had to deal with the crowds before. Normally she traveled by taxi. But now that she was a working woman, and as a democratic gesture, she had decided to brave the unfamiliar subway. It had been a nightmare. She had avoided the first train because she didn't want to crush into the hordes of people pushing and wedging themselves into the cars. But the platform filled up again before the next train arrived, and by that time she realized that she would have to push and shove like everyone else in order to get to work on time. It was an unnerving experience, but for the first time she felt part of the main tide of the city. Hundreds of bodies pressed up against each other. Good smells, bad smells. She had hugged her handbag close to her chest as the screaming train careened uptown. In New York, there were pickpockets even at nine in the morning.

The lobby of the Solow Building was spacious, cool, and impersonal. She found the proper bank of elevators, and rode to the forty-eighth floor. When she stepped off the elevator she stood, wondering where to go, what to do next. She was surrounded by a futuristic-looking reception area, with high-gloss pale-gray walls that still smelled strongly of paint. Twin-sized canvases by Roy Lichtenstein dominated the wall behind a plush gray velour sofa. The floor was carpeted in a gray-and-white geometric pattern by Patterson, Flynn and Martin. Before her was a lacquered gray reception desk, vacant at the moment, and behind it, floor-to-ceiling panels of tinted glass looked over Central Park as it stretched greenly north to 110th Street. The morning sunlight caught the windows of the stately apartment buildings along Central Park West, turning them to glittering mirror bursts of fire.

The elevator whirred open behind Tyger, to let out an

attractive woman of about thirty-five, wearing a navy-and-white Adolfo suit, and carrying a Zabar's shopping bag and Gucci briefcase. The woman looked around too, and then smiled at Tyger.

"Is this your first day?" Tyger nodded. *"Moi aussi.* I'm Connie Larcada, advertising lady." She laughed.

They shook hands. "I'm Tyger Hayes. But what I'm doing is still a big question mark. I'm assistant to the president."

The receptionist returned, flustered to see Tyger and Connie standing there. "Oh, I'm sorry," she apologized, "I didn't think anyone would get here so early. I just went to . . ."

Connie laughed commiseratingly. "I could stand to go to the same place myself. But first you'd better show us where our nameplates are."

Workmen were still busy in the halls. The sunny yellow paint in Tyger's office was not yet dry. Nevertheless, Tyger felt a thrill, walking into it for the first time. Her own office. It was reasonably spacious, and possessed one window with the same breathtaking view of Central Park, white wicker furniture, and a white Parsons table as a desk. On it sat a vase containing a dozen roses, with a card from Hugh Marshall: "Welcome aboard." Tyger sat down and called Jake, who was already involved in a shooting session and too busy to talk.

Connie Larcada walked in. "Your roses are yellow, mine are red. I wonder what that means." She laughed. "The first day at a new job always makes me feel as if I'm all dressed up with no place to go."

"You can't feel it as much as me. This is my first office job."

"I've installed a filter coffeemaker in my office. The water should have dripped through by now. Shall we have our first coffee break?"

Tyger laughed. "I'm certainly ready for a break. All this hard work is getting to me."

The two women spent the next hour filling in on each other's backgrounds.

". . . I know I've led a pretty privileged existence, but now I'm eager to earn my own way. It sounds corny, but I guess I'm trying to find meaning in my life." Tyger smiled, slightly embarrassed at letting her hair down so soon. But Connie Larcada was a warm, earthy woman, and it was impossible not to be honest with her.

"Well." Connie poured them each another cup of coffee. "It's not bad starting at the top. You were right to use your connections. It's taken me nearly twenty years to get where I am. I had to drop out of college when my father died, and start working. Eighty bucks a week as a receptionist—after taxes all I got to take home was fifty-five. I didn't have any connections—Dad was a pharmacist in Indianapolis—so I had to learn to recognize and grab opportunities faster than anybody else." Connie dumped a drugstore packet of sugar into her cup. "I've also had to put up with my share of male chauvinists . . . I deserved a vice-presidency at the agency—five years before they actually gave it to me." Her voice held no malice. "Don't worry, kid. You'll learn fast. And I'm always here if you need any advice."

Tyger liked Connie. She wasn't a tight-lipped, hard-nosed career woman at all. She looked like the quintessential earth mother, a little plump, but dressed imaginatively enough to conceal it. Before the hour was up, Connie had confided that her fortieth birthday was coming soon. She had never married, but had legally adopted her late sister's child, an eight-year-old girl named Tina.

"Oh, here you are. This place is like a morgue." A chipmunkish man, in his early forties, stood in the doorway.

"Come in," said Connie. "You have to be Jess Leibowitz, head of marketing."

"I don't have to be . . . but I am." Jess smiled, and they introduced themselves. Jess was wise-cracking, good-natured, and a mediocre dresser, who looked as if he would be easy to get along with. He chatted over coffee with them, and then pulled a report out of his briefcase.

"Tim Yates sent this over. Basically, it says that the Matt Phillips negotiations are going well. They expect to have a contract signed by next week."

"Great," said Tyger. "What do we do while we wait for the deal to go through?"

"Proceed as if the deal has already been signed," Jess said. "I mean, even if it comes to an unexpected dead end with Phillips, they'll hook up with another designer. All the designer does is lend us a name. It's up to us to market the product." Jess talked fast, with enthusiasm.

"You're jumping the gun, Jess," Connie interrupted. "We have to decide what the product is going to be before we can market it."

"I thought it was all decided . . . perfume," said Tyger.

"Right. But is it going to be thirty-five dollars an ounce perfume, or one hundred dollars an ounce?" Jess broke in.

"Do we want a scent for virgins or sophisticates? Teens or geriatrics?"

Connie leaned back in her chair. "Hmmm, I love creating new products."

Jess turned to Tyger. "Marshall says you're hooked into the lives of New York's trendiest young women. The conference room will be ready in a couple of days. Why don't you set up a series of informal marketing panels here, maybe four or five . . ."

"Wait," Tyger said. "You're going too fast . . . I've got a lot to learn. I don't know the first thing about marketing panels."

Jess was not bothered by Tyger's inexperience. He explained that marketing panels were merely selected groups of people, gathered in a room to discuss, in this case, the creation of an imaginary new product. The panels were overseen by a moderator whose job was to steer panelists in the right direction, and keep the discussion from digressing onto other topics. He continued, "So, basically, you select a group of so-called knowledgeable consumers to create your product, by telling you what they want or need that doesn't yet exist."

"In other words," said Tyger, "you put your friends to work for you."

"In this case, yes. Your friends, Tyger, know a lot about fashion and fragrance. Even if we don't ultimately go with their opinions, their ideas will give us a base to work from."

"Wait a minute," said Connie. "I've just thought of a hitch. Keller Perfumes is still a secret. Tyger's got to figure out a way to get her friends here, pick their brains, and not have them gossiping around town about what we're up to."

Jess wrinkled his brow. "Good point, Connie."

Tyger agreed. "All my friends do is gossip. How on earth can we keep them quiet?"

"I have an idea," injected Connie. "They're going to learn a lot by just coming to this office. Have you told anyone that you're working here?"

"No one that I'd call for a panel."

"Then why not have them come to your apartment? Give 'em wine and cheese. Tell them you're taking a course in marketing at the New School . . . that you have an assignment. You need their help in creating an imaginary perfume."

Tyger applauded. "Connie, you're terrific!"

Sheldon Shaw arrived on Thursday morning. He called

Connie Larcada, Jess Leibowitz and Tyger into his office for a general get-acquainted briefing.

Well into middle age, Shaw still possessed a full head of predominantly brown hair, but whiskey and defeat had begun to soften the line of his jaw into jowls. There was a pallor to his skin except at the cheeks and nose, where a network of tiny veins brought forth a parody of ruddy health. His suit was expensive, but bunched awkwardly about his medium frame as he slumped in his chair at the head of the conference table.

His manner was formal. "I want to welcome you all to Keller Perfumes . . ."

Connie interrupted breezily. "We should be welcoming you. We've had three days on you at this point."

Shawl smiled absentmindedly. "Ah, you're right. Well, we've all got our work cut out for us. Miss Larcada and Mr. Leibowitz . . . I'm pleased to have you on the team. I've studied your backgrounds, and I'm impressed." He looked at Tyger. "Miss Hayes . . . you seem to be a fledgling in the corporate world. . . ."

Tyger had been expecting that, and decided the friendly approach would be best. "I sure am, but I don't plan to be for long. I'm anxious to learn as much as I can, as fast as I can. I'm looking forward to working under your guidance." She flashed a disarming smile which seemed to be lost on Shaw. He appeared to be thinking of something else.

"Well, ah, Hugh Marshall seems to have confidence in you. Let's hope you live up to his expectations."

Tyger, smarting, sat back in her chair and observed Sheldon Shaw as the meeting continued. She could hardly fault him for being less than enthusiastic about her. Still, there was something about the attitude behind his remark that made her suspect that Shaw disliked Hugh Marshall. She guessed that Shaw resented the fact that Marshall had hired her rather than allowing Shaw to pick his own assistant.

Tyger concluded that the professional thing to do was to reserve judgment on Sheldon Shaw. First impressions were not always accurate.

CHAPTER EIGHT

TYGER spent the day on the phone, setting up product development panels. By quitting time she had arranged six of them, each to be composed of seven to ten women, in various age ranges. Connie advised her against hiring a professional moderator, since it was important that the panels look impromptu. Tyger opted for holding them at Bobbie's duplex, since her own place was still practically empty. Her friends and acquaintances were not the sort to rough it by sitting cross-legged on the floor. She would have to serve tea and wine, some good Brie and mountains of *crudités* for the dieters. Everyone bought the premise that she wanted their opinions for a school marketing project. The only person to shower her with skepticism was her best friend, Julia Hatcher.

"Since when," Julia asked over the phone from East Hampton, "were you the sort of person to take courses at the New School? Besides . . . it's the first of August. Odd time for a class to be beginning." Julia paused. Tyger could hear Julia lighting one of the pastel colored cigarettes she always bought at Nat Sherman's. "C'mon, Tyger, 'fess up. What's going on?"

Tyger wanted to tell Julia the truth, to tell her all about the job, but that was out of the question. Julia's life revolved around her kids, and gossipy long lunches with friends. "Really, Julia. Why can't you believe that I'm changing my life around? I told you . . . I want to start working. I've decided it'll help me to take some practical business courses."

"Okay . . . but the *New School*?" Julia was tough to placate.

"Look, Julia, all I'm asking is for you to invite some of your beach cronies over this weekend when I'm out there. So I can interview them. Will you do it, or won't you?" Tyger realized that she was beginning to sound belligerent.

"Okay, okay. You don't have to get nasty. How many women do you want me to line up?"

"Thanks, love. I knew I could count on you. What about six or seven . . . ?"

"I'll see what I can do. I still think you're up to something fishy, but I'll let you have your little secret," Julia announced patronizingly, and sighed dramatically. "I'm sure you'll confide in me sooner or later."

Tyger laughed. "You know I always do, kid. Thanks a bunch."

Connie Larcada, Jess Leibowitz, Sheldon Shaw, Tyger and Tim Yates were already assembled in the boardroom. Tim had just finished pouring the coffee when Hugh Marshall appeared and greeted them each swiftly.

Marshall was handsomely dressed, as always, in a European tropical worsted wool suit of charcoal brown. He rested his monogrammed silver-headed cane by his chair and sat down at the head of the conference table.

"I have good news. We've just completed negotiations with Matt Phillips. He has licensed us his name to use for a woman's perfume. To be followed, in due time, by a man's scent. Then, if all goes well, cosmetics. He'll get a hefty fee up front, as well as royalties. He'll act as a consultant in an advisory capacity for the line, and he's agreed to give us final approval on packaging, marketing, promotion, and the scent itself." Marshall paused, and looked around the table for reactions.

"Great!" Connie cheered. "You mean he's not going to get in our way."

Marshall smiled. "Right. Oh, he'll take an interest, but contractually he can't clog the works if he doesn't approve of the marketing scheme you come up with. Not that I foresee any problems. I have full confidence that you will create a product that satisfies everyone." He glanced quickly at Tyger, who was watching him with rapt attention.

Jess broke in. "Thanks, Hugh. Now that we have the go-ahead, let's have the bottom line. What's the schedule you're thinking about?"

"You mean Sheldon hasn't told you?" Hugh Marshall shot an impenetrable look at Sheldon Shaw, who was doodling on his yellow legal pad. "I want to launch the Matt Phillips fragrance in March."

"March?" Tyger let her amazement show. "But that's only eight months."

"Exactly." Marshall's face was businesslike. Tyger could feel the toughness underneath his smooth veneer.

Connie sighed, and then broke into a grin. "We're going to be busy little beavers, but it's not so bad. We can do it."

Hugh Marshall stood up and took hold of his cane. "I wouldn't have picked any of you if you couldn't." He looked at his watch. "Sorry. I must rush to the airport. Tim will be our liaison for this project. He can fill you in on any details I've missed." Marshall limped gracefully out of the room.

Following Marshall's exit, they all sat there, in silence. Jess looked over at Sheldon Shaw. "Boy, you sure can keep a secret," he said. "I know this is all hush-hush, but that's ridiculous."

Shaw looked ill at ease. "I dictated a memo to my secretary. It must have gotten lost."

"Well," said Connie, pushing back her chair, "we have our work cut out for us. Let's see . . . was Rome built in eight months?"

"Tyger . . . we've spoken on the phone so often lately, I was wondering if you'd like to have lunch. . . ." Tim Yates came up to Tyger as the meeting broke up.

"So we can talk in person. . . . I'd love to."

Tim Yates had begun finally to relax around Tyger and was not as shy as he had seemed in the beginning. She was glad to establish a contact who was so close to Hugh Marshall. Over a salad at O'Neal's, Tyger took the opportunity to glean as much information as she could about Kellerco and its president.

"I've known Matt Phillips since my modeling days. He's a real perfectionist. I can't believe he'd give up creative control of a product his name was associated with," Tyger said.

"Well," Tim began, "he's getting half a million dollars up front. Plus royalties."

"Hmmm, I guess that kind of money *can* influence people's decisions." Tyger took a sip of her club soda.

Tim lowered his voice, and Tyger had to lean forward to hear him above the din of the restaurant. "There is a little more to it. Want some good office gossip?"

Tyger's face lit up. "It'll be my first participation in corporate intrigue."

"You know, of course, that Matt Phillips lives with that model, Garry Gray?" Tyger nodded. "Well, he insisted that Kellerco launch a men's line, with the stipulation that Garry be the model and spokesman for all of the print and TV ads."

"Wow! He gave up his creative rights for that leech? I can't believe it!" Tyger was astounded.

"It's true. I sat in on the negotiations."

"I know Garry. At least I've chatted with him on numerous occasions. I just can't figure out what Matt sees in him."

"Is it true that Tasha Powers is still bitter?"

Tyger nodded. "She took it pretty hard. I mean, anyone would, under the circumstances."

"I hear she's very competitive professionally with Phillips. I guess she'll be upset when she learns about Matt's perfume. You know, she was our second choice. . . ."

Tyger was anxious to steer the conversation around to Hugh Marshall. She decided to be candid.

"Tim, I'm a bit confused about something. . . ."

"What?" He lit a cigarette.

"Hugh Marshall's obviously very interested in Keller Perfumes. But this is just one of dozens of companies owned by Kellerco. . . ."

"Well, he's wanted to take Kellerco into the so-called glamour money fields for a long time. But the board, especially Nelson Bachrach, the chairman, has been against it. This is the first time they've voted one of Hugh's glamour ideas through." Tim looked around quickly, anxious to make sure that none of his colleagues from Kellerco were sitting nearby. "It's possible they want the division to fail . . . then they can boot Marshall out."

"Boot him out? But he's president, and has a lot of power. Why? Hasn't the company prospered under him?" Tyger asked.

"Of course. But there are those who don't give him credit. Because he married into the Keller family they don't believe that he's actually a top-notch businessman."

"It sounds as if you admire Hugh Marshall, though."

Tim paused, thoughtfully. "I do. I have tremendous respect for him. I *know* how hard he works. Some people dislike the social image he projects, but a lot of his social life is for the sake of business."

Tyger perked up. "Really?"

"Well, he never discusses his personal life with me, but I don't think he's interested in anyone special. He's too busy. He thinks about Kellerco twenty-four hours a day. . . ." Tim laughed. "He probably dreams about business at night. Hugh Marshall's made a lot of enemies because he expects the people around him to be as dedicated as he is. If he suspects that one of his executives is putting forth less than one hundred percent, then that person is either kicked out or banished to the hinterlands. . . ."

"Which makes me wonder about Sheldon Shaw. . . ."

Tim scrutinized Tyger. "What about him?"

"Well . . . I don't want this to go any further. It's just my observation. . . ."

Tim leaned forward. "Don't worry, Tyger. All of this is completely off the record."

"It seems to me that Sheldon doesn't do anything. I mean, if Hugh cares about Keller Perfumes, why did he appoint Shaw as president?"

Tim lowered his voice and glanced around the restaurant again. "Actually, Shaw wasn't Marshall's choice. He was Nelson Bachrach's. Shaw has been with the company for a long time. I think Mr. Bachrach wanted someone from the old guard there to keep an eye on Marshall."

"But . . . isn't Hugh Marshall's position at Kellerco secure enough? Even if the perfume division were a bust, it wouldn't make any difference, would it?"

"That's the million-dollar question, Tyger. These days who knows? One day you're president of a company, the next . . . Some ex-corporation presidents don't ever know what hit them. They arrive at work and find that the door to the executive suite is locked. . . ."

"Oh, Tim, you're exaggerating."

"Not at all, Tyger. No one has it completely made. Once you've fought your way to the top, you have to fight even harder to stay there." He crushed his cigarette out. "But Hugh Marshall's tough. He has amazing stamina, and he's smart."

Tim paid the check, and he and Tyger strolled down Fifty-seventh Street toward her office.

"What about you, Tim? Where are you heading?" She laughed. "I mean, career-wise."

Yates smiled, and a veil of shyness initially concealed the

impact of his words on Tyger. "I'm ambitious," he said. "I want to run the show someday."

"You mean Kellerco?"

"Kellerco, or someplace else. I'm young, but I've got a lot of experience. I see a lot, and hear a lot, and people trust me."

Tyger smiled back at Tim. She trusted him, too. But suddenly she wondered whether or not she should.

CHAPTER NINE

AT five-thirty, the sidewalk was crowded and there was only a whisper of an August breeze as Tyger strolled down Fifth Avenue. She had spent the past week, including the weekend at the Hatchers' in East Hampton, conducting marketing panels. Now the information had to be compiled into a report, and she had a full night's drudgery ahead of her. On impulse, she decided to drop by Jake's studio. She walked the entire distance, to Twenty-first Street.

The elevator door opened into Jake's loft. A tall, breathtakingly beautiful brunette stood in front of a blue backdrop, bathed in hot arc lights. Jake crouched before her, talking to her in intimate, suggestive tones, and clicking pictures. Ellie Baerwald, his assistant, hovered nearby, changing film and handing him cameras as he asked for them.

Tyger recognized the model. She was Kate Cassell, and it was impossible to read a magazine, pass a newsstand, or go through the checkout line at any supermarket in the country without seeing her wide, full-lipped, spectacularly American face. She was currently the country's number-one model.

Many models look ordinary in the flesh because the camera adds another dimension to their looks; not Kate Cassell. In person, she possessed an additional spark, a special character which took her features past the current standards of perfection. Tyger often wondered how Jake could stand being around so much beauty, day in, day out.

Jake clicked the last shot and handed his camera to Ellie.

"Okay, Kate, that's it for today." He smiled. "You were sensational, as always."

"I feel like a melted marshmallow. I'm sure I smell like a skunk." Kate laughed. "C'mon, Jake, when are you going to jazz up the air conditioning in this barn?"

"You give me the money, Kate, and I'll do it."

"Well, on second thought . . . it's not so bad. God! It's late. I've got to get out of here. . . ."

"Am I as bad as all that?"

"Worse," Kate called sassily as she headed for the dressing room to change back into her street clothes.

Jake spotted Tyger, who had been standing off to the side. She would never interrupt Jake in the middle of a shoot. "Hi, uh . . . I seem to have forgotten your name, stranger." He came over and gave her a kiss.

"Don't get your hopes up, Jake. I'm here on borrowed time."

"Haven't you finished that damned marketing study yet? God, you're slow."

"Can I go now, Jake?" Ellie Baerwald asked. "Everything's set for tomorrow."

"Great. Take off then. Have a good evening," Jake said.

Kate Cassell breezed back through with her gear and rang for the elevator, acknowledging Tyger with a wink and a smile. "By the way, Jake, when are you coming with me to see Madame Doris?"

"Don't hold your breath, love."

"You'll be sorry. She's getting old. She could retire any day now."

"Or die," offered Jake.

"Jake, you're scum!" The elevator arrived, and both Kate and Ellie disappeared.

Tyger sat down on a crate. "Now that's an intriguing bit of conversation. Care to elaborate?"

"Madame Doris is some palm reader that Kate swears by. Been going to her for years. Claims the old lady has predicted all of her fame and fortune, in stages. And that she pinpointed exactly when and where it would all occur."

"Impressive. You may not be interested, but I'd love to see her. I haven't been to a good clairvoyant in ages."

"There you go with your California talk again. Crazy, weird, all of you."

"Are you referring to Californians, or women?"

"Take your pick. I do not believe in palmists and mind

readers. At least not the ones who give you twenty minutes for twenty bucks, while the line forms around the block. People with real extrasensory gifts don't sell them for money."

"Don't be ridiculous, Jake. Everyone barters their best assets on the marketplace. Look at Kate Cassell. She earns a lot more money, I'm sure, than a poor old seer. Kate'll be able to retire for life by the time she's thirty."

"How old do you think she is?"

"Oh, twenty-five, maybe."

"Well, she's at least thirty. And she *has* to keep hustling. She hasn't saved a dime."

"How do you know so much about her?" Tyger was curious.

"We used to be an item a while back. Didn't you know that?"

"I should have. Is there any female in this city you haven't had a fling with?"

Jake changed the subject. "Will you play hooky long enough to have dinner with me?" He came up behind her and gently began massaging her neck and shoulders.

"Hmmm . . . that feels wonderful. I'd like to, Jake. But, with you, one thing leads to another. I've got to have this summary done by tomorrow."

"Okay. But tomorrow night we're having a proper date. An all-nighter. I miss my bed."

"It's my bed now. You gave it to me."

"I forgot to mention that I come with it."

"You *come* with it? Not bad, Jake."

Jake kissed the nape of her neck, and then began nuzzling her ear. "No pun intended. . . ." He was irresistible.

"I've changed my mind, Jake. I'll spend an hour with you before I head home. No dinner, though, just dessert."

What influences your decision when you select a new perfume? The actual smell, or . . . Tyger's recorded voice boomed out into the night, accompanied by the sounds of her tired fingers clicking away on the typewriter.

It was four in the morning and the marketing report was still a mess. Just as Tyger thought the end was in sight, she had happened upon a tape in the bottom of her totebag that Ginger McShane, the secretary she shared with Sheldon Shaw, had forgotten to transcribe.

Hopped up by five cups of coffee and beginning to feel almost ill, Tyger tried to compile the findings of her marketing panels into a succinct summary, but there were so many facts and opinions that she kept getting bogged down. Her brain was stale. She couldn't think linearly. Her mind was jumping all over the place, from the caffeine, no doubt. She felt like talking to Jake, but decided it would be cruel to ruin his sleep. *If* he was asleep. He might be with another woman. Tyger didn't care whether he saw other women, but she didn't want to know about it while it was happening.

Then the sound of her phone pierced the stillness. Tyger was so startled that she let it ring three times before she answered.

"Hello, darling. I'm terribly sorry to wake you." It was the faraway voice of her mother. Bobbie did make calls at odd hours. She rarely stopped to work out time differences.

"You didn't wake me. I was up . . . working."

"Working? At this hour? Really, darling, that's taking your job much too seriously. Anyway . . . I'm in Madrid and my plane's about to leave. I'll be in New York later today. Marta called. Elaine Talbert died. A sudden heart attack."

"Oh . . . I didn't know. I'm sorry." Her mother and Elaine were old friends. Elaine had taken young Bobbie Taylor under her wing when she had first come to New York from Philadelphia's Main Line, long before Bobbie had met and married the first of her four husbands, Harry Hayes.

"Oops, must run. They just announced my plane. Have dinner with me tonight. I have a lot to tell you. 'Bye, dear. Love you." Click. That was Bobbie.

Tyger went over to the window and looked out. All around her there was silence. No drunks singing in the streets. No traffic sounds, except for the monotonous hum of a distant garbage truck. She turned and looked around the room. The walls were still bare, and the chairs she had ordered from Bloomingdale's had not yet arrived. Without rugs and pictures and memorabilia the place was cold. There was just an ugly typewriter looming up at her from a makeshift table, and that report to finish.

Her foot began to tickle. She looked down and a cockroach jumped off her toe and scurried across the room. She rushed after it and stomped on it. Then again, and again. Nine hundred dollars a month, and the apartment still had bugs. God, she hated this place. Taking off her shoes, she flung them against the fireplace. She was shaking, then unexpectedly she heard a sob penetrate the silence. Her sob, followed by a stream of tears rushing down her face. Tyger sank into the only chair in the room and cried hysterically. She was overcome with fatigue and frustration. She hated herself, and she hated the fact that she was incapable of stopping the flood.

Finally, the tears ran out. She walked slowly into the bathroom, splashed cold water on her face, and looked into the mirror. Her nose was beet red, her cheeks and neck all splotchy. She looked as ugly as she felt inside.

Going back into the living room, she sat before the typewriter. No matter what, she had to finish. But before she started working again she had to talk to Jake. She dialed his number. It rang eleven times before she hung up, feeling rotten and more alone than ever. Tyger wandered into the bedroom and lay down on top of the covers. Just before she dozed off from exhaustion she managed to set the alarm for seven. She would go to the office early, and finish the report there.

Sheldon Shaw sauntered into Tyger's office around ten-thirty. The crinkles around his eyes appeared deeper than usual. He looked the way Tyger felt. She had been at work since eight and was still suffering the jittery effects of her coffee hangover.

"Tyger," he snapped, skipping amenities. "What's the story on those marketing panel reports? We need them."

"I've finished," Tyger announced triumphantly. "Ginger's typing up the final draft right now."

Shaw cleared his throat. He had obviously assumed that Tyger would drag it out until the end of the week, and was taken aback that she had the matter well in hand. "Good," he said grudgingly. "I appreciate your efficiency."

Up close, Shaw looked something more than tired. Tyger noticed that his razor had missed a thin line of whiskers trailing down his right cheek. He turned and left her office, without any further dialogue.

Shaw closed his office door behind him and walked across the tan carpet to his desk. He took a small key from his breast pocket and unlocked the top right-hand drawer of his desk. Picking up a bottle of vodka, he shakily unscrewed the cap and took a swig. He waited a moment, as if considering what to do next, then took another swallow. He locked the bottle out of sight again and sat down at his desk.

Sheldon Shaw had spent most of his working life at Kellerco. He had witnessed its growth into a multi-conglomerate, and finally Bachrach had rewarded him with this presidency. Most of his colleagues, the ones his age who had stuck with the company, had been promoted to top positions long before. And yet, he had played the game. Dragging his wife and two kids around the country while Kellerco transferred him at whim. Putting up with his wife's complaints of no friends, his children's difficulties in adjusting to a new school every year or so. Louise had begged him to change jobs, to stay in one place, but whenever he actually began looking around he'd back down. So his wife had started to drink, and he drank with her. Night after night, year after year; nothing changed. Finally, they were back in New York, settled in one place at last. But the kids were off at college, gone. Louise still had no friends, and stayed in an alcoholic haze most of the time.

Shaw looked through a few reports on his desk, then tossed them aside. The pressure to prove himself in this job was unbearable. There was so much to learn about the perfume business. Too much. He wasn't a kid any more, anxious to tackle a challenge. He wanted to relax.

He wished he could have brought Dave Kirshenbaum, his former assistant, along with him to Keller Perfumes. But Hugh Marshall had vetoed Dave in favor of Tyger Hayes, a young jet-set beauty Marshall presumably had the hots for. Tyger Hayes was an eager beaver, but he could tell that she was after her own glory, not his.

His intercom buzzed. It was Ginger McShane, his secretary. "Everybody is assembled in the conference room, Mr. Shaw."

His mind was blank. "Conference room?"

"The Tuesday meeting," Ginger reminded him. "You sent out a memo last week to the staff, saying that there was to be a regular meeting every Tuesday at eleven."

Shaw was silent. His mind would not focus on what she was saying. Memos. Meetings. Shit.

"Shall I cancel it, Mr. Shaw? Are you all right?"

"I'll be right there. Just getting some papers together." He unlocked his desk drawer again, reached for the vodka and took another drink. That one cleared his head.

While the confidence was still warm in his body, he picked up his briefcase and hurried to the conference room. He forgot to return the bottle to the locked drawer.

" . . . And so there are many elements to be decided on before we have any tangible evidence of our efforts. . . ." Shaw had kicked off the meeting with a rehash of steps of which everyone was acutely aware.

"Now, Shel, why don't you bring out your whip and remind us of the deadline," Connie injected fliply.

Shaw's face went blank. It was evident that once again he had forgotten the date.

Tyger looked at the calendar on the date book she had with her. "March fifteenth. Seven and one-half months, to be exact. We're going to be very busy."

"Unfortunately, that's not a prediction. It's a fact," sighed Connie.

"We can do it," Jess assured. "When I first started out in this business we had an assignment to create an entire line of cosmetics in that amount of time. Creams and lotions, and a complete range of makeup colors. We worked until the last minute, but we did it. Even delivered the first shipment to Saks ourselves, in a station wagon. Coming up with one fragrance ought to be a cinch."

"You're right. It ought to be, but experience tells me it won't," Connie said. "Okay, who's doing what?"

Tyger reported on her marketing panels. "Ginger will get copies to you later today. But the upshot of it all confirms a great deal of what we thought we knew already. There was great controversy among the panelists as to what made them buy a perfume. Many started out saying it was the actual scent itself, then most agreed that the designer's name, the bottle—and to a lesser extent the model and ads—were all prime factors. Word of mouth plays a big part, in-store sampling and impulse buying, too. . . ."

"What sort of fragrance do they want?" Connie asked.

"Opinions varied but the majority wants a sophisticated, long-lasting, evening fragrance." Tyger put down her report and looked around the room. "It boils down to the fact that they'll buy anything that smells good and has Matt Phillips's name on it. . . ."

"Most interesting," Shaw conceded, quickly turning to Jess Leibowitz. "What's going on in your corner?"

Jess opened one of the half-dozen folders resting on the polished ebony conference table. "I've been working with the comptroller over the financial breakdown. Tim Yates called me to stress that Marshall wants a class perfume. Matt Phillips is not to be mass-marketed."

"At least, not for a few years," Connie interposed.

"Right," Jess agreed. "We're talking about a fragrance that will sell anywhere from sixty-five to a hundred dollars an ounce. Now we've got to decide just *where* between those two figures."

"That depends on whether we decide that Matt Phillips is as prestigious as, say, Yves Saint Laurent," Connie stated. "Of course, Saint Laurent didn't begin with Opium at a hundred bucks an ounce. His other perfumes, like Rive Gauche, are popular and sell for considerably less. According to the current designer market, my instincts tell me that we have to stay middle-of-the-road expensive."

"Affordable for a lot of women, a splurge for some," Tyger agreed. "Besides, it's the fifteen-dollar spray cologne and the purse flacons that sell the most anyway."

Jess broke in. "You've both got the idea." His brown eyes sparkled. "By midweek, I'll have cost projections done up for perfumes selling from sixty-five to eighty-five dollars. I don't think we should go over that. At least not for the first Phillips fragrance."

Shaw cleared his throat in an attempt to get back into the flow of conversation. "Don't think in terms of future products. Consider this the one and only."

Connie, who was riffling through papers in front of her, spoke up. "You're right, Shel. And it could be, if we don't deliver a first-rate perfume that women flock to the stores to buy."

She continued, "I have a stack of facts and figures in my office that reaches halfway to the ceiling. Christ, anyone would think I'm doing a master's thesis on the fragrance industry. Demographics, statistics . . . every perfume ad for every scent that's graced a shelf in the last three decades. And lists of possible names for our perfume. I've worked up a preliminary budget for both a print campaign in local papers and national magazines, and a combo print-TV launch. Just in case Kellerco decides to shoot the works."

Ginger McShane, who had been on the telephone, entered hurriedly and took her seat. "Mr. Marshall's secretary just phoned, Mr. Shaw. Mr. Marshall wants us to arrange a meeting with Matt Phillips just as soon as we have something concrete to tell him. Apparently, Mr. Phillips is now quite nervous about having signed away his creative rights."

Connie laughed. "The man himself? It's amazing how you can get caught up in a product, and forget all about the person who's *supposed* to be causing it all to happen. Well, I know his breed. No matter what we do, he'll want to devour us for breakfast and throw our leftovers to the sharks."

"I know him," Tyger said. "And it's true, he has a large ego. But he's reasonable. I'm sure we'll come up with a perfume that will be the essence of what he would have designed." She gave a quick laugh. "No pun intended."

"Oh, Tyger, I love you," Connie announced. "So chic and naive at the same time. Matt Phillips will *never* like what we do. For the reason that *we* are coming up with it, and not him."

Tyger felt as if she should stand up for her old acquaintance. "But we can't treat him like an ugly stepchild. Even though he doesn't have final approval, he's still our consultant. He's a brilliant designer. He's bound to have a lot of good ideas. Why not listen to them?"

"You're right, I know," conceded Connie. "No matter what, we have to hear him out . . . and try to tread carefully on his ego. We want him in our corner—so he'll do in-store promotions for us when the perfume is launched. . . ."

Jess broke in. "I've just had a thought. Shel, why not make Tyger our ambassador to Matt Phillips? She knows him. Maybe she can unruffle his feathers, and keep him off our backs."

"Good idea, Jess." In fact, Shaw had been thinking along the same lines himself. It was perfect. It would keep Matt Phillips from breathing down *his* neck, and if Tyger was not up to the assignment Shaw would have good leverage with Hugh Marshall for getting her out. Then he could bring in his old assistant Dave Kirshenbaum, who had always made him look good, and the pressure would be off. Shaw smiled. "Will you do it, Tyger?"

"Sure, if you'll give me a title. What about vice president in charge of Matt Phillips?" Tyger grew serious then and said, "It won't be easy, but I'll try."

Shaw cleared his throat. He was pleased by the latest turn of events. "Well, then . . . it's settled. I'll check with Hugh Marshall to see if he has any objections." Having gained everyone's attention, Shaw continued, "Connie . . . I think everyone should give Ginger lists of possible names for the perfume. She can type them up and circulate copies for consideration and elimination. And, ah, Jess, what about the fragrance manufacturers?"

Jess pulled out another of his manila folders. "Got it well in hand, Shel. The half-dozen or so top fragrance manufacturers, both here and in France. I'll contact their salesmen with our requirements. Just as soon as we know what we want."

"What about the design for the bottles and packaging?" Shaw asked.

"Didn't you see that memo that Marshall sent over? He has some specific ideas on designers." Jess shrugged. "We have to listen to him. He's the boss." Sheldon Shaw bristled a bit. Marshall usually left his presidents alone, to run a company as they saw fit, but obviously he was not going to do that this time.

Connie rolled her eyes, as if she were reading Shaw's thoughts. "I know this is a pet project of Marshall's. I just hope he won't breathe down our necks as much as Phillips probably will. Why won't they just let us experts alone to do our jobs?"

Jess laughed. "Now who sounds naive, Connie? You've been in the business long enough to know the answer to that one."

"By the way," Connie changed the subject, "while we're getting this product together, what should we call it?"

"What's wrong with what we've been calling it? The Matt Phillips perfume?" Tyger asked.

Connie chuckled. "Have you no sense of cloak-and-dagger? Remember, we're in the 'top secret' business."

"Oh, you mean a code name!"

"That's what Charles Revson did at Revlon. All their products had code names. He was afraid that competitors would find out about new products before they were launched. I have a friend who used to work there, and she said the tags were unbelievable, things like Ritex, and Tylex. Only the key people knew what the products actually were, never the secretaries or suppliers or people bottling the stuff. Before its launch, she told me that Charlie was referred to as Cosmos. Sabotage exists everywhere, but Revson was known for his obsession with keeping things top-secret. Anyway . . . what's our code going to be?"

"Number One?" Jess suggested.

"What about Essence?" Tyger said. "Or Bare Essence, since we don't have anything else besides a code name."

Connie clapped her hands. "Great! I love it."

Shaw's brow furrowed. "I don't think . . ."

Connie was used to having her way, and settling matters quickly. "Oh, Shel. We could spend all day on this if we wanted, but we all have too much to do. I vote for Bare Essence, or BE for short."

"Fine with me." Jess nodded. He looked at his watch. "I've

got a meeting in five minutes with some bottle fillers, to get estimates."

"I think we've touched on everything," Connie said. "Let's get back to work."

Shaw agreed, slightly disgruntled that it wasn't he who had formally closed the meeting. He was still ill at ease with his new staff.

Suddenly, on impulse, Shaw decided to do something relatively unprecedented for him. He brushed past Tyger, who was in consultation with Ginger McShane, and caught up with Connie Larcada.

"Ah, Connie." He broached everything seriously, even his impulses. "Perhaps we could have lunch this week?"

Connie's lips opened into her Midwestern grin, which was not quite toothy enough to be overbearing. "That means today. I was booked solid, but Ginger just informed me that I've been stood up by a sickly *Vogue* editor."

"I'm free today, too." Shaw was beginning to feel an agitation in the pit of his stomach. Maybe he shouldn't have asked her out. Perhaps he should have made it a rule to only see his colleagues at the office.

"Where'll we go? I'm starved." Sheldon Shaw half smiled at her openness, and for a split second Connie saw a shy attractiveness that must have been quite engaging to women when he was young. He would still be attractive, she noted, if it weren't for a slightly hangdog look that exaggerated the lines around his eyes and mouth.

They settled on Orsini's, on Fifty-sixth Street, and Connie went back to her office to grab her jacket. She was pleased at the opportunity to get to know Sheldon Shaw better. Thus far, he had kept himself aloof from the rest of the action. She hadn't seen enough of him yet to make up her mind as to whether or not he was a strong silent leader who would be there in the crunch, or merely a man who had reached the level of his incompetence. After lunch, she would have a reasonably good fix on the sort of person he was.

The dark restaurant, with its red velvet walls and love seats, was crowded, but they got a table at the front of the main dining room. Shaw ordered a vodka martini, and Connie decided on a bloody Mary. When the drinks arrived, Shaw told the captain to bring them another round, along with the menu.

"I've seen you before, you know," Sheldon Shaw said,

almost shyly. "At a space buyers' convention in St. Louis a couple of years ago."

Connie smiled, flattered. "What an amazing memory," she said. "I'm afraid I . . ."

"We didn't exactly meet. I was only there for an afternoon, but I heard your talk on magazine strategy. You were very impressive."

"You should have seen my knees knocking behind the podium. I was afraid if I stopped talking I'd collapse in a heap. Oh, I wish you'd come up and told me."

"I had a plane to catch."

"That's no reason to keep a lady waiting two years to hear her reviews."

Shaw laughed. The captain appeared and reeled off the day's specialties. Connie ordered *gnocchi* in pesto sauce, and Shaw the *osso bucco*. He selected a 1971 Bolla Amarone from the wine list.

Over the entrées, they discussed the challenge of creating Keller Perfumes.

"As I see it," Shaw summed up, "our immediate goal is to define our target audience in regard to life-style and mood orientation. . . ."

Connie nodded, repressing a smile. She remembered the exact phrase from a recent fragrance report in *Women's Wear Daily*. Well, Sheldon Shaw might not be an original thinker. But he was a good study. And there was something appealingly vulnerable about him.

"Oh, let's not talk perfume any more," Connie said. "Let's turn our minds to dessert. Feel like ordering something and giving me a bite?"

Sheldon Shaw glowed, from both the full-bodied wine and the company of his attractive companion. "Nothing would give me greater pleasure," he said, summoning the waiter.

In a few minutes, two espressos and one *zuppa inglese*—a rum-and-almond-flavored cake with layers of chocolate, custard and apricot preserves—were placed before them.

"Oh, heavenly sin," Connie said, taking a bite. "This cake is richer than it has any right to be. For the sake of my figure I suppose we should have gone with the gorgonzola."

"You have nothing to worry about," Sheldon assured her. "You know, I don't think I've shared a dessert with anyone since I was eighteen. Back in Seattle," he remembered. "I had a girl friend named Evelyn Evans. She was a cheerleader and I was on the football team. Every afternoon after practice

we'd stop in the local drugstore and demolish a banana split."
He broke off, laughing. "How did I get off on that tangent?"

Connie shook her head. She was glad she had taken off
early yesterday afternoon to have her hair trimmed and
restreaked at the Suga salon at Bergdorf's. She was pleased
that Sheldon Shaw liked her figure, even if it was twenty
pounds fuller than it should be. "Sheldon, let's order another
espresso. I want to hear more about your past."

"And I'd like to hear about yours. Another *zuppa inglese?*"

"You're wicked, Sheldon. Any more suggestions like that,
and this may be our last meal together."

By the end of lunch, Connie still was not sure how good a
president Sheldon Shaw was for Keller Perfumes. She was
pretty sure, however, that she would wind up having an
affair with him. His marriage was wretched. His children
were grown. He drank a great deal, out of unhappiness, she
surmised. Connie Larcada knew better than to be suckered
into such a situation. But in three weeks she was going to
turn forty. That meant the chances were high that she would
remain single for the rest of her life. She needed something to
look forward to. Sheldon Shaw was not so bad. In fact, sitting
across the table smiling at her, he looked pretty good.

CHAPTER TEN

OVER a hundred bottles were scattered about on Tyger's white Parsons table-desk: round, square, elliptical, teardrops, pear shapes, Lalique crystal flacons, apothecary bottles with glass stoppers, and more. They represented a sampling of the inventory of Bloomingdale's perfume department, where Tyger had spent her lunch hour.

Surveying the stock of scents before her, she felt like a small child who had been given *carte blanche* at F.A.O. Schwarz. Next to the famous fragrances stood tiny flasks of essential oils—enough single-flower notes to fill a greenhouse, as well as herbal essences, even vegetable extracts.

She called out to Ginger McShane. "How'd you like to smell like a carrot?"

"What?" Ginger walked in.

"Or parsley. Or a rose geranium . . ."

"Tyger . . . I think all this has gone to your head." She surveyed the selection of bottles on Tyger's desk. "You're definitely crazy."

"Well, you know, when I'm interested in something I take to it with a vengeance."

Ginger went back to her office, and Tyger began comparing smells, determined to develop her olfactory awareness and become a "nose," as they said in the trade. She opened bottles greedily, sniffed, and dabbed fragrances up and down both arms. Within minutes her nose gave out. All the aromas blended together and she could no longer distinguish one fragrance from another. She decided to spend Saturday at the library, learning the chemistry of perfume and what went into making a fragrance woodsy, mossy, floral, spicy. . . .

Her direct line rang. The voice was Bobbie's, sounding tired. "I'm afraid I'll have to cancel dinner tonight. I promised to help poor Marta with the arrangements. Elaine's funeral will be Thursday. . . ."

"Are you all right, Mother? You sound so . . ."

"Oh, I'm fine . . . under the circumstances. Look, let's make it tomorrow evening, shall we? Just us, at home? If you can still find your way . . ."

"Of course, Mother. I'll look forward to it." Bobbie had not been at all pleased when Tyger had told her about her apartment in the Village.

"I could smell this office from the other end of the floor." Tyger looked up to see Hugh Marshall standing in her doorway.

"Oh, hello! Come in . . . what are you doing here?" Tyger's small sofa was piled with books and magazine clippings. She quickly cleared a space for him, but he shook his head.

"I just had a meeting with Shaw, and now I have to go down to Wall Street. I just thought I'd take a minute to look in on you." He stared at the bottles. "What're you up to?"

"I'm trying to learn everything I can about perfume." Tyger was flattered that Marshall had stopped in. Although his tan had faded and for the first time she noticed that he was beginning to gray at the temples, he looked sensational. His summer tweed suit obviously had been tailored specifically for him.

He smiled, displaying those perfect teeth. "Sheldon told me he wants you to be Keller Perfumes' official link with Matt Phillips. . . ."

"Handholder is more like it, I suspect. Is Matt really agitated about giving up his creative rights?"

Marshall laughed briskly. "Agitated is a mild word for it. Anyway, I complimented Shaw on his recommendation. You can smooth things over with Phillips, if anybody can."

Tyger was pleased by Marshall's vote of confidence. "Well, I'm meeting Matt for drinks after work. It remains to be seen whether I'll succeed or not."

"You will." Tyger wasn't sure whether Marshall was assuring her or ordering her. Whatever it was, the contact of eyes was exciting. The man did something to her. No question about that.

Bill's, on West Fortieth near Seventh Avenue, was crowded with after-work regulars, all involved in one way or another with the fashion industry. Matt Phillips sat at the bar, chatting with some colleagues. He spotted Tyger as she came in and rose to greet her.

"Ah," he said, "the lady Benedict Arnold." He kissed her perfunctorily on the check, and they found a table toward the back, away from the din of the bustling bar.

They ordered drinks, and then Matt lit into her. "I don't understand, Tyger, how you got yourself involved with that tacky crew. What do you *do* at Keller Perfumes, anyway?"

"I'm assistant to the president . . . a rather catch-all job. So far I've been doing a little of everything."

"Oh? I didn't think anyone over there was doing anything at all. Here I am allowing my name . . ." He glanced around, then lowered his voice, ". . . *my* name to their fucking perfume, and I have yet to receive so much as a phone call from the janitor! It's insulting. I'm still the creative consult-ant on this project, you know. So far, not one single question has been directed my way." He gave her a piercing look, and paused as the waiter set their drinks on the table. "You can understand that I'm feeling less than indispensable.

"Hugh Marshall," he continued breathlessly, "hit me with such a snow job in the beginning. Kellerco was to do this and that and the other thing. . . . The *only* thing they've done so far is hire a bunch of incompetents to sit around on their asses." He smiled brittlely. "No offense intended, Tyger."

"Obviously offense *was* intended, Matt." She looked at him sympathetically. "Believe me, I understand your feeling. It's your name we're using. And we are all anxious for you to exercise full control as creative consultant. I agree there's no excuse for my boss, Sheldon Shaw, not calling you, but he just transferred over from another Keller company. He's been busy . . ."

Phillips interrupted her. "Dammit, I don't care how busy anyone is. You'd *think* I'd get priority, some sort of preferen-tial treatment. After all, none of you would be there if it weren't for me." He poured the rest of the bottle of Heineken's into his glass, and signaled the waiter to bring them another round.

Tyger smiled. "Matt, things are just shaking down. We'll be organized in another few days. . . ."

"And another thing . . ." Matt hadn't heard a word she had

said. "I haven't even seen the Keller Perfumes offices."

"You will, Matt. Probably more often than you'd care to by the time the perfume's launched."

"After all," he steamed ahead, "I know my audience. My experience may be with clothes and not perfume, but I know the women who want the Matt Phillips look. The aura of the fragrance should reflect my designs. I really can't understand why you aren't on the phone asking my advice every day. You saw the piece *Newsweek* did on me last month, didn't you?"

Tyger nodded. Matt had been featured in the cover story on America's current "in" designers. "Matt . . . calm down. Don't blame me. I *agree* with you."

He was somewhat taken aback. "You do?" He opened a silver Navajo pillbox and pulled out a white tablet the size of a dime. He swallowed it, washing it down with a sip of beer. "Just a Quaalude," he said to Tyger, "to mellow me out. Want one?"

Tyger shook her head and continued, "The whole thing's been handled messily. But it's a new company, and it's taken us a few weeks to get our equilibrium. We wanted to have a full report for you by the time we had our first meeting. To impress you. The only way we can work together is if you have the respect for us that we have for you."

Matt smiled smugly. "Surely, love, you can't expect me to regard all of you as highly as myself?"

Tyger could see from a twinkle in his eye that he meant the remark lightly. "Of course not, Matt. But you get my point."

"Hmm." He nodded. "But as far as I'm concerned you and your colleagues still reside behind the line, in enemy territory."

Matt still wasn't appeased. Tyger continued her original tack. "We know if it weren't for you we wouldn't have a product to sell. You are as important to us as the fragrance we finally come up with. . . ."

"Bullshit!" Matt reached into his breast pocket and pulled out a small silk scarf, one of his designer trademarks. He laid it in his lap, out of sight, and poured into the center of it a little white powder from a hand-painted oriental china vial. He raised the scarf to his nose and sniffed the powder in both nostrils. "This is sensational coke, Tyger. The best. How about a sniff to clear your head?" He passed her the china vial and scarf.

Tyger was tempted, but she felt uneasy about taking drugs

in public. In fact, she had lost interest in cocaine in recent weeks. Her job was much more stimulating. "Again, I'll pass," she said.

"It's your loss." Matt shrugged. The Quaalude and the beer and the coke were working. He felt better. "Well, Tyger, at least I know one sympathetic person at Keller. Now if you only . . ."

Garry Gray, Matt's lover, appeared at the table, interrupting. "My goodness! I can't believe my eyes. You're sitting at a table with Tyger Hayes. Will wonders never cease?"

"Hi, Garry." Tyger attempted sweetness. "Why don't you join us?" Tyger had to admit that Garry was good-looking, but generally he had little to say that was not mundane or, in his quicker-witted moments, bitchy. Usually he exuded a congenial blandness that Tyger found boring. She assumed that he must be a hell of a good lover to keep Matt's interest after all this time.

"Tyger and I are semi-friends again. Sit down and be nice to her," Matt commanded gently. "Want a drink?"

"No . . . some coke."

"Christ, have you already gone through today's allotment? You're disgraceful," Matt chided lovingly. He handed the Chinese vial to Garry.

"Thanks, pal. Guess what I just heard? There's trouble in paradise . . . Tasha and Billy Youngblood."

"Since when is that news? I know Tasha much too well to think that she's attracted to anything about Youngblood except his money. . . ." Garry put his arm around Matt and whispered something in Matt's ear. Then he put his hand in Matt's lap.

"Why don't we go back to your office for a few minutes," Garry whispered, ignoring Tyger.

"Okay, honey." Matt gave him a loving pat. "I'll be with you in a minute. Tyger has finished her spiel."

Garry left without saying goodbye to Tyger. She had to make one last stand. "Matt, before you leave, let me stress again how much we're going to rely on you." She realized that she had been underestimating his ego. She was going to have to keep treading water.

"We'll see about that. Anyway, I'm extremely busy now, designing my spring collection. If you need my help, you'll have to wait for it. . . ."

He was determined to be difficult, and Tyger knew she had to play along with it. "Of course, Matt. I understand. We'll try to use your time as efficiently as possible. Anyway, there'll be a meeting next week. To bring you up to date."

"It's about time." He noticed Garry standing near the door, tapping his foot impatiently. "Well, darling, have a nice night. *Ciao*."

Tyger took a last sip of her drink, paid the check and headed out to Seventh Avenue to hail a cab for Jake's. It was not going to be clear sailing as far as Matt Phillips was concerned.

CHAPTER ELEVEN

MARY Rogers hugged Tyger when she stepped off the private elevator into her mother's apartment. Mary Rogers looked concerned. "Your mother won't admit it, but I think something's wrong. Something other than Miss Elaine's death."

Tyger nodded. "Me, too. I'll get to the bottom of it. Where is she?"

"In her room. Changing. She told me to send you right up."

Tyger headed up the apricot-carpeted stairs and knocked on her mother's door. "It's me, Mother."

"Come in, darling."

Bobbie was reclined on top of the bedcovers, in an old silk Pucci robe that Tyger hadn't seen in years. She was surprised Bobbie hadn't weeded it out of her closet ages ago. Tyger kissed her mother and gave her an affectionate hug.

At forty-six, Roberta Taylor Hayes Prather McNeeley Rowan was unquestionably a fabulous-looking woman. She did everything a female of her position and means was supposed to do to keep in shape: the exercise, diet, massage, and cosmetic surgery. And it worked, in aces. She had an exuberance for living that kept all of her energy forces flowing. She never ran down. People loved being around her; both socialites and celebrities turned down other invitations to be present at her soirées. She was always the center of attention, captivating both men and women. She was, and always had been, extraordinarily popular.

Bobbie sat up, bringing her knees to her chest, her arms

encircling them. "Sit here on the bed. Let me look at you."
She quickly appraised her daughter's current look. "Smashing.
As your mother, of course I take full credit."

"You deserve it." Tyger was surprised to see that tiny lines
were beginning to etch themselves in certain areas on her
mother's face, around her eyes and near her mouth. Her
makeup was less than impeccably applied, totally un-
characteristic of Bobbie. Tyger noted that her mother didn't
exactly look older, more as if her sharpness were losing its
edges. She looked worn out. Tyger was somewhat taken
aback. It's not that people's parents didn't age. Harry had
been twenty years older than Bobbie, and had looked it. But
over the years Bobbie had never changed, except in style and
hair color.

As if she were reading her daughter's thoughts, Bobbie sat
up and lit a cigarette. "I'm suffering from delayed jet lag.
Yesterday I was fine. There was too much to do to be tired.
Today I feel as if a bomb had been dropped directly on top of
me." She tossed her pack of Dunhill's to Tyger. "Have a
smoke?"

"I quit. Don't you remember?"

"Oh, of course I do." Bobbie nodded vaguely. "I will soon.
I've already started cutting down."

"Mother, you've been saying that for years. You don't want
to quit because you're afraid you'll gain that automatic ten or
fifteen pounds."

"Well, it'd be awful. It's hard to lose weight at my age."

"Cancer would be awful, too." Tyger tossed the pack of
cigarettes into the wastebasket.

"My disapproving daughter. . . ." Bobbie started to say
something else, but changed the subject. "Why don't you fix
yourself a drink? I'll be dressed in two minutes."

Tyger headed down to the living room. She knew her
mother loved her, but there was always some other emotion
lurking near the surface. Bobbie camouflaged it well, but not
completely. Perhaps that was why she didn't see her mother
any oftener than she had to. Over the past few years since
Bobbie had married Jimmy, Lord Rowan, their meetings had
been even less frequent. All of Jimmy's business dealings
were in England or on the Continent; he had a personal
loathing for the States. Jimmy seldom accompanied Bobbie
when she jetted over to see friends, shop and check on her
investments.

Mary Rogers had placed a crystal bowl of Russian caviar on

ice. It rested on the coffee table, surrounded by crisp toast points and lemon wedges. A bottle of Stolichnaya vodka was chilling in the silver champagne bucket. Tyger settled herself on the sofa and glanced at the latest issue of *Vogue* while she waited.

Bobbie appeared shortly, her makeup reapplied. She seemed revitalized. Her figure was like Tyger's, slim and busty, but not too busty to wear clothes well. She had changed into silk chiffon harem pants by Mary McFadden, and a black satin wrap top patterned with jet beads and chenille.

"Caviar. Vodka. What's the occasion?" Tyger asked. "I haven't forgotten your birthday have I?" She stopped to calculate the date.

"Of course not, darling. It's been such a depressing day I decided I needed a lift. And I wanted to celebrate seeing you."

Mary Rogers served them the vodka in tiny silver thimble cups. Bobbie raised hers. "And here's to your job! You have to tell me all about it."

For the next few hours, over drinks, then dinner, Tyger and Bobbie chatted, catching up on gossip and events from the past month since they had seen each other. By ten o'clock, after many thimbles full of vodka, and wine with dinner, they were both feeling giddy. Bobbie ordered a bottle of champagne, to finish off the evening. She seldom drank that much, and after a toast to the future, she became pensive.

Tyger knew something was wrong. She was anxious to dig for it. Until now Bobbie had purposely kept the conversation breezy, but now Tyger recognized the cue Bobbie was giving her. Her mother was ready, and drunk enough, to unburden herself. Tyger's head was less than clear, but she was prepared. Everyone who knew Bobbie well was aware that she liked to dominate the tides of an evening. She thrived on dictating the moods of those around her.

"What's wrong, Mother?"

Bobbie sighed, and remained silent. Tyger was trying to decide how to proceed when Bobbie finally spoke. "I'm afraid that I have recently made a big mess of my life." She paused and lit a cigarette.

"It seems," she continued, "that I may be back in New York for good. Jimmy's thrown me out." With that news expelled, she took a sip of champagne, and began giggling. "If you hadn't been so busy worrying about that silly job, you would probably have heard rumors flying about town. . . ."

"Don't leave me hanging. Give me the details."

"You know that actor, Tom Galvani?" Tyger knew. He was a young star, still on the rise, and extremely sexy, with black hair and smiling blue eyes. On the strength of his latest box-office smash, a disco movie, he commanded half a million a picture, plus points. "I met him at Jimmy's daughter's wedding and . . . it was instant. I'm twenty fucking years older than him. Of course, it's no secret that he likes older women. . . ." A thought struck her suddenly. "My God, Tyger . . . he's younger than *you*." She took a breath and resumed. "Anyway, he fell madly in love with me. Like a lovestruck teen. Phone calls, flowers, notes, little rendezvous in secluded places . . ." She giggled again. "Completely sappy . . . and utterly romantic."

Bobbie was beginning to relish telling the story. "At first, I was just flattered by it all and went along for a lark. Jimmy knew this movie star was paying me lots of attention, and he was frightfully amused. He knows me well enough to know that I don't fall in love with my admirers. I enjoy them . . . but I'm always faithful to my husbands. . . ."

Tyger could remember times when Bobbie had not been faithful to Harry, but she let the thought rest. "Mother, you're rambling. Hurry and get to the scandal."

"Don't make fun of me, Tyger. You aren't exactly the vestal virgin. . . ."

Tyger nodded. "We'll get to me later. Right now you're leading up to why Jimmy's thrown you out of the castle."

"All right. To make a long story short, I finally succumbed to Tom's charms. God, all that New York Italian virility. I've never been with such an incredible man in my whole life! A 'fucking machine,' as they say. . . ." She laughed awkwardly.

"Where was Jimmy all this time?"

"He was racing around, working with the Swedes on some deal. He didn't want me along because it was one of those all-business jaunts he knows I hate. So Tom and I sneaked off to Spain, and rented a wonderfully secluded villa on the Costa del Sol. We had a splendid week or so. Then Jimmy tracked me down, and demanded that I return to London. Tom's director had also been calling from Paris every ten minutes . . . they needed him for some reshooting." Bobbie took a few more sips of champagne, and lapsed into a memory.

"You're leaving me panting." Tyger was spellbound. Her mother had never spoken to her so candidly. It was unlike Bobbie to talk about a torrid affair.

"Well . . . we had two choices. To return to our respective lives like obedient little children. Or take off, and try to camouflage our trail."

"I can guess which alternative you chose." Tyger poured herself another glass of champagne.

"We hired a yacht, and cruised around the Mediterranean for a few weeks. Idyllic. Just like the movies." Bobbie sighed deeply. "Tom made me feel twenty-five again, and absolutely gorgeous. We talked about coming out into the open: I'd divorce Jimmy, and live with Tom. Then it happened. Overnight. Tom changed. He became restless and edgy. He began alluding to his commitments. He was desperate to talk to his agent, he had to get in touch with some friends in New York. He began brooding . . . then he closed me out entirely. We returned to Spain. He said goodbye to me at the Barcelona airport and took off. No mention of our ever getting together again. . . ." Tears welled up in her eyes, but she took a deep breath to gain control. Bobbie had always been able to stop herself from crying. She knew it made her look wretched.

"And that, as they say, is that," Bobbie continued. "I felt used . . . taken advantage of. Oh, I know I could have been the one who tired of him first. Aside from sex, we had very little in common. It was bound to end. I just made the fatal mistake: carrying it one step too far in my fantasies." She shrugged. "Anyway, when I returned to London, Jimmy had moved into his club. He refused to talk to me, just left word that his lawyer had already begun proceedings." Bobbie opened a new pack of cigarettes and lit one. "Then I went back to Madrid . . . to be alone and think. I'd been there only two days when Marta called to tell me about Elaine. So here I am. A damned fool. What a charade it's all been!"

"Is there any chance of reconciling with Jimmy? I'm sure he still loves you. After all, it hasn't been very long. . . ."

"I considered going to him, hat in hand. But why? Jimmy's wonderful, and very rich, but he loves business more than anything . . . and he's always been a rotten lover. What's there to go back to?" She poured the rest of the champagne into their glasses.

"It could be worse," Tyger said brightly. "You're still young. You look great. . . ."

"Hmmm. I feel old as hell. I've made an appointment to have cosmetic acupuncture. Maybe that will help." Bobbie laughed. "Perhaps I should start a career too. Do you think Hugh Marshall can come up with something for me?"

"Hands off, Mother. He's mine."

"Yours? What's been going on behind office doors?"

Tyger backtracked. "He's not mine exactly. I mean, the job is. As far as my love life is concerned I'm still occupied with Jake Danton."

"Occupied? What do you mean by that? Are you in love with him?"

"I don't think so. . . ."

"Now it's time for me to get motherly. Do as I say, not as I do, you know." She laughed, then assumed a sterner tone. "Tyger, you're much too indiscreet. You're twenty-six. You've had God knows how many lovers. And married twice. . . ."

"Only once technically, Mother," Tyger reminded her. "You had the first one annulled, remember?"

Bobbie sidestepped. "I know I sound like a broken record, but it *is* time you settled down. You'll be bored with this job in no time. You have to think about your future."

"I am. That's *why* I got a job."

"Oh, face it. This is just a whim, like all of your other hobbies. You aren't the sort to be a committed career woman."

The comment stung. "I'm *changing,* Mother! I'm getting older."

"Well, you weren't raised to be a nine-to-five drudge. It's time for you to latch onto someone dependable. You're spoiled, Tyger . . . and not very realistic."

"And you are?" Tyger hated Bobbie in this mood. Too much alcohol transformed Bobbie's personality, a fact of which she was well aware, and so Bobbie seldom drank too much. From past experience, Tyger knew it was time to leave, before they each blurted out things they would regret later.

Tyger stood. "Mother, I don't feel the need to justify my job or my life to you. We've both had a little too much to drink and it's late. I should be getting home." She leaned over to kiss her mother goodbye.

With a jolt, Tyger felt the blow to her right cheek. Bobbie slapped her, hard. Tyger staggered sideways, tripping over the coffee table. She caught her balance by grasping onto the grand piano behind her.

"I'm not ready for you to go yet. I have a lot more to say!" Bobbie's face had taken on high color with her indignant fury. All signs of fatigue were gone; she looked radiant.

"You've said enough already!" Tyger's cheek smarted, and she felt dizzy, off balance. She fought back an impulse to cry.

Instead, she stood rigidly still, trying to regain her composure. Bobbie waited, poised for Tyger's next move.

Tyger stared back at her mother, while her emotions scrambled between fury, hatred and humiliation. Tyger's mind leaped backward to a time long ago. She was in the living room of the mansion in Beverly Hills, and she was young, ten or eleven. Bobbie had accused her of lying about where she had been that day, and then had hit Tyger, totally unexpectedly.

Both times, then and now, Tyger had been caught off guard. An unexpected rage had welled up in Bobbie and exploded through her usually collected exterior. But it was the vindictiveness behind the blow, the power of the slap itself, that had astonished Tyger more than the momentary pain of the actual strike.

"I'm sorry, Tyger, I . . ."

Tyger recovered her senses and knew that she had to get out of there. She headed for the hall. "Goodnight, Mother."

"Tyger! You come back here this minute . . ."

Rather than wait for the elevator, Tyger went to the kitchen, exiting through the service entrance, down the back stairs. She didn't want Bobbie coming after her, if indeed she would even bother to try.

Once on Park Avenue, Tyger walked briskly for nearly fifteen blocks before she had calmed down enough to hail a cab. All the way home, Tyger tried to figure out why her mother felt the way she did about her. Bobbie had spent her life charming people, getting what she wanted. But underneath it all, many layers down, there was a desperation. Bobbie wanted, *needed,* to control her own life and the lives of those about whom she cared. When circumstances, or will, caused someone to rebel against her, something snapped within her. Fortunately, most of the time people did what she wanted. Bobbie was an expert at manipulation, but Tyger was no longer willing to let herself be manipulated.

It was daybreak before Tyger fell asleep.

CHAPTER TWELVE

"DARLING, is that you?" Bobbie's voice took on a clipped English tone when she was ill at ease.

"Of course, Mother. I was just about to ring you to check on the time of the funeral." Tyger was determined to be civil, and prepared to ignore last night's skirmish. With Bobbie, unpleasantries were always swept under the rug, with the understanding that in time they would magically disappear.

"It's at noon. Shall I have Mary swing by your office on the way? We can go together. . . . I hate these things."

"Oh, Mother, I think I'll walk. It's only fourteen blocks, and I need the exercise."

Bobbie sighed. "You're determined not to forgive and forget, I see. Well, let's not rehash this over the phone. I have to get dressed. We'll talk later."

Of course they did not talk later. The funeral was mobbed, and Bobbie felt it her duty to look after Marta to keep her from caving in. Elaine had stipulated, in a will she had drawn up years before, that her body be cremated. She did not want gawkers staring at her lifeless body smiling out waxily from an open coffin. She had often told Marta that when her time came she didn't want a big fuss made over her death. However, she was Elaine Talbert, and a big fuss was in order.

There was a circus atmosphere overriding the solemnity of the occasion. Photographers snapped furiously as celebrities rushed from their limousines up the steps to St. James Church at Seventy-first and Madison. And, if for no other reason than to be seen, everyone was there: Elaine's friends and enemies from fashion, business, publishing, international banking. Diana Vreeland, Governor Carey with Anne Ford Uzielli, James Brady, Dina Merrill, Helen Gurley Brown, Laurence Rockefeller, C. Z. Guest, Bill Paley, Chessy Rayner and Mica Ertegun, Joyce and David Susskind. That sort of celebrity funeral even attracted New York's regular party crashers. Tyger guessed that there was only a handful of sincere mourners.

When the service was over, Tyger stood on the steps outside and watched the congregation stream out, their expressions of mournful piety dissolving into questions about where to have lunch. Bobbie emerged, and blinked a moment in the bright sunlight until she shielded her eyes with a pair of Dior dark glasses. Then she saw Tyger and came over to her.

"The best-dressed funeral of the decade," Bobbie said. "I think Elaine would have been pleased."

"Hello, Mother. How's Marta holding up?"

"Poor dear, she's dissolved. Her sister arrived from Minneapolis. She's taken her under her wing."

Tyger looked past her mother and saw the tall figure of Hugh Marshall emerging from the church. Bobbie followed her glance, just as Marshall spotted them and made his way over.

"Hugh!" said Lady Rowan. She pushed the dark glasses up over her head. Her eyes sparkled. "Goodness, it's been ages since I've seen you."

"It has been a long time, Bobbie. You spend entirely too much time in England." He smiled engagingly, then greeted Tyger. "I suppose Tyger's filled you in on her new job?"

"Of course." Bobbie flashed her perfect teeth back at his. "I'm terribly grateful to you for hiring her on. I've been meaning to write a note to thank you."

Tyger felt like a small child being talked about over her head. She was annoyed, but kept a pleasant expression on her face.

"Tyger got the job on her own initiative, I assure you." Hugh glanced at Tyger and smiled. Other women nearby paused to gaze at him. He turned back to Roberta. "You look marvelous, Bobbie. Are you in town for long?"

Bobbie fluttered her long fingers and gave a helpless sigh.

(121)

"Goodness only knows. I'm at the mercy of my lawyer and my stockbroker. As long as they tell me to stay, I stay." She laughed. "Business! I'm afraid I don't have a head for it."

"I'm sure you manage superbly," Hugh replied gallantly.

Tyger was beginning to seethe. *Do I have to stand here and listen to this?* she thought. But she was reluctant to leave Hugh alone with Lady Bobbie. It was hard to believe he did not see through her mother's pose of helpless femininity. But he stood there, smiling.

"I imagine I'll be here at least a couple of weeks," Bobbie said.

"Good." He leaned forward and kissed her cheek. "Perhaps we'll see each other again . . . under better circumstances." He turned to Tyger, but refrained from kissing her cheek, said "I'll see *you* soon," and vanished into the crowd.

"Mother, I thought you knew Hugh Marshall only casually."

"Oh, yes." Bobbie nodded vaguely. "I haven't seen him since I was married to Cappy. You know, the horse-breeding set." She paused. "I'd forgotten how attractive he is."

"Well, Mother, you've been busy working the Continent."

Bobbie's eyes narrowed. "How sharper than a serpent's tooth. Et cetera. Shall we bury the hatchet and have lunch?"

"Sorry, Mother." Tyger looked at her watch. "I have to get back to the office. But consider the hatchet buried."

Bobbie kissed Tyger's cheek automatically. "I'll let you know my plans. I may go to San Francisco for the weekend."

"Well . . . keep me posted."

Tyger thought about her mother as she strolled toward Fifth. There wasn't much else to do but forgive and forget. They were stuck with each other, mother and daughter. The patterns were etched; nothing ever really changed between them. Tyger was aware of the unspoken, ever-present competition between them, as if they were, actually, sisters. Except that Bobbie held a psychological edge.

Tyger wondered if Hugh Marshall was attracted to her mother. Had they had a fling in the past? Or worse, a flirtation that had never been consummated and still lurked in the back of their minds?

Hugh Marshall's limousine turned left at Seventy-second Street onto Fifth Avenue. The telephone buzzed once and Marshall put down his *Times.*

"Yes, Tim. What's up?"

"I just heard from Mr. Bachrach," the young Englishman said. "He's been detained in Chicago, and cannot make lunch. He will see you at four instead."

"Did you move up my four-o'clock appointment with O'Hara and the British group?"

"Yes, sir. To two-thirty."

"Fine, Tim. I'll see you then."

Marshall gazed idly out the window onto the tree-lined avenue and spotted Tyger Hayes, strolling down the park side of Fifth, oblivious to the admiring stares of a group of teenaged softball players waiting for their bus.

Marshall pressed the button to lower the window which separated him from his chauffeur. "Curtis, pull up alongside that young woman there, in the brown linen suit." He pressed another button and lowered his window. "Tyger!"

Tyger slowed warily, then smiled as she turned and recognized Hugh Marshall. "Oh! Hello again."

"What's the matter? Don't we pay you enough to cover transportation?"

Tyger's full-lipped smile broadened to a grin. "You don't pay me nearly enough. But that's not why I'm walking. You may not have noticed . . . but it's a beautiful day."

Marshall glanced past her into the park. "So it is." Behind them, an impatient taxi driver honked for the limousine to move along. "Come on, Tyger. I'll give you a lift."

Tyger stepped quickly into the car and settled herself next to Hugh Marshall against the beige ultrasuede upholstery. She stretched her long legs out in front of her, aware that she was showing them off to their best advantage, and aware that they had not escaped Marshall's notice.

"Where to?"

"Back to the office, monsieur."

"But it's lunchtime. Don't you have a date?"

"Only with a container of yogurt and a stack of Jess's demographic surveys."

Hugh Marshall paused for a moment while he made up his mind. "How about having lunch with me? Tim just informed me that my schedule's been switched around."

Tyger's mood shifted into high gear. Ten minutes before she had been speculating about her mother's past relationship with Hugh Marshall. Now it was she and not her mother who was going to spend an uninterrupted hour with the handsome enigmatic president of Kellerco. "The yogurt will be furious . . . but I'd love it."

*   *   *

Manhattan Market on Second Avenue at Fifty-fourth Street was brimming with its lunchtime devotees of Americanized *nouvelle cuisine,* but Hugh and Tyger were shown immediately to a choice table near the rear glass wall with its sunny view of an adjacent park. The rest of the large dining room was unobtrusively handsome, with floor-to-ceiling gray suede walls displaying blown-up black-and-white photographs of New York.

"Bring us an order of bread and Brie-butter right away," Tyger instructed the pleasant young waiter as he seated her. She smiled at Hugh. "They have the best homemade bread in New York here."

"I agree it's good. But not the best. The best is made about twice a year by none other than your lunch companion."

"Hugh, I don't believe it! You? Baking bread?"

"Why not? One can get rid of a great deal of pent-up hostility with all that kneading and punching."

"This is a side of you that *People* would love to get its cameras on."

"Promise me you'll never tell them. It's one of my best-kept secrets. I have an old Navajo-Irish cook on my ranch in Colorado. She taught me how to bake bread years ago. I was recuperating from an accident, and . . ." He stopped. "I'm in danger of losing track of time. Are you ready to order?"

Hugh Marshall had let her see more of himself than he wanted to. Tyger was fascinated and desperately curious . . . but she knew better than to press. The waiter came, and she ordered a salad with goat cheese and roasted pecans and *carpaccio*—thinly sliced raw beef with fresh parsley and lime sauce. Marshall chose the seafood pasta with crabmeat and vegetables, and a California Chardonnay. Then he turned the conversation toward the safe confines of business.

"Are you making headway with Matt Phillips?"

"I met with him the other evening in an effort to stroke his ego. . . ." Tyger broke off a piece of bread. "He's determined to be difficult. I calmed him down a bit, but I'm afraid it's going to be uphill all the way."

Marshall looked at Tyger kindly. The thin lines around his mouth softened again. "You'll have him eating out of your hand in no time."

"If not, he can sulk all the way to the bank." Tyger laughed and so did Marshall, a deep hearty laugh that caused the couple at the next table to glance over at them. Tyger recognized the woman. She was the gossip columnist Liz Smith.

"Oh, dear." Tyger lowered her voice. "Don't look now but I think we're going to be an item tomorrow."

Hugh Marshall glanced across and caught the columnist's eye.

"Hello, Hugh . . . Tyger," Liz Smith said.

"Put away your notebook, Liz," Marshall said with a grin. "Tyger works for me. This is strictly business."

But as Hugh Marshall looked back at her, Tyger thought she saw more than "strictly business" in his smile. She felt suddenly giddy, almost tipsy, although the waiter was just now pouring the wine.

Lunch was served. They talked business. Tyger hardly touched her food. Her stomach was in a knot, and her mind kept replaying that smile.

After lunch, Hugh Marshall dropped Tyger off at her office and headed for his two-thirty appointment. There was something about Tyger, he had concluded, something tremendously appealing, and that worried him. He did not want to get too close to her, but seeing her so often, working with her, it might be difficult not to.

Bobbie McNeeley . . . Lady Rowan now. Years ago, in Kentucky, there had been a spark between them. It might be worth fanning now. He would think about it. If he were seeing her mother it would be protection against any involvement with Tyger. He could control himself and his emotions when it came to most women. With Tyger, he was not so sure.

Magnet. Dance. Pizazz. Eclipse. Cantata. Jubilee. Revelation. City Lights. Aura. Magic. Everyone at Keller Cosmetics had been suggesting name possibilities for the new perfume. Connie complained that she couldn't sleep; mysterious voices spit names out at her all night. Tryst. Pomegranate. Casablanca. Ginger compiled lists of the suggestions. These were narrowed down to the best. Then they started all over again.

Connie and Jess were already in Shaw's office when Tyger walked in. "I just spoke with Matt Phillips, and mentioned some of our best name ideas. He nixed them all. He did mention the name he thinks we should use." Tyger sank down in her chair.

"Oh, God," breathed Connie. "I'm afraid to ask. . . ."

"Well, actually, we have a choice: Matt Phillips, or Perfume by Matt Phillips."

Connie groaned.

"His point," Tyger explained, "is that Ralph Lauren's perfume is called Lauren, and Oscar de la Renta's is Oscar. There's Halston and Adolfo and . . ."

"Yes, yes," sighed Connie, "I know. But Matt Phillips just isn't as classy-sounding as Lauren or Halston."

Everyone agreed. "Unfortunately, he has his mind set on having *only* his name on it," Tyger emphasized. She had spent an uncomfortable half hour arguing the point with Matt Phillips that morning in his office.

Sheldon Shaw looked at her. "Well, he'll be at the meeting next week with Marshall. We'll talk it over with him then. Of course, you know, it's possible that Phillips does have a point. . . ."

Connie pounded her fist on Shaw's desk. "No! We need a better name. We haven't come up with it yet, but we will. There's time."

Jess broke in. "Let's change the subject and pin down the fragrance profile. I'm setting up a meeting with the fragrance manufacturers for next week, after we've had the session with Marshall and Phillips." He looked at Connie. "There's not as much time as you think. It's almost Labor Day."

The rest of the afternoon was spent in heavy conference. By five, Jess, Connie and Tyger had nearly completed the official fragrance profile for "Bare Essence." All their information, interviews and statistics had been translated into the target market—the women to whom the perfume would be directed. In addition, they sketched out how the fragrance would be stored and shipped, the distribution outlets and all other pertinent information the fragrance manufacturer needed to know before they could begin coming up with a scent.

"The scent," Connie said with a tired sigh. "Sooner or later we had to get around to that. What do we shoot for—a knock-off of an existing fragrance, or something totally new?"

"Look . . . it's going to be much easier to pick a fragrance we *know* our target market buys, like Chloë or Halston or whatever, and have it duplicated. On the same track . . . but different enough." Jess rubbed his hands over his cheeks and felt the scratchiness of his five-o'clock shadow against his fingers.

"With a 'twist,'" said Tyger. Everyone looked at her.

"That's a term perfumers use. 'Give us Opium . . . with a twist.' "

"I think we should aim for something new," announced Connie. "Well, realistically, with all the perfumes on the market, I guess it can't be too new. But you know what I mean."

Tyger agreed. "Matt Phillips feels that way, too. He doesn't want his perfume compared to another designer's. His ego is at stake . . . and the individuality that he puts into his designs."

"Let's face it," Jess interjected. "We don't have much time. Ultimately we're going to have to settle on what we can get."

"True. A perfumer can spend years creating a new fragrance," Tyger said, brimming with the knowledge of her recent research.

"But many perfumes are done in a few months. I've read about some being whipped up in a few weeks," Connie added.

"Not totally new smells, though," Tyger said. "To have something that fast, it would be a duplication of an existing perfume. Back to the 'twist.' "

Connie leaned back in her chair. "Well, I still feel we should aim for something new. If nobody comes up with it, then we'll have to settle for less. But *not* until we get down to the wire. . . ."

Back in his office, Sheldon Shaw fixed himself a drink. "Ginger," he said into the intercom, "hold my calls and give me an outside line." He took a black notebook from his vest pocket, looked up a number and dialed. As the call raced through clicking interchanges to Phoenix, he took a long swallow of vodka. He felt ill at ease with Nelson Bachrach even on the phone.

"Hello?" The chairman's voice barked into his private line.

"Good afternoon, sir. Sheldon Shaw, here."

"What's going on back there, Shaw?"

"Well, sir, things seem to be coming along pretty well. Not quite as quickly as I'd hoped. I think our problem is this assistant Marshall has saddled me with, Tyger Hayes. As I've told you before, Mr. Bachrach, I don't feel comfortable working with an assistant who's so totally without a business background. I think I could get a lot more accomplished if you'd give me the authority to dismiss her and bring in my man, Dave Kirshenbaum."

"Forget it, Shaw," Bachrach snapped. "I don't want anyone more accomplished. This Hayes girl is just fine."

"But sir, I . . ."

"Kellerco's no goddam beauty parlor. If Hugh Marshall wants to impress his society friends, let him do it. Let him hire all the debutantes he likes. This is Marshall's main event, Shaw. You're just in there to keep score."

Sheldon Shaw took a quiet swallow of vodka. "I'm not sure I understand, Mr. Bachrach. You're not saying . . ."

"I'm not saying anything. Just sit back and relax, Shel. You're doing fine. Keep me posted."

"Of course, sir. But should I . . ." The line was dead. "Goodbye, sir," Shaw said automatically, and hung up the phone.

Shaw took the cap off the Smirnoff's and poured the rest of the contents of the bottle into his empty glass. He realized that his hand was shaking, and he had the sudden awful awareness that he was all alone.

What did Bachrach want, anyway? Didn't he see what was going to happen with people like Tyger Hayes worming their way into positions of power? Did he *want* this company to fail?

Of course, that was just what Bachrach wanted, or he was convinced that it was inevitable, which came to the same thing. Bachrach was going to sit back and watch Keller Perfumes crumble, and then sweep Hugh Marshall out with the debris.

And he, Sheldon Shaw, would be part of that debris.

Shaw stood gloomily at the window and looked down on the park below. Riders cantered along the bridle path. Hansom cabs mingled with cyclists, roller skaters and skateboarders on the blacktop drives which were closed to cars until sundown. Rush-hour traffic prowled the streets around its perimeters.

Oh, God, he thought, *why does this have to happen to me?* It was a no-win situation. Whichever way the chips fell, they were sure to fall on him.

Unless he could think of something. He would have to start sharpening his own knives if he was going to cut himself out of this situation.

CHAPTER THIRTEEN

"WHY is it . . . that when you sleep in a strange bed you have vivid dreams?" Tyger asked. She was sitting at Jake's kitchen table, adding the finishing touches to her makeup. She was wearing yesterday's outfit, but she could change into the extra outfit she kept at the office. She was not in the mood to go home and change before work.

"Thanks a lot. After all this time you still consider my bed strange? I'm insulted." Jake refilled their mugs with coffee from the electric percolator.

"You know what I mean. I seem to dream more clearly here than at home. It's not that I don't sleep well, I'm just able to remember everything better."

Jake was rooting through the refrigerator for something to eat. "No bread for toast," he said. "Wanna go around the corner to the coffee shop, and get some eggs and English muffins?"

"Jake . . . stop talking about food! I'm trying to tell you about this idea I got in my dream."

"Tell me at the coffee shop. I'm starving."

"No, I'll be late for work. Let me tell you my idea. Then you can go get fat while I head uptown."

Jake sighed, and sat down in a canvas director's chair. "Okay. You know, other people's dreams are always boring."

"Well . . . this is more of a sleeping brainstorm than a dream."

"Tyger, stop stalling while I collapse from hunger. Tell me!"

"I'm trying to!" Tyger snapped, then she sighed. "For weeks now, I've been dreaming about work—visions of perfume dancing in my head. But last night it all came together. I was walking through a big store. Probably Bloomingdale's, but it didn't really look like it. . . ."

Jake glanced at his watch. "I'm giving you one minute."

"I saw a huge display of Matt Phillips's dresses. Hundreds and hundreds of them. I went over to look, and on the tags were bright little scratch-and-sniff cards. They read: 'Try a whiff of Matt Phillips's new perfume.' "

Jake stood up. "That's great, love. Let's go for breakfast." He rang for the elevator.

"Jake, it's a brilliant idea! Scratch-and-sniff labels attached to Matt's clothes would sell a lot of perfume. I'm talking about his ready-to-wear line, not the designer collection. It's a hell of a gimmick. It's revolutionary!"

The elevator arrived. Jake stepped in and held the door so it wouldn't close. "Maybe they'll elect you to the perfume hall of fame," he quipped. "Coming?"

Tyger gathered up her gear and brushed past Jake, into the elevator.

"You may have trouble finding a cab this time of day," he said. "Why don't you change your mind and have breakfast with me?"

Tyger said nothing. The elevator opened onto the ground floor. She exited and walked quickly out of the front door, onto the street.

Jake hurried to catch up with her. "Hey . . . what's the matter? Why aren't you talking to me?"

Tyger continued to ignore him. Sixth Avenue was jammed. There were no empty cabs in sight, so Tyger headed for the bus stop on the next corner. Jake followed her.

"Tyger! This is stupid. Why are you mad?"

She glared at Jake. "If you can't guess . . ."

"Just because I didn't turn somersaults over your nocturnal brainstorm . . . ?"

"There was no need for you to be so fucking obnoxious about it. You could see it was something I was excited about. You could have shown a little enthusiasm." Tyger extracted two quarters from her change purse as the Number Six bus pulled up next to the curb.

"You're making a mountain out of this. But I'm sorry, I really am . . ." Jake called out as Tyger ascended the steps into the crowded bus.

Tyger inched her way to the rear and found a seat. She looked back and saw Jake still standing on the sidewalk, looking forlorn. She realized that she had probably over-reacted, but Jake had annoyed her.

As the bus crept uptown, Tyger began to think about him, about them. Regardless of this morning's altercation, she liked Jake. He was easy to be with. She had gradually stopped seeing all of her old standby escorts in favor of him. Their sex life was terrific. Perhaps that was it. They had a good time together, but their relationship was primarily sexual. Tyger knew that if they were going to fall in love with each other it would have happened by now. She guessed she wasn't emotionally ready to fall in love at the moment. Her job was the main priority of her life these days. Unless, of course, Hugh Marshall were to show a little more interest.

"Tyger, are you ready to head over to Marshall's office? It's time for the meeting." Jess Leibowitz had put on a Countess Mara tie for the occasion, and was looking a little more dapper than usual.

"Coming, Jess. Where's Connie?"

"Shaw just walked in. She's in his office briefing him on the events of our meeting this morning. They'll join us over there."

Sheldon Shaw had missed the regular Tuesday-morning meeting, without checking in at all. Jess and Connie, howev-er, had responded enthusiastically to Tyger's dream idea. They had also nailed down the last details of their presenta-tion to Marshall and Phillips at the meeting.

Tim Yates greeted them outside the Kellerco boardroom. "I'm sorry we had to move up the meeting like this. Hugh has to rush to Arizona. There's a crisis at Keller Copper, and who knows how long he'll be out there." He lowered his voice. "Matt Phillips is already inside."

Hugh Marshall moved down the hall at a fast clip, despite his limp, and joined them. "Good afternoon, Jess, Tyger. Shall we get underway?"

Tim spoke up. "Connie Larcada and Sheldon Shaw will be here in a couple of minutes."

As they entered the boardroom, Matt Phillips stood up. He wore one of the originals from his men's-wear collection, an easy-fitting suit in greige linen with a foulard tie. He looked a bit too dashing for the Kellerco boardroom. His spirits were up. Tyger guessed he had just sniffed some cocaine.

"Hello, darling." He kissed Tyger on both cheeks, then shook hands with Marshall and the rest.

"Shall we get started. I've got to catch a plane at five," Marshall announced.

The door opened behind him, and Shaw and Connie hurried in.

"Sorry, Hugh," Sheldon Shaw said. "Some last-minute details."

Marshall waved his hand impatiently. "What do you have for us today?"

Shaw cleared his throat and took a sip of coffee. "Well, ah, things seem to be moving right along." He picked up the notes from this morning's meeting that Connie had given him. He had trouble focusing. The paper trembled in his hand, and he put it back down again. "Let's see, ah, Jess—why don't we start with the fragrance profile?"

Jess sat forward. "Sure, Sheldon." He looked at Phillips, then at Marshall. "I have appointments with the top eight fragrance manufacturers later this week. I'm asking them to get back to us with their submissions by November first."

"What if no one comes up with an exceptional fragrance?" Matt Phillips asked. "We can't just settle for anything."

"We're dealing with the best people in the business," Marshall soothed.

"But what if you don't get a good enough fragrance by launch date? We can't just bottle anything. My *name's* going to be on it!"

Marshall was cool. "Don't worry, Matt. We'll have a terrific scent by March. If we don't, it's not the end of the world. We can change the formula later."

"What? Start out with one perfume, and end up with another . . . oh no!" Matt's face was anxious.

"It has been done in the past," Tyger said reassuringly.

"Sure has," Connie said. "According to my inside sources at Revlon, Charlie has changed its formula several times."

"And Norell, Replique, Arpège . . . they're all different from the way they started out," Tyger added.

"Anyway, Matt, rest assured. When the bottles are shipped to the stores next spring, they will contain a quality product." Marshall looked at Jess. "We seem to have gotten off the track. You were going to read us the fragrance profile that you'll submit to the perfume manufacturers."

Jess sat forward. "Right. Here it is." He picked up his dossier and read: "The perfume, code-named 'Bare Essence,' is to be 'American.' It is to be a long-lasting 'evening' scent. Sensual, spirited, evocative of many moods. Not a single-note floral or garden smell, but a more sophisticated, complex blend of ingredients. Heady, but not heavy. The woman who wears it is—or aspires to be—a trend-setter, an individualist. A woman who dresses for herself without losing her awareness of her environment or the opposite sex." Jess turned the page.

"Exactly the sort of woman who wears my clothes," Matt Phillips said approvingly.

"The distribution," Jess continued, "is to be select, concentrating on stores which do a large volume in Matt Phillips clothes. The launch will be at either Bloomingdale's or Saks Fifth Avenue, depending upon which will give us the best floor space and cooperative promotion." He paused, to let the facts rest for a moment, and lit a cigarette.

"We'll aim for Bloomingdale's," Marshall cut in. "They've just redecorated their main floor. It will give us greater impact."

"Right." Jess nodded. "The packaging, by a well-known designer, will be exclusive, expensive-looking. The perfume manufacturer who develops the scent will make up the concentrated formula and ship it to our bottler, who will add water and alcohol, fill the bottles, and store them in a climate-controlled warehouse. The cases will be shipped in specially air-conditioned trucks, so that under no circumstance can the fragrance be damaged in transit."

Jess cleared his throat. "The Phillips perfume is to sell at retail for eighty-five dollars an ounce; the eau-de-toilette, for fifteen dollars a bottle. As of now, there are to be no auxiliary products—bath oil, powder, soap, et cetera. The Phillips men's fragrance will be introduced within a year after the women's perfume hits the market." Jess finished, and looked up.

"Good work—all of you," Hugh Marshall said. "I'm pleased."

Jess handed a list to Marshall. "Here are the names of the fragrance manufacturers I've contacted."

Marshall scanned it quickly, and nodded his approval. "Okay, what's next?" He directed his question to Sheldon Shaw.

Shaw went blank for a second, and looked down at his notes. His head felt lousy, but he had to keep up a good front for the others, especially Marshall. "Oh, ah . . . regarding promotion. Besides the regular methods—ads, in-store sampling, scented mailers, gift-with-purchase giveaways—I've, ah, had an additional idea: scratch-and-sniff perfume tags, to be attached to the labels of Phillips's ready-to-wear clothes. That way, the buyer can sample the scent while she's trying on the dress. . . ."

Matt Phillips smiled. "Oh, I love it! . . . I *love* it."

Marshall agreed. "First-rate. Ingenious!"

Tyger was stunned. She looked at Shaw, but his eyes were lowered to the paper in front of him. Jess and Connie shot Tyger glances to indicate that they, too, were astounded. Tyger opened her mouth to say something, then reconsidered. It would seem unprofessional to haggle in front of Marshall. She sat back in her chair and kept quiet.

Tim Yates broke in. "Hugh, I'm afraid that it's time to go."

Marshall stood. "Good meeting. I'm extremely pleased. Sorry to rush off like this." He closed his briefcase. "Tyger, I want you to ride with me to the airport."

"Of course." Tyger caught Sheldon Shaw glancing at her, and she could read jealousy and uneasiness in his eyes. She knew he was wondering what she would tell Marshall. *Well, let him worry,* she thought. She returned his stare evenly and his eyes fell away.

The Kellerco Mercedes was comfortable but not lavish. There was a telephone and a bar but no TV or recording system. Hugh Marshall and Tyger were speeding toward La Guardia Airport, where Marshall would take the company jet to Phoenix. They would be there in less than fifteen minutes, and Tyger wished they were headed for Kennedy so she could spend half an hour longer with him.

Marshall opened his briefcase. "Still like the job?"

"I love it. I'm really lucky to . . ."

"Luck has nothing to do with it," Marshall interrupted. "You were right for the job . . . and you're handling it well." He smiled at Tyger. For a moment it seemed to Tyger as if he were looking deep behind her eyes, contemplating her, perhaps desiring her. There were warm sapphire lights glimmering in his eyes. But Marshall glanced down at his briefcase, and when he looked back at Tyger, the familiar opaque curtain had been lowered behind his pupils, camouflaging what she thought she had seen a moment before. He cleared his throat. "We don't have much time. What do you know about a woman named Martine Rainier?"

"She's a top French jewelry designer. About thirty. She's very current, very chic . . ."

"In Europe," Marshall said. "She isn't well known here."

"Not *well* known, perhaps, but she's beginning to gather a reputation. Tiffany's carries her jewelry. . . ."

"Do you know her?"

"Never met her myself, but we have some friends in common. I hear that she's . . . a bit difficult."

"I want her to design the bottles for our perfume."

"That's fabulous," Tyger said. "She'd be perfect!"

"My sources tell me that she's not keen on America. Or American businesses. She won't be easy to convince. We can offer her a lot of money, but I understand that's not what she bases her decisions on. Anyway, Tyger, I want you to go to Paris and talk her into working for us."

"Me?" Tyger was astonished.

"I can't think of anyone who stands a better chance of getting through to her. You're young, and you run in the same circles."

"I'll certainly try. When do you want me to go?"

"Tomorrow. Or the day after. There's no time to lose." He handed Tyger a portfolio containing clippings and background about Martine Rainier. "You can read this on the plane over."

The limousine pulled up in front of the Marine terminal. The driver got out of the car, pulled Marshall's suitcase out of the trunk and opened the door for him. "I see your plane parked on the runway, sir."

"Thanks, Curtis. Let them know I'm here and ready to leave immediately." Hugh turned back to Tyger. "I'm confident that you'll succeed with the enigmatic Miss Rainier. If you need anything, Tim will make the arrangements." He reached over and shook Tyger's hand, then got out of the car quickly.

Marshall sat alone in the blue-and-white custom-decorated passenger cabin of the company's Gulfstream, sipping his martini. The steward had just taken his dinner order: rare steak, salad, no dessert. Hugh looked out the window at the clouds thousands of feet below him. The setting sun glared in, and he pulled down the shade.

Marshall pulled out the dossier on Keller Perfumes. He sipped his drink, and thought about this afternoon's meeting. It had gone well. Even Matt Phillips had seemed reasonably satisfied, mainly due to the scratch-and-sniff idea. Odd . . . it did not seem to be the sort of concept that Shaw was likely to come up with. No, more likely Connie Larcada or Tyger Hayes. Yes, quite possibly Tyger. In spite of her lack of business credentials, she was working out well. She had energy and fresh ideas. Marshall was pleased that his hunch about her had proved correct. Tyger was . . . *No,* he thought. *No point in dwelling on her.*

He poured himself a second martini from the silver shaker that sat on the chrome-and-glass coffee table in front of him, and focused his attention on Sheldon Shaw. The man had seemed vague today, a little shaky. On the other hand, Marshall did not expect, or want, much from him. Nelson Bachrach had appointed Shaw to the presidency in order to have a conduit into Keller Perfumes. Shaw was a weakling. Did Bachrach count on him to drag the entire division under with his ineptitude? It did not make any difference to Hugh Marshall, because Shaw's presidency was working to his advantage. If Bachrach had brought in one of the stronger executives for the job, there would have been friction. Marshall would not have been able to call the shots as easily. No, Shaw was just fine, for now. When the company got off the ground, and the perfume was launched, Marshall would be ready to back out of active participation. Then he would appoint a more dynamic president to take over.

Marshall closed his eyes and rested his head against the back of the navy velour sofa. He propped his feet up on the coffee table. The next moment, the steward appeared with his dinner tray.

CHAPTER FOURTEEN

TYGER had Hugh Marshall's chauffeur drop her off at the office. It was past five, and the place was empty except for the cleaning lady who was vacuuming the reception area. In her office, on her desk, was a basket brimming with coral roses. There was a note: "For sniffing only—don't scratch yourself. Forgive me for being a bore. Love, J.D." Tyger smiled. Good old Jake. He wasn't so bad after all.

She went through her desk, and chose the pertinent information she would need to show Martine Rainier in Paris: the Bare Essence fragrance profile; a portfolio on Matt Phillips; a file full of American perfume ads. She was elated by the assignment Hugh had given her. He trusted her to handle an important project, and she was determined to succeed. It would also be fun to get back to Paris.

Tyger gathered up her briefcase and handbag and headed down the hallway to the elevators. She ran into Sheldon Shaw, emerging from the men's room. "Oh," she said, startled. "I didn't know anyone else was still here."

"Only me," he said, somewhat breezily, "burning the midnight oil." He kept his gaze fixed on her. Tyger felt uncomfortable.

"Well, as long as you're still here . . . I wanted to talk to you. About the board meeting today. I had to rush out afterward, but . . ."

"Yes," he sneered. "A chummy little heart-to-heart with Marshall out to the airport."

Tyger could smell whiskey on Shaw's breath. "Well, he has an assignment for me. He wants me to go to Paris and talk to a designer—Martine Rainier—about doing the bottles and packaging for us."

Shaw pointed his finger at Tyger. There was something menacing in the gesture. "Ah ha! Lucky little girl."

"This is sort of a special case. You see, Miss Rainier's supposed to be difficult. She doesn't like Americans or American businesses, and so . . ."

"And so," Shaw picked up, "since our Tyger here is an international jet-setter, she's the perfect choice." The lines in Shaw's face wrinkled with contempt.

"Hugh Marshall offered me the assignment, and I accepted it," Tyger snapped. "And while we're on the subject of mutual disapproval, I want to know why you presented my idea at the board meeting without mentioning that it was mine."

"I don't know what you're talking about." Shaw appeared indignant. The accusation seemed to make him stand taller. His conservative gray suit looked less disheveled when his shoulders weren't hunched over, as they often were.

"You know . . . my idea for the scratch-and-sniff clothes labels. You told them that *you* had a terrific idea. . . ."

"My dear young lady," Shaw said patronizingly, "when I said '*I* had,' I meant that I had the idea submitted to me. I'm sure that Marshall and Phillips gathered that, as president, I was speaking for the rest of my colleagues."

"I don't think anyone gathered any such thing," Tyger retorted.

"Well, isn't it convenient that you had a chance to plead your case to Marshall . . . in private?"

"I didn't bring it up, and I certainly don't intend to."

"Remember, Miss Hayes, we're all in this together. If you don't want to play ball with the team, then you can leave."

"Are you asking me to hand in my resignation?" It had never occurred to Tyger that Shaw could fire her.

Shaw backed off, realizing his position. "Tyger, my dear, don't be melodramatic. It's just a question of your remembering that we're all in this together . . . a company effort. You've got to learn to keep that inflated ego of yours under wraps."

Tyger was furious. Her face burned a bright shade of crimson. She wanted to say something cutting; instead she took a deep breath. "I'll let Ginger know where I'll be staying in Paris . . . and when I'll be back in the office. Goodnight, Sheldon."

Sheldon Shaw watched Tyger Hayes stalk down the corridor. She deserved a bit of comeuppance. He would love to have fired her, but that would cause too many repercussions. Hugh Marshall would probably hit the ceiling, and Bachrach would not be pleased either.

He returned to his office. Connie Larcada was sitting on the sofa, nursing a scotch and water.

"Who were you talking to, Sheldon? I heard voices. . . ."

"Oh, just Tyger," Shaw said evasively. He poured himself another drink. "Marshall's sending her to Paris. She wanted to ask my advice about something."

Tyger settled back into her purple-cushioned seat in the first-class section of Air France Flight No. 171. Her earphones were in place, and she was listening to some jazz, vintage John Coltrane.

Jake Danton nudged her. "Champagne?"

"Of course!"

"Except for a couple of boring weekends in Long Island, do you realize that this is our first real holiday together?" Jake kicked off his Tony Lama boots and stretched out his legs.

"Holiday for you, love, not for me." Jake had insisted on coming to Paris with Tyger when he heard about her assignment. He'd been working hard lately, and felt himself due for a little relaxation. "I'll be working my ass off." Tyger pulled out her folder of information on Martine Rainier.

Jake frowned. "Don't tell me you're going to start working now?"

"I've got to have all this down cold. I want to be superprepared when I meet with Martine Rainier."

"*If* you see her," Jake reminded her. "She may refuse to grant you an audience."

"Oh, I'll think of something. . . ."

Jake smiled, and lifted his armrest so that he could nestle closer to Tyger. "I'm sure you will." The flight attendant brought a bottle of Veuve Cliquot. Jake poured two glasses and leaned over to whisper to Tyger: "Ever done it in a 747?"

Tyger's friend Jacqueline Aubier was in Singapore on assignment for *Elle*, but she had left the keys to her apartment with the concierge so that Tyger and Jake could stay there. Kellerco would have footed the bill at the Ritz, but luxury hotels were not Paris to Tyger. She preferred the freedom and anonymity of a private apartment. The large studio was four flights up at 10 rue du Dragon, right around the corner from St.-Germain-des-Prés in the sixth arrondissement on the Rive Gauche. The studio was cluttered and cozy. Jacqueline, a writer, had filled the place with books, posters, old photographs and memorabilia. Large plumes and assorted colored feathers were displayed on the pale-pink walls; oversized pillows made from antique tapestries were stacked on the floor in lieu of chairs. Walking into the apartment made Tyger feel as if she were walking back in time. It was the sort of place where Colette might have lived and worked.

Replacing the phone, Tyger called to Jake, "I got her! Martine's busy today, but will meet me for lunch tomorrow." Tyger sat down on a cushion and wrote in her appointment book. "I lied. I said I was in town for the weekend, and had all sorts of messages for her from mutual friends. Jesus, suddenly I'm nervous as hell."

"You know everything there is to know about her." Jake indicated the Martine Rainier portfolio sitting on the desk next to Jacqueline's typewriter. "You're as prepared as you'll ever be. Anyway, that means we have a full uninterrupted day to play. What'll we do first?"

Tyger looked out the window. "We're in Paris!" she said with unexpected glee, and giggled with delight. "Let's go to Bertillon first for ice cream. Then let's just play it by ear."

"God, the light's fantastic. Take your clothes off, Tyger." Jake pulled out his Nikon, and snapped Tyger against the hazy radiance of late morning, as she stripped down to nothing.

Tyger moved sensuously before the camera, responding to Jake's suggestive commands. Through the window came the soft gray brightness of Paris after a summer rain. It fell across Tyger's skin, casting the swell of her breasts and thighs into dark relief. Her auburn hair tumbled loosely around her shoulders and swung back and forth as she moved her head.

"That's it, Tyger, arch your back. More, babe, more. Let me see those nipples. Twist this way. That's it! Open up your thighs a little. Lick your lips. Come on, babe. Give it to me . . . fantastic!" Jake looked up. "That's enough for art. . . ." He set his Nikon on the table behind him and dove for Tyger among the pillows.

An hour later, they were walking down the rue de Fleurus, past the one-time residence of Gertrude Stein and Alice B.

Toklas, and through the wrought-iron gates of the Jardins du Luxembourg.

Lilies and poppies bloomed. Skinny little boys sailed toy boats in the pond. Little girls nursed dolls while their young *au pairs* chatted noisily to each other, keeping their faces pointed upward to catch the sun's rays. Tyger and Jake walked around the Latin Quarter, across the Pont Neuf and up the rue de Rivoli, all the way to the Champs Elysées. When their feet finally gave out, they hailed a taxi to the Place de la Madeleine.

They spent an hour at the new Fauchon which had risen like a phoenix from the ashes of the original buildings bombed in a 1977 terrorist blast. Produce from all over the world—strawberries from California, mangoes from Manila—displayed with an artist's hand glistened like jewels in bright clean bins on the main floor of the east building. Shelves upon shelves of condiments, biscuits, tinned delicacies, *confitures* and honeys, vinegars and twenty-three kinds of mustard laced with fruits, herbs and spices lined the walls. There were foods, exotic and ordinary, from every country imaginable.

The wine and spirits section offered a similarly catholic range, with Kentucky bourbon rubbing labels with Chinese vodka, awe-inspiring champagnes cloaked in mantles of dust, and Fauchon's own private line of unique liqueurs. The gastronomy department displayed a lavish assortment of pâtés, terrines and elegant cooked dishes created by leading chefs such as Paul Bocuse, and the Troisgros brothers, whose gourmet goodies were trucked daily from their three-star restaurant in Roanne.

Fauchon's north building housed the *patisseries*, created by twenty in-house chefs, and chocolates made by artisans working exclusively for Fauchon. There were also ice creams and sherbets—in unusual flavors such as litchi and passion fruit—made on the spot. Chauffeur-driven limousines lined the block while well-bred ladies dashed in for unusual mouthwatering morsels to round out that evening's dinner party.

"What a show this is," Jake marveled. "Think we can afford our own jet to carry back all the stuff I'd like to buy?"

"Oh, they'll ship it for you. Except the sherbet. I think we'd better eat that here. . . ." Tyger laughed.

"And *now*. What flavor do you want to indulge in?" Jake ordered mango sherbet.

"Oh, I think I'd rather devour a *mille feuilles*," Tyger said.

"Nobody will believe we've been to Paris if we don't put on a couple of pounds. . . ."

"Oh, Tyger," Jake said. "If your mother ever heard you say that she'd probably have your tastebuds surgically removed."

Tyger laughed. "Come on, let's hit the pastries."

Before they left, Jake and Tyger bought a melon from Morocco for their next morning's breakfast, a jar of curry-flavored mustard, a quarter kilo of thinly sliced *jambon de Parme*, and a bottle of Fauchon's *liqueur de coriandre*. Afterward they walked over to the Trocadero to catch a screening of Hitchcock's *Spellbound*, in English with French subtitles, at the Cinémathèque.

Around seven, Tyger and Jake dragged themselves up the four flights to their flat, and collapsed. Tyger drew hot water into the tub, to soak her feet. "I wish I'd worn sneakers. My feet are full of blisters. You may have to rent me a pair of crutches for the evening."

"Where'll we eat? I'm starved." Jake changed the film in his camera, and snapped Tyger sitting miserably on the rim of the tub.

"It depends. Do you want to go to an expensive, touristy three-star restaurant . . . or a charming dive where the Parisians hang out?"

"A touristy three-star gourmet glutton meal . . . rich sauces, many courses, incredible wine. Total excess is what I crave."

"Me, too." Tyger thumbed through her *Guide Michelin*. "Lasserre's closed until September. It'll have to be Tour d'Argent. I'll telephone for a reservation."

The Tour d'Argent didn't disappoint Jake. Their table bordered on the picture windows overlooking the Seine, the Gothic towers and buttresses of Notre Dame, and the sparkling Paris lights. Jake started off with the *potage* Tour d'Argent, a thick but delicately flavored black-bean soup, then opted for a house specialty—pressed duck and *champignons à la Bordelaise,* and wound up with the Tour d'Argent's aristocrat of desserts, Grand Marnier soufflé. Tyger chose smoked salmon, filet of sole with a truffle sauce, braised endives, and *pêches flambées*. The wine was a 1971 Meursault.

As he leaned back in his chair sipping the house's special cognac, Jake looked around the sumptuous room. "I feel as if this ought to have been my last meal. Nothing else I will ever eat can compare to this. Remember that old W. C. Fields flick? I think it was *My Little Chickadee,* when they're getting ready to hang him, and they ask him if he has any last request. He thinks for a minute, and then he says, 'Yes . . . I'd like to see Paris before I die. . . .' "

Tyger laughed. "That was one of my father's favorites. He used to screen it all the time in his projection room. . . ."

"I can't begin to imagine what your life must have been like, growing up in Hollywood. Amazing!" Jake shook his head in wonder.

"And I can't imagine what yours must have been like. Omaha, Nebraska, seems as exotic to me as Hollywood must seem to you. I mean, what did you *do* in Omaha . . . to pass the time?"

Jake laughed. "Ask Nick Nolte. He lived across the street from me. A lot of celebrities come from Nebraska . . . Henry Fonda and Dick Cavett and Johnny Carson. They couldn't wait to get out! Anyway, I'm sure we did the same things you did . . . got drunk, got laid, drove fast. Just that the cars we drove weren't Ferraris, they were souped-up vintage '55 Fords. And we saw our movies at the drive-in, not in projection rooms. . . ."

"Poor baby. Say, what time is it? We're supposed to meet Pascal and Françoise at midnight."

"We have about forty-five minutes." Jake drained his brandy snifter. "Want another cognac?"

"No, I can barely breathe I've eaten so much. I need air. Why don't we walk over to Montparnasse? It's not so terribly far."

"Aw, let's stay out and take a taxi over. Besides, I thought your feet were ruined for life."

Tyger opened her handbag. "This time I'm prepared. I brought a pair of flat-heeled sandals, for walking. C'mon, Jake . . . before all that food turns to fat." Jake groaned and pulled out his American Express card to pay the check, which came to over two hundred dollars, with tip.

"No, Jake. Put that away. My treat. I have an expense account, remember?"

Jake looked upward. "Thank the Lord for equality!"

The enormous main room of La Coupole was as crowded and busy as a train station at rush hour. The famous *brasserie* on the Boulevard Montparnasse was the largest in Paris, and had been a favorite haunt of the Parisian "in crowd" since the golden days of the Twenties. Its muraled pillars, painted by aspiring artists of that day (one said to have been done by the great Jean Arp), reflected the electric glamour of the Paris of the Jazz Age, and in a city where hardly any place remained fashionable for more than a year or two, La Coupole remained *the* late-night spot, year after year, decade after decade.

It was midnight now, the hour at which La Coupole hit its stride. Everyone came there as the night wore on, and by now things were at their noisy, smoky, glittering peak. The fashion world, the Parisian aristocracy, came slumming to the determinedly unelegant atmosphere of the vast, brightly lit restaurant, and table-hopped relentlessly among their own crowd. Karl Lagerfeld held court at a fiefdom of tables at the center of this group.

The theater people established their beachhead in another section, where Peter Brooke could be seen surrounded by his international group of actors. The film world sprawled through its own network of tables, where a visitor could spot such celluloid-familiar faces as Gérard Départieu, Jeanne Moreau, François Truffaut, and Agnes Varda, among the legions of the lesser-known.

There were musicians, too, and writers, poets, artists. Shirley Goldfarb, an American painter, had been a fixture with her sculptor husband, Gregory, at the same small table every night for a quarter of a century or more. The room was in constant motion as people circulated from table to table, exchanging greetings and kisses, seeing and being seen, sometimes wedging in for a drink and then moving on. But always within their own group; the fashion people never mixed with the actors at La Coupole, the painters kept to themselves.

Tyger led Jake through this labyrinth, peering around in the blue haze of Gitanes smoke for her friends.

"Tyger! *Chérie! Par ici!* Hello!" She turned at the sound of the familiar booming voice.

"Pascal!" Tyger made her way to the table where the burly Frenchman towered with his arms flung wide in greeting. He was over six feet tall, a massive figure in a blue Chinese peasant jacket, his ruddy face dominated by a fuzzy blond mustache. Tyger had known the director and his photojournalist wife Françoise Carrière for years, since they had met on a train in Chile where Pascal had been shooting a film.

"Let me look at you." He beamed. "Fantastic! Not bad for an old lady. . . ." He kissed her again, and greeted Jake. "Sit down! My dinner's getting cold. Have you eaten? But of course you've eaten. You're Americans," he teased. "You eat at five in the afternoon. But then you must be hungry again."

A waiter brought a couple of chairs, and they squeezed around the table, making a total of eight people at a table for four. At La Coupole this was standard, and the waiters adapted with stoic indifference.

"This is Tyger Hayes, my favorite American friend, and *her* favorite American friend, Jake Danton." Pascal made the introductions. Pascal's and Françoise's table included Darius Cottrell, a pleasantly shaggy young producer; Baron von Lipschitz, an Austrian who restored castles and invested in films; Chantal Rossignol, a film critic who headed the selection committee for the Cannes Film Festival; and Nicole Maurice, one of France's top models, who was making her screen debut in Pascal's current film.

"So tell me about this job, Tyger," Pascal said. "How wonderful. You are a worker at last! Now you can become a member of the Partie Communiste, and join the struggle."

Tyger laughed. "Sorry, Pascal. I'm not that kind of a worker. I'm management—assistant to the president. Still a capitalist, after all." She described her new life as a working woman in New York. "It's all still top-secret. But I'm here to meet with Martine Rainier about package design. Do you know her?"

Françoise made a face. She was wearing a green-and-brown babushka around her blond hair, and looked like a beautiful Russian peasant. "Ugh, I cannot stand that woman Rainier. I was doing a piece on her last year for *Vogue*. We would make appointments, and she would not show up. I'd ring her assistant, and she would say, 'Oh, Martine's in Milan today' . . . or Tangier, wherever. She just takes off whenever she feels like it. It took me a month to get the story, and it should have taken no more than two days."

Pascal kissed Françoise on the cheek. "Sour grapes," he said. "My darling wife does not like Martine because I had an affair with her," he explained to Tyger. His blue eyes sparkled with amusement. "It was years ago . . . nothing more than a short fling. Martine's *très gentille* . . . if you know how to handle her. You must not allow yourself to be intimidated by her."

Françoise saluted her husband with a sweeping right hand. "Ah, Pascal . . . the world's greatest lover!"

Nicole, the pouty young actress, spoke up, in French. "Everybody's had an affair with her—men, women . . ."

"Probably even children," Darius interjected devilishly.

"And I agree with Françoise," Nicole continued, sullenly. "Martine's a bitch. She uses people. Oh, I know she has a lot of friends, but she drops them, too. She is a female barracuda."

Tyger switched the conversation back to English, for Jake's sake. "Oh God, now I'm more apprehensive than ever about meeting her."

"You could meet her tonight," Pascal said. "She's probably here." He half-rose, looking around.

"No! Not tonight. I need to be prepared."

Pascal patted Tyger on the head. "Don't worry, *chérie*, you'll get along fine."

Tyger pretended to be offended. "And just what do you mean by that, Pascal?"

Pascal summoned the waiter and ordered more oysters on the half-shell for himself, and wine for the table. "Just don't listen to the others. Martine's a nice girl."

"Ha!" added Françoise, getting in the last word.

CHAPTER FIFTEEN

THE Brasserie Lipp on Boulevard St. Germain was packed as usual with an eclectic lunchtime crowd of the literary, social, and diplomatic elite. Tyger, calling upon a longtime acquaintance with the maître d'hotel, had wangled a late reservation at a small table in the mirror-lined main room. She had been waiting there for half an hour, doing her best to ignore the glares of latecomers being shunted to the upstairs dining room. Twice the waiter had been over to inquire if Tyger's guest was coming and if she would like to order. Tyger hated waiting. She remembered what Françoise had said: "Martine makes appointments and doesn't show up."

"Another *eau minerale,* mademoiselle?" The waiter cleared away her empty glass. "Would you like to see the menu now?"

"Not yet. Bring me a glass of white wine."

Two tables down, Jackie Onassis was talking quietly with her daughter, Caroline. Harry Ashcombe and the beautiful Elizabeth, Lord and Lady Ashcombe, were laughing with friends at a larger table in the center of the room. Tyger could hear Simone de Beauvoir noisily arguing with a flock of her admirers, seven in all, young poets, writers or, possibly, her students.

The waiter brought Tyger's wine, and she forced herself to take small sips. She wished she had brought along a book, or magazine. She tried to figure out just how long she should remain there before concluding, for certain, that she had been stood up by Martine Rainier.

"Tyger? It *is* you! Why haven't you telephoned?" Tyger looked up to see the Contessa di Brunesi, a great friend of her mother's. The countess had begun life as Carlotta Crane, the daughter of a well-to-do doctor from Devon, Pennsylvania, one of the key posts along Philadelphia's fabled Main Line. She and Tyger's mother had been childhood friends and, later, roommates at Miss Porter's School in Farmington, Connecticut, where Bobbie and Lolli achieved legend as the "Second Story Twins" for their midnight exploits in sneaking out their dormitory window. Over the intervening years of husbands and titles they had remained close.

"Lolli!" Tyger stood up and kissed her cheeks. "I tried to reach you this morning. You'll find my message when you get home."

"Good girl," Lolli said. "You look marvelous, darling!"

"So do you. What's this new look?"

Lolli laughed. "Quiet elegance." Lolli, a flamboyant beauty, normally was given to color-drenched Saint Laurent fantasy clothes. But today she was a picture of understatement in a beige Dior fitted suit set off with simple gold-and-diamond ear clips from Van Cleef's, and Hermès shoes and handbag. Her long chestnut hair had been pulled back severely into a tight chignon. "I must look as if I'm headed for the convent. Actually I'm getting ready to marry a Swiss banker. Terribly conservative. No title, but scads of money." She rolled her eyes. "My dear, I have to think about my security."

The countess slipped into the seat next to Tyger and lowered her voice conspiratorially. "We must get together for tea. I've heard rumors about Bobbie. I want to know which ones are true."

Tyger grinned. "What have you heard?"

"Well," Lolli began, and then stopped as she became aware that someone had come up to the table. "Martine, darling!" she exclaimed. "Tyger, you know Martine Rainier?"

"No, actually. But we are having lunch together." Tyger extended her hand to Martine, who shook it lightly, as if reluctant to make physical contact.

"How do you do," Martine said without much interest, and then turned to Lolli and began chatting in rapid French, leaving Tyger to reflect that the stories she had heard of Martine's rudeness were not exaggerated.

"Il faut que tu nous joins pour déjeuner," Martine said to Lolli, but to Tyger's relief the countess declined.

"No, no, darling, I can't possibly. I'm joining Lord and Lady Ashcombe." She kissed the younger women goodbye. "Tyger, we'll have our talk soon. I'm dying of curiosity!"

Martine took Lolli's place in the chair next to Tyger. She was wearing a slinky white Thierry Mugler dress, with printed silk scarves tied around her neck, waist, and thigh which peaked out through the high slit in her skirt. Cadaverthin, she was darkly tanned, and her olive skin glowed.

"Well." Tyger smiled. "Another mutual friend we didn't even know about. You know Lolli well?"

"Yes."

The waiter arrived with the menus, providing a temporary distraction to the impasse. "Now would you like to see the menu?"

Martine shrugged. "I'm not hungry. You go ahead and order."

Tyger was starved. But she knew better than to concede an early round in one-upmanship to Martine. "No menu, *merci.* Just another wine." She smiled cordially at Martine.

Martine lit a Gauloise. She held it between her thumb and index finger, like a man. Her curly black hair was closely cropped, and her wide brown eyes were framed by heavy black lashes and brows, naturally thick without the aid of mascara. She wore dark plum eyeshadow, rouge, lipstick and nail polish. Martine's lips were full, sensual, and yet she tensed them in a certain way so that her mouth appeared set and determined. Inhaling on her cigarette, she looked distractedly around the crowded room, in search of familiar faces. She waved and nodded at several people, then turned her gaze back to Tyger, although she remained silent.

Tyger decided to get straight to the point. Social niceties, she realized, were wasted on the unpredictable designer. "I'm not really here to talk about mutual friends. I've come to make you a business offer. If you're interested I will go into detail. If not, then there's no need to waste each other's time."

"Yes," Martine said carelessly. "I know why you are here."

"You do? How?"

"One has friends. One hears things. I must say I am surprised. The Tyger Hayes I have heard about was not much involved with business, I do not think."

"Well, I am now," Tyger said, matter-of-factly reaching for her briefcase. "What I wish to discuss with you is confidential."

How confidential could anything be in Paris? She wondered which of last night's La Coupole coterie had gone to Martine with the news. Nicole Maurice, the pouty actress, she guessed.

"The project is, for now, top-secret. The company is a large American conglomerate. The product is an American designer's perfume. We want you to design the bottles." Tyger stopped short, sipped her wine and waited for Martine to speak.

"You know, I don't much like American businesses," Martine said. She extinguished her Gauloise and lit another.

"I know that."

"Then what makes you think that I would be interested in this job?"

"You're the toast of Europe, but you're not yet a household name in America. Even though you may dislike Americans, as a businesswoman you can hardly afford to turn your back on the American market. You must know this. Otherwise you wouldn't have agreed to meet with me, knowing what I was here to talk to you about. . . ." Tyger paused, for effect. She was beginning to enjoy her role, although she wondered how Hugh Marshall handled situations like this.

"True," Martine conceded.

"Are you bored, or do you want me to continue?"

Martine seemed a bit more relaxed. "Let's order more wine. I am intrigued by what you are saying. Only intrigued, that is all."

The waiter set two more glasses in front of them, and presented Martine with a note. She read it quickly, and said to the waiter, "Please tell monsieur that I am in a business consultation now. He may call me this evening." She smiled at Tyger. "A certain man follows me everywhere. He sends notes to my table, as if to remind me that he is always near. . . ."

"God, doesn't that make you uncomfortable?" Tyger asked.

Martine shrugged. "Oh . . . I find it amusing. Some men are such asses, don't you agree?" She didn't wait for an answer. "Now tell me . . . who is this American designer who is launching a perfume?"

"You understand that this is confidential . . . ?"

"Much of the work that I do is involved with companies who are afraid that their secrets will be stolen. I am too busy to gossip about which company is launching what."

Tyger handed Martine the folder on Matt Phillips. The Frenchwoman was impressed. "I have always liked his clothes.

They appeal to me. What other information can you give me?"

Martine read the fragrance profile, and Tyger explained about Hugh Marshall and Kellerco. Martine listened, and seemed receptive to Tyger's proposals. "All right. Now let's have what you Americans call the 'bottom line' . . . how much money will you pay me?"

"You'll be well paid," Tyger assured her. "But you'll have to discuss price with Hugh Marshall. I'm not involved in the financial side of this."

"Well, Tyger . . ." Martine smiled for the first time. "I will say this. I am interested enough in the deal to think further about it. You understand that I cannot commit myself here and now?"

"Of course, I didn't expect you to."

Martine threw her cigarettes and Dunhill lighter into her straw purse. "I must get back to work. If you want to walk with me, I will show you a wonderful antique clothes store. It is down a *cul de sac* and you would never find it on your own. A friend of mine just opened the shop. It's full of one-of-a-kind treasures."

Out in the Paris sunshine, Martine chatted with Tyger as if they were old friends on a lazy afternoon's shopping spree. They walked up the Boulevard St. Germain to the rue de Buci, and off down an alleyway to a tiny shop on the ground floor of an apartment house. Martine introduced Tyger to her friend Laura, the shop's owner. When she turned to go she kissed Tyger on both cheeks. Her attitude toward Tyger had changed dramatically over the past hour.

"I almost forgot," Martine said. "I am having a party this evening. Can you stop by?"

"I'd love to." It was business, after all. "If I can bring a friend."

Martine shrugged. "But of course, bring anyone you like. Eight o'clock. Thirty-one Quai de l'Horloge. *Ciao*," she said, and left quickly.

"Hell, why do you drag me into your business shit? I thought I could have you all to myself tonight, just the two of us spending a romantic evening in Paris." Jake and Tyger were relaxing at the Café Flor, near their apartment, and mapping out the schedule for the rest of their stay.

"Look, I'm trying to get Martine to agree to do the Kellerco project. She's tough, Jake. But by the end of our meeting she

(151)

had begun to warm up to me, and I don't want to snub her now. We only have to go there for a bit. Or . . . I could go alone and meet you afterward." Tyger sipped her espresso, aware of the admiring stares of the Frenchmen seated nearby. Her hair was pulled back, but a halo of frizz still framed her face softly. She was wearing white Moroccan pants with a yellow silk T-shirt, belted with a nostalgic whimsy she had found in Laura's shop: a wide-banded Fifties cinch belt, with metallic emblems of vintage cars stapled into the leather. Around her neck she wore an antique lavender satin ribbon to which she had pinned several yellow tea roses. Regulars at the Café Flor noticed her and decided that she was probably an American film star.

"Oh, I'll go," Jake relented. "But let's not stay long." Jake looked dashing, too, in a white Giorgio Armani suit, with a wide-brimmed straw hat tilted gangster-style down over his forehead. Tyger had given him one of her yellow tea roses for his lapel.

"It's getting late." Tyger drained her demitasse of thick black coffee.

Jake signaled the waiter. *"L'addition, s'il vous plaît.* We still have an hour or so to kill before we go to Martine's. What'll we do?"

"Let's head back to the apartment. I'm sure we'll think of something."

Jake laughed. "Yeah, you can quiz me on my French phrases."

Just past ten, Tyger and Jake ascended to Martine Rainier's top-floor flat, riding in a creaky brocaded wrought-iron elevator, a remnant of the distant past. Tyger's hair was down around her shoulders now, and she brushed a lock back off her forehead.

"Don't worry. You look terrific." Jake tweaked her cheek.

"Don't do that! I'm not worried." But she was apprehensive about the mercurial Martine.

A bearded young man let them in, and disappeared into the crowd.

Perhaps fifty people were milling about, and nearly as many cigarette ends circled smoke into the air. Tyger and Jake found their way to a lacquered table against the far wall, where beneath a Magritte canvas stood bottles of uncorked Baron Philippe de Rothschild private reserve champagne.

"Bubbly?" Jake offered gallantly.

"I've never turned it down."

Martine's apartment was done in a sharply focused minimalist decor. Walls and upholstered furniture were covered in a beige fabric of the same shade as the wall-to-wall carpeting. Concealed perimeter lighting illuminated the room with inconspicuous but dramatic effect. French doors, framed in polished stainless steel and covered with sparkling curtains of cellophane mesh, led out to a terrace that overlooked the Seine. An unbanistered stairway spiraled up to another floor, and down those carpeted steps Martine now appeared.

She was wearing skin-tight brown leather pants with a cerise silk chiffon bikini halter. She had painted a green-and-magenta dragon across the width of her bare midriff, and her spiky heels made her a good five inches taller. Both of her ears were pierced in three places, and each sported a different earring. Her makeup was softer, much less severe than it had been earlier. She was lean and dazzling.

"Good God!" Jake whistled under his breath. "Would I love to photograph her!"

"Tyger!" Martine called cordially from across the room. "You made it! There are some friends I want you to meet." Martine came over to them and kissed Tyger warmly, quickly, on the lips. She looked at Jake, sized him up and gave him a cool greeting. Still, she kept her eyes on him as she led them over to meet a young Iranian prince, a cousin of the former royal family, who was now living in exile in Paris.

Jake spotted Marisa Berenson across the room and headed over to talk to her. Tyger soon ran out of small talk with the prince and excused herself on the pretext of a telephone call. She looked for Jake, who had disappeared again, and finally found him on the terrace, discussing a possible business deal with a French agent. Tyger wandered back inside to the champagne table to refill her glass.

"Allow me." A man picked up a bottle and poured. She looked up and recognized Tom Galvani, the young movie star who had jilted her mother.

"Oh," she said. "It's you."

"Yes," he agreed. "I know this sounds like an old routine . . . but you look familiar. Haven't we met before?"

"Not exactly. I think you know my mother."

Galvani looked puzzled for a moment. Then his face broke into a dimpled smile. "Hey . . . you're Tyger Hayes, aren't you?"

"That's right."

"Sure, I recognize you from your pictures. You also look a lot like your mother." He paused. "How is Bobbie?"

"She's fine," Tyger said coolly.

"Hey, look," said Galvani a bit uneasily. "I hope you don't think I'm a grade-A shit."

Tyger shrugged. "My mother's affairs are . . . her affair." She smiled. Galvani was attractive, all right, even more so in person than on screen. He was shorter than she had imagined he would be, but with an unmistakable aura of star quality. Since her childhood Tyger had always been fascinated with that quality and had been unable to decide which came first—the stardom or the quality. But Tom Galvani was not her type. Nor, she would have thought, her mother's, but Bobbie had been unusually rhapsodic about his skills as a lover. Tyger was almost tempted to find out.

"I'd like to see more of you. Why don't we go someplace and have a quiet drink?" Galvani spoke softly. "There's a nice bar over near the George V where I'm staying."

"Sorry," Tyger said. "I'm here with someone."

"Then tomorrow?"

Tyger shook her head. "No, I . . ."

Galvani sighed. "Well, maybe another time, another city." He gave Tyger the sincere vulnerable smile for which he was famous.

The living room was hot from the assembled bodies, and stank with the thick vapor of French and Turkish cigarettes. Tyger ambled aimlessly down the hallway and walked into a library that appeared to be Martine's office. There were sketches tacked on the walls, askew, and the desk was piled with papers and sketch pads and other paraphernalia of her trade. Next to the sofa, a round beige lacquered end table held dozens of photographs in Art Deco frames. They were of Martine, her family and friends. Tyger picked up one picture of a teenaged Martine in what must have been her first ball gown. The expression on Martine's face was one of exhilaration and self-consciousness. Tyger could remember a similar photo of herself, at fourteen, on the terrace at her father's estate.

"Ah, you are one of those people made curious by other people's photographs?" Tyger turned to see Martine standing behind her.

"Oh . . . I hope you don't think I'm being nosy. I had to get away from the smoke. I was just thinking how much this display resembles the one on the grand piano in my mother's living room. The faces are different, that's all."

Martine picked up an intricately inlaid frame. "My mother. She died of cancer last year. She was only forty-six. . . ."

"My mother's age. How terrible . . . I'm sorry."

"Yes. More really for my sister than for me," Martine said, picking up on the thought. "She was much closer to Mother than I. My mother disapproved of my working. She felt it was a scandal, a disgrace for someone from my background. I would try and explain to her how much my work means to me, but she could not understand. Her age was young, but many of her ideas were of an older generation."

Martine replaced the photograph and reached for Tyger's glass. "May I?" Tyger nodded. Martine sipped thoughtfully. "You know, we have many things in common . . . I feel it. I sense that deep down we are very similar. *Tu comprends, ma chère?*" She handed Tyger back her champagne, and went over to her desk. "Come here. I will show you some sketches I am doing for a company that manufactures ornamental faucets and spigots. It seems mundane, but these are quite extraordinary, don't you agree?"

Tyger nodded. "Wonderful." She wanted to ask Martine what her feelings were about the Kellerco job, but she bit her tongue. If the subject was brought up at all, Martine had to do it.

As Tyger stood next to Martine, looking at the sketches, Martine draped her arm around Tyger's waist. "I really did not think I was going to like you," she said. "But I do. You are *très sympa.*" She kissed Tyger's cheek. "I must return to my guests."

As she walked back toward the living room Tyger tried to figure out how to read Martine. She had a reputation for contrariness; and yet with Tyger, aside from those first fifteen minutes at Brasserie Lipp, Martine had been warm and friendly. If the friendliness held up, the Kellerco deal looked like a sure thing. But somehow Tyger still felt uneasy. She kept waiting for the trap door to open.

Tyger spent the next half hour listening to a renowned archaeologist, who fascinated a small group with tales of legendary hexes and spells associated with discoveries of the ancient world. Out of the corner of her eye, Tyger noticed Jake talking to Martine. She saw them head toward the library. After a moment, Tyger slipped away and followed them, to see whether Jake was ready to leave.

From the doorway of the library Martine's back was to Tyger. Jake's arms were around Martine and they were kissing. Tyger stood there a moment, immobilized more by surprise than jealousy. Then, before she could turn and duck out, Jake's eyes opened.

"Hi, Tyger," he said. "You finally got away from that old guy?"

"He was interesting. Anyway, if you want to go to Régine's, we should think about heading off."

Martine turned around, trying to read Tyger's reaction to the kiss. "Don't go yet, Tyger. I want you and Jake to join me for a quiet supper after the others have left. I make an inspirational *soufflé au fromage*. You can go to Régine's later. . . ."

Tyger felt intuitively that it was time to go. It did not seem likely that Martine wanted to discuss business, and Tyger did not want to press her luck on her friendship with Martine. Until the deal was signed she thought that relationship would best be handled in short takes.

She shot Jake a look to indicate that she did not want them to stay. Jake read her signal but chose to ignore it.

"We'd love to," he said. "I want you to let me photograph you. . . ."

Martine smiled. "I would like nothing better. You have quite a reputation, Monsieur Danton."

Tyger couldn't decide whether Martine was genuinely attracted to Jake, or whether she was flirting with him because he was there with Tyger.

"*Ah, bien, mes chères.* I am delighted that you will stay and keep me company. I do not like to sleep. I much prefer talking at night with my friends. . . ."

The archaeologist and his band of admirers came to bid Martine goodnight. She took them to the door, and Tyger was alone with Jake. "Dammit! Couldn't you tell that I wanted to leave? You don't seem to realize that I'm conducting business with Martine. Now you're carrying it over into a personal thing, and it's not going to work."

Jake put his hands on Tyger's shoulders. "Martine fascinates me, that's all. Staying here for supper is *not* going to jeopardize your chances of getting her to design the bottles for your precious little perfume. Just cool it, Tyger. You're getting uptight over nothing. Besides, you don't want to offend Martine. That would be bad business."

"You don't care about me, or my job," Tyger snapped. "The

only thing that interests you is being superstud, and adding another female to your collection. I know for a fact that Martine is notoriously unpredictable. If you get something going with her it could backfire, in *my* face!" Tyger's brow was wrinkled with irritation.

"Then you *are* jealous," Jake said. "Look, okay, okay . . . we'll go. You make the excuses, though." He walked away from her to the window, and then turned back. "And you know, if Martine decides to do the Kellerco job, it's going to be because they'll pay her a lot of bread to do it. And because she *wants* to do it. Her decision isn't going to be based on anything you do at all. You're self-dramatizing."

"All right!" Tyger retorted loudly. Then she lowered her voice. "All right. We'll stay for supper with Martine. Does that make you happy?"

Jake smiled. "Yes. It does."

CHAPTER SIXTEEN

ONCE the rest of the guests had gone, Martine brought Tyger and Jake back to her kitchen. Clearly the Frenchwoman enjoyed cooking, because the kitchen contrasted with the austere simplicity of the rest of the apartment. It had a cheerful provincial quality with a huge old-fashioned wrought-iron stove and a wall oven. Copper pots and pans hung gleaming from a horizontal carriage wheel extending from the ceiling. The walls were all hand-painted Mexican tile, and the floor was Spanish terrazzo. Herbs grew in little pots in a windowbox overlooking the garden of an inner courtyard, six floors below.

"I have some fantastic hash from Morocco. Want some?" Without waiting for an answer, Martine reached into a tea canister and produced a clay pipe and a wallet-sized brick of hashish. She cut off a small greenish-brown chunk, placed it in the pipe and lit it. Then she passed it across the counter to Tyger.

Tyger drew in the sweet fragrant smoke, pulling it deep into her lungs. It bit against her throat and she went into a fit of coughing. "That's stronger than I thought," she gasped, handing the pipe to Jake. "I haven't had hash like that in a long time."

Martine separated eggs for the soufflé and began making a *roux* in a porcelain saucepan. "Tyger, there are greens in the vegetable bin, and perhaps a cucumber. Would you mind making a salad?"

"I don't understand how anyone who loves to cook can stay so thin," Jake said, grating gruyère into a copper bowl.

"I like to eat . . . in small amounts. But cooking relaxes me. It . . . helps me unwind." She accepted the pipe as it made another round. "So does this." Martine added milk to the butter and flour and stirred the mixture with a wire whisk. "Jake, are you finished with the cheese? I need it, *mon cher.*"

Jake handed her the bowl. "Here it is, along with a bit of scraped finger, for added flavor."

Martine laughed throatily. "Ah, Jake, it will make the soufflé more perfect than usual." She added egg yolks, poured the mixture into a glass soufflé dish and beat in the stiff egg whites. *"Voilà!"* she said, popping it into the oven. "I am going up to change into something cooler. This leather looks nice, but it doesn't breathe. Tyger, why don't you come with me? Jake," she commanded, "open another bottle of wine."

Tyger followed Martine up the floating staircase. Her head felt light. The hashish had swept away her reservations about staying at Martine's. Why had she been so worried? She was there. She might as well enjoy herself.

Martine's bedroom floor was covered by a thick beige carpet. In the middle of the room, a large mattress rested on a platform half a foot above the floor, surrounded by gigantic pillowy soft sculptures. A huge Mark Rothko canvas dominated one wall. The other end of the room was covered with bookshelves, filled with books, geological rock specimens, miniature replicas of antique furniture, a collection of hand-painted ostrich eggs, and the miscellaneous mementos of a traveler.

Martine walked over to her closet. "I brought a pink-and-gold silk caftan back from Tenerife last week . . . but now I have, oh, buyer's remorse. It would be just perfect for you, with your coloring." She pulled the caftan off a hanger. "If you like it, I will make you a present of it. Here, try it on. I am going to run some cool water in the tub, so I can splash my body. It's hot tonight, no?" She headed into the bathroom, unhooking her chiffon halter and throwing it down on the floor as she went.

"What the hell," Tyger whispered to herself. Jake was right about one thing. Martine wanted to write the scenario, and Tyger might as well go along with it. Her reactions would probably have something to do with Martine's business decision, regardless of what Jake thought. The evening would have to be played out to its logical conclusions. Besides, the hashish made her feel a bit reckless.

The caftan lay where Martine had tossed it, on the bed. It was exquisite. Tyger unzipped her clingy black Matt Phillips dress and slipped it down over her hips.

"Well, try it on!" Martine had reappeared, naked, in the doorway.

Tyger pulled the caftan over her head and down over her body. "It looks sensational, Tyger," said Martine. "Come into the bathroom and have a look in the full-length mirror."

Tyger followed the naked Martine into the multi-mirrored bathroom. "It's beautiful, Martine. Thank you. You have until the end of the evening to change your mind."

"Stay with me. I'll just be a minute. Poor Jake must be wondering what has happened to us. I hope he is keeping his eye on the soufflé. . . ." Martine sank to her knees in the large circular tub, and splashed herself with running water from the tap. Tyger watched her as she scrubbed off the hand-painted dragon decorating her abdomen. Martine's dark tan was even, with no sign of a bikini line on her bony torso. Her breasts were those of an underdeveloped fourteen-year-old, except that the nipples were dark brown instead of virginal pink. There was a smoothness to Martine's boyish body, a slight rounding of the hips, that kept her from looking unsexy.

"Are you hot, Tyger? Will you join me and cool off? This tub is large enough for two, *n'est-ce pas?*" She laughed, scrubbing her thighs with a loofah.

"Why don't you, Tyger?" Jake's voice rang out from the doorway. He was carrying a bottle of wine and three glasses. "I'll serve your wine *dans le* . . . bathtub."

"Oh, Jake . . ." Martine twisted around so she could see him. "What about the soufflé?"

"I turned the heat down. It'll be ready in an hour."

"But it won't rise if you cook it that way," Tyger said.

Jake set the glasses down by the sink and poured the wine. "It'll still taste good by the time we get around to it. Go on . . . hop in!"

Tyger hesitated; but it seemed ridiculous to refuse. She slipped off her clothes and stepped into the tepid water, causing little waves to splash up around Martine's breasts. Tyger felt as if she were entering the arena for the preliminary event; from now on there was no turning back. She sank down into the tub, facing Martine, her back resting against the cool porcelain. Her leg brushed against Martine's body, and she was aware of its softness, the slippery sensuality of two female bodies touching underwater. She smiled at Martine. She was determined to show that American women could be as sophisticated as Europeans. She began to relax. Hugh Marshall and Kellerco seemed very far away at the moment.

Jake handed the two women their glasses of wine.

"Jake, would you be a love and get the dope? I have some in an Indian brass kutch box, next to my bed."

The hash pipe was passed around again while Tyger and Martine continued to recline languidly in the tub. Jake sat in a wicker chair he had brought in from the next room. Before long, they were all floating.

Martine lifted Tyger's feet into her lap and began playing with them, idly pulling on the toes and massaging her arch.

Tyger settled back, relaxed, and remembered something that had happened long before. "I had two great chums when I first moved to New York. Bob, and his lover, Sinclair. I wasn't dating anyone special, so I went out with them two or three times a week. Bob was the funniest person I'd ever met. He was also attractive, and if he hadn't been gay I might have fallen madly in love with him.

"One night, late," Tyger continued, "we were sitting around Bob's place, drinking straight tequila with salt and lime slices. Bob and I started flirting ... and one thing led to another. Before long, we were all in bed together. Sinclair went along with it because he took all his cues from Bob. They were kissing and massaging my body and I was really digging it. Then presto! I passed out. A little while later I woke up and saw Bob and Sinclair making it with each other. I pretended I was still out of it, but I watched the whole thing. It really turned me on. . . ."

"Men with men," said Martine. "It is something I fantasize about sometimes."

"Not me," said Jake. "Women with women. There's nothing better."

"Hmmm. That's true also." Martine grabbed the sponge and squeezed water over Tyger's shoulders. "You have beautiful breasts," she whispered. "Doesn't Tyger have *the* most beautiful breasts, Jake? Full ... but not too big." Martine's hand casually brushed against Tyger's right nipple. "Oh, for just one day I should like to have a body like yours, Tyger." She kissed Tyger on the lips, quickly. "Jake ... aren't you going to join us? Or do you prefer the role of voyeur?"

"Right now, I'm happy to watch. You two both look ravishing. I wish I'd brought my camera."

"Oh, I'm glad you didn't." Martine smiled. "I don't want to be blackmailed someday by incriminating pictures."

"Not a chance, Martine," Jake replied. "The word 'incriminating' insinuates that a crime has been involved. You and Tyger taking a bath together is about the farthest thing from a crime that I can think of."

Tyger was soaping and rinsing Martine's back now. "We'd better get out. Your skin is full of goose bumps."

Martine looked puzzled. *"Qu'est-ce que c'est* 'goose bumps'?"

"Oh, *les chairs de poule,* I guess. Here . . . look at these." Tyger trailed her fingers down Martine's arms, pointing out the tiny bumps.

"Oh, you're right. Jake, will you hand us the towels?" Martine ran her fingers and palms right up her scalp, so that her short hair was sticking straight up when she finished. Tyger smoothed Martine's hair back down again for her and grabbed a towel from Jake.

Jake reached over to dry Martine. He pulled her to him and pressed his nose into her flat chest, but she pulled away, nonchalantly.

"I feel much better now," she said. "I'm going to put on some music."

When Martine had left the room, Jake kissed Tyger's belly and nuzzled his nose into her bellybutton. "This is turning into a nice evening. Aren't you glad we stayed?"

"Hmmm," Tyger said absentmindedly, thinking about Martine and wondering whether the Frenchwoman's performance was calculated entirely to arouse Jake's interest, or whether she was truly attracted to Tyger. Was she trying to prove to Tyger that she was in complete control of every situation? Or was Martine merely a compulsive *femme fatale,* desperately anxious to make love to anyone who captured her interest, male or female? Tyger was intrigued.

"Come into the bedroom when you're ready. I've put on some records—Blondie, Neil Young, Willie Nelson, Alan Price . . . you like?"

Tyger and Jake joined Martine, who had pulled the white spread off of her king-size bed and was lounging on Clarence House floral sheets. She wore only a thin gold chain around her waist, with her initials, M.R., forming the clasp. She held some gold chains in her hand.

"Do me a favor, Tyger. I have been experimenting with some designs for breast jewelry, but up to now I have been using myself as model." She laughed. "Not a good model for breasts, am I? Here. Will you try these on?"

"Sure. I love breast jewelry."

"Yes? Me, too. It's been done before, but it's usually uninteresting and uncomfortable. I want to design a whole line—for the beach, for disco . . ." She wrapped the gold chains around Tyger's breasts, and attached them with a golden leaf pin at the back of her shoulder blades. "This is the simple version." She rooted through a box of ornaments and attached some decorative Art Deco pins to the shoulder chains. Producing a hand mirror, she said, "See? How do you like it?"

Tyger gazed at her breasts in the mirror. The jewelry suited her. "Fabulous! I want one . . . very ornate and outrageous."

Martine put her arm around Tyger affectionately. "I'll design a very rococo one with you in mind." Tyger draped her arm around Martine in an effort to appear casual. Sitting there, they looked like teenaged girl friends at a slumber party. Except they were both naked.

"I'll design penis jewelry with *you* in mind, Jake." Martine began unbuttoning Jake's pink silk shirt.

"It's been done. You should see what they sell at those gay shops in New York."

"Oh? Do you go often to these gay shops, Jake?" Martine teased. "Perhaps that is why you prefer to simply observe. Hmmm, Jake, is that right?" She helped him out of his shirt, and began rubbing her hand over the rise in his jeans.

"Come here, wench, and find out for yourself." He unzipped his jeans. Martine slithered closer to him and cuddled up in his arms. She motioned for Tyger to join them.

Tyger was getting in the mood. She had never been with a woman before, but realized that she only had to do to Martine what she would like done to her. Experience was a state of mind, and the hashish had made her mind receptive. She nibbled Jake's toes, and then Martine's. She rubbed her hands over their legs. One was muscled and hairy, the other smooth and silky soft. The tactile difference between male and female bodies was amazing.

Martine turned around to face Tyger as Jake ran his lips up and down her thighs. Tyger enveloped Jake's erection with her mouth and began sucking, while Martine held

Tyger's hair away from her face and ran her lips along Tyger's shoulders.

As they hugged, Tyger was struck again with Martine's softness, her fragility, in contrast with Jake's muscular roughness. Tyger's previously pent-up curiosity about women, and the taboos of making love to them, melted away into the sensuality of the moment and the haze of hash. She could feel Martine's kisses spiraling pleasure through her erect nipples as her left hand moved slowly up and down Jake's penis.

Tyger wanted Martine. She pulled her into a long, experimental kiss. The mouths of the two women met, their tongues twisting around each other.

Tyger's fingers cupped and squeezed Martine's soft buttocks, and explored the wet cleft below. Every touch was amazing, a totally new sensation and yet strangely familiar too, like exploring an imprecise copy of herself. It was wildly narcissistic, and disconcerting, and exciting, and she could feel herself responding as Martine's lips and fingers mirrored her own, and Jake moved and moaned between them.

But in the midst of it all a doubt entered Tyger's mind, and she opened her eyes to find Martine's open too, and fixed on her with what seemed an almost detached curiosity. Tyger felt her passion begin to abate against a slight suspicion—was Martine really into it? Was she truly aroused, or was she just pulling strings? Tyger could not be sure. She drew away from Martine and focused her attention back on Jake. Martine sensed the shift, and followed suit.

"Jake," Martine said, "You American men are so well built. It turns me on like crazy." She moved around and sat down on top of him. He moved in and out of her slowly while his right hand found Tyger's breasts and squeezed them gently. Martine's fingers rubbed Tyger's clitoris, faster and faster. Tyger and Jake and Martine came almost at the same time, in a chorus of heaving sighs, their bodies crumpled limply, entwined around each other.

A new record dropped down on Martine's phonograph, and the gravelly voice of Captain Beefheart pierced the still Paris night. After a while, Tyger and Martine finished off the remaining wine. Jake continued to lie there, savoring the aftermath of total carnal enjoyment. No one spoke. A breeze began stirring, to cool the hours before sunrise, gently blowing the curtains into the room. Martine rolled a joint and passed it around.

"A beautiful *partouze*." Martine sighed. "You were wonderful, my friends." She spoke to them both, but she was looking at Tyger.

"I hate to bring it up," Jake said, "but I'm afraid our soufflé has probably baked away, bowl and all."

"Ah, *merde!*" Martine leaped from the bed and raced down to the kitchen. Tyger and Jake looked at each other. It was nearly four a.m.

The next morning, in their rue du Dragon flat, Tyger sat on a chair, towel-drying her freshly washed hair. She was in a rotten mood, and the weather was in sympathy. Paris looked dreary as black rain clouds planted themselves over the city.

Jake called out from the kitchen. "You almost ready? If we rush we can make it to the Pompidou museum before it starts raining."

"You go alone. I've seen it," she said petulantly.

"Oh, Jesus, I thought you'd gotten out of your funk. . . ." Jake and Tyger had been arguing since breakfast about the previous night's episode with Martine Rainier. Jake had had a great time, and wanted to see Martine again, for a rerun of the action. Tyger was hung over and full of misgivings. Jumping into bed with Martine was probably the worst thing she could have done.

"No, I feel crummier than ever. What if I completely botched Kellerco's chances of getting Martine? And *you* helped me. . . ."

"Wait a minute. Don't blame me for your lusts!" Jake snapped.

"I wanted to leave, remember? You were the one who insisted that we stay. Because Martine was coming on to you, and you wanted to get into her pants. You can't stand not to make a conquest, can you?" Tyger threw her wet towel at him.

"You bitch!" He hadn't been this angry at a woman in a long time. "You can't just do one thing one minute, and then . . ."

The doorbell rang. Jake and Tyger both froze for a second, staring at each other with contempt. Then Jake went to answer. He returned with a letter to Tyger from Martine.

Tyger grabbed the letter, but paused without opening it. "This is not good news. I feel it. . . ."

"Oh, just read it, Tyger. Skip the dramatics."

Tyger read aloud: "Tyger, Sorry to kiss and run, but I had the urge to go to St. Tropez. By the time I return, you and

Jake will have left Paris, but perhaps we will see each other again one of these days. X. Martine. P.S. I will wire Hugh Marshall with my decision when I have made it."

Tyger crumpled the letter in her hand and threw it at Jake. "Shit!" she screamed at the top of her lungs. "Shit! Shit! *Shit!*" She stormed into the bathroom and slammed the door. The wood was swollen from age, and it wouldn't close completely. Tyger kicked it with her foot.

Jake shouted through the door. "I'm not sticking around for your histrionics. I'm going out! I'll call later, and if you've calmed down maybe we can do something together this afternoon."

"Fat chance!" Tyger screamed back. She reached for her makeup and was applying gray eye pencil when she heard Jake slam shut the front door of the apartment.

It was Sunday evening, nearly dark, but the lights had not been turned on at the apartment on Jane Street. Tyger had been back from Paris for two days. She had flown out a few hours after she had received the note from Martine, without saying goodbye to Jake. She had left a letter for him with the concierge, telling Jake that he was welcome to remain at Jacqueline's apartment for as long as he liked. So far, Jake had not tried to telephone her in New York. She didn't really expect him to.

Everything was going wrong: no more Jake, and if Hugh Marshall received a negative decision from Martine, perhaps there would be no more job.

Tyger sat cross-legged on the floor of the still-bare apartment, watching the darkness deepen. It was nearly a month since she had taken the place, but the rooms still looked as if they were waiting for their tenant to arrive. It was a cheerless place to be alone in while the world was falling apart.

If she had a pack of cigarettes she would start smoking again. If there were liquor in the house, she would get drunk. Instead, she sat listening to the street sounds of Labor Day traffic in the dark. Finally, she dragged herself into the bedroom and forced herself to go to sleep.

CHAPTER SEVENTEEN

TYGER munched on a bagel with cream cheese, and reread the page she had just finished typing. Her report on the Paris trip was not ready, and Hugh Marshall wanted to see her at five. She had nothing to tell him. Or nothing that she *could* tell him. The truth—that she had had lunch with Martine Rainier and then jumped in bed with her—was out of the question.

"Oh, shit," she said to herself. She tore the paper out of the typewriter and tossed it into the wastepaper basket already brimming with her other false starts. There was nothing to write. She could give her report orally, and get it over with quicker.

Tyger finished her bagel. She hadn't eaten a decent meal for nearly three days.

As Tyger emerged from the elevator onto the thirty-fifth floor of the Kellerco Building, she ran into Tim Yates.

"Oh, hello, Tyger." The young Englishman smiled warmly. "Hugh's quite anxious to see you."

"I know," Tyger said. "Wish me luck." Any other time, the fact that Hugh Marshall wanted to see her would have cheered her up. Now, she could not bear facing him with the fact that she had failed her mission. He had given her a big assignment, and she had blown it.

Annie Johnson showed Tyger into Marshall's office immediately. Marshall's jacket was off, but his tie was in place and his shirtsleeves were not rolled up. He stood, smiling, and extended his hand to Tyger, shaking it genially.

"Congratulations, Tyger! You must have done some selling job on Martine Rainier. She's thrilled to be doing the bottles and packaging for us. I've just ironed out the money end. Of course we're paying her an arm and a leg, but I expected that."

Tyger was stunned by the news. "That's terrific! She, ah, didn't give *me* a firm commitment. . . ."

"Well, you obviously handled the matter like a pro. Martine will be coming to the States in a couple of weeks, and of course she'll expect special attention. I'll assign you to keep her occupied, since you're obviously on her wavelength."

"It seems I am." Knowing the kind of special attention Martine would want, Tyger was not anxious to repeat the Paris episode, but for Hugh Marshall's sake she would deal with Martine as diplomatically as possible.

"I'm very impressed, Tyger. Not that I doubted you could do it, but it was a tough assignment. Let's have a drink to celebrate."

"Love one. It's the end of a long day."

Marshall moved over to a louvered oak panel and pressed a button. The panel slipped open to display a well-equipped bar. "What'll you have?"

"Dry vermouth on the rocks, please." Tyger watched her boss as he poured the vermouth, and fixed a vodka martini for himself. She decided that if he were cast as an executive in a movie no one would buy it—he was too good-looking for the role. No doubt that was the reason some of his colleagues mistrusted him. She could tell that she would have to go slowly if she was ever going to attract Hugh Marshall.

"My predecessor in this job kept a bartender on staff for occasions like this. A waste of money. . . ." Hugh smiled at Tyger as he brought her drink over and handed it to her.

"Ah, but what if I'd ordered something tricky, like a Singapore Sling or a Golden Dream?"

"Easy. I would have handed you the bar guide and told you to help yourself. Corporation presidents are experts in delegating responsibility." He walked around his desk, pulling one of the leather armchairs around so that he faced Tyger.

"To Martine . . . and the fabulous bottle she's going to design." Tyger paused. "You know, Matt Phillips won't be particularly pleased that we've got Martine. He left a message for me saying he wants the bottles designed by his friend Jeff Stein—the SoHo artist."

Hugh waved his hand to dismiss Matt Phillips. "Martine's the best. Stein wouldn't have been a bad second choice . . . but we don't have to worry about that now. I want Martine's touch to balance the 'American-ness' of the scent. Her name has clout in Europe. It will add international glamour to the perfume . . . for the women who care about that sort of thing."

"You'd be surprised how many women care about that sort of thing."

"Do you?" Marshall asked, smiling.

"Only if it's company policy. I'm all business these days."

Marshall laughed. "I saw Andy Parrish last weekend. I thanked him for sending you to me."

"How is Andy? I haven't seen him in months."

"He's fine. Has a nice yearling he's excited about. A Secretariat colt."

"Should bring a lot of money at Keeneland."

"Andy's not selling him. Going to train him himself and race him. Andy sees this colt as his big chance to take the Triple Crown."

Tyger grinned. "The latest in a long line of immortal hopefuls." She liked seeing Marshall laugh. It gave his face a warmer, more human look that she had seldom seen. There was a man behind the executive mask, but Tyger guessed that Hugh Marshall did his best never to let him show.

"Your glass is empty. Have another drink, Tyger?"

She couldn't tell from his voice whether he wanted her to stay or not, and decided not to push it. Leave 'em wanting more. "No, thanks. I have to go. Unless there's something else you want to discuss?"

"I think we've covered it all." He looked at his watch. "Oh, it's later than I thought. I'm entertaining a group of Brazilian diplomats this evening. To set up distributorships for one of the newer subsidiaries." He walked her to the door. "I'm sure your evening will be much more interesting than mine."

"I hope so! See you soon, Hugh." Tyger's evening was going to consist of a deli sandwich and an old movie of her father's on TV.

Adjoining Hugh Marshall's office was a bath and a small dressing room, where three suits and a dinner jacket hung behind the sliding doors of a narrow closet. As soon as Tyger left, he went in to shave and change for the evening.

He was pleased with Tyger for the job she had done, and pleased with himself for sending her. Bachrach would never have chosen someone like Tyger. Bachrach would have sent a Sheldon Shaw, and Martine Rainier would have turned him down flat. But what Tyger Hayes lacked in business experience she more than made up in poise and intelligence. And she was a woman, and young, and from a background someone like Martine Rainier could be comfortable with. No, Tyger had been the right one to send, all right. And the results had proved it.

As he splashed on Bill Blass's aftershave and reached for a clean shirt, Hugh wondered whether Tyger would stick with this job, or if it was just a passing fancy. He decided that as long as the job was challenging she wouldn't be bored. He could understand that. Making deals, calling shots, keeping on the move was what it was all about. It was what made life interesting, unpredictable. In his case, overseeing a corporate empire was the only thing he had found to capture his attention for longer than a few weeks. That, and his children. But he didn't see enough of them to become bored. If he had to be around them all the time, perhaps he would tire of them, too.

His thoughts shifted back to Tyger. Perhaps he should have brought her along tonight, to help deal with the Brazilians. She was articulate and attractive, and she probably even spoke a little Portuguese. She certainly would have helped the deal. But then he dismissed the thought. The line was too thin there between business and pleasure, and he knew he had better keep Tyger firmly on the business side. She was becoming too valuable at Keller Perfumes, and if he were to allow even a suggestion of romance to creep in . . . well, women were unpredictable, except that you could always predict with certainty that something would go wrong. And there was no time on the tight Keller Perfumes timetable to replace a Tyger Hayes.

There were plenty of beautiful women in New York for him to take out who were not connected with business. Unfortunately, there were damned few he actually enjoyed talking with.

Choosing a Matt Phillips tie to go with his navy linen Phillips suit, he pulled it around his collar. Tyger Hayes had a natural acuity for the glamour business, and he liked talking with her. He decided he had better leave it at that.

* * *

On Thursday of that week, *Women's Wear Daily*, the *Wall Street Journal*, and the style page of *The New York Times* all ran features on Tasha Powers and the signature perfume she was launching, to be called Disco. It was scheduled to hit the stores in March.

By ten o'clock Thursday morning, a few hours after the papers had come out, everyone at Keller Perfumes was assembled in Hugh Marshall's office in an extreme state of agitation.

Matt Phillips was hysterical. "I wanted to make the announcement about *my* perfume weeks ago. But no, *you* said"—he glared hostilely at Marshall—"that we should keep it top-secret until fall. Now, no matter what we do it'll look as if I copied Tasha. Oh God, I can't stand it. . . ."

"Calm down, Matt. This has come out of left field. There's nothing to do but deal with it. We'll have to hold a press conference, and announce your perfume as soon as possible."

"No!" Matt shrieked. "Make my announcement on top of Tasha's? I will not be accused of imitating her."

Jess Leibowitz jumped in. "I know that it'll look a bit anticlimactic. But on the other hand, we can't overlook sales and publicity. Tasha Powers will cop it all for herself if we don't follow up immediately. We have to let the buyers know that you're in the running, too. We've got to land the best stores and the best space for ourselves. If the buyers don't know about us, they'll make commitments to Powers. We *have* to announce, as soon as possible."

"I agree," Connie said. "Look at it this way, Matt. You'll take the wind out of her sails by upstaging her."

"Everyone on Seventh Avenue will say I'm copying her. Our rivalry isn't exactly a secret, you know."

"Well, Matt," Tyger said, "let's take advantage of the rivalry and squeeze as much publicity out of it as we can for ourselves. In the long run, no one's going to care whose perfume was announced first."

"How do you suppose Tasha found out about Matt's perfume?" Connie asked.

"Billy Youngblood makes it a point to know everything about everybody. He tried to give me the third degree last month at a party. He seemed to know something then," Tyger remembered. "Maybe Garry inadvertently let it slip. . . ."

Matt lashed out. "Garry would do no such thing! Tyger, what makes you so sure that *you* didn't spill the beans?"

"It wasn't me. Billy had a spy somewhere," Tyger speculated.

"Okay," said Marshall. "What's done is done. I imagine Tasha Powers found out about our perfume, one way or another, but *how* 'doesn't matter now. . . ." It did matter to Marshall. If there was a leak he wanted to know where it was. But that was not the question of the moment.

"You're right, Hugh," Connie said. "And if Tasha copied the idea from Matt then she has even less time than we do to put together a perfume."

Marshall nodded. "All right. Matt must make his announcement as soon as possible. Now, what's the best way to do it?"

"Yes," Connie said, "the way that will sound *least* like Matt's saying, 'If she can do it, I can do it.'"

"I have a couple of thoughts." Tyger looked at the notes she had been jotting down. "First, Tasha's announcement, according to the *Times*, was rushed. She held a press conference in her office. So we should throw together a splashy press party."

"There's nothing at all unique about that," Matt sulked.

"That leads to my second thought. Why not announce Matt's *men's* scent at the same time . . . instead of waiting until after the women's perfume is out?"

"But we won't be ready to put out a men's fragrance in March," Jess objected.

"We don't have to launch it in March, just *announce* that it will follow the women's scent. It will sound as if we're farther along with the planning of our line than Tasha. . . ."

"Tyger's right," Marshall agreed. "No point in holding off the men's announcement until later. Except that I don't agree with you, Jess. We *can* put out both fragrances at the same time. And we will! Put together a profile for the men's line, and get back to the fragrance manufacturers with it. No reason they can't come up with two scents. Sheldon, you haven't added your thoughts about this. . . ."

Shaw looked up. "I, ah, think it'll mean working 'round the clock, but I certainly agree that it will look good to launch both fragrances at the same time." That was what Marshall wanted him to say, Shaw thought, and what the hell did it really matter? "We can have two products by March, Hugh."

"I'm glad you concur. Tyger, you handle the press party. I'll host it on behalf of Kellerco, and let's do it right away. You figure out when and where. Connie, we want the press and department-store biggies. Matt, give Tyger a list of the Seventh Avenue people you want included. Tyger, pull together some celebrities, too. But keep the list small, because in the spring, for the launch, we'll have to do the whole thing all over again, only a bigger splash, with more people."

Matt stood and paced the office with fretful steps. His impeccably dressed bantam body twitched with displeasure. "Well, I suppose we're making the best out of a bad situation. But what about the packaging and bottle design? As you already know, I am not at all pleased with the choice of Martine Rainier. Oh, I don't deny she has talent. But she's French. The whole point of my scent is that it's American. . . ."

"But, Matt, we've been over and over this." Tyger was impatient. "Martine's participation can only increase the prestige of your perfume. . . ."

"Perhaps." Matt Phillips stood with his back to them, shoulders squared combatively as he stared out the window. "But she's only been commissioned to do the women's fragrance. Nothing's been said to her about the men's scent, has it?"

Marshall looked at Tyger, who shook her head. "What are you driving at, Matt?"

Phillips turned to face them, a sharp, sudden movement, like a mechanical toy on a spring. "Jeff Stein—an American designer, and, in my opinion, the best. I want him for the men's fragrance."

Marshall sat looking thoughtful. Everyone else remained silent. "Not a bad idea, Matt. Two different looks, two different markets. . . ."

Tyger and Connie were appalled at the idea. Connie spoke first. "But two designers! What if their ideas clash? After all, most lines aim for a synergism between their men's and women's products. Look at Jovan—their male and female bottles fit together, like a puzzle."

"There are no rules to this sort of thing," Marshall pronounced. "We have two markets, and two different fragrance statements to be made." Hugh Marshall was firm.

"But what about Martine?" Tyger asked. "She's going to be upset when she learns that there's a men's scent and that someone other than she will be doing the packaging."

"If there are any problems, Tyger, I'm sure you can handle them. Besides, Martine's being paid a hefty sum. Women are the ones who are going to be impressed that we chose her, because of her jewelry. Men won't give a damn. No, Matt's right on this point. Jeff Stein is the perfect choice for the men's bottles. Matt, you and Jess try to get to him today, okay?"

It was, Tyger decided, an object lesson in executive generalship. The meeting had begun in disarray, with Matt Phillips in near hysteria. But thanks to Hugh Marshall's handling of the packaging matter, they were adjourning in a buoyant mood, with Matt looking positively smug. Knowing where to make the right concessions was a key part of a job like Marshall's. Tyger only hoped that this concession had been the right one.

The next week, for Tyger, was a blur of phone calls and racing around Manhattan arranging all the details of the party. Due to a last-minute cancellation, she was able to line up an upstairs room at "21." She stood over the printer to make sure the invitations came out perfectly, had them hand-addressed by a calligrapher, and delivered by messengers to two hundred influential people. Connie and Matt had helped her with the guest list, an ordeal that had lasted until well after midnight one evening. The final number of guests had been pared down from over twice as many top candidates.

At six o'clock the following Thursday, a week after their initial decision, Hugh Marshall toasted Matt Phillips with champagne to celebrate the Kellerco-Phillips association. The dark wood-paneled upstairs room at "21" had been transformed into a jungle of Chinese orchids, gardenias, angel roses and stephanotis, and the heady aroma set the mood for the fragrance announcement. Since it was too warm for a fire, a large basket of oriental lilies replaced the logs of the woodburning fireplace and spilled out over the hearth. Champagne and assorted hot and cold hors d'oeuvre were passed around by deft waiters, and Tyger had pulled together press kits for the reporters. Butlers circulated, passing out Havana cigars to the men and Matt Phillips silk scarves to the women. A small string quartet played unobtrusively in the background.

Tyger stood next to one of the tall potted palms, rented specially for the occasion, and took a moment to look around. Flashbulbs clicked at the far end of the room as Matt Phillips and Hugh Marshall talked to reporters from all the local papers, national magazines and television stations. The Baron and Baroness di Portanova, new owners of "21"—he had bought the restaurant for ten million as a gift for his beautiful wife, Sandra—mixed with the other guests. Lee Radziwill was there, and Lucie Arnaz, and a throng of Seventh Avenue celebrities. Even Billy Youngblood had shown up, Tyger was surprised to see. He was talking to Tim Yates, who introduced him to Sheldon Shaw. Yates quickly extricated himself and came over to Tyger.

"Excellent turnout." The young Englishman smiled.

"Yes. I haven't checked the list with Ginger yet, but I'd guess we have pretty nearly a full house."

"Things seem to be going splendidly. A waiter bumped into Angela Lansbury and *just* missed dousing her with champagne. Thank God she has a good sense of humor. . . . Oh, oh, Hugh's summoning me. . . ." Yates rushed to the other end of the room.

Connie Larcada, wearing a Ralph Lauren Donegal tweed jacket, gray silk charmeuse blouse and charcoal velvet skirt, made her way through the crowd with a glass of champagne for Tyger. "You haven't had anything to eat or drink all evening. The party's a success." She surveyed the crowd. "Everyone's here. Even the Kellerco bigwig, Nelson Bachrach."

"I'm too nervous to eat, and I'm afraid that if I drink it'll go right to my head. That's all I need . . . to stagger around." She lowered her voice. "I am worried about Sheldon, though. He seems a little bleary."

Connie looked alarmed. "Oh, dear. I've been busy talking with the press. I haven't seen Shel in about half an hour. It's not too obvious, is it? Marshall hasn't seen him, has he?"

"I don't think so—in answer to both your questions. I saw Sheldon talking to Bachrach a while ago, but he seemed okay then. He's over there now." Tyger looked into the crowd. "Or, at least, he was . . . talking to Billy Youngblood." Tyger was suddenly aware of Connie's concern over Sheldon Shaw. Connie seemed to have taken him under her wing recently. Tyger wondered if there could be something more to it than that, but dismissed the thought. Surely Connie would never become involved with someone as unappealing as Sheldon Shaw.

"Well, I'm off to circulate some more. By the way, Tyger, the flowers are incredible. How did you manage to get so many? I feel as if I'm at the Rose Bowl Parade." She laughed.

Matt Phillips came over and kissed Tyger. "You did an amazing job of coordinating everything so fast. I'd say it's going quite well, wouldn't you? By the way, you look smashing tonight, my dear."

Tyger's gold-flecked auburn hair was pulled away from her face and held in place by two Cartier pavé diamond haircombs which Bobbie had given her for her birthday. She wore an electrifying royal-blue off-one-shoulder Phillips original, its straight skirt ending just above her knees. To keep in the mood of the occasion, Tyger had wound a four-foot boa of black silk cord and fresh white freesia blossoms around her neck. "Your friend Tasha seems to be absent from the festivities, but Billy Youngblood was here for a while."

Matt made a face. "Just as crass as ever. It serves me right for insisting that Tasha be invited. Thank God, he didn't stay long. I saw him talking to Sheldon Shaw for a few minutes. Shaw's about the only person I know who could bore even Billy Youngblood into leaving a party. . . ."

"Now, Matt. Don't be catty. After all, I saw him talking to Garry, too."

Matt raised one eyebrow, a facial gesture he had worked hard at perfecting. "Now look whose claws are coming out. Why don't you like Garry?"

Tyger hedged. "I don't dislike him. But . . . I think you deserve better. I'm sorry, I guess that's being too frank."

"Well, you aren't the only one who thinks that. But I can't help it. I'm as hooked on Garry as I am on cocaine. Speaking of which, would you like to slip behind the potted palms and have a sniff?"

"*I* would, pal." Garry pranced up in time to hear the word "cocaine." He and Matt dashed off, laughing, to the side of the room.

Tyger wandered around, chatting with guests and looking for Hugh Marshall. She spotted him next to the fireplace, deeply engrossed in conversation with her mother. Tyger had not spoken to Bobbie since Elaine's funeral, but she felt that the press party would be a good opportunity to smooth things over. After all, Lady Bobbie was the sort of celebrity that the press looked for at these gatherings.

"Hmm, your boss and your mother. Looks like you could be part of a different sort of threesome now."

Tyger reeled around to face the familiar voice. "Jake! What are you doing here?"

"I came with Barbara Reed." He pointed to a reporter from one of the local TV stations. "I didn't realize whose party it was until we got here. Sorry. I would've stayed away if I'd known."

"That's okay, Jake. I've cooled off. I apologize for the way I acted in Paris. Can we be friends?" Tyger knew she didn't love Jake. That evening in Paris, and their fight afterward, was only an excuse for their breaking up. But she still liked him, and missed talking to him.

"Just friends?" asked Jake. He looked at Tyger with concern.

"Yes, Jake. I need time to myself these days."

"Don't tell me you need space." Jake grinned. "The epidemic disease of modern woman."

Tyger smiled back at him. "It's the space age, Jake."

"Well, I'm sorry, I miss you. But it's up to you, kid. Like they say on the late show, we could have made beautiful music together." He lit a cigarette. "Let me know if you want to get together and hum an occasional tune."

"Okay." Tyger laughed. "You always had a good ear."

"Ear? Is that all?" But Jake noticed that Tyger was no longer smiling, and he followed her gaze. Bobbie and Hugh Marshall were still locked in conversation. "What's the story with your mother and Marshall?"

"Why does there have to be a story, Jake?" Tyger snapped. "They're old friends."

"That wouldn't be jealousy rearing its ugly head, would it? I always suspected there was more than business between you and Marshall."

"I'm sorry, Jake. No, there's nothing between us, really. There can't be." She smiled ruefully. "Just keeping up with the business end is tough enough."

"You look like a girl who needs someone to talk to over a cheeseburger at P. J. Clarke's."

"I'd love it. But don't you have plans with Barbara Reed?"

"Barbara? No. We're just old friends. Like . . ." He gestured with a nod of his head toward Lady Bobbie and Hugh Marshall.

Tyger ignored the implication. "I can't leave here for at least a half an hour. Can you wait?"

"Forever, my darling."

Nelson Bachrach ordered a scotch from the bar, and went over to join Hugh Marshall and Roberta Rowan.

"Hello, Bobbie," he grumbled. "Surprised to see you."

"Nelson! I was hoping you'd be here. My little girl Tyger's working at Keller Perfumes these days." Bobbie looked stunning in a black velvet Oscar de la Renta evening suit with a hand-beaded camisole and a seed-pearl lariat by Angela Cummings tied at her throat.

(177)

"Has Hugh been telling you how unreasonable I am? That I'm dead set against this subsidiary . . ."

Bobbie smiled. "Oh? Hugh didn't mention it. But if you are, then shame on you. Getting into perfume is a marvelous idea. Even my granddad and Sam Keller would have come around to the idea. . . ." She flashed a coquettish smile.

Bachrach lit a cigar. "Bobbie, you're a beautiful woman, but what you don't know about business would fill a trunk or two."

"What? You should ask my stockbroker. He says I have an uncanny ability to predict trends. . . ."

"Hmm. I see you've been brainwashing her, Hugh."

"I didn't have to." Marshall was calm.

Bachrach glared at him. "This is quite a party. Must've cost a year's salary for somebody."

"I assure you, Nelson, we're on budget."

"I hope so. Sheldon Shaw told me that things are proceeding at a slow pace over there." Bachrach gloated.

"This is the kind of product that comes together at the last minute. You know that."

"I only know that I have to protect the interests of our stockholders, like Bobbie here."

"But, Nelson," Bobbie said, "I'm absolutely in favor of Matt Phillips's perfumes. . . ."

"I'm not going to get into an argument with you, Bobbie. You're probably as stubborn as your granddad was. Besides, you don't want your daughter to lose her job. . . ."

"Oh, Nelson," Bobbie said diplomatically, "you can see through us all. But I'd still lay odds that Keller Perfumes will be a winner."

"No, Bobbie, I wouldn't want to take your money like that." Bachrach tossed his cigar into the lily-laden fireplace. "Hugh, I'm going to be watching the expense sheets on this project. Shaw tells me you've been encouraging him to spend money like water."

"Oh? There must be some misunderstanding," Hugh said.

"I hope so. Anyway, I'm going now," Bachrach said abruptly. He kissed Bobbie formally. "Better tell your daughter to start looking for a new job." He left without saying goodbye to Hugh Marshall.

"My, my. What do you think of that?" Bobbie asked Hugh.

He smiled. "Part of a day's job, Bobbie. Have dinner with me later, and I'll tell you more about it."

"Love to, Hugh."

*   *   *

The Russian Tea Room was bustling with after-theater activity. In the cheerful dining room, girdles of tinsel and red balls encircled the ceiling lamps and sprouted from the walls, in celebration of Christmases past and Christmases yet to come. Waiters in braid-trimmed red tunics hurried back and forth through the close-packed tables, bearing trays of *blini* and caviar and chilled vodkas from Russia and Eastern Europe. The dark-turquoise walls were adorned with paintings —large ballet murals of a limited palette toward the front of the room, smaller canvases of varied period and style closer to the kitchen. Beautiful silver samovars perched on shelves along the length of the restaurant.

Lady Rowan and Hugh Carlyle Marshall III were seated at a front banquette. The room was filled with the establishment's characteristic mix of the famous and the ordinary. Next to what appeared to be a theater party from Westchester, Vladimir Horowitz unwound after a triumphant recital at the adjacent Carnegie Hall. Chevy Chase hosted a table that included Candice Bergen, Paul Simon and Peter Sellers. From across the room Ahmet and Mica Ertegun waved a greeting to Lady Bobbie.

"Your *blini* look delicious," Bobbie said enviously, as Hugh spread a piece with red caviar and sour cream.

"Please, have some."

"Oh, Hugh, how can you be so cruel? Get thee behind me. I think I've gained five pounds just looking at them!"

"I'm sure five pounds wouldn't do you a bit of harm."

"Hugh, you *are* wicked! Well, perhaps just . . . no, I can't. I remember Ruth Gordon once told me that her secret for staying thin was that she hadn't eaten anything she really liked in forty years."

"What a depressing thought." The waiter brought him another round of chilled vodka flavored with peppercorns. "Now that I think about it," he went on, "you used to eat pancakes. Remember that New Year's Eve in Lexington? Nine years ago, I think."

"Can it be? I suppose it must. Cappy and I were still together, and . . ." Bobbie broke off, delicately avoiding direct mention of the late Sarah Marshall. "But pancakes?"

"Sure. You had that Chinese cook. You'd ordered crêpes for a late-night supper for a few of us, around three in the morning, after the party had broken up. Won Lee, or whatever his name was, came in with a tray of Moo Shu Pork and a stack of Chinese pancakes."

"Oh, I remember." Bobbie laughed. "He never did understand crêpes!"

"But he made a terrific Moo Shu Pork."

"We did have fun back there in those days, didn't we, Hugh?" She covered his hand with hers for a moment and looked into his eyes. "We've all come such a long way since then."

"You haven't changed a bit, Bobbie."

"Oh, Hugh!" She tossed her head, pleased. It was true, she thought. She had not changed. Not much, anyway. Religious dieting, the daily torture of exercise, massage, acupuncture, creams and potions from all corners of the globe, and the impossible-to-detect skills of a Park Avenue specialist, applied at the crucial moment several years ago before she really *needed* any cosmetic surgery—these had kept time standing still for Bobbie's reflection that she scrutinized in the mirror every morning. But how much longer, she wondered, could she hold the vicious markings of age at bay?

"We never saw enough of you in Kentucky," she said.

"A couple of weekends a year is about all I've ever been able to manage down there."

"Ah, but they were always the best weekends."

Hugh raised his glass to her. Bobbie toasted him back with Perrier. "Here's to Kentucky," Hugh said. "What was it they used to say . . . 'Land of fast horses and beautiful women'?"

"I think it was the other way around." Bobbie laughed. "Oh, Hugh, do you remember that midnight swimming party at your farm?"

"Oh, God . . . where you were accidentally changing in the wrong bath house, and I walked in on you?"

"Yes, only I have a confession to make, after all these years. It wasn't accidental. And I wanted you to stay."

Hugh Marshall looked agreeably shocked. "Why, Bobbie, I never guessed . . ."

"Yes, I know. Oh, well . . . and when I think of all the delicious scandals that were daily fare down there in the horsy set. We would have been a tasty one, wouldn't we?"

"On your account certainly . . . not mine."

"Don't be so modest. You were the talk of the powder room back then. And you've only grown more attractive."

"Well . . . perhaps I could walk in on you again sometime."

Bobbie smiled. "Perhaps you could."

* * *

Tasha was in her study-office, going over some sketches for her spring collection, when Billy Youngblood returned home, drunk and singing to himself.

"Ah, here you are, my lovely." Billy blew Tasha a kiss on his way over to the huge mahogany bar he had had imported from his favorite pub in England.

Tasha didn't bother to look up. "Tell me the truth. Did you go to Matt Phillips's press party?" They had fought about it earlier. She had refused to go, and had forbidden Billy to.

"Of course, honey. It's important to show up at those shindigs. Tim Yates introduced me to that guy Shaw, the president of Keller Perfumes. He was sloshed and didn't realize who I was until the end of the conversation. . . ."

Tasha cut him off sharply. "You *know* I didn't want you to show your face at that party."

"The point is . . ." Billy sauntered over to the sofa and flopped down with his feet up. "The point is that I found out some useful information."

"Stop beating around the bush! What did you find out?"

"First of all, they're not much farther ahead of schedule than we are. They don't have names for the fragrances yet. *Or* the fragrances themselves . . . or the packaging. And Shaw told me that Matt Phillips was beside himself when you announced our perfume first. . . ."

"It's not 'our' perfume, it's my . . ."

"Now, darlin', keep things in perspective. It's our perfume because I'm putting up the money for it. According to the papers we've signed, you've *leased* me your name for a perfume. According to these very same papers, you don't have enough influence to amount to a hill of beans over the Tasha Powers perfume. . . ."

"*What?* The papers I signed didn't say any such thing."

"The papers you *signed* certainly did. The papers you looked at *before* you signed . . . were a little different. I made a few last-minute changes to protect myself and my investment."

Tasha turned white. She raced across the room "You double-crossed me! You rotten son of a bitch . . ."

"Now, now, sweet lamb. It's *my* money, and you haven't been very nice to me lately. I just need a little insurance that you're not gonna take my money and run. You know I'm just wild about you, my little hothead." Billy smiled triumphantly

(181)

at her. "Now . . . if your temper tantrum's over, why don't you fix your sweet Billy another bourbon?"

Tasha felt numb with loathing. She was a hell of a good designer, but she knew she wasn't much of a businesswoman. She walked slowly over to the bar and fixed Billy a drink. Then she poured one for herself. Billy had the upper hand, but only in this round. She would get the best of her husband one of these days.

Hugh Marshall drew up the knot in his Cerruti tie. Before putting on his jacket he came and sat again on the edge of the bed where Bobbie lay, her slim body covered only by the peach satin sheet trimmed in lace. He ran his hand along her side and over her breast. She smiled up at him.

"I wish you didn't have to go."

"I'm sorry. I have some papers to go over tonight, and a couple of children who expect Daddy to be there in the morning."

He stood and put on his jacket. His eyes fell on a photograph of Tyger, smiling from a jeweled frame on the dresser.

Marshall's driver was asleep behind the wheel of the long black Rolls-Royce Silver Shadow II. Marshall climbed in and tapped the window. The chauffeur woke up and started the limousine, and they drove home through empty streets.

He would have to be careful, Marshall thought. He did not want to become involved with Roberta Rowan. He did not want to become involved with any woman now. But especially Bobbie. She was Tyger's mother, though they could easily pass for sisters, and Bobbie was enormously, dangerously attractive. But it came too close to violating his cardinal rule on the separation of business and social life.

It was more than that, too, he knew, but he would not let himself think about it.

CHAPTER EIGHTEEN

"I LIKE Magic," Jess said.

"I'm leaning toward Jazz Age, or maybe Pizazz," Connie said.

Tyger consulted the master list of potential perfume names. "What about just plain Jazz? It says it all . . . hot, cool, sophisticated, earthy. It has a lot of possibilities for ads and promotion. . . ."

"Hmmm. Jazz. Yeah, I really like it," Connie agreed. "What do you think, Shel?"

Shaw was distracted. He often was at their Tuesday-morning meetings. "I'm sorry. What did you say?"

"Tune in, Sheldon. We're going over perfume names, remember?" Connie was annoyed with Shaw, and she was the only one who dared ride him when he appeared preoccupied. "What do you think about Jazz?"

"It's good . . . good."

Jess hung up the phone. "I tried it out on my wife. She has a great sense about these things. She loves Jazz. I'm going to take a straw poll around the office." He left the room.

Connie dug back into Shaw. "You only think it's good? Do you have any better ideas?"

"No, Connie. You misunderstood me. I really like Jazz. It's the one I've been zeroing in on."

Jess returned. "Thumbs up. Shall we adopt it?"

"I vote yes," Connie said. "Or we can live with it for a couple of days and make sure it wears well. . . ."

"No, this has to be the final decision." Shaw pulled himself together. "The designer has to do up the logo. The Rainier woman has to get started with the packaging. We have to commit."

"You're right, Sheldon. I agree." Tyger had been making an effort to get along with Shaw. They didn't like each other, but she knew she was the one who ultimately had to make the best of it.

"Call Matt Phillips and fill him in," Shaw ordered. He was glad that Tyger had to deal with Phillips. At least she was good for something.

"Okay, now what about the men's fragrance? Are we going with Matt Phillips for Men?"

"I think so," Connie said. "It's straightforward. I don't like macho names for men's products anyway. Jess?"

Jess nodded. "I don't think we can go wrong with that. They're doing a big push on Matt's new men's-clothing line, and we'll get a good free ride off that."

"Sheldon?" Connie asked.

"Yes." Shaw penciled it in on his yellow pad. "It's a name men will be comfortable with."

"It's certainly a name Matt will be comfortable with." Tyger laughed. "Great. I'll give him both decisions right away."

"Oh . . . the most important news, and I almost forgot to tell you." Jess was beaming. "Hold onto your hats. Tom Sullivan, the best salesman Halston's got, is coming over to us. He says he wants a challenge . . . the job at Halston's getting too comfortable for him." Jess laughed self-consciously. "I assured him that working at Keller Perfumes should be challenging enough."

"Terrific, Jess," Connie enthused. "Sullivan's supposed to be the one who really made Halston a big honcho in the designer perfume market."

Shaw looked annoyed. "You should've checked with me first, Jess. It's up to me to approve new appointments."

"Sorry, Shel, but there wasn't time. Tom was available, and everything just fell into place. Marshall told me to line up the best salesman in the business, and to make it worth his while to come over to us . . ."

"Who are you taking orders from?" Shaw exploded. "Me or Hugh Marshall? *I'm* the president of Keller Perfumes. Don't forget it."

Jess's face turned red. "I know, Shel. It's just that . . ." He shut up. "Sorry, Shel. It won't happen again."

After the meeting Connie Larcada marched into Shaw's office and closed the door behind her.

"What was that all about? Poor Jess. You embarrassed him to death, in front of us all. What got into you? Sometimes I can't figure you out."

Shaw was still seething. "Dammit, Connie, it's about time things got straightened out about who's running this company. I'm the president. But every time I turn around Hugh Marshall's butting in, until my own staff doesn't know who to listen to! What does Marshall think I am, some sort of office furniture?"

"I'm sure he doesn't mean it that way," Connie soothed. "But you know how important this company is to Marshall. He's probably just . . ."

"Important to him? What about *me?*" Shaw's face was so red now that Connie began to grow alarmed. She was relieved when he loosened his tie and unbuttoned his collar. "I've worked my whole career for Kellerco. I've gone where they wanted and done what they wanted . . . I've shaken the right hands and said the right words and kissed the right asses, and finally Nelson Bachrach notices and gives me the job I should have had ten years ago. President of a company. A goddam perfume company, but a presidency, at last. And what happens? It's the pet project of Hugh Marshall, pride of the Harvard Business School, the boy wonder who started at the top! Well, I want him off my back, Connie. It's my job, *my* company, and I want him off my back!"

"Well, then, get him off!"

"What?"

"Get him off. Take charge, Sheldon. Take control. You can do it!"

"Yes, well, that's easy to say." Shaw opened the desk drawer where he kept a glass and his private reserve of vodka, and poured a fast drink. When he had downed it, he refilled the glass. He looked at Connie, breathing hard still, but calmer. "That's easy enough to say. With a man like Marshall, though, you've got to be careful. You can't just come right out and tell him to fuck off. . . ."

Connie shook her head. "There's a lot more you can do just by taking hold here, Shel. You know, just . . . being here in the office more, being on top of things . . . reading the staff

reports more carefully. Sometimes at meetings it seems like
. . ." She broke off. He was glaring at her with such anger that
it frightened her. "I'm not trying to tell you your job, Sheldon.
It's just . . ."

"Yes?"

"Nothing . . . I don't know. . . ."

"It's just that all of you think you can do it better than me.
That's it, isn't it? You, Jess, and that little bitch, Tyger. You
all think you know so goddam much! Well, let me tell you, I
was organizing companies when you were swapping comic
books. I was mentioned in *Business Week* back in 1965 as a
young executive to watch, when you were still learning how
to use carbon paper! I know what I'm doing here. . . ."

"Then *do* it, Sheldon." Connie's eyes were shining, and she
took hold of Sheldon's arms. "You're fabulous when you're
like this. You can do anything, I know you can. You make up
your mind, darling, and there's nothing you can't do."

Shaw put down his glass and pulled Connie to him. He
kissed her savagely, exultantly, and she could feel him hard
and throbbing against her belly. As his hand slid up the back
of her skirt and began to tug down at her panty hose, she
pulled her mouth away.

"Sheldon, we can't, not here . . . Ginger might . . ."

Without stopping what he was doing, Shaw reached across
and turned the lock on his door. Then he lowered Connie
until she could feel the cool leather of the sofa against her
naked buttocks and thighs. She knew that there was nothing
she could say to stop him; and even if she had thought
of something, she would not have dreamed of saying
it.

Tyger met Tim Yates for lunch at Pearl's, on West Forty-
eighth. Miss Pearl greeted Tyger, inquired about her mother,
and cast a cool, appraising glance over Tim before seating
them near the center of the long, narrow room with its dark
mirrors and slanting ceiling. Tyger, leaning forward to be
heard over the room's impossible acoustics, filled Tim in on
the morning meeting.

"I like the names," he said. "What was Phillips's reaction?"

"He liked Jazz, in spite of himself. And he's wild about
Matt Phillips for Men."

"I should rather think he would be. It reflects his own
sexual philosophy."

"He was actually in a pretty good mood today. I suppose a

lot does depend on how things are going with Garry Gray at any given moment.'"

"So then . . . everything's in good shape?"

Tyger grimaced. "Comparatively speaking. I'd be happier if we weren't constantly having to play catch-up with Tasha Powers."

Tim nodded. "Extraordinary thing, isn't it? It does sometimes seem that when an idea gets in the air, everybody starts grabbing at it."

"I hope that's all it is." Tyger sighed. "I don't know. Billy Youngblood seems to be keeping a step ahead of us at every turn, and I just don't believe he's that smart."

Yates looked interested. "What do you mean?"

"Oh, I don't know. He could have a spy . . . but I suppose it's nothing that dramatic. I guess it's hard to keep a project like this from leaking a little here and there. But I don't trust Youngblood. I don't think there's a principle in his entire body."

"I don't know him personally . . . but from what I've heard, you're probably right." Yates let his neck fall forward while he quickly massaged it with one hand. There were lines of strain around his eyes.

"You look as if you've been up all night," Tyger said.

"The past three. I don't know how Hugh can do it. He's forty, I'm twenty-nine, and he has ten times the energy I have. He thrives on work. . . ."

"What's going on to keep you so busy?"

"A merger. Keller Copper has just taken over Consolidated Metals, and it's a bloody mess. ConMet's a disaster. It's all very complicated, and Nelson Bachrach isn't helping things any. If he'd just let Hugh handle it, but, you know, he won't give Hugh credit for anything."

"Surely he agrees that Kellerco's doing better than ever under Hugh's leadership. Kellerco's moving up on *Fortune's* Five Hundred list. Eight years ago it wasn't even listed. . . ."

"Sounds as if you've been reading our annual report. I think Bachrach has some sort of personal grudge against Marshall. Probably because of Hugh's upper-class background. Bachrach worked his way up and obviously feels everyone else should do the same."

"But who does Bachrach think would run the company better?" Tyger picked up her chopsticks and took a bite of Pearl's famous lemon chicken.

"Oh, God, who knows? Perhaps the old goat is getting

senile. I suspect he's jealous of Hugh. I think he hates being at the end of his career. He wants to be forty, like Hugh." Tim sighed. "For that matter, who can blame him? I bloody well don't look forward to getting old."

Tyger laughed. "Well, Tim, you have a way to go yet."

"I don't know. I'm going to be thirty next month. I'm not going places as fast as I'd hoped." Tim pushed his sea bass with pickled cucumber and scallions around on his plate.

"What do you mean? You're Hugh Marshall's right-hand man. You have a lot of responsibility. Thirty's not very old, you know," Tyger reminded him.

"It is when you've decided to be a millionaire by the time you're thirty-five. Right now I have five thousand dollars in the bank . . . and a long way to go."

Tyger realized that he was serious, and was intrigued. "Oh, Tim, you're going places. Anyone can see that."

"Well," he said quietly, "I have some irons in the fire."

The check came.

"Your expense account or mine?" Tyger asked.

"Mine." Tim laid his American Express card on the check, and the waiter took it away. "I say, Tyger, you wouldn't like to go out with me sometime, would you? In the evening, I mean?"

"Oh, Tim, I . . ."

He laughed nervously. "After all, we're both such slaves to Kellerco . . . who else would go out with me? The woman I've been seeing for the last few months finally told me to call her if I ever get a divorce from Hugh Marshall."

"What a great threesome we'd make." Tyger laughed. "You, me, and Hugh! Actually, Tim," she said kindly, "it's sweet of you to ask . . . but I've just broken up with someone. I've sworn off men while I try to get my life in shape."

She was sorry to hurt him. Tyger could tell that Tim Yates was shy with women, and that it had cost him to ask. But she also suspected that his interest in her was as much for her glamour—Tyger Hayes, Beautiful Person, International Set, Daughter of the legendary Harry Hayes and Lady Rowan—as for herself. And she did not want to become involved in that.

"Well, maybe next year," Tim said, camouflaging his disappointment. "In the meantime, at least, we have our lunches together. That will keep me going."

Tyger smiled. She looked forward to their lunches for another reason: Tim's closeness with Hugh Marshall.

* * *

From the bedroom came the muffled sound of televised laughter, and above it the sound of snoring. Louise Shaw had fallen asleep watching *The Tonight Show*. Sheldon Shaw sat in the living room, and J&B on the rocks on the table in front of him, alongside his open briefcase. He had used it as an excuse to send Louise to bed alone. He knew she would be snoring before *The Tonight Show* was half over. He wanted to think.

He could not stay with Louise much longer. She had grown old and defeated with him, and she accepted his defeat. She asked nothing of him now but financial support and occasional sex. The former he could give her; the latter was becoming more and more repugnant.

Connie Larcada was different. She was not young, but still sexually magnificent, with her red mouth and full, pillowy breasts with their dark nipples that stiffened to acorn hardness and made her cry out when he seized them in his lips.

And Connie believed in him. With Connie beside him, perhaps he *could* still do it. Perhaps he could pull it off, after all.

But at Kellerco . . . things had started so badly there. If he had a new start, a clean slate.

Perhaps he would call Billy Youngblood after all. At the press party at "21" Youngblood had seemed very anxious to talk to him about a job. Well, it couldn't hurt to hear what he had to say.

Inside the silver Bentley, rented for the occasion, Andy Parrish poured two mint juleps out of a pewter shaker. A man only in his middle thirties, his red hair was already interwoven with silver, but the freckles still abounded on his gently handsome, good-natured face. His black dinner clothes covered his lanky frame with elegant ease. Andy spoke with his characteristically slow Lexington accent.

"Ah know you were expecting champagne, but when you're with me you have to drink bourbon."

"I'll try, Andy. But you remember that night out on the south forty when you were trying to unbutton my blouse . . . and I threw up all over you. I haven't touched bourbon since then. That evening was not one of my finest moments."

"Oh, just part of growin' up." Andy laughed. "I had my heart set on scorin' that night, too. I hope you can hold your bourbon better tonight. I sure don't want you to embarrass me in front of all the celebrities," he teased.

They were on their way to a star-studded gala at Tavern on the Green for the "I Love New York" campaign. Andy Parrish came up from Kentucky a couple of times a year and always took Tyger out. He would have liked to be with her every night, but he knew she was not interested in him romantically.

The huge party was exactly as expected: crowded and boring. Tyger had been to a hundred such events and she could walk through them in her sleep. The food was predictably spectacular, the music expertly unobtrusive. The faces were the same ones that appeared with regularity in the society columns of Eugenia Sheppard and Suzy Knickerbocker. John and Mary Lindsay, Liza Minnelli, Halston, Bill and Pat Buckley, Andy Warhol with his pet tape recorder "Sony," Betty Bacall, Beverly Sills, Marylou and Cornelius Vanderbilt Whitney, Joseph Papp, and several hundred other famous New Yorkers mingled and mixed in the Garden, the Crystal Room and the Elm Tree Room.

Andy got a kick out of checking out the season's crop of debutantes. Tyger entered into the spirit of the party by helping him figure out which ones he could go to bed with after one date or two. Andy eliminated the ones who would take longer than two evenings.

"Look at that blonde over there, the one with her hair in Bo Derek braids around her head. What do you think?" Andy asked.

Tyger scrutinized her. "Yours in about ten minutes."

"Well, you're wrong. I took her out last time I was in town. She required two dates . . . including dinners at Le Cirque *and* the Palace. Hey! Look over there. Isn't that Bobbie with Hugh Marshall? Well . . . well. Lightnin' seems to be strikin' twice."

Bobbie looked marvelous in a green taffeta-and-velvet ballgown by Galanos. She was surrounded by half a dozen men, captivating them with effervescent chitchat. Hugh Marshall was standing next to her, as apparently mesmerized as the others. As Tyger watched, Hugh put his arm around Bobbie's shoulder, whispered something into her ear, and they melted away from her admirers and off into the crowd together.

"I didn't know Bobbie and Hugh were an item these days," Andy said.

"I didn't either." Tyger tried hard to stifle her jealousy. "Andy . . . what did you mean by 'lightning striking twice'?"

He shrugged. "It was a rumor—I'm not at all sure it was true—that when Bobbie and Cappy were married she had an affair with Hugh Marshall." Andy steered Tyger through the crowd. "It's hard to believe, because Hugh's never spent enough time in Kentucky to get anything going. He flies in for a weekend now and then. Come on, let's find them. I want to say hello. . . ."

Tyger wasn't sure she could stomach seeing Bobbie with Hugh Marshall, but had to make the best of it. Her mother spotted them first, and rushed over.

"Why, darling! You look divine, absolutely shimmering. You seem only to wear Matt Phillips's clothes these days. Well, never mind. They suit you. Andy! How lovely to see you. I was thrilled when your horse won the Derby this spring. You know, I miss Kentucky. . . ." She paused for breath.

Andy beamed. Even though she was eleven years older than he was, Bobbie had always attracted him. "Why don't you come down and visit me? Everyone in Lexington is so impressed that you became a lady after you divorced Cappy. . . ."

"Oh, Andy," she cooed, "you know I was a lady even when I was married to Cappy. How is he anyway?"

"Fine. He and Lucy Anne just had a baby girl. . . ."

"My God! At his age?"

While Andy and Bobbie gossiped about mutual friends, Hugh Marshall turned to Tyger.

"You always look smashing, day and night." He continued without waiting for her flattered response, "I tried to reach you at the office this afternoon but you had already left."

Business, Tyger thought, always business. "I left early to drop some things off for Matt Phillips. . . ."

"I heard from Martine Rainier. She's coming to town in two weeks to show us her rough ideas for the bottles."

"Great . . . terrific," Tyger said automatically.

"That doesn't sound very enthusiastic," Hugh said. "What's the matter? Has Matt Phillips succeeded in turning you against Martine?"

"Of course not, Hugh. I'm not impressionable." Tyger's temper was showing, and she tried to smooth it over. "I guess I am dreading Martine's appearance. There'll be a real clash of egos between her and Matt. And I'm going to be right in the middle, trying to field the blows."

Hugh laughed. "Let's hope it doesn't come to that. I see what you mean, though."

Bobbie flashed Hugh a warm smile and slipped her arm in his. Hugh looked at her, then back at Tyger, slightly distracted. It was impossible for Tyger to tell what he was thinking as he looked from mother to daughter. Or what he felt about Bobbie. "You can handle Martine," he continued. "You obviously impressed her in Paris."

Obviously, thought Tyger. If Hugh only knew the half of it. "I'll do my best."

Bobbie broke in. "Tyger, dear, let's have a long lunch soon. To catch up."

"Love to, Mother." Tyger had to get away before she exploded. "Andy and I were just heading off, to a livelier party downtown. See you soon." She grabbed Andy, and they hurried away.

"Jesus, Tyger," Andy said in the limousine, "Ah was havin' a real good time. It was lively enough for me there."

"It was *too* lively for me. Can you take me home, please?"

"What's the matter? Ah thought we were goin' to another party."

"There *isn't* another party. I just wanted to leave that one. You can go back after you've dropped me off."

"What's wrong? You're mad about somethin'. Are you mad at me?" Before she could answer, he went on, "Is it because I was flirtin' with your mother? I know she's your mother, but she's so good-lookin'. and ..." He trailed off. "I was only flirtin', Tyger. That's *all.*"

Even Andy was a member of Bobbie's fan club. It was almost too much to bear. When Tyger was around her mother she still felt as if there were braces on her teeth, and ten additional pounds plastered on each hip. "Oh, Andy, I'm not jealous of my mother. Really. No, the truth is, I have a splitting headache. Working too hard. . . ."

"Partying too hard would be more like it. Come on, Tyger. Having a job can't have changed you that much."

"It *has!*" Tyger snapped, then sighed. "Sorry, Andy, I didn't mean to bite your head off." The limousine pulled up in front of Tyger's building on Jane Street, and she got out quickly. "Go back and have a good time. And ... please forgive me. Call next time you're in town."

"Oh, Ah will, Tyger. Ah always love seein' you. Wait, let me take you to your door. . . ." But Tyger was already inside the lobby by the time he had finished the sentence. "Might as well head back to Tavern on the Green," Andy told the driver.

Tyger smoked half a joint and called Jake. "Are you busy?"

"Believe it or not, I'm in the darkroom."

"Well, get into the bedroom. I'm coming over."

"Sure," said Jake, surprised. "Great!"

"No strings, though. Just a good time."

Jake sighed. "Okay, Tyger. I guess I have to take what I can get. Come on over."

In five minutes, Tyger had changed from her gown into baggy jeans and a pink silk T-shirt, and was racing in a cab toward Jake's. She was still ticked off about this evening, ticked off at Hugh Marshall, ticked off at her mother, and ticked off at herself for being ticked off. Sex, at least, would be distracting for the time being.

CHAPTER NINETEEN

BY EARLY October there was a chill to the air. Joggers in Central Park had to run through a thick carpet of golden leaves. At Kennedy Airport, the skinny trees near the International Arrivals building were already bare.

An impatient Tyger paced near the arrival gate watching the passengers from Air France Flight No. 458 trickle out of customs. Where in the devil was Martine? As a first-class passenger she should have been through passport control and customs long before now.

"Oh, Tyger! Tyger! Over here!" Martine waved from a nearby exit door. She looked awesomely chic, wearing a man's gray fedora and a patchwork coat by Chantal Thomass. *"Merde!* They have managed to lose one of my valises. Or maybe it's been stolen. I knew I never should have come to New York. Bad things always happen to me when I'm here." She stopped complaining long enough to kiss Tyger on both cheeks. "Hello, *ma chère*. It is wonderful to see you again." Martine headed off, cursing in French, to report her loss.

Tyger wished Martine had mailed her sketches instead of bringing them over, since duty as Martine's official escort would not be confined to the hours between nine and five. But she didn't have a choice. Hugh Marshall was relying on her to keep Martine in good spirits during her visit. If things didn't go well, Martine might quit and take her designs right back to Paris.

First on Tyger's agenda, in the limousine into Manhattan,

was to inform Martine that Jeff Stein was doing the bottles for Matt Phillips for Men.

"Merde! Merde! Merde!" was Martine's response. "The look between the two perfumes should be in *harmony*. This idea of two different designers is a disaster! Whose idea was it, anyway?"

"I don't remember . . . but it was decided on by Hugh Marshall and Matt Phillips. Hugh knew that your name would add *éclat* to the women's perfume, but felt that men wouldn't . . ." Tyger stopped short, realizing that she had said the wrong thing. People with egos as large as Martine's expected *everyone* to know who they were. "I mean . . ."

"I know what you mean, Tyger." Martine lit a Gauloise and exhaled noisily. "Let's drop it. I am much too busy to do the men's packaging anyway." She shrugged. "It's their loss. My designs for the Jazz bottles are incredible. You will love them."

Tyger accompanied Martine to the suite at the Carlyle Hotel which Kellerco owned. When the company was not using it for clients, the Carlyle rented it back to accommodate their overflow.

"You must be tired," Tyger said. "Why don't you get some rest before the meeting?" She looked at her Cartier tank watch. "I have to get back to the office, but I'll send the car to pick you up at quarter of four. The bar and icebox are stocked, but if you need anything . . ."

"I'll be fine, *ma chère*." Martine kissed Tyger on both cheeks. "See you later."

Martine kicked off her boots and went into the kitchen. After pouring herself a glass of Badoit she sauntered back into the living room to get two aspirin from her handbag. The large room, decorated to Kellerco's specifications by Angelo Donghia, was carpeted in a practical chocolate brown. Two suede Casa Bella sofas rested at angles in front of the black marble fireplace, and between them nestled a knee-level Victorian roulette table. Over by the enormous picture window overlooking Central Park, two bamboo-printed swivel chairs flanked a lacquered backgammon table.

Martine lit a cigarette and wandered into one of the two bedrooms. She sat on the chrome-and-mirrored king-size bed. "I will remain pleasant," she whispered to herself, stretching out and laying her head back on the pillows. "I will be calm. . . ." She was, in truth, angry that she had not been hired to design the men's packaging for Keller Perfumes. She leaned over and crushed her cigarette into the ash tray on the bedside table.

Martine had made a decision: it was time for her to become as in demand in America as she was in Europe. There was a lot of money to be made on this side of the Atlantic. And she needed money. She had a habit of spending it as fast as she made it, but she had recently turned thirty, and she had to start saving for the villa in Cap d'Antibes. It had been built by her grandfather in the early Twenties. Her father had been forced to sell it when he went bankrupt in 1970, shortly before he died. Now it was owned by a loathsome bourgeois family who were letting it fall into disrepair. She had to get it back from them, at any cost.

Jess brought Tom Sullivan, the new head salesman, around to Tyger's office to introduce them. Sullivan had just started work at Keller Perfumes. He looked boyish, with carrot hair and freckles left over from a summer of sailing in the Sound.

"Tyger, I have a hunch you may be able to help Tom. He's practically got Marge Francisco at Bloomingdale's eating out of his hand. . . ."

"Nothing's set," Tom hastened to add. "You have to keep your fingers crossed in this business." Tyger was surprised by Tom's softspokenness. She had expected someone overbearing, boisterous. "Marge Francisco, especially, is a will o' the wisp," Tom said. "Anyway, I had lunch with a mutual friend today and discovered something I never knew. Marge is an admirer of your mother's. . . ."

"This is where you come in, Tyger," said Jess.

"Okay. I'll ask Mother to fit you in for a lunch."

"By tomorrow, Tyger? Or the next day, at the latest?"

"Jesus, you guys don't ask much, do you? Don't you think I'm busy enough without running little errands for you?"

Tom smiled. "I'm prepared to bribe you with two tickets to *Tosca* at the Met. Dress Circle. Pavarotti. Tonight."

"It's a deal. I'll give her a call after the meeting."

Tyger looked at her watch. Three. Time to call Martine at the Carlyle and wake her: she was to present her sketches in an hour.

Everyone was assembled in the conference room at Keller Perfumes, except Matt Phillips. Hugh Marshall as usual was pressed for time, and anxious for the meeting to begin.

"I can't imagine where Matt is. I spoke to him an hour ago,

(196)

and he was on his way." Tyger dreaded the encounter between Martine and Matt. She had a feeling that they would hate each other on sight.

"Never mind, Tyger," Hugh Marshall said. "This gives me a chance to welcome Mademoiselle Rainier informally. Let's see, Martine, has Tyger introduced you to everyone here?"

"Bien sûr . . ."

At that moment, Matt Phillips arrived—with Jeff Stein, the designer for the men's packaging. After the introductions, Martine flashed Tyger a look that would wither daisies. Hugh Marshall glanced at Tyger with astonishment. Tyger shrugged, to indicate that she had had no idea that this was going to happen. Matt, however, bailed her out.

"I was leaving my office to come here when I ran into Jeff, with his roughs for the men's line. I decided to bring him along so he could show them to you directly." He looked at Martine, who was frowning. "You don't mind, do you, Miss Rainier?" He mispronounced it Rain-near instead of Rain-ee-yea, on purpose.

Tyger scribbled a note, in French, to Martine, apologizing for Matt's thoughtlessness, although she was sure that Matt was being rude deliberately. Martine had figured it out, too, and appeared tense.

"All right," Marshall said. "Let's get on with it. Martine, we're ready to see your designs. I feel like a kid on Christmas morning, anxious to see what Santa's left under the tree." Hugh Marshall seldom resorted to such blatant folksiness, but the circumstances demanded it. The atmosphere in the boardroom was as heavy as the air before a summer cloudburst.

With the composure of a professional, Martine rose and walked over to a large easel and propped her sketch boards against it, still covered. "First, let me say that I am pleased that Keller Perfumes wanted me as their designer for Jazz. And for giving me free rein of my imagination. Many companies want a designer, but it turns out that they already have a specific idea in mind. All they really need is a draftsperson. . . ." Martine paused and looked around the room, establishing eye contact with everyone present except Matt Phillips, who was examining his fingernails.

"Bien . . ." she continued. "I am most excited . . . both with the concept of your perfume and with my designs. Sometimes I must struggle to get what I want. Other times there is a flow. It is as if the idea is waiting in the air for the right

person to transform it into a realistic design. Those compositions are always the best—and the ones that win awards. I know you will like what I have created for Jazz, because these designs are absolutely right for your perfume. And *voilà* . . ." She showed her series of sketches. Martine was right; false modesty would have been out of place, as well as out of character. Her designs were spectacular. The perfume bottle was sleek and beautiful: a vertically pentagonal crystal-clear flacon with an opaque crystal trumpet sculpted onto the stopper. The cologne bottle was a larger version, without the trumpet. Instead, black-painted music notes framed the red lettering of "Jazz" which ran vertically down the bottle. The boxes were patterned in red-and-blue foil with red-and-blue embossed "Jazz" letters—the "ja" etched in blue on red foil, the "zz" in red, on blue foil. Everyone in the room was impressed. Even Matt Phillips nodded, grudgingly.

It was a hard act to follow, and Jeff Stein's look for Matt Phillips for Men was more conventional. Hugh Marshall voiced several objections, although the others thought the large brown rectangular bottles were workable. Marshall, however, had specific suggestions for Stein, and Stein agreed to modify his designs accordingly, and to change the color to navy, so the men's and women's colors would be complementary for combined display.

The afternoon was a triumph for Martine Rainier. In spite of her haughty French indifference, Tyger could see that she was pleased by the reception. Her high spirits when the meeting was over indicated to Tyger that Martine had been nervous about submitting her designs. She was not as secure as she appeared to be.

After the meeting, Tyger arranged the luncheon for Tom Sullivan, and then she and Martine went for a drink with Connie. Martine was relaxed, and was as effervescent as a girl who has received an invitation to her first prom.

"Did you see Hugh"—she pronounced it "you"—"Marshall's face when I showed my perfume-bottle design? He looked like a proud papa! He was so pleased."

"Matt Phillips was prepared to hate your designs, but aesthetically you're on the same wavelength, if nothing else." Connie liked the young Frenchwoman, even though she knew she would never be that young again, or that skinny, or that chic.

Tyger nursed her white-wine spritzer. "Tomorrow I'll talk to the prospective bottle and box manufacturers and get prices. Then you can interview them, Martine, and figure out which one will work best to your specifications."

Martine looked at Connie. "Is Tyger always like this—work, work, work?"

"Yeah, lately. I think she's hooked on it. Just like you, I'd guess. Me, too, only with a difference."

"What?" Tyger asked.

"I *have* to work. To support my expensive life-style—you know, eating, living in a tiny penthouse with a twenty-degree slice of the East River . . ."

Martine lit a Gauloise from her second pack of the day. "I grew up with everything. My mother was even minor royalty. But my father was a gambler, of sorts. He lost it all. My mother married my sister off to a rich Swiss architect. When it was my turn, I chose design school instead. I also worked as a model. My mother was horrified when I announced that I preferred working to settling down with a boring young man with a golden future. Until the day she died, she thought I was some kind of freak." Martine laughed. "Now whenever I visit my sister, *she* tries to play matchmaker. But I'll never get married. I like my life just as it is."

"I feel pretty much the same way," Tyger said. "But that's with two mistakes behind me."

Connie smiled ruefully. "I wish I could be twenty-six again and feel that way. I always wanted to get married and never had the right offer. Oh, there were proposals here and there, but I was always looking for . . . well, I guess I'm not sure what I was looking for. But I never expected the time to go by so fast. . . ." She finished her scotch. "Well, I'm happy now raising Tina—my sister's daughter. My life would be pretty empty without her. Don't either of you think about having a child someday?"

Martine's face hardened. "No. Never! Why would anyone want to bring a child into today's world? It's madness!"

"What about you, Tyger?" Connie asked.

"Oh, I don't know what my life's going to be like tomorrow, much less a few years from now. No plans." Tyger smiled. She supposed she fit in somewhere between her two friends. She was not sure she never wanted children. She had always vaguely supposed they would come in time, like crow's feet. But she was not anxious to have them any time soon.

Tyger looked at Connie with curious sympathy. *I never expected the time to go by so fast. . . .* Connie did not seem so very much older, and yet so much was already closing off to her.

After the opera that evening, Martine tried to convince Tyger to go to Régine's.

"No, Martine. It's been a long day. I'm tired."

"But, Tyger, some friends are meeting me there. I think you will like them. . . ."

"No, really, I'll pass." She kissed Martine's cheeks. "See you tomorrow."

Tyger was relieved to be rid of Martine for the rest of the night. So far, neither of them had made any reference to that night in Paris.

Tyger was sound asleep when the phone jarred her. She reached for it slowly.

"Hello, Tyger, sorry to wake you. . . ." Martine's voice spilled rapidly into the phone. "But I am so angry I could scream. I am ready to cancel the deal with Keller Perfumes. I don't care about the money . . . I've had it!"

Tyger sat up in bed and turned on the light. She tried to conceal her anger at being awakened in the middle of the night. She wasn't in the mood to play games. "Martine, please. Tell me what's wrong."

Tyger could hear the Frenchwoman lighting a cigarette. "I can't go into it over the phone. I will come over. . . ."

So that's what it was all about, thought Tyger. Martine wanted an excuse to visit her at home. "Okay, Martine. Twelve Jane Street."

"I'll be there in five minutes."

For the next hour, Martine ranted nonstop. The object of her tirade was Matt Phillips. She had run into him and Garry Gray at Régine's and they had been totally obnoxious to her. She had risen above Matt's rudeness at the afternoon's meeting, but she was deeply offended by his nocturnal behavior.

"He said the most appalling things to me! I know he was drunk or stoned . . . but that's no excuse. Matt was being vulgar on purpose. He introduced me to his friends as 'the famous French bitch'!" She took Tyger's hands and held onto them tightly. "Oh, Tyger . . . I refuse to have my name associated with that man! I cannot give my talent to *his* perfume."

Tyger could understand why Martine was upset, and knew she would have to do some fast talking to get Martine to change her mind about walking out on Kellerco. "I don't know why he behaved that way. He liked your designs at the meeting today. . . ."

"Of course he did. My bottles are great—any fool can see that. He's jealous!"

"Hmmm. You're probably right. He agreed to give up creative control, and is only a consultant. I know he regrets that decision. . . ."

"Wait until he takes one of his collections to Paris," Martine interrupted. "I'll make sure he gets the same treatment there that he has given me. Only double!" She was getting worked up again. "God, I hate bitchy, self-indulgent men. They think they're so much better than women. But we know women are better! In every way. . . ." Martine's voice softened. She still held Tyger's hands.

Ever since the Frenchwoman had arrived Tyger felt that Martine was particularly warm toward her. But Tyger had not figured out whether Martine's feelings were sexual or not. The French were more openly sensual and tactile than the Americans. They touched each other more, out of habit.

Tyger did not want to go to bed with Martine. On the other hand, she could hardly make an issue of it until she was absolutely certain that Martine was angling in that direction. First she had to smooth things over so Martine would not head back to France with her designs. Hugh was counting on her; she could not let him down.

"Martine, the Jazz bottles are fabulous. You're getting a lot of money for them . . . and we'll gain a lot of prestige by having your name associated with our perfume. . . ."

"That's just the point! My name is *not* going to be linked with Keller Perfumes . . . but with Matt Phillips. That pig! I would rather die than have his name on my bottles."

"But the promotion will say, 'Bottles by Martine Rainier.' That gives you credit, separate from Matt. . . ."

"No . . . not even if Matt Phillips crawled on his belly through that door, not even then would I forgive him! And that *trou de cul*, his lover . . ."

"Garry."

"He's worse than Matt. Do you know he even insulted the friends I was with? And Régine, poor thing, was so upset that it was happening in her club. . . ."

"Martine, I can't make excuses for Matt. Who knows what goes on in his mind? But you can't let yourself take it personally. . . ."

"Not take it personally!" Martine's voice trembled with rage.

"Wait! Listen . . . you've done the Jazz bottles—and they're brilliant. You're being well paid, and you're heading back to Paris in a few days. You never need to see Matt Phillips again. . . ."

"Merde!" Martine threw her cigarette into the ash tray.

"Martine, Jazz will make you famous over here. Other American companies will fight to get you. Don't run away now."

Martine opened a new pack of Gauloises and lit one. "Oh, I don't know. I hate Matt Phillips! Flashes of what he said tonight keep coming back to me."

Tyger was exasperated. Martine was not giving up, and she and Matt both had such overblown egos. Tyger knew there was not a chance in the world of persuading Matt to apologize. She tried again. "Martine, you've got to turn the other cheek. You're a professional, hired for a specific job. There's an American expression, 'Take the money and run.' "

Martine sipped from the snifter of cognac Tyger had poured her. She put the glass down and ran her hands through her short hair, bending her neck and letting her head tilt toward her lap. She took a deep breath and expelled it slowly. Then she sat up again. She said nothing.

Tyger sighed. "Look, Martine, I'll level with you. I brought you in on this . . . and it's going to look really bad for me if you back out now. We need you, Martine. I need you."

Martine brought her head slowly around until her eyes met Tyger's. The smoke from the Gauloise that dangled from her lips rose like a mist between them. It shielded Martine's eyes from Tyger.

"Poor Tyger," Martine said. Her voice was softer now; softer, but not quite yielding. *"C'est très important, hein?* It means very much to you?"

"My job, probably. And the project. We've all worked pretty hard on it."

"You would be unhappy to lose your job?"

"You know I would."

Martine reached out and trailed her fingertips along the line of Tyger's cheekbone. "I do not want you to be unhappy," she murmured. She dropped her cigarette into the ash tray, and through the smokeless air her brown eyes seared into Tyger's.

Well, thought Tyger, *it's happening.* She had known this

moment would come since she had learned from Hugh of Martine's visit to New York. She had alternately put it out of her mind and planned sophisticated ways of handling it. But coming now, in this mood, in this context—would she have to make love to Martine to keep her job?

She was stunned by the thought, and by the hypnotic deep stare of Martine's eyes, and she scarcely realized that Martine's fingers were traveling down the polished shell buttons of her robe, deftly flicking them undone. Tyger's mind was racing, but her hands never moved from her sides as the robe fell open. Martine eased it back from her shoulders, and it slipped to her naked waist.

"Tyger," Martine said huskily, "I love you." She caressed the tips of Tyger's breasts, and then her arms encircled Tyger and drew her close into a deep, probing kiss.

Tyger felt neither revulsion nor passion at the embrace. She felt only a sharp pang of pity. She waited a moment, and then pushed Martine gently away.

"I'm sorry," she said. "But no, Martine. I like you very much. I want us to be friends. But that's as far as it can go with me."

For a moment there was anger in Martine's eyes, then hurt. And then there was something more painful that Tyger had never seen there before: confusion. "But Tyger," she said, "in Paris . . ." Martine shook her head, a quick, angry movement, but this time the anger was directed at herself. She turned away and lit another cigarette, and when she turned back again there was a wry, controlled smile behind the blue curtain of smoke.

"I know." Martine nodded. "It was Jake. He wanted it, not you. You only went along."

"I enjoyed it," Tyger admitted.

"But once is enough, eh? And only if there is a man around." Martine shrugged. "I like men too. I like both men and women. In the past few years I have come to prefer women. But you are the first woman since my dancing-school teacher that I have ever felt I loved."

"I'm fond of you, Martine. . . ."

Martine stood and walked over to the window. Tyger watched as she stared out into the empty Village street. Her body looked frail and weary slumped against the window casing.

"I once lived with a man for three years," Martine said. "Henri Lemoine, the Grand Prix racing driver." Tyger did not follow auto racing, but the name triggered a memory for her. "It was all very exciting. He was ridiculously handsome, *très romantique,* a fantastic lover. And the living with danger, too, with death—you cannot believe, Tyger, what an aphrodisiac. To know each time you hold your lover between your legs and caress him, so strong and alive, that it may be the last. . . .

"But I stupidly became *enceinte*—pregnant. And at first Henri seemed happy, and I was too, to be having a baby, his baby. But as my belly grew, he became more distant. He became afraid. This man, who was afraid of nothing, who could push a racing car to the edge of impossibility, was terrified to be the father of a little baby. And so finally I tried to abort myself. But it was too late. Then the baby was born two months early, dead, strangled with the umbilical cord around its neck. When Henri came to see me in the hospital, he looked so relieved, as if he had walked miraculously away from a terrible accident. And he said he was glad to see me looking so well, and that perhaps it was better if we decided not to see each other for a while."

"How awful." Tyger went and put a hand on Martine's shoulder. Martine's shoulders rose and fell with deep breathing, but she was not crying. Then the memory that the name had triggered came to Tyger.

"Henri Lemoine . . . he was killed last year, wasn't he?"

"Testing a new car for the Agnellis."

"Oh, Martine . . ."

Martine's face was pale and haggard in the gray light that was beginning to come in the window. "I'm so tired," she said. "Can I sleep here?"

Martine fell asleep without undressing. She was still asleep a few hours later when Tyger left for the office. Tyger had not asked her again what she intended to do about her Keller Perfumes commitment. She thought Martine's rage had burned itself out. But Martine was nothing if not unpredictable. However, Tyger decided, there was nothing more that she could do about it.

CHAPTER TWENTY

SHELDON Shaw felt better. He had not actually told Louise he was leaving her. He had said that he needed to get away and think for a few weeks. In the meantime, Connie had helped him move into an apartment that belonged to a friend of hers who was going to be away until January. By then, he would have broken the news to Louise, and he could move in with Connie.

He had cut down on his drinking. He had not had a single drop today. Of course, there was a reason: he had an appointment with Billy Youngblood. They were meeting for drinks after work, and Shaw didn't want to appear fuzzy.

Billy Youngblood had told Shaw at the Phillips press party at "21" that he would love to have a good man like Shaw in his camp. Shaw had been thinking about it more and more. He was leaving Louise; maybe he should leave Kellerco, too. There was not enough for him to do with Marshall taking such an unusual interest in the company. Shaw decided he would be in a stronger position with Connie, and feel better about himself, if he were hired away from Kellerco while he was still president of Keller Perfumes, before Marshall sacked him or the company failed and Bachrach kicked them both out. At any rate, it wouldn't hurt to have a drink with Youngblood, to put out feelers.

They met at Teacher's Pub on Broadway and Eightieth. Shaw had insisted on an out-of-the-way place where no one from Kellerco would be apt to run into them.

"Well, Sheldon, how the hell are you? I was glad to get your call." Billy Youngblood was sitting at a round table near the bar, wearing his usual Texas-Western garb.

"Hello, Youngblood."

"Call me Billy. My friends do."

The waitress came around, and Shaw ordered a martini.

"I'll have the same. On the rocks, with bourbon, and skip the vermouth and olive." Youngblood laughed loudly. "Well, Sheldon, I don't want you to give away any trade secrets, of course, but how's it goin' at your place?"

Shaw cleared his throat nervously. He wished the girl would hurry up with the drinks. "Oh, things are coming along fine. Right on schedule. How's your operation?"

"Great. Tasha's right on top of it. She's designin' great bottles. They're gonna cost me a fortune to have made up." He laughed jovially. The drinks arrived, and Shaw was relieved to hear Youngblood tell the waitress to bring another round.

Before long, they were on their third drink. Shaw liked Youngblood. He felt as if they were old friends. Youngblood was easy to talk to.

"What do you say we have one more?" Billy Youngblood said. "You're not in any kind of a rush, are you?" He paused. "You know, I'm not goin' to mince words. I like you, Shelley. Mind if I call you that? I have a feelin' that we're goin' to be great friends and drinkin' buddies. I like a man who can hold his liquor. And I have to say it . . . I wish you were workin' for me instead of Kellerco. We sure could use someone like you, with your experience in the field. . . ."

Shaw tried not to appear eager. "I appreciate that, Billy. It's a competitive business, no doubt about it. One has to keep on top of things."

"Mind if I level with you?" Youngblood said with sincerity.

"Of course not. Feel free."

"Well, the truth is, I'm not too interested in the perfume business. I started this company for Tasha, but as soon as it gets off the ground I'm pullin' out of the day-to-day operations. I want to free myself up for my other deals. Frankly, I've been lookin' for someone to take over, and head up Powers Perfumes for me. We're goin' into a lot of new products—hair, bath, cosmetics. I've been lookin' for a man like you." He leaned back and fished a long cigar from the pocket of his gaudy jacket. His eyes stayed on Shaw as he struck a match and held it to the tip. "Of course, I know it'd take a hell of a lot to lure you away from Kellerco. You've been there for twenty-five years."

"How did you know that?"

"Oh, when I'm interested in someone, I do some checking up. You're a good man, Shelley. I'm not goin' to pretend I don't know it."

"Thank you, Billy." Shaw cleared his throat again. "I've had a good run with Kellerco. I'm not anxious to leave. Of course, one has to keep an open mind to new opportunities. . . ." The meeting was going even better than Shaw had hoped.

Youngblood smiled. "I'm glad to hear it. What do you say? Let's have one more. . . ."

"Well . . . okay." Shaw seldom came across anybody else who could match him drink for drink.

"As I said, I know it'd take a lot to get you to leave Kellerco. But, Shelley, I'm prepared to offer you a helluva deal. Now, hear me out before you say anything . . . okay?"

"All right. I'll listen."

"I'm goin' to tell you somethin' that's top-secret. I trust you. I don't want it gettin' back to Marshall or Phillips or anybody. . . ."

"It won't. You can count on me. . . ."

"Good. I knew I could. First of all, let me tell you what's on my mind for you. I'm thinkin' the top job at Powers Perfume . . . runnin' the whole shebang. With a startin' salary of seventy grand, a percentage of the company . . . and . . . two hundred thousand dollars. As a bonus, you might say." Billy paused. He could tell he almost had Sheldon Shaw eating out of his hand. His information had been accurate; he knew Shaw wouldn't turn down an offer like that, regardless of what was involved.

"Nearly a quarter of a million dollars . . . as a bonus?"

"Well, there's a small favor involved. I want you to understand . . . I need you, Shelley. And, according to my inside sources, I don't think they appreciate you at Kellerco the way they should. They don't know what they've got. Marshall probably has some little idea, but he's afraid of you. Afraid you'll take his place."

"Well," Shaw demurred, "that's not for me to say. But tell me, Billy, what's this favor?"

"My car's waitin' outside. Why don't I give you a lift home, and we'll discuss it."

* * *

The last weeks of October were hectic at Keller Perfumes. They were making tangible progress, and the March deadline had begun to seem a realistic goal. To Tyger's relief, Martine had returned to Paris without further incident, to begin designing a promotional Jazz pendant. Manufacturers had been selected to execute her designs for bottles and packaging. Jeff Stein had come up with the final look for Matt Phillips for Men, and a supplier had been contracted. Marge Francisco, the Person Who Counted at Bloomingdale's, had been won over. Negotiations had gone smoothly, and Keller Perfumes had signed an exclusive agreement with Bloomingdale's for the introduction of the Matt Phillips line. The exclusive would give Bloomingdale's a one-week head start on the rest of the country. Tom Sullivan had buyers from the two hundred best stores around the country so enthusiastic about Jazz they could hardly wait until March. In addition, an art director named Davis Chipps had joined the staff.

The deadline had arrived to choose the actual scents. On the first of November, eight fragrance companies submitted their entries, two fragrances each for Jazz and Matt Phillips for Men. Within hours after the perfume samples had arrived the offices at Keller Perfumes were saturated with the fragrances. Secretaries rushed around smelling each other's wrists. Messengers arriving with deliveries were not allowed to leave without sniffing bottles and stating their preference.

Jess Leibowitz's wife, Gloria, had even joined in the sniffing and voting—so she wouldn't accuse him of being involved in a record number of extramarital affairs, Jess joked. Each night when Jess arrived home Gloria was expected to sniff the various scents and voice her reactions on a scale of one to ten. She was then given samples to try on herself and friends, with instructions to make notations as to who preferred what.

Back in the office, all other business took second priority.

"Hey, how's this one? Smell my arm." Connie sauntered into Tyger's office with a Styrofoam coffee container in one hand and a perfume bottle in the other.

"Hmmm, not bad. Try my neck." Tyger bent over so Connie could smell the back of her neck.

"Not good."

"What do you mean? Tyger's neck's my favorite so far." Ginger McShane, the secretary, called in.

And so it went, for days. Everyone at Keller Perfumes and

their friends were on the scent. Samples were sniffed and eliminated one day, reinstated the next. Tyger organized more marketing panels, and she and Connie and Ginger stayed late after work tabulating the results. Slowly, the samples were narrowed down to three contenders for Jazz, and two for Matt Phillips for Men.

Hugh Marshall and Tim Yates joined in the evaluation of the fragrances still in the running. Everyone gathered in Sheldon Shaw's office to hear their reactions. Tyger had not seen Hugh for weeks. She knew Bobbie had not seen him either, because her mother was visiting friends in San Francisco. Tim had reported to Tyger that the atmosphere around Kellerco had been tense. The merger with ConMet, the copper company, had been slow and tedious. The final contracts were finally signed six weeks after the original takeover was planned. For the first time since Tyger had known him, Hugh Marshall showed strain. He looked tired, thinner, and his skin paler.

"I like this—number one—for the men's cologne. For the women's, I don't know. None quite make it. Number two . . ." He sniffed again. ". . . is on the right track." Tyger was pleased that Hugh Marshall was leaning toward the same ones as she.

"I like this men's scent." Tim picked up number one. "And I'd go along with Hugh's choice for the women's. Number two."

"My wife and her friends kept fluctuating." said Jess.

"I agree about the men's scent," said Connie. "But I'm in a complete dither about the women's. One morning I lean toward one, by afternoon I've changed my mind. I don't think any of them is perfect."

"What happens now?" Tyger asked. "None is exactly what we had in mind for Jazz. But we have to have something on the department-store shelves by March."

"We *will* have a product on the shelves in time," Sheldon Shaw said. "Any of these will do. They're all perfectly adequate. We just have to decide on one."

"But Jazz has to be special. . . ." Tyger protested.

"It's the advertising and promotion that makes a perfume *special*." Shaw mocked her emphasis of the word. "Who cares what it smells like as long as it doesn't stink?"

Tyger looked at Hugh Marshall.

"Sheldon's right," Hugh said. "We have to create a market for Jazz. The actual smell of the perfume is of minor consequence." Tyger's face fell. "But I agree with Connie and Tyger. Jazz has to be a real winner. I want it to become a classic, like Chanel's Number Five or Lauder's Youth Dew. A great perfume." He pointed to the samples. "We don't have it yet."

"But what if we don't get it? We *have* to pick something," Tyger pursued her original question.

"Exactly," Shaw said. "Whether it's 'special' or not. What you have to understand, Tyger, is that the bottom line is to have a product to sell."

Tyger bristled at his patronizing tone. But Hugh Marshall stepped in smoothly. "We still have time to get it right. Or, if we don't get it by the time we need it we'll bottle the best choice and keep working."

"The perfumers haven't had much time," Tyger added. "If we go with the best we have so far, and that company's perfumer perfects it, then we could still wind up with something terrific."

"Right. Now, which will it be?" Marshall asked.

An hour later the decision was made. Sample number one, made by the International Fragrance Group, was to become Matt Phillips for Men. Sample number two, by DeHavilland Fragrances, a French company, was unanimously selected as the base note for Jazz. It was good, but needed work.

At six-thirty, Tyger straightened her desk and slipped some papers into her briefcase. She had a dinner date at La Grenouille with Dane Easton, an investment banker who played polo and had the sort of white-teethed good looks that one found in the fashion ads of the Sunday *New York Times Magazine*. Easton had been calling her for weeks, and although Tyger was not particularly interested in dating him, she had finally given in to his persistence. She would go over the papers later, if she did not get home too late.

She gave herself a quick spray of the winning DeHavilland perfume sample and put on her coat. Her hand was on the doorknob when her private line rang.

"Tyger? Glad I caught you," Hugh Marshall said. "I have an assignment for you. My car will pick you up downstairs in five minutes. You can ride home with me. I'm running on a tight schedule. I'm flying out to Phoenix later tonight. Better plan to stay to dinner, I've got some things to go over with you."

He did not ask if it was convenient. It did not seem to occur to Hugh Marshall that Tyger might have other plans. Still, as she walked across the lobby ten minutes later, with Dane Easton now a peevish voice in her past, Tyger was not unhappy. At last she would get a firsthand glimpse of a rare and fascinating sight: Hugh Marshall at home.

The chauffeur held open the door of the limousine. Hugh Marshall was already in the back seat.

"I hope you feel like a long plane ride, Tyger," he greeted her as she got in. "I'm sending you and Jess to Grasse to make the final arrangements with DeHavilland. You're booked on Air France tomorrow evening. Can you make it?"

There were thirty thousand things that she had to do. There were contracts to go over, meetings to cancel, phone calls, Matt Phillips, letters . . . not to mention packing. She did not even know how long she would be gone.

"Of course, Hugh," she said.

"Daddy! You're home early!" Eight-year-old Leslie Marshall squealed.

Angus, ten, slid down the hallway on a pair of cross-country skis. "Hey, Dad, aren't they neat? Nanny took me to buy them this afternoon."

Marshall laughed. "I don't think you'll have much use for them in Dallas." He introduced Tyger to his children and their governess.

"Daddy, I wish you were coming with us." Leslie pouted.

Hugh had taken off his coat and picked her up in his arms. "I told you, sweetheart, I have a business trip. But I'll stop in Dallas on my way back and spend a day or so with you. Then we'll all fly home together."

"But I want you to stay with us the whole time. . . ."

Hugh laughed. "Well, Leslie, I'll tell you what. For spring vacation, I'll take you and Angus to the Bahamas, and we'll be together the entire time."

"Hurray! What about Nanny? Can she come, too?"

Hugh looked at Nanny and winked. "She'd better. I don't know how I'd handle you myself. You'd starve."

"Yes, 'cause you don't know how to cook, do you, Dad?" Angus said.

"That's okay. I can cook for you," Leslie said. "My class at school made cookies today, as a special treat."

Nanny, a tall, thin blonde from Minnesota, laughed. "Well, then, if you can make cookies for us, that's all we need. Come along. Let's get ready for dinner with your father."

Throughout dinner, Hugh Marshall chatted and laughed

with his children. Tyger wondered if many women had been invited to observe Hugh in this setting. Tyger had never seen Hugh so relaxed. A layer of tension had been peeled away, like a rubber mask. He seemed younger when he was at ease.

After dinner, Marshall read the children a chapter from Tolkien's *Lord of the Rings*. Then he kissed and hugged them warmly, and they grudgingly headed off to bed.

"Come into the study, Tyger," Hugh said. "I want to brief you on this assignment."

Tyger gathered her briefcase and followed him. The study was an elaborately ornate room with an intricately patterned eighteenth-century Agra rug, and Louis XV fauteuils covered in gold Scalamandré brocade. K'ang Hsi dynasty porcelain birds perched on the mantel above the gilt-inlaid fireplace. The room did not fit Hugh; it was too fussy.

"Let me light a fire first. Would you like a cognac?"

"Love one." As Hugh poured the drinks, Tyger wandered around the study. "This room . . . doesn't look like you."

"I know. A couple of years ago my sister, who's a decorator, decided the apartment needed to be redone. I gave her *carte blanche* to keep her happy . . . and this is the result. I can't hurt her feelings by telling her I don't like it. Besides . . . I don't care that much. Rooms are just backdrops."

"But colors and textures reflect feelings. People are supposed to be most comfortable surrounded by things they like."

"I guess if I felt that way I'd have this room done in shades of brown. All dark. And on the walls, Impressionist paintings of beautiful women in their boudoirs. . . ."

"Boudoirs?" Tyger grinned.

Hugh nodded. "You know how the *Oxford Dictionary* describes a boudoir?"

Tyger made a guess. "A room where a woman can be alone with her thoughts?"

" 'A room to sulk in' . . . and a place where she can receive intimate friends. I ran across that meaning when I was a student, and it struck me as apt."

"It's a wonderful description. . . ."

"It seems fitting for a study, too. I sulk in here quite often." He smiled at Tyger. "But I seldom receive intimate friends." Then, as if afraid he had become too personal, he retreated quickly to business ground.

"Now, you and Jess will be dealing primarily with Pierre DeHavilland, and with his head perfumer, a fellow named

Guy Saint Denis. Saint Denis has the reputation of being a genius. I hope it's true, because we want a lot out of him."

"If there's a spark of genius there, I'll dig it out."

"What you've got to do is get across to him the subtleties of what it is we want for Jazz. He's on the right track with the sample they sent, but he's going to need guidance."

"How long should I be prepared to stay? It could take a long time."

"Yes it could, and we can't spare you. So what you've got to do is persuade Saint Denis to come back to New York to work. DeHavilland's got a laboratory in Brooklyn. He could set up operations there."

Tyger smiled. "Made in Brooklyn. That's the American touch we've been looking for."

"You'll have to handle him carefully, Tyger. He's supposed to be temperamental—one of the occupational hazards of genius, it seems. That's why I wanted you in on the negotiations."

"There are a lot of French people who are perfectly even-tempered." Tyger sighed in mock complaint. "Why do I always end up with the touchy cases?"

"Your lot in life, apparently. Brush up on your German and next time I'll send you there. They're a pretty stolid bunch." He poured more cognac. It was a Rémy Martin Louis XIII Rarest Reserve, and the peaceful-looking amber liquid sent up deep, penetrating fumes. "Here's to Jazz," he said, touching his glass to hers with a delicate crystal ping. "And to the success of your mission."

Tyger sipped the cognac, holding the pear-shaped goblet in both hands. She gazed into the fire for a moment, watching the flames dance like orange pennants in a brisk wind. "We will get what we want, won't we, Hugh?"

He came and stood beside her, following her gaze, so that, although they stood side by side and did not look at each other, their eyes seemed to meet in the fire. "I think we will," he said. "I usually do."

He turned and faced Tyger directly. "I imagine you do, too."

She looked up at him. She had never been that close to him before. "Not always," she said. "But I try."

The moment hung suspended, like a raindrop trembling on the edge of a leaf. And then it was gone. There was an instant when she was sure he would kiss her, and then it was too late, and he was walking over to his desk. Tyger felt deflated and numb.

"Well, keep on trying, Tyger. You've done one hell of a job for us so far—a lot more than I expected when I hired you."

"Thank you. I've learned a lot, working with you . . . and Connie and Jess." If they were talking business, she would keep it business. She would not pursue romantic double meanings once he had withdrawn. Hugh Marshall was not playing hard to get. He *was* hard to get.

Marshall took a folder from his briefcase and handed it to her. "Here's the background on DeHavilland that you'll need to go over with Jess. I have to get going now. I have a plane to catch in an hour."

"Of course. I've got a lot to do myself if I'm going to be ready to fly to the Riviera tomorrow."

He walked to the front door with her. "I'm afraid I'll need the car. I'll have them call you a cab."

"Don't be silly, Hugh, I can manage."

"Well, good luck, then."

The elevator arrived. They shook hands, and Tyger stepped in.

"Have a good trip. But I warn you, Grasse is a pretty dull place." Hugh smiled.

"I'm terrific in dull places."

"Good luck with Monsieur Saint Denis. Bring him back alive."

He stepped back. The elevator man took the cue, and the oak paneled doors slid shut.

"Don't worry about me," said Tyger wryly as the elevator began its descent. "I always get my man." She realized that she had spoken aloud, but the uniformed operator did not react.

CHAPTER TWENTY-ONE

THE air trip from De Gaulle Airport in Paris to the south of France was turbulent. The jouncing did not bother Tyger, but Jess Leibowitz was not a happy flier. In the States, he admitted to Tyger, he always went by car or train unless he had to get somewhere fast. Tyger chatted nonstop, trying to relax him, but Jess merely sat upright, grimly clutching the arm of his seat.

At last, they burrowed through the clouds and touched down on the rain-drenched runway of the Nice–Côte d'Azur airport. Jess had calmed down a bit by the time they were settled in the limousine sent for them by Pierre DeHavilland, the president of DeHavilland Fragrances.

The trip to Grasse was forty-two kilometers of narrow, winding, hilly roads. The rain beat down in torrents.

"Well, out of the frying pan . . ." Jess was nervous again, and looked warily out the window. "Don't you think the driver's taking the curves too fast? The road's slick."

"French drivers, you know. They don't honk and wave their arms as much as the Italians, but they're mad, just the same. I think they're all in training for the Grand Prix." She laughed.

"Well, tell him to take it easy."

Tyger leaned forward and tapped on the window which separated them from the driver. *"Pardon, monsieur, voulez-vous conduire moins vite? Mon ami à du mal."*

The young man grinned and nodded. *"Bien sûr, mademoi-*

selle. Nous serons à Grasse dans dix minutes." He slowed down a fraction.

"We'll be there in ten minutes. . . ."

"I wish I hadn't finished off the Dramamine," Jess said miserably.

Pierre DeHavilland looked proudly out of the window to the city below, then turned back to Tyger and Jess. "Grasse has been the center of our French perfume industry for nearly two centuries."

Tyger and Jess were sitting in DeHavilland's white-and-chrome office, sipping coffee and listening politely to the portly businessman's introductory travelogue.

"Quel domage," DeHavilland continued, "that you have come to see us in November, in the rain. Three weeks ago you would have been able to see the last crop of jasmine blossoms being harvested at dawn. That is when the fragrance is strongest." He offered Jess a cigar, and lit one himself. The pungent smoke drifted through the room, in curious counterpoint to the floral fragrances he was describing. "In the summer, you know, we have one great flower garden from Grasse to Nice. Besides jasmine, we grow tuberoses, iris, hyacinths, *roses de mai,* jonquils, lavender, orange flowers, violets, mimosa, carnations, acacia, reseda, narcissus, even more. There are seventy-five hundred acres in this area devoted to the cultivation of flowers for the perfume industry." Pierre DeHavilland clearly loved the perfume business. His puffy red cheeks glowed when he spoke about his favorite subject. "How many jasmine blossoms—handpicked and hand-pressed—would you guess it would take to produce one pound of absolute oil?"

"I couldn't begin to guess," said Jess.

"Neither can I." Tyger knew the answer from spending so many hours at the library, but didn't want to ruin DeHavilland's punch line.

"One ton of blossoms. *C'est incroyable,* no? But come with me. You will have a tour of our factory."

Pierre DeHavilland had carried on the traditions set forth by his great-grandfather, but under his leadership DeHavilland Fragrances had grown into an international company, with a modern factory in Grasse, a branch in New York, and subsidiaries in fifteen countries. DeHavilland's son, Albin, was in charge of production of the flower fields the company owned, located in Grasse and around the world—Algeria, Morocco, Egypt, Indonesia and South America.

Before they left DeHavilland's office he led Tyger and Jess over to a large household refrigerator that contained bottles of every perfume currently on the market. "Perfume must be kept cold, so it won't spoil or evaporate. Always keep it refrigerated," he advised Tyger, "unless you use the same fragrance every day and go through it quickly."

Tyger nodded. "By the way, what are those cubicles over there?" They had wandered into a small room where four white booths were lined up against the wall.

"Those are our candle rooms. To test the aroma of scented candles when they burn. This allows the testers to determine the trueness of a scent, as well as its longevity. Later on, you'll see our temperature-controlled testing unit. We use it to see how a scent reacts in different climates. You know, something may smell marvelous in Alaska, but react differently in the tropics. Every fragrance that is created must go through stability testing, even the aromas of household products. If you have a cleaner for rugs, for example—something that may stay in the kitchen cabinet for a long time—we have to know it will not make a stink when you get around to using it again." He chuckled. He was proud of the English slang he had picked up over the years. "You know, everything has an odor. Even a product such as a deodorant which is specified as 'unscented' has a scent—to cover up the product's chemical smell."

DeHavilland led Tyger and Jess down a narrow corridor into a large sterile-looking room. Floor-to-ceiling gray metal shelves lined the walls. Each shelf was crowded with brown-tinted glass bottles, mostly pints, some larger. Technicians wandered about, wearing white starched laboratory coats.

"There is great competition among fragrance manufacturers," he said. "We all work on new perfumes, as well as on scents for household products and cosmetics. And flavors, too—for gum, cake mixes, everything." As if on cue, a young man rushed into the room carrying a tray with small paper cups.

"Ah, Monsieur DeHavilland . . . I have been looking all over for you. Here are the samples for the Piña Colada."

Pierre DeHavilland handed paper cups to Tyger and Jess, then took one for himself. "This is a new product for us. You have it in America. Drinks . . . ah, cocktails . . . which are already mixed and ready to serve. What do you think?"

Tyger took a sip. It was sweet, but Piña Coladas tended to be. "It's . . . good."

"Delicious," Jess added enthusiastically.

"*Ah, bien.*" He spoke to the young assistant holding the tray. "*Merci*, Henri. We will talk later."

DeHavilland took Tyger and Jess over for a closer look at the shelves along the south wall, opening bottles at random to let them smell the aromas. "We have more than four thousand essential oils to work with—flower, fruit, animal extracts, gums and resins. Some are natural essences, some are synthetic. You know, every fragrance manufacturer specializes in its synthetics. Some of us have developed synthetics for which only we have the formula, and other companies must buy from us if they wish to use them. In the trade, these are called 'captive chemicals.' Here at DeHavilland we have had great success with them."

"Are synthetics new to the perfume industry?" Jess asked. "The best perfumes don't contain artificial ingredients, do they?"

"Ah, good questions, Monsieur Leibowitz. A Frenchman named Coumarin developed the first synthetic over a hundred years ago, in 1868. He created the scent of 'new-mown hay.' It is a smell we all recognize, but it must be created chemically to exist for a perfumer. You cannot grow new-mown hay and extract the aroma, can you?" DeHavilland laughed robustly. "There are exceptions, of course, but today two-thirds or more of the ingredients in a perfume are synthetic. Partly due to the cost of natural essences, because crops are at the mercy of nature, and partly due to the shortage of the natural product. There are many people wanting perfumes and yet there are only a few places where we can grow flowers of the quality needed for the perfumer. Especially when you remember that it takes one hundred million rose petals to make one pound of attar of rose. Around Grasse, we can produce seventeen tons of *roses de mai* every year, or a little over eight pounds of essential rose oil."

DeHavilland took a bottle off the shelf, sniffed, and held it out for Jess and Tyger to smell. "This is the attar of *rose de mai*. Nearly every quality perfume contains rose, but did you know every type of rose has a different smell? Gertrude Stein said, 'A rose is a rose is a rose,' but it simply is not so."

"Does where it's grown make a difference?" Tyger asked.

"*Mais oui,* like wine. The quality of the grapes depends on the soil, the slope of the hill, the temperature, the amount of rain. So it is with flowers. The hybrid tea rose smells fruity. Fragrant Cloud produces an aftertaste of cinnamon; the roses of Bulgaria differ from the ones grown in France." He opened another bottle for them to smell. "You know, every flower produces a complexity of aromas. There is no *single* odor, but a blending of overtones and undertones. That is what makes the art of perfumery so unpredictable for the perfumer. . . ."

"You mentioned earlier that jasmine blossoms are harvested at dawn," Tyger noted. "*Why* is their aroma strongest then?"

"It is just before fertilization takes place," DeHavilland explained. "At that time they are highly charged with essential oil. After that, the oils descend into the stems and become diffused into every part of the plant. Different kinds of flowers smell stronger at different times of day. That is why each type of flower must be harvested at the precisely right moment, day or night."

"So you use synthetics to keep the cost of perfume down?" Jess asked.

"Yes, and no. Some snytetics are not necessarily cheaper, but they can be produced in greater quantity. On the whole, they are more consistent, their scent is more predictable than the natural essences. Many perfumers, however, believe that a synthetic odor lacks the warmth, the bouquet, of the real scent. That's why the great perfumes are mixtures of real essences and synthetic ones. You know, Chanel Number Five was one of the first perfumes to use synthetic ingredients, back in 1923. . . ."

The tour continued. Pierre DeHavilland loved showing clients around the laboratories. His running commentary had been polished over the years. "The greatest contribution of the chemist to the perfumer is the group of synthetics that are not merely copies of the natural scent, but man-invented. Some of our most sophisticated modern perfumes could never have been created without a group of artificial chemicals called aldehydes. Some fifty of the world's most famous perfumes are either floral aldehydes, like Arpège, or floral-woodsy-powdery aldehydes—Chamade or Rive Gauche."

DeHavilland paused for a moment, to take stock. "And, of course, there are fresh mossy aldehydes, such as Ma Griffe and Crêpe de Chine. But . . . I fear I am getting too technical."

"Are there any natural essences that can't be duplicated synthetically?" Tyger asked.

"Jasmine," DeHavilland stated emphatically. "Therefore, it is one of the essential oils found in the most expensive perfumes, like Joy. Now, come with me. I have something interesting to show you."

Tyger wondered when they would get to meet Guy Saint Denis, the chief perfumer, but knew there was no way to rush DeHavilland. For the next half hour he showed them through the laboratories used for stability and climate testing, the flavor labs, the rooms in which aromas were developed for household products, as well as for all types of cosmetic and beauty products. "You know," said DeHavilland, "a perfume's odor changes sometimes when you're making soap or talcum. You cannot always use the same formula as the perfume's, even though it is to be marketed under the same name."

Tyger and Jess were led into a room filled with computers. "Suppose that you came to me," DeHavilland continued, "requesting a perfume that would duplicate a certain scent, such as Shalimar. We would give a bottle of the scent to the instrumentation lab. With machines, the chemists are able to extract the oil, put it through our computer, and obtain a readout of the synthetic materials which exist in the formula. Computers, however, cannot read most natural essences . . . they tell us what *percentage* of the whole is real essential oil. So with our computer, we can quickly determine eighty-five to ninety percent of a perfume's formula. Then our perfumers must figure out what real oils are used to make up that remaining ten to fifteen percent. Interesting, no?"

DeHavilland led them over to a large boxlike machine. "To get the real essence, the scent is put into here." He pointed. "Then the perfumer must sniff the vapor which is emitted here." He indicated a small slot. "He must smell it the moment the vapor comes out. If he cannot identify the scent, he must collect condensed crystals of the scent, and try to identify those. There is one other problem: this one comes with the synthetics. If a perfume contains a 'captive chemical' —one which has been developed by a specific fragrance manufacturer—then there are additional problems in duplicating the scent."

Tyger and Jess followed the president of DeHavilland Fragrances down a winding corridor to a small laboratory. "And now I want you to meet our genius, our head perfumer, Guy Saint Denis." They walked into the empty room. DeHavilland called out to an assistant who was passing by. "Violette, please find Guy. I have some clients for him to meet."

DeHavilland turned back to Tyger and Jess. "While we

wait I will show you his 'organ'—a perfumer's research bench." He led them over to a rounded laboratory table, surrounded by vertical and horizontal rows of shelves, holding hundreds of ounce-sized bottles of raw materials. "You see, the bottles look like the keyboard of an organ. The perfumer can sit here, in the middle, and have every essence he needs merely an arm's length away. And these"—he pointed to long thin strips of white paper—"are called *mouillettes*, blotting paper on which to test the fragrances. A creative perfumer is known in the trade as a 'nose.' It is his job to blend a variety of odors into a new and salable scent. He is an artist, not just a mixer. When two aromatic substances are put together they react unpredictably. You can easily wind up with a stink instead of a perfume."

A voice interrupted from behind them. "I am sorry to have made you wait."

They all turned to see Guy Saint Denis. Tyger was riveted. For some reason, she had expected a little man with thick glasses, and an enlarged nose, bulbous and red from all the sniffing he was compelled to do. Instead, Guy Saint Denis resembled the actor Richard Gere. He appeared to be in his early thirties, with penetrating chocolate-brown eyes, olive skin, and perfectly proportioned features. There were no glasses, and his nose was straight and aristocratic. He was tall for a Frenchman, an inch or so over six feet, and slim.

DeHavilland made the introductions. "I can see from your face, Miss Hayes, that you are startled that our famous perfumer is so young. Most people are. But the art of perfumery has been handed down through his family for generations. Guy came to us when he was still a boy. He created his first important fragrance for us when he was only twenty-three."

"I am equally surprised that an executive for a large American company can be so . . . lovely." Guy Saint Denis stared at Tyger in a way that was far from professional. Then he smiled, rather shyly, and turned his eyes back to his employer. "What questions do you have for me?"

"I am taking our guests for dinner this evening, and I want you to join us. You can explain more about perfumery. That is, if Miss Hayes and Mr. Leibowitz are interested. . . ."

Tyger spoke quickly. "Oh, yes, we are anxious to learn as much as we can." She was also anxious to observe Guy Saint Denis outside of the laboratory. And dinner would give her and Jess an opportunity to convince Saint Denis to come back with them to the States.

"I would be most happy to join you," Saint Denis said. "I have much to do today, so I will meet you at the restaurant."

DeHavilland smiled with relief. His chief perfumer could be most uncooperative at times, often when it involved courtesy to important clients. "*Ah, bien,* Guy. Eight o'clock at Poêle d'Or, in Cannes where our guests are staying."

Guy Saint Denis said goodbye to the Americans and watched Tyger Hayes walk down the hallway until she turned a corner and disappeared.

The Poêle d'Or restaurant in Cannes rated two of the *Guide Michelin's* coveted stars. Pierre DeHavilland was a frequent patron, especially during the off season when many of the other restaurants on the Côte d'Azur were closed. He was anxious to please the Americans. The negotiations with Keller Perfumes had been completed that afternoon, via transatlantic phone with Hugh Marshall. Everything had gone well, but there was another bridge to be crossed. They wanted Guy Saint Denis to go to New York to work on Jazz.

DeHavilland dreaded bringing up the subject with Guy. Grasse was the Garden of Eden as far as the young man was concerned. DeHavilland had no idea how he was going to convince Guy to go to America, and if Guy refused, there was the possibility that Keller Perfumes would cancel the deal.

"I am sorry to be late. It is hard for me to stop working. I forget to check the time," Guy Saint Denis apologized self-consciously. Dressed in a conservative but well-cut gray three-piece suit, Guy looked more like an English banker than a French perfumer.

"We really haven't been here long." Tyger smiled.

"Work, work, work, this young man." DeHavilland chuckled. "It is difficult to get him to leave his beloved laboratory." *But not, let us pray, impossible,* he thought to himself.

DeHavilland raised a pudgy hand, and a waiter materialized. DeHavilland glanced carelessly at the menu and turned to Tyger and Jess. "May I suggest to begin, the *belons au champagne?* Oysters are done particularly well here. And perhaps a Chevalier-Montrachet? The 1976 is quite satisfactory."

He shepherded them through their choices, settling on a *filet d'agneau en croûte* for himself and Leibowitz—a safe choice, lamb, for an American businessman. To Tyger he recommended the *filets de turbot aux concombres,* while Guy ordered his standard Provençal favorite, *sauté de scuipons à*

(222)

la Niçoise, a dish of squid prepared with tomatoes and anchovies. As the dinner progressed, DeHavilland sat back and listened as Leibowitz bombarded Guy Saint Denis with questions.

From time to time, DeHavilland noticed, his young head perfumer would steal glances across the table at Leibowitz's assistant, Tyger Hayes, who spoke less but listened attentively. She looked like a Renaissance beauty, in a soft brown crêpe de chine dinner dress with lace at the collar and cuffs. There was something out of the ordinary in Guy's look—a warmth, almost a shyness. DeHavilland relaxed a little and began to enjoy his *filet d'agneau.* Perhaps there would be a way out of this dilemma after all.

"How do you start to create a new perfume?" Jess asked.

"With a theme ... an idea. Or if we are working for a specific client, like Keller Perfumes, then we follow their guidelines. . . ." He smiled at Tyger. "After that, it is trial and error, like a composer writing a symphony."

"In fact," DeHavilland interjected, "a hundred years ago one of our countrymen, named Piesse, attempted to compare odors with sounds. He believed there was a harmony in smell, as in music. He created an octave of odors."

"How poetic. . . ." Tyger sipped the Bellet, a local wine DeHavilland had insisted they try, with cheese, for dessert. "Certainly odor can affect one's mood, just as sound does. . . ."

"Bien sûr, Miss Hayes." Guy nodded, not taking his eyes away from her. "Smell also influences our attraction to others. In animals it plays a necessary part in courtship. And in humans it is said that a kiss is a greeting by smell. Did you know that in many primitive cultures the words for 'kiss' and 'greet' are the same as for 'smell'?"

"I guess that's why the perfume business is so big," Jess said. "Humans are the only ones who get to choose *how* they're going to smell."

Guy shrugged. "It's part of our image. A perfume—like the clothes we choose—says a great deal about us."

"Someone once said that a great perfume makes a man curious and another woman envious." DeHavilland chuckled.

"I knew a Haitian woman . . ." Tyger said. "She told me to put clove oil behind my ears and under my left arm. According to voodoo legend, it would attract my true love. . . ."

"And what happened, Miss Hayes?" Guy sat forward with interest.

Tyger laughed. "Well . . . one man told me I reminded him

of his dentist, who recommended clove oil for toothaches. Another friend said I smelled like a bakery at Christmas."

"Ah, but you know," said Guy, "many perfumes contain the essence of cloves . . . so your voodoo friend was not altogether wrong. Smells are very elusive. The violet, for example. Actually, it does not lose its fragrance . . . we lose our ability to smell it."

"Our sense of smell goes in daily rhythms," said Pierre DeHavilland. "Sharper in the evening than when we wake up. Our laboratory is working on a timed-release fragrance . . . to give off a succession of scents, each becoming subtler as the day wears on."

As the dinner drew to a close, DeHavilland began to grow apprehensive again. There was certainly a chemistry between his head perfumer and the beautiful young American, but would that be enough to influence Guy's antipathy to travel? He ordered Armagnac, from the province of Gascony near the Pyrenees, and waited for the moment to seem opportune. He regretted that Tyger Hayes was wearing Farouche—a nice fragrance without a doubt, but Nina Ricci was not a DeHavilland client. Guy could sometimes be temperamental over such small matters.

". . . something so invigorating about New York," Tyger was saying. DeHavilland's attention perked up. "It's one of my favorite cities—New York, and of course, Paris. But there's a creative pace to New York that really gets in your blood."

"I should like very much to go there someday." Guy smiled.

Eh bien, DeHavilland said to himself, *c'est le moment.* "Guy, it may be that this will be possible very soon. Keller Perfumes is most anxious to have you go to New York to work on the Jazz fragrance. So that you will be nearby. It would be only for a short while, of course . . . until you finished . . ."

Pierre DeHavilland trailed off awkwardly. Guy looked at him, then at Tyger Hayes and Jess Leibowitz. There was nothing in his brown eyes to give any clue to his thoughts. Tyger looked pale and tense. Jess Leibowitz fidgeted with his Armagnac.

At last Guy spoke; and although he addressed Pierre DeHavilland, his eyes were on Tyger. "All right, Pierre," he said simply. "I will go."

There were exhaled breaths around the table. DeHavilland nearly choked on his brandy. Tyger broke into a happy smile, and the smile reflected on the face of Guy Saint Denis.

Pierre DeHavilland watched, and smiled a smile of his own. It had not been such a complicated problem after all. The solution was easy to discover: *Cherchez la femme.*

"We'll try to make your stay in New York as pleasant as possible," Tyger said. Hugh Marshall would praise her for another job well done, Tyger thought. But as she gazed across the table at the good-looking Frenchman, Hugh Marshall seemed far away. Tyger was glad that Guy Saint Denis was coming to New York.

CHAPTER TWENTY-TWO

IN her townhouse on East Sixty-first Street, Tasha Powers was going over some details on the look for Disco. Saks Fifth Avenue was set for its introduction, and production was rolling along. Like the Matt Phillips fragrance, Disco was due to hit the shelves in March.

Billy Youngblood arrived home, soaking from an unexpected thunderstorm.

"Billy! How many times have I told you to leave your boots in the hall? How can we keep this carpet white if you're going to track all over it?"

"No problem. When it's dirty we'll have 'em lay a new one. You worry too much, honey. You're not poor any more. . . ."

"You could still take off your boots at the door," Tasha said. "Besides, you're too *old* for the cowboy look." She turned to her assistant. "That'll be all for today, Rita. Remember, I'll be in the office late tomorrow. I have to speak at that Fashion Group breakfast."

When Rita had gone, Billy Youngblood took off his left boot and flung it against the wall, shattering the glass on the Warhol lithograph. "Goddammit, Tasha, why do you like to insult me in front of other people? Especially Rita. You know she's a gossip." He poured himself a bourbon. "And I'm not too old for the *cowboy look*. I'm from Texas. That's the way we dress down there. . . ."

"Oh, skip it. It's your house and your carpet, anyway." Tasha took the glass out of his hand and took a sip.

"I have somethin' to improve your mood." He reached into his coat pocket. "Harris Fragrances sent over two more perfume samples. One of them's really dynamite."

Tasha grabbed them out of his hand greedily. She unscrewed the tops, closed her eyes, and smelled one, then the other. "Which one of these is dynamite? Tell me . . . I'd like to know. Shit, Billy, the only smell you can identify is good bourbon."

"Tasha, face it. You're bein' too particular. So far, you've turned down twenty-three submissions, and we're gettin' to the bottom of the barrel. You've got to select one and be done with it."

"I can't just pick anything. I'm competing with that schmuck Matt, and my perfume's got to be better than his."

"Stop shoutin', honey. Your perfume'll be fine. Don't you think the folks at Keller Perfumes are goin' through the same thing as us? Look, sweetie, I've put together a whole perfume company for you. You don't have to do anything except pick out bottles, decide on a logo, and choose the scent. That's not so much. Out of twenty-three choices, you ought to find somethin' pretty nice . . ."

"None of them are right for Disco," Tasha shrieked. "I can't believe that in this whole world someone can't come up with a decent fragrance. . . ."

Billy fixed another drink. "You're bein' too choosy. Remember, we haven't got much time if we want to beat Phillips into the stores. . . ."

"I'd just as soon bottle piss as the stuff that's been submitted so far." Tasha began crying out of exasperation. "Oh, Billy, why can't you understand? Disco is so important to me."

"All right, baby. We'll get you a good perfume. You won't have to settle for second best." He put his arms around Tasha. She let him hold her for a minute, then she broke away.

Tasha smiled coquettishly. "If you come up with a spectacular perfume for me, I'll . . . I'll let you do something you've always wanted to do. In bed."

Youngblood's face lit up. "You've got yourself a deal, my love." He held up his empty glass. "Meanwhile, how about another bourbon?"

"Of course, Billy." Tasha poured him a double, and looked at the clock on the wall behind the bar. Only seven-thirty, and they were not going out. She was anxious to get him drunk enough to fall asleep early so she wouldn't have to put up with him all evening.

"Matt, this is terrific! Women will fight their way to the Jazz counter." Connie Larcada was not fond of Matt Phillips. She had the impression that he tolerated only thin women, and, consequently, felt like a cow when he was around. But, giving him his due, his designs for the look of the department-store counter were very good.

Hugh Marshall threw the sketches back down on the conference table. "Fantastic . . . but not feasible. Recreating Bourbon Street is too expensive."

"I'm *not* recreating Bourbon Street. The counter is an impression of the aura of jazz. It's got to be different. You don't want our display to blend in with all the others, do you?"

"Matt . . . this budget is way out of line. You'll have to come back with a more realistic figure. Either that, or rethink the whole concept." Tyger was surprised at Hugh's sharpness. Was he really beginning to worry that Keller Perfumes wouldn't be a success? This was the first meeting where he had shown signs of pressure.

"Matt took it pretty well, considering," Tyger remarked when the meeting was over. Hugh Marshall had paused at her office door on his way to the elevator. Out at Ginger's desk, Tim Yates was busy on the phone.

"We're all beginning to feel the pinch of pressure," said Marshall. "Even Matt. It's beginning to get through to him that there's no time for hysterics any more." He ran a hand wearily over his eyes. "Speaking of the artistic temperament, have you got Monsieur Saint Denis installed and happy?"

"Installed, anyway."

"Well, keep him happy. You've done a great job once again. DeHavilland practically wept when I told him that we wanted Saint Denis over here. I think he was ready to send us his wife instead. He didn't seem to think he could persuade his genius to leave. My guess is that the credit goes to you."

"Not really. All I did was look interested, which wasn't hard at all. Guy didn't take very much convincing."

Marshall looked at her quizzically. "Well, whatever. Keep up the good work. See that he gets everything he needs."

A little later Ginger McShane came in with some letters

for Tyger to sign. "Poor Mr. Marshall." She sighed. "He looks so tired. I'm glad he's getting away."

"Getting away?"

"Oh, I thought he must have told you. He's leaving tonight for a long weekend. That's the most time off he'll take, poor man. Mr. Yates was just booking his flight to Nassau. Isn't that nice?"

"He certainly needs a rest," Tyger agreed, wondering why Hugh had not mentioned it to her.

She signed the letters and went through the pink memo slips detailing her phone calls. She sorted them into business and personal, and made the business calls first. Among the personals was her mother. She and Bobbie were penciled in for lunch tomorrow. Tyger guessed cancellation, which was fine with her. Toward the middle of the afternoon she dialed her mother.

"Tyger darling, I'm terribly sorry, I can't make lunch tomorrow after all. I'm going off to Nassau for the weekend. The Whitneys' yacht. I simply couldn't refuse. You understand, don't you, darling?"

"Of course." Tyger felt a clenching in her stomach. "Nassau? Who are you going with?"

"Why, Hugh Marshall," Bobbie said. "He can't work all the time, Tyger, even if he is your boss. Mustn't begrudge the man a little holiday."

Though it was only midafternoon, Tyger left the office and walked the two blocks north to Central Park. An early winter wind slapped her face once she was no longer shielded by the tall buildings. With the chilly air, the city had speeded up. People scurried, no one lingered. The park benches were empty now, except for the occasional dog walker or bag lady taking a rest. As Tyger observed the changing city scene, she realized that a great deal had happened to her in the past few months. It wasn't merely the job. She had begun to question things she used to take for granted. By taking responsibility for her life, she supposed she was finally growing up. Just one thing bothered her, and it bothered her a lot. She couldn't stop thinking about her mother and Hugh Marshall. They were having an affair. . . . She was going to have a hard time dealing with that.

Tyger had helped Guy Saint Denis get settled in the Kellerco suite at the Carlyle, the same one Martine had occupied during her visit. She also leased him a Peugeot so he could get back and forth from Brooklyn easily, but he soon turned it in, explaining that New York taxis were far preferable to coping oneself with the New York traffic.

Tyger invited Guy to her apartment for dinner several nights later. She told herself that it was for the good of Keller Perfumes that she take an interest in his well-being, but she knew better.

Guy arrived an hour late, wearing the same gray three-piece suit he had worn that night in Cannes.

"I am sorry. I decided to try the subway, and I ended up at something called Shea Stadium. That's a long way, no?" Guy handed her a wilted bunch of violets. "I bought these for you so long ago that they are dead."

"Poor Guy. You'll find your way around soon." She took the flowers and put them in a small Steuben glass vase. "There . . . they'll bounce back. What will you have to drink?"

"Do you have Campari?"

"Yes."

"And soda, please."

"Coming up." She fixed the drinks. "How do you like New York so far?"

Guy shrugged. "It's better than I thought it would be. This is the nicest part I have seen . . . your apartment."

"Tomorrow's Saturday. I'll take you sightseeing, if you don't mind going antique hunting first. This place still needs a lot of filling out. . . ." Tyger's apartment had begun to come together in the past month. On her working woman's salary she had overlaid the floors with natural-colored Chinese rush tile matting from Conran's, and filled the living room with contemporary Italian wicker chairs, baskets, and natural cane pendant lamps from a sale at Bloomingdale's. For color, she had covered an entire wall with framed French watercolors of exotic birds which she had unearthed at a flea market on Canal Street. The other walls she had kept beige, but had spent one entire weekend varnishing them to a high gloss. For the dining alcove Bobbie had given her a carved enamel Japanese screen from the Momoyama period, more expensive than the other furnishings in her apartment put together. Over the tomato-red-clothed round dining table—salvaged from a curbside furniture pile on Hudson Street late one night—Tyger had hung a lacquered Japanese parasol, from Azuma, upside down to camouflage the spot lighting. Over-all, she was pleased with the effect, although she still had a lot to do. The bedroom still had only the queen-sized bed that Jake had given her and a bureau.

"Anything I do with you will be wonderful, Tyger." He looked at her with his warm brown eyes.

They talked perfume and cuisine at dinner. Tyger had prepared a roast duckling stuffed with minced fresh vegetables. To set it off she had splurged a little on a 1974 Spring Mountain Chardonnay, a stylish California white, to introduce Guy to California wines. She had been rewarded when the condescension on his face had changed to surprised approval as he first sniffed and then sipped the wine.

After dinner, over sliced chilled kiwi fruit and some ripe Brie and crackers, with a white Bordeaux, Tyger got Guy to talk about himself.

"My father was a perfumer, and my grandfather too. I am third-generation."

"So, the nose runs in your family," Tyger said. Then, hearing how it sounded, she burst into a fit of giggles. Guy looked on uncomprehendingly.

"Qu'est-ce que c'est?"

"Oh, it sounds terrible in English." She translated and Guy laughed. It eased the mood between them, which had been a bit formal and tentative.

"Did you never want to be anything else?" Tyger asked.

"Oh yes . . . a cyclist. I dreamed of winning the Tour de France. I used to train very hard. I wanted to be another Eddie Merczx."

"A bicyclist?"

"Yes. I know you do not have much bicycle racing in this country. But in France it is tremendously popular. I wanted to be a great sports hero. I thought perfume was very—how do you say?—sissy."

"But you still became a perfumer. . . ." Tyger poured more espresso into Guy's demitasse.

"I was always interested at heart, I think. When I was a little boy I was exceptionally good at identifying smells. I could tell what fish my mother had brought home from the market—turbot, rouget, rascasse—when I was still too small to see into the basket on the table. And of course there were always wonderful perfume smells around our house. It was never a case of 'the shoemaker's wife goes barefoot.' My mother always smelled heavenly."

"Well, I'm glad you followed . . . in the family tradition."

Guy's eyes sparkled. "You were going to say, 'I'm glad you followed your nose.' "

"I was not! You're as sensitive as Cyrano!" They both laughed. "I'm sure you would have made a wonderful cyclist," Tyger said. "But then we probably would never have met."

"Thank you, Tyger." He reached out and took her hand. "By the way, I appreciate your thoughtfulness."

"What do you mean?"

He brought her wrist up to his face and sniffed. "It is one of my creations. You were not wearing it that night in Cannes."

Tyger smiled. "I did a little research. It's a wonderful fragrance, Guy."

"It suits you." He kissed the soft inside of her wrist; then, with his eyes on hers, he returned her hand slowly to the table. "But it is not good enough for you, Tyger. With Jazz, I will do even better. With you in mind."

She sent him home finally at two o'clock, calling a taxi so that he would not get lost again. They stood by the window looking down into the street while they waited for the taxi to arrive. When it pulled up below them with its "on radio call" message glowing impatiently, Guy pulled Tyger to him and kissed her on the lips.

"Do not walk me to the door," he said in French. "Wait here by the window so that I can see you as I drive away."

From the street beneath her window he waved at Tyger, and then signaled again through the rear window of the cab as it eased down Jane Street and turned to head uptown. Tyger waited until he was out of sight.

She would have to go to B. Dalton and stock up on cookbooks, she thought, as she undressed and slipped into bed. There were bound to be more dinners coming up. And very likely breakfasts, too.

CHAPTER TWENTY-THREE

BOBBIE looked elegantly sporty in her wool tweed riding jacket which she wore over a huckleberry-colored cashmere turtleneck and gray wool gabardine skirt. Her blond hair had grown to shoulder length, and was loosely curled. She was blonder than ever from the sun in the Bahamas. No one in La Caravelle who didn't know her would have guessed she was closer to fifty than thirty.

"Oh, darling, everything I want to order is fattening. I suppose I'll have to go with the asparagus *sans* Hollandaise. I gained two pounds in Nassau. You have to get it off right away. That's the secret, Tyger." She leaned back against the red velvet banquette, under one of the Parisian street-scene murals.

"I know, Mother. But I'm having something substantial . . . I missed dinner last night."

"Hmmm." Bobbie absentmindedly checked out the outfits of the two young women who had just sat down at the next table. Miniskirts again. She had never thought she would live to see the day. "How did you happen to miss dinner? Working late?"

"Yes, actually. I went out to DeHavilland's lab in Brooklyn after work to meet Guy for dinner, but he worked till midnight. I seem to have become an unpaid perfumer's apprentice."

"How's it coming? Has Jazz been born yet?" Bobbie laughed.

"Not yet. Guy's working hard, but it takes time. A perfumer can spend years creating a great fragrance. Guy has only two months. . . ."

"What happens if he doesn't make the deadline?"

Tyger smiled and took a bite of her *celeri rémoulade*. "Birth of the blues for Keller Perfumes, I guess. But he'll do it. . . ."

"Well, I know Hugh has great confidence in him." It was the first mention of Hugh Marshall. Tyger had been waiting for her mother to bring him up.

"By the way, how was your trip? Tim Yates told me that Hugh looked well rested. . . ."

"We had a fine time, but constantly surrounded, you know. You can't be alone on a yacht full of people."

Good, thought Tyger. Then she took the plunge. "You're seeing a lot of Hugh these days, aren't you?"

"Not a lot. He's always off on business. Just like Jimmy. Which reminds me . . . I may be getting a dandy settlement after all. I found out—through secret sources—that Jimmy's been having an affair with his best friend's widow off and on for several years." Bobbie smiled. "Isn't that marvelous? Gives me great leverage—since he was so outraged by my affair with Tom Galvani. Oh . . . and more news. Lolli left her banker waiting at the aisle. Got cold feet at the last minute, and decided she couldn't do it, even for money. . . ."

For the rest of lunch Bobbie gossiped about friends, keeping the conversation light on purpose. She was careful to avoid any scenes with Tyger.

Tyger had hoped the conversation would come back to her favorite topic, Hugh Marshall. She was extremely curious to know the extent of her mother's involvement with him. Finally, as they were sipping espresso, she decided to abandon subtlety.

"Mother, when your divorce from Jimmy comes through, what are your plans?"

"Well . . . I was thinking of taking a place in Palm Springs for the winter. Or maybe Gstaad. I can't decide between sun and snow."

"Then you and Hugh aren't that . . ." She couldn't bring herself to say more.

"Well, darling, one has to play the game. He doesn't want a woman who'll just sit around waiting for him to call." Bobbie wondered why Tyger was so interested in her affair with Hugh. Was it merely curiosity, or was it more? All at once it dawned on her: Tyger's interest was not as a daughter, but as a rival. Bobbie realized that she would have to be careful about what she told Tyger from now on.

After lunch Bobbie spent an hour browsing through Bendel's. She found an attractive set of handblown glasses on the first floor which she had sent to her weekend hostess as a bread-and-butter present.

But it was Tyger who was on her mind. Tyger, and Hugh Marshall. Bobbie realized now that she should not have been surprised. Of course her daughter was interested in Hugh. Why else would she have taken that silly job? A young woman like Tyger did not suddenly develop an interest in business unless there was a man in the picture. It had been careless of Bobbie not to have seen it sooner.

She guessed that there had not been very much between Tyger and Hugh, outside of the office. Certainly Hugh had betrayed no sign of it. Nor had her daughter, whom Bobbie could read somewhat better. Still, it was strange to think of Hugh as she had been with him on the yacht in Nassau, and to wonder whether he had ever done those things with Tyger.

In a curious way, Lady Rowan found that she rather enjoyed being in competition over a man with her daughter. Especially in view of the fact that she appeared to have the upper hand. Of course she did not want to see Tyger hurt. But even less did she want to be hurt herself. Tyger was twenty years younger than she was. Hugh was six years younger. Bobbie was forty-six years old, and she was afraid she might be running out of chances.

Nelson Bachrach waited impatiently in Hugh Marshall's office. He despised tardiness, in any situation, and he was to meet his wife at the St. Regis in half an hour. They were going on a vacation. Bachrach was not looking forward to it, but Mrs. Bachrach's health was poor. The doctor had suggested a cruise, and Mrs. Bachrach had been wanting to see the South Pacific for years, ever since the opening night of the play when she had gone into a swoon over Ezio Pinza. So the South Pacific it was, on the *Kungsholm,* leaving New York that evening. They would be away for two months, which was the main source of Bachrach's discontent. He was not anxious to leave the company in Hugh Marshall's hands for that length of time.

Hugh Marshall entered. "Good afternoon, Nelson. All ready for the trip?" He shook the older man's hand formally.

(235)

"Mrs. Bachrach is," Bachrach grumbled. "She's taken care of everything."

"You're like me, Nelson," Hugh said pleasantly. "I know you aren't looking forward to being away."

Nelson Bachrach resented any suggestion of a similarity between himself and Marshall. In any case, he was in no mood for small talk. "Fill me in on ConMet."

"Our people are walking in on Monday. After all the harassment, their ex-president, Evans, is finally cooperating. By the time you get back, the shakedown will be complete. . . ."

"And what about that damned perfume? Shaw tells me you're set to go in March. Except you don't have a perfume to put in those expensive custom-made bottles." Bachrach glared at Marshall. "Did you get my memo last week to cut back on expenses?"

"Yes. We are. And we're hot on the heels of a great fragrance. Look, Nelson, a year from now you'll have changed your mind about this division."

"I doubt it, although Mrs. Bachrach is pleased as punch. Says we're finally making a product she can give away for gifts. Anyway, Hugh, you got this one past the board, but don't think this is the start of a trend. As long as I'm around I'm not going to watch the birth of Keller chocolates and towels and baby food. . . . Someone has to protect Sam Keller's memory!"

"Nelson, Sam was an entrepreneur, an innovator. Believe me, if he were alive now he'd be over at the lab mixing essences himself. He was always in favor of diversification."

"*Not* in the way you're doing it! You're spending too much money to get this thing off the ground."

"Be reasonable, Nelson. You know as well as I there's no way to get a new venture rolling without investing a hell of a lot of capital. And we can't expect to start seeing a profit for at least two years. You know that."

"I don't like your style, Marshall. I've never kept that a secret from you. You and your Harvard M.B.A.! You got where you are by marrying Sarah Keller. That's a fact you tend to forget."

"No, Nelson, I haven't forgotten Sarah. . . ." His voice was dry ice, a hoarse whisper. He waited a moment, then continued. "Yates has compiled the information you requested. Here it is." He handed Bachrach the folder. "*Bon voyage.* My best to Mrs. Bachrach. Now if you'll excuse me, I have to get to a meeting." He left the room quickly.

Hugh Marshall knew how he had gotten where he was. Why couldn't they all leave him alone and let him run the damned company? If Bachrach would face facts he would realize that Hugh was as good an administrator and innovator as Sam Keller had been, maybe better. But Nelson Bachrach was Hugh's cross to bear until the old man retired from the board. Unless, of course, Bachrach managed to get Hugh out first.

"I convinced Shel to go with your recommendation, Tyger. Jake Danton's the perfect photographer for our ads." Connie Larcada was sitting in Tyger's office, eating her midmorning snack from a small enamel tray. She had joined Weight Watchers and, so far, had lost eight pounds.

"Great! I'll call him today and give him the good news."

"Have you talked with Eileen Ford yet about models?"

"Yes ... and Stewart and Zoli. I also want Jake's recommendations, since he works with them all." Tyger was taking advantage of their coffee break to paint her fingernails.

"I want Kate Cassell," Connie stated. "She's very American ... but with enough mystery to carry off the Jazz campaign."

"I think so, too, but she gets top dollar. Tim Yates told me that Hugh suggested we look for an unknown. You know, make her a star, the Jazz woman."

"And when Hugh suggests, we listen, right?" Connie's dig, Tyger guessed, was motivated by her loyalty to Sheldon Shaw. Tyger was certain that they were having an affair. Tyger had to admit that Shaw was not given much to do around Keller Perfumes. Lately all he seemed to do was show up for meetings and take three-hour lunches.

"Has your ad budget been approved yet?" Tyger asked.

"Yep ... three hundred thou for a print campaign ... local papers and national magazines."

"What about TV?"

"Too expensive for now. If things go well I think I can get a budget increase next year."

"How soon do we need our Jazz model?"

"Right away. Have Ginger do the preliminary screening. We'll shoot the men's ads first since Garry Gray's all set."

For the next week, tall young women with black leather portfolios streamed into Ginger McShane's office. The search for a promising unknown was on. There were possibilities, but no one seemed quite right.

Tyger called Jake. "You still haven't recommended anyone for the Jazz model."

"I know. I've been thinking. You remember that Swiss girl, Astrid? The one who gave me the cuckoo clock?"

"Oh, yeah. She's great-looking . . ."

"And versatile. She has about a hundred different looks. Ford handles her."

"Okay, send her over. How'd the session with Garry go?"

"Ah, not too good. We're reshooting tomorrow."

Tyger reached for her handbag and paid the delivery boy who had just walked in with her iced tea, rare hamburger and cottage cheese. "What's the problem?"

"The guy's a stiff. I don't like him."

"Well, they say the true professional rises above . . ."

Jake laughed. "Cut the shit, Tyger. I'll bring Garry's proofs over on Thursday. You can take me to lunch after."

"I got you the Keller account. You can damned well take me to lunch." Tyger was glad she and Jake were buddies now. It was more fun with the pressure off.

By the end of the week, the model choices were narrowing. Connie liked Astrid, but still wanted Kate Cassell. There were two other young women in the running, too. Jess wanted Gaby Prouvost. Davis Chipps, the art director, was leaning toward a stunning black model, Jean Lee.

Kate Cassell walked into Tyger's office, unannounced. one day at noon. "Hi, Tyger. Can I take you to lunch?"

"I'd love it, but I'm booked."

Kate dropped her huge canvas bag on the floor and sat on Tyger's small sofa, stretching her long legs out in front of her. "I won't budge, Tyger. I'm pissed off as hell that you haven't called me about the Jazz campaign. Every model in town's been up here."

"You're too expensive, Kate. You'd be perfect . . . but we have a budget."

"We can talk price. I'm not *that* expensive . . ."

"But Kate, you can have any job you want. Why are you interested in this?"

"I have my reasons."

Tyger didn't press. "You know, Tasha Powers has a perfume coming out. I heard they have a huge ad budget."

"Tasha's doing the ads herself. Listen, Tyger, I want to be

(238)

the Jazz lady. Believe it or not, I've never gotten in at the beginning of a new product. And if the scent's associated with me, they have to keep using me, right?"

"Sure. They'd want to."

"Oh, shit. I'll level with you, Tyger." She lowered her voice. "I'm thirty-three. I want the contract with Keller, for security. I'm tired of hustling, and my movie career's a bust . . . did you see the reviews of *Goin' West?*" Tyger shook her head. "Well, the offers haven't exactly been pouring in since then."

"Kate, you'd be fabulous for Jazz, but there are a couple of other contenders. Budget's the issue. Besides, it's not my decision anyway."

Kate perked up. "Oh? Whose is it?"

"Hugh Marshall has final approval."

Kate stood and collected her gear. "Well, thanks, Tyger. We'll have lunch another time. Promise not to tell anybody my age, okay?"

Tyger wondered how long it would take her to get to Hugh Marshall, and if Kate would convince him to meet her price.

The next day, Tyger was summoned by Hugh Marshall to discuss the choices for the Jazz model. After a meeting earlier that morning in Shaw's office, the decision of the Keller Perfumes staff was to go with Astrid, if they wanted a relative unknown, or Kate Cassell, if Kellerco was willing to meet her price.

Tyger sipped the coffee Annie Johnson had brought in. "Astrid's terrific for print. The only problem would be later, with TV. Her Swiss accent might detract from the American aura we're projecting. . . ."

"Good point, Tyger." Hugh looked at Astrid's photo again. "She's a good-looking girl, but I've made up my mind. I want Kate Cassell. She'll make Jazz immediately identifiable as a quality product."

"But Tim told me you wanted an unknown to keep the budget down. . . ."

"That's what I said, all right. I've been haggling with the chairman of the board over the budget, with a lot of pressure to cut costs. . . ." He looked toward the window, lost in thought. Then he turned back to Tyger and pounded his fist on the desk. "But dammit, Tyger, this is a first-class product. It has to be done right!"

"Spend money to make it. . . ."

"Of course. Kate Cassell is willing to sign an exclusive

agreement with us . . . for Jazz and subsequent products. For a little extra money she can be *all* ours. That's worth a hell of a lot."

"I agree."

"I'm going to tell you something, Tyger. Something I don't want spread around. . . ."

"You can trust me, Hugh."

He looked at her for a moment, as if trying to decide whether to go ahead. "Yes, I know I can. You know, Keller Perfumes is my baby. I've fought for it all the way . . . and I'm not going to cut corners now. If the company fails I may go down the drain with it."

Tim Yates had insinuated as much, but Tyger still couldn't believe it. "What? You're indispensable here. . . ."

"Nobody's indispensable, Tyger."

Hugh looked as surprised as Tyger did at his own vehemence. He grinned, a bit self-consciously. Tyger found it enormously attractive. "No matter how much power you have, Tyger, there's always someone—higher than you, or lower—anxious to pull the rug out from under your feet."

"It's not so different from Hollywood, really," said Tyger. "You're only as good as your last picture. If you're at the top—which means your pictures make a hell of a lot of money—you're allowed a picture's grace, one flop. Like Steve Spielberg—after *Jaws* and *Close Encounters*, he fell down on *1941*. They're still glad to see him, but I imagine there's some strain behind those smiles now, and they'll be doing a lot more looking over his shoulder. And if you miss twice—well, look what happened to Peter Bogdanovich."

"He missed twice, did he?" Hugh came around and sat on the front of his desk.

Tyger nodded. "My father used to quote Sam Goldwyn, who was always spoken of around our house as the Legendary Sam Goldwyn: 'It's a dog-eat-dog business, and nobody's going to eat me!' "

Hugh Marshall laughed. "Perhaps Hollywood was a better training ground for a business career than I thought."

"Oh, we learned the basic values. 'Never give a sucker an even break.' " She paused, her tone becoming serious. "Don't worry, Hugh. Jazz has the best producer in the business. It's a sure hit."

Marshall smiled, unexpectedly touched. "Thank you, Tyger. You're good for my morale. I wish I could have you around all the time."

Their eyes met. *You could,* she thought, and although she had not said it aloud it was as if he had heard her. They looked at each other and thoughts passed between them too swiftly to put into words.

The intercom buzzed. Tyger started. Marshall turned around distractedly and switched it on.

"Yes," he said in a strained voice.

"Excuse me, Mr. Marshall, but it's twelve-fifteen. Miss Hayes wanted to be reminded of her lunch appointment."

"Thank you, Annie."

"I could break my appointment, Hugh, if there's . . . more to talk about."

"No, no," he said gruffly, walking back around his desk and making a show of flipping through his appointment book. "You'd better run along. I'll call you tomorrow with my final decision on the Jazz model."

Tyger's lunch was with Jess Leibowitz and a vice president of Marshall Field, but she let Jess carry the conversation. Her mind was on Hugh Marshall. The man was attracted to her, she was sure of it. But why was he fighting it so hard?

CHAPTER TWENTY-FOUR

THE next day was a busy one for Tyger. She was in her office early, and had lunch at her desk. Around midafternoon the phone rang. It was Hugh Marshall.

"I've made my decision, Tyger," he said. "Let your people over there know that Kate Cassell's got the job."

"Great, Hugh. I think she'll be perfect."

She had scarcely hung up when there was a tap on her door and Matt Phillips walked in.

"Hello, sweetie. I was just looking for you. I ran into Kate Cassell at Studio 54 last night. She hinted that she might get the Jazz job."

"News travels fast. It's now a fact . . . Hugh Marshall just okayed it."

"Well, I'm glad. For once, I approve of what you're doing over here." He pulled an antique gold pocket watch from his jacket. "I must get back to my office. Why don't you come with me? I have a dress for you."

"I was heading down to see you today anyway. To show you the ad copy. . . ."

On the way to 555 Seventh Avenue, Matt's mood shifted. He fished the oriental cocaine bottle out of his pocket. "Want some?" Tyger shook her head. "Just as well," he said. "I'm running low, and my dealer's out of town." He sniffed the coke and became silent for the rest of the ride.

By the time they were settled in his office, Matt was snapping into the intercom at his secretary. "Why didn't you leave those fabric samples in here? And what about those checks I'm supposed to sign? Do I have to remind you of everything?" He turned to Tyger. "Fix me a club soda, would you? And whatever you want. God, I can't believe it! I leave the office for twenty minutes and the place falls apart. Skip the soda and pour me some coffee, black. I'm supposed to lay off caffeine . . . but I need it." He began sorting through the closet. "Oh, shit, where's that dress. . . ."

"It's okay, Matt. Forget it."

"It's *not* okay, Tyger. This office is an ode to inefficiency! Nothing's where it should be. You heard, of course, that Edgar's deserted me?"

Tyger nodded. Edgar Newhouse had been Matt's chief assistant. "I read in *W* that he's starting his own line of ready-to-wear."

"That's what happens. You train people . . . teach them everything. Then they go out and compete with you." He searched through his desk drawers. "Shit. You don't have a Quaalude, do you?"

"Sorry."

"Oh God, what a day." He sank down onto the paisley chaise.

"You look exhausted, Matt."

"I can't sleep. Everything's wrong. Edgar's leaving. I *hate* my latest sketches. My creativity . . . my spark, it's gone . . . and if I don't get it back . . ." He lit a cigarette. Tyger watched his hand shake.

"You obviously need a rest. Why don't you take a trip?"

"Too busy for that." Matt leaned back and pressed his fingers to his forehead, to ease the ache.

"Look at yourself. Coffee, drugs, pills, cigarettes. Out at discos every night. How long do you think you can keep up this pace?"

"Oh, even if I could get away, Garry wouldn't go."

"Don't take him! If he goes, you'll wind up doing everything you do here. . . ."

"I won't go without Garry!" Matt poured some water in a pitcher and sprinkled the plants in the window.

"I was only making a suggestion, Matt. . . ."

"You hate Garry. You'd do anything to break us up!"

"What nonsense! It's true I don't like him, but it's your life. All I said was that you look strung out, and need to take it easy."

Lois Gerd, Matt's secretary, walked in with a special-delivery letter.

"Lois, how many times have I told you to knock!" Matt shouted. "That's it . . . I've had it with you! You're fired. I'll have Marcy send you a check for two weeks' severance."

Lois broke into tears. "Mr. Phillips, I'm so sorry. Please . . . I didn't mean . . ."

"Leave, you bitch. Now!" Matt stood and grabbed a catalog from his desk and flung it at the sobbing young woman. His aim was off, but she screamed and ran from the room.

"You pay people a bloody fortune and they don't give a damn," Matt said to himself. He sat down at his desk with a low moan. "I can't stand it! I can't take any more." He gazed at Tyger with the eyes of a wounded fawn. "Now I'm going to have to find another secretary."

"Matt," Tyger said calmly, "you need to get away for a couple of days."

"I can't." .

"*Look* at yourself. You're at the pinnacle of your career. Don't blow it."

Matt took a series of quick shallow breaths. "If only one area of my life were going well I could cope. But there are so many problems—at work, at home. . . ."

"Well, you can't solve them in your frame of mind. Go lie on a beach someplace. Problems have a way of sorting themselves out when you get away from them."

"Thank you, Ann Landers," he said sarcastically.

"I'm only trying to help." Tyger picked up her portfolio and handbag. "I'll leave a copy of the ad proposals here. . . ." She placed it on his desk.

"Wait, Tyger! Don't run off mad. Look . . . I'll think about what you said." He paused. "If Lois is still out there, send her in. I'll give her another chance."

Lois had already cleared out of her office, but Garry Gray was sitting on her desk smoking a joint. He nodded to Tyger and headed in to see Matt.

"I thought you were shooting a commercial today," Matt said.

"Oh, ah, it's been postponed. Listen, pal, I'm out of cash and it's after three. The bank's closed."

"I put fifty on the table next to the bed before I left this morning. Didn't you see it?"

Garry sat down on Matt's chaise and propped up his feet. "Yeah, but I've run through it."

"How? What did you spend it on?"

"I don't know." Garry laughed. "Fifty doesn't go far these days. Double-digit inflation . . ." He smiled. "Where's the coke? I want some."

"Shit . . ." Matt said. "I gave you two grams yesterday."

"I know, but I've used it all."

"By yourself? I doubt it." Matt glanced at his blond friend. "Who have you been with?"

"Nobody."

"Nobody? Ha! I *know* you're seeing someone. . . ."

"I'm not, Matt. Honest. You know I love you."

"Then come here and show me."

"Let me have just a little snort first."

Matt handed him the Chinese vial. "Here."

Garry spooned some of the powder into his nose and sniffed deeply. "Come here," he said, and Matt obeyed. Garry kneeled on the floor, unzipping Matt's pants and pulling them, along with his bikini briefs, over Matt's slim hips.

Matt stood tall, his feet apart, and moaned softly when Garry took hold of his growing erection. As Garry's lips worked faster and faster, and Matt's penis disappeared deep into his lover's throat, Matt felt the tension drain from his aching head and flow into his loins. It was excruciating. It was unbearable. It was exhilarating. Matt needed this. He pulled Garry's head closer and dug his fingers into Garry's scalp. "Oh . . . oh, no . . . oh, *God!*" Matt screamed. His eyes were closed and he tossed back his head and moaned. The sound came deep from his gut. "Now, Garry . . . *now!* Oh, my love!" Matt came quickly, twitching jerkily while his lover swallowed the juices of his passion.

Running his fingers lovingly through Garry's blond hair, Matt said, "I have a wonderful idea. Let's hop a plane and spend a week in Acapulco."

Garry pulled away, stood, and reached into his hip pocket for his comb. "I can't leave now. Maybe next month."

"I *need* to get away now."

"So go alone. I'm busy," Garry said.

"Doing what? And who with? I thought you'd *like* a trip."

"I told you, Matt," Garry hedged. "I can't go now."

"Why? Tell me!"

"Oh, just a lot of stuff going on. It's a bad time to leave town." Garry had been looking through the large clothes closet. He pulled out one of Matt's worsted wool blazers and put it on.

"Well, *I'm* going," Matt said. "You stay here. It'll do you good to make some money. Buy your own drugs. Get your own place. . . ." Matt slammed the closet door shut.

"Cool it, pal. I still love you. . . ."

"You're seeing someone else! What kind of a fool do you take me for? You only got the Keller Perfume job because of *me,* you know, and that's the only thing you've done since summer." Matt turned away. "I hope your new friend is as generous as I."

"Listen, Matt," Garry came over and touched Matt's cheek lightly. "I don't have a new friend. Nobody special. You've always known I fool around a little during the day. I mean, you work." He kissed Matt's lips. "I need a lot of sex . . . but none of them mean anything. You're the only one I want." Garry held Matt in his arms.

"All right," Matt conceded. "Call TWA and make reservations for us."

"Sure, Matt. But for next month. . . ."

Matt twisted away from Garry. "You leech!" he shouted. "Get out of here. Get *out* of my life!"

Garry looked contrite. "Shit, Matt. You don't own me. Try to understand. I can't do everything at your beck and call."

"You don't have to. Ever again." Matt pouted and turned to look out the window at the traffic down below. He kept his back to Garry.

Garry came over and stood beside Matt. "Look, love, be reasonable. . . ."

"Get the fuck out of here," Matt said evenly. Going to his desk, he picked up the phone, dialed TWA and asked for the time of the next plane to Acapulco. "Okay . . . I'd like to make a reservation for the eight-o'clock flight. Yes, for one." He gave the clerk his American Express number.

Garry remained at the window for a minute. Then he strode quickly out of the room.

Matt was certain that Garry would be on the plane.

CHAPTER TWENTY-FIVE

ON her way home from work Tyger picked up bread from Balducci's, flown in fresh from Paris that day, along with some *pâté de campagne,* a wedge of gruyère, roast breasts of chicken with *herbes de Provence,* spicy Moroccan olives, and a bag of Famous Amos chocolate-chip cookies. At the liquor store she purchased a good bottle of California Cabernet Sauvignon, and hailed a cab for the DeHavilland factory in Brooklyn.

The night watchman let Tyger in. Everyone else had left for the day. Guy was in back, in the special laboratory that had been fixed up for his stay in America.

"Surprise, Guy. I brought a picnic."

Guy put down a glass vial and came over and kissed her. "Oh, Tyger, how wonderful. You are very nice to me."

"Not a bit. I'm only protecting the interests of Keller Perfumes. If you starved to death what would we do?"

Guy touched her breasts. He could see the nipples becoming erect underneath her mauve silk shirt. "And is it *only* the interests of Keller Perfumes you care about?"

"Oh, perhaps I have a few interests of my own." She put her arms around him. "I think I should move my bed over here to the lab. This is where you spend most of your time. . . ."

"All for you, *ma chérie.*" He kissed Tyger lightly on the nose. "And of course for Monsieur Leibowitz and Monsieur Shaw and Monsieur Marshall and the board of directors of Kellerco. But it is your skin, not theirs, that I keep in mind as

I work." He ran a fingertip up along her throat to her earlobe.

"I'm not only flattered as a woman, I'm reassured as a perfume executive."

"Aha . . . speaking of that, let us see how you are developing your talents. Come over here, I have something for you to sniff." Guy dipped a piece of blotting paper into a tiny bottle.

"Hmmm. What is it?"

"Guess. You said you wanted to become a 'nose.' This is tonight's lesson."

Tyger sniffed the liquid again. "A mixture—gardenia . . . jasmine . . . rose . . ." She looked at Guy.

He shook his head. "It is only one essential oil, one of the most expensive absolutes. Tuberose. My grandfather used to compare its smell to a well-stocked garden at sunset."

"Well, I have a lot to learn. But I read the results of a study at Yale that says women have a better sense of smell than men. So there!" She smiled, her eyes teasing him.

"Not *exactly* true." Guy kissed her forehead lightly. "Women have a better odor vocabulary and sensory identification."

"Meaning?"

"Women are better than men at *identifying* smells. But everyone can develop their olfactory awareness . . . although some people are more smell-oriented than others."

"Okay, try me again," Tyger said.

Guy opened another small bottle for Tyger to smell. She recognized the scent.

"That's easy. L'Air du Temps," she said. "Nina Ricci."

Guy smiled. "Right. But what's in it?"

"Well . . ." She smelled it again. "Carnation . . . and something spicy . . ."

"And, I would guess," said Guy, "that the formula would include a page and a half of other ingredients."

Tyger threw up her arms. "It's impossible!"

Guy put his arm around her. "Don't forget. I've been doing it all my life."

"Guy, tell me something. Does a nose ever lose his sense of smell? You know, from overuse?"

"It depends. There are famous perfumers in their seventies. Women, however, don't smell as well as men after menopause . . . estrogen affects their olfactory perception. . . ." He handed her another vial. "Try this."

"Okay. I recognize it—patchouli."

"*Très bien.* In perfumery, it is used as a fixative . . . it makes a perfume long-lasting. The skill of a perfumer is best demonstrated by his ability to handle fixatives. They are also called the 'base notes' of a fragrance—the heaviest, longest-lasting. They are warm, woody, animal scents."

"This is fascinating," Tyger said, looking around the laboratory with its tiers of bottles, vials and equipment. "What's next?"

Guy came up behind her and put his hands on her shoulders, pressing his lips down against the curve of her neck. "Next . . ."

Tyger leaned back against him, and he slipped his hands down inside her shirt. "No, Guy, not here. . . ."

"Why not?"

"It's not . . . romantic."

"Ah, Tyger, you are wrong." He turned her around to face him. "Will you let me show you?"

Guy's eyes were gentle and loving, and lit with a warm gleam of humor. Tyger smiled, and nodded.

Guy untied the silk Laura Eastman scarf from around Tyger's waist and held it up to her eyes. "Don't worry," he chuckled softly. "This is only for romance." He drew it over her eyes in a blindfold and knotted it at the back of her head. Then he took her again by the shoulders and turned her slowly around three times. "Now," Guy said, "we are no longer in a *laboratoire* in Brooklyn. We are in the south of France . . . in a flower garden . . . at sunset."

And suddenly her nose caught the exquisite fragrance of a blooming garden. There was the dusky sweetness of roses, a hint of ripe gardenia . . . it was the tuberose essence, of course.

"A soft, warm breeze . . ." Guy said, and Tyger heard the quiet hum of his heater fan, and felt the warm air stirring at her legs. She was reminded of a similar scene in one of her father's old movies, where the couple danced together on an empty sound stage. In the Harry Hayes version, the camera faded away to the clouds right after the couple embraced. Tyger was glad that real life was X-rated. She felt Guy unbuttoning her shirt with one hand; with the other he brought another fragrance to her nose.

"Lily of the valley?"

"Oui, ma chère." Guy loosened Tyger's purple wool skirt and let it fall. Then he took the elastic of her panties in his fingers and drew them down her legs. He held her hand and guided her, naked, to where her toes felt something soft and warm. "Come, my darling, and sit here beneath this flowering

tree," he whispered, and Tyger smelled an intoxicating spring bouquet of lilac. Guy lowered her down, and her thighs and buttocks met not a hard cold floor but a mossy cushion. What was it? She felt it with her fingers . . . her silver-fox coat.

"The sun is setting, and the lovers are in their secluded garden, enjoying a *pique-nique sur l'herbe*. There is music from the village. . . ." Tyger heard a click, a cassette snapping into Guy's tape player, and the opening strains of Beethoven's *Pastorale* swelled into the air. "It is a very sophisticated village," Guy explained. "Pierre Boulez is the concert master."

Now Tyger felt Guy's fingers touching her cheek, and moving softly down her neck, over her body. At the same time, one after another, floral fragrances appeared for her to smell.

"Orange blossom . . . violet . . ." The fingers of one hand moved gently, barely touching, raising gooseflesh of desire wherever they passed. The fur on which they were sitting tickled erotically at the tender flesh between her thighs. Tyger's voice trembled. ". . . jonquil . . ."

"Mmmm." Guy's fingers were trailing down her spine, over the swells of her buttocks. "And this?"

"Ugh . . . I don't know. . . ."

"Pâté." He slipped a sliver into her mouth. "Remember the lovers are having a picnic." A moment later she heard the sound of the wine being uncorked.

"Cabernet Sauvignon," Tyger pronounced. "Chapelet, 1976. You forget . . . one of the lovers prepared the picnic." A cool glass pressed against her bottom lip, and she drank. The wine was velvet and delicious.

"And now," she heard him say, breathing faster, "the lovers have finished their picnic. . . ."

Guy's arms wrapped around her, and his naked body pressed hers firmly onto the soft garden floor. His penis filled her, and went deep inside. For a while their pelvises danced to the idyllic strains of Beethoven, but all too soon the urgent needs of their bodies brought them to a crescendo, out of synch with the music. And afterward, as Tyger lay in Guy's warm arms and licked his nipple tenderly, she felt that Guy might be all she ever needed.

"*Vive la France,*" she whispered into his ear.

The art director, Davis Chipps, and Tyger and Connie were glum. Jake had done his best, but the proofs of the ads featuring Garry Gray were disappointing. The door opened, and Hugh Marshall entered the conference room.

"Sorry I'm late. What's the problem?"

Tyger handed him the photos and layout. "This. Garry projects as much personality as a grapefruit."

Connie interrupted, laughing. "From what I hear, he *is* a grapefruit."

"Anyway, Hugh," Davis Chipps said, "these are the results of the fourth photo session. I don't believe the fault lies with Jake Danton."

Marshall studied the evidence. "I see what you mean. Can I see the proofs from the other sessions?" Tyger handed them to him, and he looked through them quickly. "You're right. Garry's bland, one-dimensional. Let's get rid of him."

"But we're stuck with him, according to the contract," Tyger said.

Marshall nodded. "Yes. But forget that for a minute. Davis, who would you use . . . if the door were open?"

"A sports figure," Davis said. "Hit the target market with someone who *represents* something. I mean, Garry Gray is just another male model . . . and not a good one at that. I think he'll give our product a weak image. Not that homosexuals don't buy lots of cologne. But it narrows your market. . . ."

"Have you anyone in mind?" Hugh asked.

"Yeah, I've thought about it. Bill Perry."

"That basketball player? He's a knockout," said Connie.

"Good idea," Hugh said. "He'd be perfect. As a matter of fact, hasn't he just written a book?"

"One on None," said Davis. "It's on the *New York Times* best-seller list. I saw him on Merv Griffin the other night. He's articulate, and he has a good sense of humor. He even wrote the book himself . . . without an 'as told to.' "

Marshall got up to leave. "Good suggestion, Davis. I'm going to think about it."

"But Hugh . . ." Tyger followed him into the hallway. "I don't see how we can break the contract with Matt. He gave up creative control to have Garry as spokesman for the line. He'll never agree to our dumping Garry. He'll sue us. Besides . . . I saw Matt yesterday, and he's in terrible shape. I think he's headed for a breakdown. If you fire Garry now, I don't know how he'd react."

Marshall waved a hand to dismiss Tyger's objections. "I can renegotiate Matt's contract, if need be. Give him creative clout on any new products we launch under his name. He'll come around. But before we do anything, let's find out if Bill Perry's interested. And if we can meet his price. Have Sheldon . . ." He stopped. "By the way, where is he? He wasn't at the meeting."

"Oh, ah, he wasn't feeling well after lunch. Connie urged him to go home early."

"Well, fill him in on all this. Let me know when you'll be seeing Perry. I'd like to sit in on the meeting, if I'm in town. See you soon, Tyger."

Tyger went back to Connie's office. "Hugh just asked where Sheldon was. I said he was sick and that you'd convinced him to leave for the day. . . ."

"Good." Connie paused. "I'm worried. I've been calling his apartment all day, and there's no answer. What could have happened? Do you think I should start calling hospitals, or . . ."

Ginger peeked in. "Connie, Mr. Shaw called when you were in the meeting. He says he's home now."

"Thank God. He's all right, isn't he?"

Ginger shrugged. "I guess so. He sounded . . . okay."

Twenty minutes later, Connie was on East Seventy-second Street, sitting in the living room of the apartment Sheldon Shaw was subletting temporarily. She was angry.

"I was frantic. Why didn't you call me right away?"

"Connie, I went to see Louise. I told her it was over. For good."

The news caught Connie off balance. "Come on, Sheldon," she said. Her voice was whispery and small.

"Connie, I want to marry you. After I divorce Louise, of course." He patted her hand consolingly. "You'll see. Things will work out before you know it. Once my life is straightened out I'll stop drinking, too."

Tears flooded into Connie's eyes. "Try to cut down in the meantime. Everybody at the office knows you drink. Tyger even covered for you with Hugh Marshall today."

"What? I don't need her doing anything on my behalf. She thinks she's such a little hotshot. . . ."

"I know you don't like her, but you're being unfair. And if you don't want her covering for you, then don't give her a reason to *have* to. Pull yourself together or . . ."

"Or what?"

Connie turned away from him.

"*What?*" he demanded, raising his voice.

"Sheldon . . . I love you. You know I do . . . and I don't want you to blow it at Keller Perfumes. You have to spend more time at the office, and less . . ."

Sheldon Shaw picked up a half-empty bottle of J&B and hurled it against the closet door. It hit with a thud and fell to the carpet below, without breaking. "Dammit, Connie, don't tell me what to do. I *told* you I'd pull myself together. Don't bug me!" he shouted. Then he sat on the sofa and hung his head in his lap. He began sobbing loudly. Connie went over to him and put her arms around his shoulders.

"It's all right," she said tenderly. "I love you. I'll help you." She brushed a lock of hair away from his forehead, and began crying softly to herself. She wished she had met him when they were young, before he had become disillusioned with his life. Things could have been so different for both of them.

The crowds bustled happily down Fifth Avenue. Christmas was all around them, and Tyger had taken Guy to the ceremonial lighting of the enormous five-story Christmas tree at Rockefeller Center. They drank hot chocolate at the Swiss Pavilion, and went Christmas shopping at Saks Fifth Avenue and Brentano's. After an hour and a half, they were both laden with shopping bags.

"Hurry, Guy. I want to check out the gift shop at the Museum of Modern Art. Then maybe we can make it to Bendel's before it closes at nine."

"Please, Tyger, no more!" Guy said, laughing. "I've had enough."

"Tyger! Darling! What a surprise to run into you. On the street, of all places." It was Lady Rowan, wearing a dark-brown fisher coat with a floppy wide-brimmed hat. Tyger introduced her mother to Guy.

"I'm meeting a friend at the Palace for dinner, but I have time for a quick drink."

"Fine," said Tyger. "What about the Algonquin?"

As Guy was checking their coats, Bobbie and Tyger arranged themselves on a Victorian sofa in the literary lobby lounge of the famous hotel.

"You never mentioned Guy was so handsome. No wonder you've been keeping him a secret," Bobbie said quickly, as Guy returned and pulled up a deep-red armchair, to face them across the low cocktail table.

After they ordered their drinks, Bobbie monopolized the

conversation, her attention focused on Guy. Tyger felt edged out. She hoped her mother would mention Hugh Marshall, but Bobbie didn't say anything about him. Tyger wondered if they were still seeing each other.

Bobbie turned to Tyger. "You'd better not let Guy loose in New York. He's so charming!" Guy blushed, obviously flattered and dazzled by Tyger's beautiful mother. "If only I were a few years younger, Tyger." She laughed. "I'd give you a run for your money."

You already have, Tyger felt like saying, but restrained herself. "What are you doing for Christmas, Mother?"

"Well, I had hoped we could spend it together, but something's come up." Bobbie's turquoise eyes twinkled as she waited to be quizzed for details.

"What, Mother? Tell us."

"Christmas. A villa in Tenerife. Dear Jimmy and I. Alone," she said dramatically.

"You're back together again?" Tyger perked up.

"Well . . . he rang and asked if I wanted to try a reconciliation. We decided to spend a few weeks together. Kind of a second honeymoon."

"Oh, Mother. I'm so happy for you."

"Well, Jimmy and I have a lot in common. Perhaps we can work it out. Oh, goodness, look at the time! I must be dashing off. Tyger, take good care of this young man. He's a dream." She gave them each a quick kiss, and was off.

Tyger and Guy stayed for another drink. "Your mother is not like any mother I have met before. She is so young . . . and lovely. You look a lot like her."

"Yes. People always take us for sisters," Tyger said, without enthusiasm.

"What's the matter, Tyger? Don't you like your mother?"

"Why do you ask that?"

"Oh . . . something about you changed when she was here. You became—*qu'est-ce que dire?*—uptight."

"I didn't know I was that obvious. I guess there's a lot of tension between us. I mean, look at the way she was flirting with you. As if I weren't here."

"Oh, Tyger, you exaggerate. She was merely being polite."

"No, Guy . . . I know her better than you do."

"So, you were jealous of your mother's attention to me? I am flattered. Maybe that means you really do care for me . . . that you are not just interested in me because of Keller Perfumes."

"Oh, Guy, you know that." Tyger smiled.

"I was not sure." He put his hand on hers. "You see, Tyger, I am in love with you." His dark eyes looked into hers. "I want you to feel the same way about me."

"I do, Guy. I . . . do." Tyger returned Guy's tender gaze, and thought about this evening's turn of events. Bobbie was getting back together with Lord Rowan, and that left Hugh Marshall free. But, surprisingly, Tyger didn't care. She looked across the table at Guy. He was a wonderful person, and she was happy with him.

"What shall we do for Christmas, Guy?"

"We shall spend it at your apartment . . . I will cook a fabulous French meal for you. I warn you . . . your Christmas present will be late. But it will be very special."

"What is it?" Tyger asked.

"Ah, no! I will not tell you. It is a surprise."

"That's not fair, Guy. Now I'm going to have to run around searching for something *really* clever for you."

"No. Just tie a ribbon around your waist. You are the only present I want."

Tyger picked up the phone and dialed. "Hello, Annie, it's Tyger Hayes. Is he in?"

In a moment Hugh Marshall's voice came on the line. "Hello, Tyger. What's on your mind?"

"Want to go to a basketball game tonight?"

"A what?"

"The Knicks against Boston. I've got two tickets at center court. Courtesy of Bill Perry."

"Good. He's interested, then?"

"Interested enough to talk. We're meeting him after the game. I've made reservations at the Ginger Man."

"Fine. I haven't been to a basketball game in years."

After she rang off, Tyger dialed another number. "This is Tyger Hayes," she said. "Is Mr. Phillips back yet?"

"I'm sorry, Miss Hayes, he still hasn't returned. We expected him in today. I'll see that he gets your messages the moment he arrives."

"Yes, please. Thank you." She put the phone back into its cradle and drummed fretfully on the table with her pencil. She hated to be meeting with Bill Perry before having a chance to explain the situation to Matt. He would throw a fit, of course, if he knew what they were up to.

And, for once, he would be right.

The Ginger Man was in the midst of its late-evening transit from busy to hopeless, as the Lincoln Center crowds began to pack in. Tyger, Hugh Marshall and Bill Perry had arrived from Madison Square Garden in time to claim their reservation, and had managed to order and receive a round of drinks before losing track of their waiter completely.

"That was a very impressive performance, Mr. Perry," Marshall was saying. The Knicks had beaten the Boston Celtics, 109–107. Bill Perry had scored twenty-three points, including the game-winner on a driving lay-up at the buzzer. "I hope it won't affect your asking price."

Perry smiled the craggy, lean-cheeked smile which was familiar to sports fans all over the country. "Everything affects my asking price, Mr. Marshall."

Tyger laughed. "I can see why you don't need an agent."

"These are tricky times for a ballplayer, Miss Hayes," Perry said, shifting his rugged six-foot-six frame around in his chair to look at Tyger, as he had repeatedly that evening, with frank approval. "The skills can lose their edge overnight. A man has to be ready to shift smoothly into the next stage of his life. The main options that interest me are politics, like Bill Bradley, or movies and commercials, like O. J. Simpson. Or broadcasting, like almost everyone else. If I decide to take a whack at politics, I can't have my opponent claiming that I don't even know how to negotiate a contract. Besides," he added, grinning again, "I *do* know how to negotiate a contract."

"I don't think we'll have a problem there," said Hugh. "But there's one small hurdle you ought to be aware of." He quickly outlined the Garry Gray situation. "We can't sign a formal contract until that's been cleared up. Matt Phillips is a man of volatile temperament, and a certain amount of stroking may be required."

"I hope *you're* not a man of volatile temperament, Mr. Perry," Tyger put in. "It seems just about everyone we've had to deal with since this project started has been."

"Only on the basketball court, Miss Hayes. And, generally, only in the final period."

"Good," said Hugh Marshall. "In the meantime, there's no reason we can't be discussing the terms of . . ."

"Oh, yes, there is," Tyger groaned. "Look who just walked in."

Matt Phillips had already spotted them, and was heading over.

"Matt, what a surprise! Won't you join us?" Marshall had risen and extended his hand.

"Hello, Hugh . . . Tyger. Just for a moment. I'm meeting somebody." He gave Tyger a quick peck on the cheek.

"Matt, this is Bill Perry, the basketball player."

Phillips smiled. "Mr. Perry needs no identification to me. I'm a big Knicks fan."

"You are?" That was a side of Matt that Tyger would never have guessed.

"And I'm a big fan of yours, Mr. Phillips," Perry said, enveloping Matt's hand in his own huge one in a handshake. "You'll notice I'm wearing your blazer."

"That sort of thing never escapes my notice."

"As a matter of fact," Perry continued, "you see a lot of Matt Phillips labels around the league these days. Basketball players tend to be a pretty fashion-oriented crew. Your men's line is really in around the NBA."

Tyger couldn't believe it. Matt was positively glowing. She caught Hugh's eye, and he nodded back at her, imperceptibly. Bill Perry's asking price had probably just gone up again, but Marshall would be happy to meet it.

Perry looked at his watch. "Excuse me a moment," he said. "I have a couple of calls to make. Mr. Phillips, if I don't see you, it's been a pleasure."

When Perry had left the table, Matt turned coolly to Tyger. "A lovely man," he said. "But what's the nature of this top-level conference? Business . . . or purely social?"

"Business, Matt," Hugh Marshall said. "We're having problems with the Matt Phillips for Men image. We wanted to begin exploring . . ."

"Problems? You mean Garry, don't you?" Matt's voice was beginning to rise.

"Matt, we . . ." Tyger began.

"You have *no* right to explore anything. We have a contract! There are no ambiguities! This is my name . . . *my* rights you're fucking with, Marshall. And you're not going to get away with it!"

Heads at nearby tables were turning. Matt Phillips stood up and flounced off.

"I'll talk to him, Hugh. . . ."

Tyger caught Matt at the bar. He had just ordered a double martini to fuel his anger.

"Matt, please, let me explain."

"You, Tyger," he seethed. "Stabbing me in the back. I thought I could trust you. . . ."

"You can, Matt. For God's sake, will you listen? I've been trying to call you all week."

"Ha!"

"It's true! But that's neither here nor there. Look, let me show you something." In her briefcase she had the shots Jake had taken of Garry Gray. She had brought them along in order to show Bill Perry the layout. Reluctantly, Matt studied them.

"They're hopeless, Matt. Surely a man of your aesthetic sensitivity can see that. Garry just doesn't project the image we want—*you* want—for Matt Phillips for Men. Look at these pictures. You know I'm right."

Matt remained quiet, looking down at the pictures in his lap and sipping his martini. When he finally looked back up at Tyger, his eyes were glistening slightly, and there was a soft smile on his lips.

"You know, Tyger, that advice you gave me was the best advice I ever had. I had a glorious week in Acapulco. Garry ended up tagging along, but in spite of him I managed to relax, enjoy myself and find someone new. A wonderful man, an architect from San Francisco. I'm meeting him here tonight. Anyway, it brought me to my senses about Garry. It was over between us a long time ago. I've been hanging on because I was terrified of being alone."

"Matt . . . I'm delighted."

Matt's face darkened. "Still, I don't like you and Marshall plotting behind my back."

"It wasn't behind your back! If you'd check in with your office once in a while you'd find messages stacked up to the ceiling from me."

"Well, I just got in tonight, in time to head straight to the Met. But I can't believe . . ."

"If you don't believe me, call your secretary at home right now. Dammit, Matt, you ought to know me better than to think I'd do anything underhanded. . . ."

Matt shook his head. "I know you wouldn't, Tyger. Apologize to Marshall for me. Bill Perry's a fine choice." He giggled. "I've always loved basketball. It's the only sport where they dress sensibly—those cute shorts and tank tops."

"Sorry to take so long, Matt," said a voice behind them.

Tyger turned to see a slim, distinguished man of about

forty-five, with hair that went from sandy brown to gray as it flared back in stylish sideburns below the ears.

"Eric!" Matt exclaimed, with a smile that lit up his face. "Eric, this is Tyger Hayes. She's with my perfume company. Tyger, this is Eric Nebelthau."

"You don't know how pleased I am to meet you," Tyger said, and chatted a few moments before she returned to Hugh Marshall.

The Silver Shadow II moved with all the smooth quiet of its nomenclature, rolling downtown along Seventh Avenue. In the back, Hugh and Tyger rode in silence.

She was an extraordinary woman, Hugh had decided. She had jumped into this job with virtually no experience, and she had handled everything he had thrown at her. And he had thrown her some tough ones. She handled herself with a poise and sureness in business matters that was instinctive, and impressive.

For many years now, the only real passion in Hugh Marshall's life had been business. It was the yardstick he measured himself against, the arena he tested himself in, the comfort and oblivion he sought against the debilitating pressures of personal and emotional life. If he appeared socially with beautiful women, it was because his business life functioned more smoothly with a certain amount of social exposure. If he went to bed with them, it was to relieve certain requirements of body and etiquette. But his passion was reserved for business; and he had never, until now, found a woman who he felt was remotely capable of understanding and sharing that passion.

But, of course, he could not allow himself to become really involved with Tyger. She worked for him; and that was an inviolable rule. Equally problematical was his affair with Bobbie. A man did not move from the mother's bed to the daughter's; not a man with any notion of decency and self-respect. The affair with Bobbie had cooled now, with her reconciliation with Lord Rowan, but the barrier to Tyger had been established.

Was that, he wondered suddenly, why he had allowed himself to be intrigued by Tyger's mother?

The Rolls turned. Midtown was behind them, and they were in the warreny streets of Tyger's Greenwich Village neighborhood. He looked at her, sitting quietly beside him.

He knew many beautiful women. What made this one's eyes and throat and lips seem different?

He knew he could not kiss her. And then, without his willing it, without his knowing it, he took her into his arms and pressed his mouth down hard on hers. He felt her lips part with a startled moan of pleasure, and his tongue probed in, and was met by her smooth, wet tongue. He squeezed her against him, violently, and her body strained against him, her hands beneath his jacket, her fingers digging passionately into his back.

"Hugh," she moaned. "Hugh . . ."

He ran his hand down her body and could feel the softness of her breasts inside her clingy Halston jersey. He could feel his desire growing, and kissed her again, gently. He wanted this woman as much as he had ever wanted anyone in his life . . . but if he went to bed with Tyger he didn't know where it might lead. And he was a little afraid to find out.

The car stopped in front of Tyger's building.

"Come up," she whispered.

He shook his head, and gently held her away from him. "No, Tyger. I'm sorry."

"Why not?"

"I'm sorry," he said again. He could see that she was hurt and angry. He could not blame her. He had acted foolishly. She had turned away from him, busily gathering her handbag and portfolio. He could not see her face, but when she looked back at him her eyes were flat and controlled.

"I'll have the lawyers draw up the Perry agreement in the morning," she said. The chauffeur came around and opened the door. "Goodnight, Hugh." Tyger got out of the Rolls and walked to her door.

Hugh Marshall waited until she was safely inside her building. Then he tapped the window with his cane, and his chauffeur started the engine, and the Silver Shadow pulled away down Jane Street.

CHAPTER TWENTY-SIX

CHRISTMAS and New Year's came and went. It was a Saturday evening in early January, and Tyger had just fixed hot buttered rum for herself and Guy, in celebration of New York City's first snow of the winter: already a foot deep, and still coming down. The streetlight outside Tyger's living-room window cast a pink-orange tint to the sparkling snow-flakes.

"When it's snowing, New York's the most beautiful place in the world." Tyger went to the window and looked out. The wind was blowing the snow into high drifts against the sides of the buildings on her street.

"Wrong. The Côte d'Azur in any season is the most beauti-ful. This snow is nice . . . but tomorrow it will be dirty. Dogs will have soiled it. . . ."

"Oh, Guy, really. Why spoil it? Where's your sense of poetry?"

"I left it in France. . . ." Guy said glumly.

"Are you homesick?"

"Yes. This New York winter is too cold. The grayness, the wind . . . I cannot get used to it."

Tyger sat beside him on the sofa and snuggled up close. "Oh, my poor darling. I keep forgetting how unhappy you must be. If you don't *want* to be here, New York can be awful."

"Oh, Tyger . . . I did not mean to hurt your feelings. I would be happy anywhere with you. You are what has made the past two months bearable." He leaned over and kissed her gently. And again. "When this job is over, you must come back to France with me. There is nothing more beautiful than walking through the flower fields. *Roses de mai* stretching as far as the eye can see. Imagine the color, the odor . . . *c'est formidable.*"

Tyger was not anxious to consider her future with Guy. Things were perfect now.

"I own some land on a hillside overlooking the jasmine fields. There is a small stone house on it. Soon, I want to fix it up, add on to it. . . ."

"It sounds lovely." Tyger changed the subject. "I have an idea. Let's get in bed and watch TV. One of my father's movies is coming on at eleven-thirty."

Guy smiled. "If you get me to bed, I don't promise to watch the movie. I only want to look at you . . . naked."

"The apartment's too drafty to lie around without any clothes on."

"I'll keep you warm." He put his arm around her and they walked to the bedroom.

The phone rang. Tyger picked it up to hear Mary Rogers's sobbing voice on the other end.

"Oh, Miss Mary. Thank goodness you're home. Please come right away! It's your mother. . . ."

Tyger felt a wave of sudden nausea. "What? What's happened?"

"I just found her. I've phoned the doctor. He's on the way, but with the snow . . . the streets are . . ."

"Mary Rogers, try to calm down. Tell me . . . is my mother alive?" Tyger asked slowly, dreading the answer.

"Yes . . . but barely breathing. There's an empty bottle of pills on her bed table. She must have taken them all . . . but I don't know how many there were." Mary Rogers burst into tears again. "Oh . . . it's so awful! I don't know how long ago she took them. She said she had a headache . . . and went to bed without dinner. That was at seven o'clock. Later the phone rang and she didn't pick up . . . I thought she had dozed off. The call was from London, from Lord Rowan. He said it was important . . . that I should wake her. So I went to her room. . . ." The Englishwoman's voice trembled with emotion. "But . . . she wouldn't wake up. Then I saw the empty bottle. Oh, please come as fast as you can. . . ."

"I'll be there right away. Drink a shot of whiskey and try to calm down. . . ."

The doctor was with Lady Rowan when Tyger arrived. Mary Rogers's eyes were red, but she had stopped crying.

"Hello, Dr. Bakst. How is . . ."

"Your mother's all right. The pills she took couldn't have killed her. I gave her thirty cc's of ipecac and induced vomiting. She'll wake up in a few hours feeling under the weather, but she'll be okay." He handed Tyger a small vial of pills. "Give her one of these tranquilizers and keep her in bed. I'll be back in the morning to have a look at her."

"Thank you for coming so quickly, doctor. It's a rough night. . . ."

"Actually, I live only two blocks away. Good exercise for me."

"Do you think . . . she took the pills by accident, or . . ."

"Tyger, no one takes half a bottle of pills by accident. Has something been troubling her?"

"I don't know. She's been away since before Christmas. I didn't know she was back in town."

"She arrived home this afternoon," Mary Rogers said. "She seemed tired, but I thought it was merely jet lag. . . ."

"Well, Tyger, you'll stay the night, won't you? Talk to her when she wakes up?" Dr. Bakst picked up his black bag. "I'll see myself to the door."

Bobbie dozed fitfully for the next few hours. So did Tyger, lying on the chaise next to her mother's bed. Around six a.m. Bobbie woke up.

"Tyger . . . what are you doing here?" she said raspily. "Oh God, my voice." She swallowed. "My throat's so dry."

"Mother, you took an overdose of barbiturates. Here . . . Dr. Bakst told me to give you this tranquilizer when you came to."

"Oh, Jesus." Bobbie began to remember what had happened. "I feel awful. Can you hand me a pillow so I can prop up?"

Tyger arranged the pillows and straightened the covers. "Would you like some tea?"

"Hmmm." Bobbie nodded. "Maybe that would help. Ohhh . . ." she moaned. "I'm beginning to remember. It was stupid of me to take those pills. . . ."

Tyger sat down beside her and took her hand. "What happened, Mother?" she asked quietly. "Do you feel like talking?"

"No!" Bobbie snapped, then, seeing the bewilderment in

her daughter's eyes, she tried to smile. "Well . . . I'll try. But first, will you get the tea?"

After two cups of tea and the Valium had relaxed her, Bobbie seemed better.

"Oh, Tyger, how ridiculous your mother is. I was in such a foul mood yesterday. The Concorde was late leaving London because of the air-traffic strike. Then the storm here . . . we had to circle JFK for hours. Once we landed there were no cabs. Finally had to share one with three loathsome people and . . ."

"Mother . . . you tried to commit suicide. It wasn't because you had a difficult trip. . . ."

"No." Bobbie paused. "No. It's . . . everything seemed so pointless. I was tired and depressed . . . and I couldn't think of one single reason to stay alive. . . ."

"Not even me?" Tyger said slowly.

"No, darling. Not even you." Bobbie sat back against the pillows with a sigh. "We're not close any more . . . I guess we never were. I've been too busy living my own life to care about yours. . . ."

"That's not exactly true. You've always had plenty to say about mine."

"Hmm. You see, you always have a dig. . . ." She lit a cigarette.

"Oh, Mother, don't smoke."

Bobbie ignored her. "Maybe if I had some grandchildren I could settle down and act my age. But I doubt if you'll ever give me any."

"I'm only twenty-six, remember? There's still plenty of time. You never can tell what will happen."

"No." Bobbie looked away dramatically. "You never can." She stared into space, lost in thought.

Tyger wanted to make a real effort. She took Bobbie's hand again. Bobbie started, then gazed at Tyger blankly.

"Mother, you're looking at me as though I'm a stranger."

"What?" She focused her eyes on Tyger. "I was thinking how little I really know you. I don't even know myself. You'd think after all these years I would . . ." Tears spilled out of her eyes.

"What's wrong, Mother? Something's happened to make you so unhappy."

"Yes. Something has. Can you get me a drink?"

"At six-thirty in the morning?"

"Lunchtime in London. No . . . forget it. Might not mix with the tranquilizer."

Tyger laughed. "That's ironic. Last night you were trying to do yourself in."

"You have a strange sense of humor, Tyger."

"No, Mother, I didn't mean . . ."

Bobbie patted Tyger's hand. "That's all right, dear. It's always been a problem between us. We stab around at conversation, but we've never been able to talk to each other."

Tyger handed Bobbie an ash tray. "You're skirting the issue right now. You still haven't told me what the matter is."

"It's not so mysterious. Mainly . . . it didn't work out with Jimmy. I went through hoops to get him back. And, it turned out, he wasn't interested." She crushed her cigarette out forcefully. "You're right, Tyger. I'm going to give up smoking," she digressed. "As you know, I'm used to getting what I want. This is hard to take. First Tom, now Jimmy. . . ."

"Mother, you're . . ."

"Don't interrupt, darling. I'm just getting started." She wound the music box on the table by her bed and the sounds of "Edelweiss" punctured the still morning air. "You know, my grandmother used to say that if you take care of your teeth, keep your hair and fingernails groomed, and read the first two pages of *The New York Times* every day, you'll always get a man." Bobbie laughed huskily. "It worked . . . but what Nonna neglected to say is that sometimes it's more important to spend time with yourself than with a man. I've never spent much time alone. I guess now that I'm middle-aged it's catching up with me." She reached for her pack of cigarettes, then pushed it away. "I'm terrified of being by myself. I guess that's why I'm jealous of you. . . ."

"Jealous of me?"

"What's surprising about that? You're young. There's so fucking much still ahead of you and . . ." She patted Tyger's arm affectionately. "You've pulled yourself together pretty well, kid. You like your job. You're not frantic to get married again. You're independent."

"Thank you, Mother."

"Don't thank me. I certainly haven't contributed to your well-being." This time she took a cigarette out of the pack and lit it. She coughed, and put it out quickly. "I can live without Jimmy. It's just the pattern. After forty-six years, what have I learned that will keep me from going out and making the same mistake again? To have four marriages behind me . . . it's really shameful. Oh, Tyger . . . what's the *point* of it all?"

Tyger looked at her mother sympathetically. "I don't know. Except that you're bound to have learned more than you realize. If you spent some time alone, taking stock . . ."

"The next thing I know you'll be telling me to write Dear Abby."

"It wouldn't hurt to get some professional help. A psychiatrist or psychoanalyst could help you sort out your feelings. Besides, everybody goes through midlife crisis. . . ."

"Yes, dear," Bobbie said mechanically. "I read *Passages*."

Tyger was becoming annoyed. "Mother, I'm only trying to help. Why won't you let me? Why *can't* we be close? I *love* you. . . ."

There was silence in the room.

"I love you, too." Bobbie began crying again. "But it's painful to be around you. I lost you somewhere along the way. You were such a sweet little girl. Painting me pictures, making me paper fans . . . but I lost you," she repeated.

Tyger put her arms around her mother and hugged her closely. "We can still be friends. It's not too late."

"Pull the curtains closed, will you?" She threw the extra pillow down on the floor by the bed. "Goodnight, dear . . . or good morning. Thank you for coming over. Now . . . I need a rest." Bobbie yawned and was asleep before Tyger had lowered the shades.

Tyger stood by the bed and looked at her mother for a few minutes. She knew that they would never be close, and it hurt. Tyger hoped that she would be happier in twenty years than her mother was—and wondered if she would be.

Another week passed, and finally Tyger found herself in a taxi racing toward Brooklyn. Guy had telephoned and told her to rush over right away. Good news, he had said.

Several other technicians were standing around Guy's lab. Guy waved to her. "Tyger! Come here! Jazz has been born."

"Oh, I'm so excited, I'm almost afraid." She took the sample vial he handed her, lifted it to her nose. There was jasmine, citrus, spice, but the overall topnote was unidentifiable. The result was sensuous . . . jazz on a summer's night. "Guy! It's terrific!" She hugged him. "Oh, darling, you've done it!"

"I am pleased with it myself. It still needs stability testing

. . . but it passes the FTC and FDA standards. The testing committee here has approved it. . . ."

"Oh, let me go call the office and tell everyone. Will you let me take you to lunch, to celebrate?"

"Bien sûr." Guy smiled. "I deserve a magnificent meal."

They went to Le Plaisir and wallowed in haute cuisine, washed down with velvety sixteen-year-old Clos de Vougeot red burgundy.

"Oh, Guy . . . I'm just so happy."

"Me, too. *Ma chère,* I love you so much." He paused. "I have something for you. Since I did not finish it in time for Christmas I was planning to save it for your birthday. But I cannot wait. I want you to have it now." He reached into his jacket pocket and pulled out a small bottle. The label was typed and fastened on with cellophane.

Tyger read it. "GSD–1122. Just what I've always wanted!"

Guy grinned. "That's just the code. The real name of the fragrance is Tyger. I created it for you."

"Oh, Guy . . . thank you . . . I . . ."

"Aren't you going to smell it?"

"Yes . . . oh, yes!" She unscrewed the top and lifted the bottle to her nose. The aroma was sophisticated and zingy, tuberose and musk, citrus and clear smoke. "Oh, Guy . . . this is fantastic!"

"What's the matter, darling? You're crying."

Tyger wiped her eyes with her napkin. "It's . . . I've . . . never had such a wonderful present. And I've never smelled anything quite like it. It's marvelous! I don't know how to thank you. . . ."

Guy laughed. "Don't worry about that. There are plenty of ways. You really like it?"

"Yes. Even more than Jazz, I think." She dabbed some behind her ears and on her wrists. "Do I get to keep this bottle?"

"Of course. You can decant it into something more beautiful, if you wish."

"What happens when I run out of it?"

"You will never run out as long as I'm around. . . ."

The more Tyger thought about it, the more she felt that the Tyger scent was better than Jazz, more perfect for Jazz than the designated one. With the stability testing completed, Jazz was scheduled to be introduced to the expectant crew at Keller Perfumes at the end of the week. Hugh Marshall was still out of town, but Tyger had told Tim Yates to pass along to him that they finally had a perfume.

"Guy," Tyger said at breakfast at the Carlyle on Friday morning, "would you mind if I let them smell Tyger . . . to consider it for the Jazz fragrance?"

Guy hesitated, then shrugged. "If you like. They are both great fragrances. This has been the most creative period of my life, to do two perfumes at the same time. I am flattered that you want to present both." A crease appeared on his forehead. "But if they choose Tyger, any woman can have it, not just you. It will no longer be special. . . ."

"No, Guy, you're wrong. It will be even more special . . . knowing that it was created for me."

Connie Larcada walked into Sheldon Shaw's office. "Are you ready for the big unveiling? I'm *so* excited."

"I'll be with you in a moment. As soon as I sign these letters."

Connie was relieved to see that Sheldon had not been drinking that morning. He had fallen short of his resolution to cut down. In fact, the problem seemed worse over the past few weeks. Connie could not bug Sheldon, because he was so defensive. He still had not actually filed for divorce, and he was defensive about that, too. Louise had contracted pneumonia and he had moved back home. Only for the time being, he had promised Connie.

"Hurry up, Shel. Everyone's waiting."

"You run along. I'll be right there." When she left the room, he poured a healthy shot of whiskey into his Styrofoam cup of coffee. Then he joined the others in the conference room.

Guy Saint Denis was there to introduce the fragrance. The entire staff, including the secretaries, was assembled and ready to sniff.

"I have prepared a number of small sample bottles of Jazz so you may each have one to keep with you. There are extras for your market testing."

The bottles were passed out, opened, and smelled, to a unanimous round of accolades.

Tyger stood. "I don't know whether I should do this to you. But in good conscience I have to." She introduced the bottle of Tyger fragrance. "This is another scent . . . one Guy created for me. And I think it's even better than the other one for Jazz." She passed it around.

Another chorus of praise followed, and another round of sniffing, first Jazz, then Tyger.

Sheldon Shaw sipped his coffee and sat. He had sniffed both fragrances and, frankly, could not tell much difference. They both smelled fine, both good perfumes.

Shaw looked at Tyger, so self-assured, confident. People like her glided through life, with lots of money and no real problems. Tyger, as he had known from the start, was part of the reason he was disenchanted with his job at Keller Perfumes. She thought she was better than he; always so gung-ho to get the job done, never missing a chance to show him up. Hugh Marshall thought she was just great; so did everyone, even Connie. Before he left Kellerco he would love to see her have some comeuppance. It would give him personal pleasure, Shaw thought, keeping his gaze fixed on her.

Then it occurred to him that he had an opportunity.

"Let me smell both those fragrances again," he said.

Connie handed the bottles to him. "My nose is shot. I can't smell anything now."

Shaw sniffed them both. "Tyger, you don't know what you're talking about. This one—Jazz—is perfect. I don't see why you had to try and confuse the issue. Hey, Jess, don't you agree with me?"

Jess was bewildered. "Well, Shel, they're both good. Golly, I don't know. Maybe you're right."

"I know I'm right. I know my fragrances," he insisted. "Mr. Saint Denis, the one you created for Jazz, don't *you* think it meets every requirement laid down by our fragrance profile and marketing survey?"

"Of course. I created it to fit the image you wanted," Guy said.

"And the scent you created for Miss Hayes—what was your inspiration for that? Was it a reject from the Jazz testing?"

"No, never. It was inspired by Tyger, and for her. I was not thinking of the Jazz theme when I was working on it."

"There! You see!" Shaw gloated. "Jazz was created for the market we stipulated. The other fragrance has nothing to do with it. There is no reason to consider it."

Tyger objected. "But I think it's better . . . more unusual."

"Or perhaps because it was created for you?"

"No!" Tyger said. "At least . . . I don't think so."

"I agree with Tyger," Connie interjected. "I like her scent for Jazz."

"I can't make up my mind," Davis Chipps said.

"I think I agree with Sheldon," Jess said. "The first one is more along the lines of our fragrance profile."

"Are we going to throw weeks of marketing analysis out the window?" Sheldon Shaw asked. "We have a darned good fragrance, made to our requirements." He looked straight at Tyger. "Tyger, I think we've got a pretty clear case here."

Tyger had never seen Shaw so positive about anything. She was surprised by his show of strength. "Sheldon, I didn't mean to open a beehive. *I* like the other scent, and I simply didn't think it would be fair not to have it for consideration."

"Yes, of course," Shaw said patronizingly. "Nevertheless, I think we've got to stick with the first scent, the one created as Jazz. We'll test it, of course, with our marketing panels. But giving people a choice will create problems. Remember, we don't have much time."

"That's true," Connie said. "We can't afford a hung jury. We've got to get into production."

"You're right," Jess said.

Tyger resented Shaw's heavy-handedness, but she had to admit he was right: they had to test Jazz and get it into production right away.

"Okay." Tyger sighed.. "You can't say I didn't try."

After the meeting, Guy went back to Tyger's office. "You know, it's not as if the fragrance I created for Jazz is not right. . . ."

"Oh, I know. I still think the other's more unique. Connie liked it, too, before Sheldon put the pressure on."

"Now, now, Tyger. Don't pout."

"I won't. There's still too much work to do. More blasted marketing panels to set up."

"I was hoping that you would take off and spend the day with me. I want to see the Magritte show at the Museum of Modern Art."

"Okay. I guess I can take an hour off. Let me make a few calls first." She leaned back in her chair. "You know, I can't understand Sheldon. I've never seen him get so worked up about anything."

CHAPTER TWENTY-SEVEN

SHELDON Shaw walked through the snowy streets to Billy Youngblood's townhouse. He was feeling good, and had been since he had managed to swing everyone's opinion for the Jazz scent away from Tyger's choice. The marketing panels had proved him out: thumbs up for Jazz. Production was moving right along.

"Come in, Shelley!" Billy Youngblood shook his hand warmly and took him into a small study overlooking the snow-covered garden. "I was just fixin' myself a drink. Have one?"

"Ah, no thanks, Billy. I'm here to talk."

"Sure, Shelley. Do you have that stuff for me?"

"Well . . . that's what I want to talk about."

Youngblood showed no reaction as he mixed the vodka martini with his index finger. "Oh?"

"Yes. You see, I've changed my mind . . . about the favor. The money would be nice, but it's a question of the ethics of the thing. I think I'll just accept the job . . . without the bonus."

Youngblood took a sip of his drink and studied the nervous man in front of him. Shaw wasn't bright enough to be bluffing, was he? Could this be a ploy to suck him for more money? "Well, now . . . what's brought about this change of mind?"

"It's . . . personal. And, I guess you could say, my conscience."

Billy reached for his cigars, handed one to Shaw and took

one for himself. "Now, let me get this straight. You're backin' out of our little deal?"

"Not at all, Billy. I'm still very excited about the job at Powers Perfumes. I just think it would be better—cleaner—without the other thing."

"Well, Sheldon, I don't think that's possible."

"What?" Shaw was beginning to feel uncomfortable.

"I mean, the favor was part of the deal . . . even though you were bein' paid extra for it. You understand?"

"Well . . ."

"To put it bluntly: no favor, no job. Are you sure you won't have a drink?" Youngblood poured himself another.

"Oh, maybe I will." Shaw was tense. Perhaps he should have seen this coming. But he hadn't. Not at all.

"And also . . ." Billy Youngblood handed him a martini and sat next to him on the red leather couch. "You don't have much of an option. About changin' your mind, I mean."

"I'm not sure I understand." In three swallows, his drink was gone. "You said you *needed* me at Powers Perfumes."

"I do . . . I do. I wanted you to do this favor for me because—among other reasons—I wanted to make sure you'd *stay* at Powers and not sashay back to Kellerco if you get homesick."

Shaw looked into his empty glass. "I thought you were offering me a job. If it's contingent on the other business, maybe I'd better turn down the offer completely." He set the empty glass down on the coffee table.

Youngblood was relieved. Shaw wasn't after more money; he really had had a change of conscience. The Texan went over to his desk, unlocked the top drawer and pulled out a tape cassette.

"You don't have a choice, Shelley. You've already come over to my camp. I have your verbal agreement . . . right here on tape. I'm sure Hugh Marshall would be real interested. . . ." Youngblood stared into Shaw's face. The president of Keller Perfumes was paler than he had been when he had arrived.

"You're blackmailing me?" Shaw felt completely numb.

"I wouldn't call it that. I'm not askin' you for any money. Hell, I'm fully prepared to pay you the bonus money. And the presidential suite at Powers is waitin' for you. It's not exactly the end of the world, is it?"

"No, I guess you're right."

"Good. I'm glad to have everything cleared up between us. Now, how soon can you get me what I want?"

Shaw cleared his throat. "Ah, I've checked. The perfume formula is locked up in the safe at DeHavilland's office in Brooklyn. It's impossible to get. I mean, without suspicion falling on me. . . ."

"That's all right." Billy Youngblood handed Shaw another drink. "I'll make it easy for you. Give me a sample bottle. I can have my lab decipher it. And don't forget the other information I need."

That evening Billy Youngblood picked up Tasha at her office.

"What are you doing here?" Tasha asked.

"We have a free evenin', and I'm takin' you out on the town."

"I'm tired, Billy. I want to go home."

"But we have somethin' to celebrate."

Tasha looked at him skeptically. "Oh? What?"

Billy opened his breast pocket and handed her a small bottle. "Smell this."

Tasha paused. Then she sniffed. "Billy! I don't believe it! This is fabulous."

"I knew you'd like it, honey. We finally have a scent for Disco."

"But I don't understand. Where did it come from? Who submitted it?"

"Well, sweetheart, I hired a freelance perfumer to work on it. A real genius, but kind of a troublemaker. He was fired from IFF a few years ago. He has his own lab now . . . in Virginia."

Tasha kissed Billy. "I can't believe it. I thought we'd have to settle for something I didn't really love. Why didn't you tell me you'd hired a freelance perfumer?"

"A surprise, my darlin'. I couldn't be sure he'd come up with somethin' you'd like." Youngblood was pleased to see Tasha so happy. "When this arrived today, I knew it was right."

"Okay, Billy. Let's celebrate. Where shall we go for dinner?"

Simon Waring, chief nose at Harris Fragrances, dialed the private number in Billy Youngblood's townhouse. It was after office hours. "Mr. Youngblood? I have to talk to you. About the fragrance analysis."

Billy Youngblood put the phone down on the amplified receiver. He liked to pace around the room when he talked business. "Have you got it all set?"

Waring hesitated. "No . . . We've deciphered about ninety percent of the formula. We're working on the rest. But there's a problem."

"What, man? Let's hear it." Youngblood was agitated that Harris Fragrances was taking such a long time getting the perfume formula worked out.

"The fragrance you gave us seems to contain two captive chemicals."

"What the hell's that?"

"Trademarked synthetics. In this case, they're owned by DeHavilland Fragrances. We'll have to buy from them."

"No! Definitely not! I don't want to bring the cost up. You'll have to make do with what you have."

"But, Mr. Youngblood," Waring protested, "it's not that simple. And . . . there's another snag."

"Tell me! Don't hedge around."

"The formula contains a high percentage of real essential oils. Jasmine, and ylang-ylang . . ."

"So what's the problem?"

"Because of too much rain, the jasmine crop was damaged. The price is up considerably from last year. And there was a drought in the Réunion Islands where we get our ylang-ylang. If you still want Disco to retail at sixty dollars an ounce, your profit margin's going to be cut substantially."

"Hell, use synthetics . . . they're cheaper, aren't they?"

"Some are. But jasmine's the one synthetic that just won't measure up to the quality of the real oil."

Billy Youngblood chewed on his cigar. This fragrance had already cost him a bundle. He had to make it up in profits, and it was too late to raise the price of Disco: they had already moved up the launch with Saks to the first of March. "Look," he said, "do the best you can. Use as much real oil as possible, and fill out with synthetics."

"Well, okay, Mr. Youngblood. But I have to warn you . . ."

"What?"

"The fragrance we provide isn't going to be as full-bodied as the sample you gave us. It can't be, on our budget, and without the captives from DeHavilland."

"Is it going to smell okay?" Youngblood demanded.

"Yes . . . but it won't . . ."

"Hell, just hurry it up. The first shipment's got to hit the stores in two weeks."

"Yes, sir, Mr. Youngblood. We'll do our best."

Tasha walked into the room. "What's the matter, Billy? You look worried."

"Nothin's wrong, honey. Just a minor problem at the lab." He laughed. "It rained too much on the Riviera last year and the price of jasmine's sky-high."

"Oh, is that all? I was afraid it was something serious."

Martine Rainier's design for a promotional gift incentive, to be sold with a purchase of Jazz perfume or toilet water, was a two-inch-long crystal music-note pendant, filled with the essence of Jazz. It was to be manufactured by Novlab, a company in Long Island City specializing in promotional premiums. However, shortly after Novlab signed the contract with Keller Perfumes there was a fire at its plant. A night watchman was asphyxiated by the fumes. In the subsequent investigation, it was suspected that this same night watchman had actually started the fire, and through his own error had been unable to escape in time.

Tyger's brainchild, the scratch-and-sniff labels which were to be attached to Matt Phillip's ready-to-wear clothes, had been infused with the Jazz scent and sent to the printer, along with various other labels and fliers to be printed for Keller Perfumes. Several days later, the factory was broken into, and the plates for the Jazz labels, among other things, were smashed and broken.

Sheldon Shaw looked harried as Connie, Jess, Davis and Tyger met in his office to discuss the realistic consequence of the two unfortunate accidents.

"This is such bad luck," Connie said. "It's as if the gods are against us."

"How much does this set us back?" Davis Chipps asked.

Tyger read from her list of notes. "I've talked to the heads of both companies. They're insured, and both have jobbers contracted to take over our account. Right now, it seems we're about two weeks behind schedule."

"Ouch," Connie said. "Does Hugh Marshall know?"

Tyger shook her head. "He's been out of town, with Tim Yates. I haven't been able to get through to either of them."

"What's happening with Tasha Powers's scent?" Jess asked. "Does anybody know?"

Tyger nodded. "Saks Fifth Avenue is giving the kickoff party on March fifteenth."

"So there's no way we can beat them to the punch," Davis said glumly.

Shaw shook his head. "This has really been unfortunate. To have accidents happen to two of our suppliers at the same time."

"I'm keeping my fingers crossed. Accidents come in threes, you know," Connie said.

"Don't even think it!" Tyger advised.

Jess drummed his fingers against the chair arm. "If you ask me, it's more than coincidence."

"Sabotage?" Tyger asked. "But who? Why? Tasha Powers's company seems to be in great shape. . . ."

Davis Chipps laughed. "Cool it, you two. You've been watching too much TV."

"Maybe . . . but I think we have to warn our other suppliers to be on the lookout for anything suspicious," Jess said.

"Good idea," Connie approved. "It certainly won't hurt. Even if it is coincidence."

"Yes," Shaw said. "Good idea, Jess."

The intercom buzzed. "Matt Phillips is here," Ginger said.

"Oh, no," Connie groaned.

"Send him in," Shaw said.

"Hello, darlings," Matt said to the group collectively. "I have my sketches for the outfit our models will wear in the stores. Here . . . very jazzy. Red velour. Slinky. Nice, no? And Tyger . . . a friend of mine is doing a silkscreen for the T-shirts. All you have to do is line up a company to make them up." He paused. "You all look so despondent. What's wrong?"

"Bad news, Matt," Tyger said. She wished, just this once, that Sheldon Shaw would step in. "There have been some production setbacks. We're running behind schedule. There was a fire at one of the supplier's factories, and . . ."

"*What?* Well, get new suppliers! I just heard from a friend of Tasha's that they've stepped up their production. Disco is being introduced on March *first*."

"Oh, no!" Connie exclaimed.

"There's nothing we can do. We're at the mercy of our suppliers. Even finding new ones will take time. . . ."

"And you're just sitting here on your asses," Matt yelled. "Just when I was beginning to think you were competent.

(276)

Well, I'm going to have a few words with Hugh Marshall. Right now!" He stormed out of the room.

"This isn't our lucky day, is it?" Connie said.

"Hugh's, though." Tyger smiled bleakly. "At least he's out of town."

A few days later, Lady Rowan walked into Tyger's office at Keller Perfumes.

"Mother! What brings you here?" Tyger was not pleased to see her mother. She had seen in Suzy Knickerbocker's column that morning that Bobbie and Hugh Marshall had been at a gala the night before. Since the night Hugh had kissed her in the limousine Tyger had been upset and confused about how she felt. She was in love with Guy . . . she thought. She was over Hugh . . . she thought. Then, that kiss, and Hugh's immediate withdrawal. It was hard enough to sort out her feelings without her mother stepping in to complicate things. Tyger didn't know that they had started seeing each other again. "I saw your picture in the *News* this morning . . . at the Lindners' ball."

"Yes, rather flattering, don't you think? I expected to run into you there."

"Guy doesn't like that sort of thing. I don't either any more. . . ."

"Well, it was a lovely party. Lots of old friends. The decorations were divine. Everything Japanese." She opened her Fendi handbag and pulled out her cigarettes. "Mind if I smoke? I'm trying to quit. See . . . this brand has the lowest tar."

Tyger found an ash tray buried under the papers on her desk. "Are you and Hugh . . . seeing a lot of each other these days?" she asked casually.

"Who ever gets to see a lot of Hugh?" Bobbie shrugged. "I'm not seeing him much. But there's always tomorrow."

Tyger was less than pleased by that answer. "I hear he's a real loner, Mother."

Bobbie was on guard. She thought that Tyger was happy with her Frenchman, but apparently she still had one eye on Hugh Marshall. "Hmmm, maybe. Anyway, I'm not actually stalking him, darling. As a matter of fact, I stopped by to tell you that I'm going to Australia."

"Australia? Why?"

"Lolli's coming with me. Her son lives there. We've rented a house on Rose Bay, in Sydney. Lolli and I haven't taken a trip together in years. It'll be like old times." She flicked an ash toward the ash tray and missed. "Lolli wants to meet a rich Aussie, and her son has all sorts of prospects lined up for her."

"How long will you be gone?" Tyger was delighted by the news.

"About a month."

"That's a long time to spend in Australia."

"It's summer there, you know."

"It's summer in a lot more interesting places than Sydney."

Bobbie giggled, and lowered her voice. "Oh, I may as well tell you. There's a fabulous plastic surgeon there. Lolli and I are going to have facelifts!"

"Mother, no . . . really? But you look terrific."

"Always the time to have it done. Anyway, I'm spending my recuperation time working on my needlepoint. Stan Grant says he'll give me a show in the spring if I can get enough together."

"I thought needlepoint was passé."

"Now, now, Tyger." Bobbie shook her finger lightly at her daughter. "Stan thinks my designs are fresh and innovative. He wants to market them. You know, in kits. Just think . . . our mother, an entrepreneur!"

Tyger grinned. "That's one way to have a career. Start your own business. Not a bad idea."

Bobbie put the cigarettes back in her bag. "Don't knock it, darling. I'm pulling myself together very well, don't you think?" She didn't wait for Tyger's answer. "I have to run. I'll call you before I leave."

Tyger walked her mother down the corridor to the bank of elevators. "I'm happy things are working out, I really am." She hugged her mother, and kissed her.

"Thank you, darling. Maybe we can take a trip together sometime. Just the two of us."

"That would be fun, Mother."

As Tyger walked back to her office she reflected that, with Bobbie's facelift, she and her mother were going to look more like sisters than ever. She wondered suddenly if this would be her mother's first.

Well . . . Australia for a month. That was good. It was a long way from Hugh Marshall. Tyger felt a lot better about Bobbie now than she had when her mother came in.

Of course, when Bobbie came back, rested and confident and looking fantastic, it might be a different story. But Tyger decided she wasn't going to let that bother her now.

(278)

CHAPTER TWENTY-EIGHT

IN spite of the setbacks, production on Jazz was catching up, and Matt Phillips for Men was right on schedule. It seemed as if Keller Perfumes would make its March 15 deadline. Tyger was in charge of the kickoff gala. Hugh Marshall had approved her ideas.

Though it was before nine a.m., Tyger figured Jake Danton would be up and having coffee. She dialed. "Hi, Jake. Hope it's not too early?"

"No, you know me—work, work, work. How's it going?"

"Well, I want you to do me a big favor. Tonight's the party at High Roller that Tasha Powers is throwing to launch her perfume. I wondered if you'd crash it. I want you to bring me back samples of Disco."

"Haven't you smelled it yet?"

"No one has. I understand that a special shipment's being hand-delivered just in time for the party. They made their deadline, but just barely. Anyway, do you mind?"

"Hell, no. It'll be fun." He paused. "Guess what . . . I have some news."

"Tell me only if it's good."

"It is. I'm getting married. To Astrid. I've just bought a bigger loft, and her son's coming from Switzerland to live with us."

Tyger felt a lump in her throat. It wasn't as if she wanted Jake any more, but it was hard to lose him for good. "Oh, Jake, congratulations. Goodness . . . I can't quite picture you as a daddy. Baseball games and all that."

"I think I'm really cut out for it." Jake was serious. "I'm ready to settle down."

"Why don't you and Astrid meet us for dinner after the party? Guy and I will be anxious to hear all about it."

"Great. Make it ten-thirty at the SoHo Charcuterie."

"See you then. *Don't* forget the perfume samples."

Hugh Marshall was on the phone in his office, but he motioned for Tyger to sit down. He finished the call, and looked at her gravely. "Have you found out anything for me, Tyger?"

"Nothing. I've been keeping my eyes and ears open, but I don't have any clues. The police haven't turned up a thing. I mean, *if* it's sabotage . . ."

"Not *if,* Tyger. I just had a call from Matt. His workshop was broken into last night, and the models' Jazz outfits were cut to shreds. Nothing else was tampered with. Matt's hysterical."

"I can't blame him. Why is all this happening?" Tyger shook her head in disbelief. "Who do you think . . . could Billy Youngblood be behind it?"

"I don't know. It could even be coming from the inside of our organization. I'm going to hire a private investigator. Let's get to the bottom of this, and fast."

"All right, Hugh." She pulled a fat manila folder out of her briefcase. "Here's a copy of the invitation. They're being hand-delivered today."

Hugh Marshall took it and read:

Matt Phillips, Keller Perfumes and Bloomingdale's
invite you to an evening of
Jazz with the Stars
in honor of
Jazz Perfume and Matt Phillips for Men
Thursday, March 15
Concert at Madison Square Garden: Eight P.M.
Party Afterwards at the Jazz Loft
12 Spring Street, from eleven o'clock

He smiled. "For once a promotional party I'm looking forward to. What musicians are lined up?"

"You won't believe it . . . Mose Allison, Art Blakey, Bill Evans, Herbie Hancock, Pharaoh Sanders and Leon Thomas . . . and Grover Washington, Jr., Bob James . . . the Crusaders, Carmen McRae . . . it's really fantastic!" She could tell that

Hugh was pleased. "We're running a full page in this Sunday's *Times*. The concert manager says it'll be a sellout beforehand. Especially because we're offering low-priced tickets."

"The concert will pay for the party and promote Jazz, too." Hugh did not try to conceal his delight. "It's ingenious, Tyger."

"We're having T-shirts and buttons saying 'I'm a Jazz Baby.' Those are for the invited guests. And we'll hand out perfume samples to everybody."

Annie Johnson quietly entered with their coffee and set it down on Hugh's desk. "Have the models been hired for the in-store promotions?" Hugh asked.

"Ginger's been interviewing them all week. We've decided to pick a group of fifteen to travel around the country and introduce the fragrance in each store. It's better in the long run than hiring local models everywhere we go."

"Good. What about the Disco launch tonight?"

"I've got it covered. My spies are infiltrating. I'll have the sample in hand by ten-thirty tonight."

Hugh smiled broadly. It was that white-toothed smile that had captivated her at their first meeting, here in this office. A lot had happened since then, but that smile still did the same things to her knees and stomach.

"Tyger, you're a phenomenon. I'm constantly amazed. Look, why don't we meet for a late supper? I'm as anxious to smell Disco as you are."

"I . . . I'm sorry, Hugh. I have a date."

His smile faded. He looked like a man who thinks he has reached the bottom and discovers there is one more step. "Of course," he said quickly. "Tomorrow morning will be fine. Have it on my desk first thing."

It was the first time Hugh Marshall had asked her out for a real date, Tyger mused as she rode the elevator down and walked across the polished lobby of the Kellerco building. Well . . . almost a real date. And she had turned him down.

It was the first time Tyger had turned Hugh Marshall down on anything.

She did not know whether she still wanted Hugh. She had Guy now, and Guy was much better for her. She hoped she did not still have her heart set on Hugh.

Still, if she did, it could not hurt to turn him down once or twice.

* * *

In spite of her hectic schedule, trying to coordinate the myriad details of the Jazz gala, Tyger was taking Guy to see the sights they had put off while he was working. Guy was spending only a few hours at the lab each day, getting the Jazz production set up. They made up the formula at the lab, then shipped it in gallon containers to the bottler, who mixed it with water and alcohol, in differing quantities, to fill the perfume and toilet-water containers.

The weather was warmer since the February thaw, and Guy was beginning to enjoy New York. Tyger hoped she could convince him to stay and work there permanently. She was happy with Guy and their quiet life. He was easy to get along with, and he had helped her relax. They had been together for only three months, but she felt as if she had known him for years. It was only when Tyger was alone sometimes with Hugh that she felt any doubts. But she would get over that, sooner or later. She had better, she told herself.

Before they went to meet Jake after the Disco party, Tyger and Guy went to see Alvin Ailey. The dance program let out at a quarter past ten, and they took a taxi to SoHo. Astrid and Jake walked out of the SoHo Charcuterie just as Tyger and Guy were stepping out of the cab.

"I forgot to make a reservation," Jake said. "There'll be a twenty-minute wait for a table. Want to stay here or go someplace else? There's the Spring Street Bar, Raoul's, Mama Sitka's . . ."

"I don't care where we go—I'm starving," Astrid said.

Guy sniffed the air. "This is peculiar." He leaned over to Astrid. "What perfume are you wearing?"

"Disco," Astrid said. "I splashed it on before I left. There was a big fountain of it by the door."

Tyger looked at Guy's face. "What's wrong?"

"Smell Astrid . . . and tell me what you think."

"Brrr," said Jake. "Let's go inside and smell each other. It's getting cold."

Tyger leaned over and sniffed Astrid's hair. "Oh, my God . . ." she said. "Disco smells like Jazz." She sniffed again. "It's a cheap version, but . . . oh, my God!" she repeated. "More sabotage."

By midnight, everyone was assembled in Hugh Marshall's office, except for Jess Leibowitz, who lived in Tarrytown and couldn't make it in time. The samples of Disco had been passed around and everyone was in a state of shock.

"The formula was stolen," Connie said. "Well, that settles the question of whether those other t' ings were coincidence, doesn't it?"

"Yes, Connie," Hugh Marshall verified. "We've been working on that premise. But so far we haven't come up with any substantial leads."

Sheldon Shaw looked peaked. It was late, and he had had a lot to drink that evening. He and Connie had gone to dinner and back to her apartment. "Well, as long as we're trying to find the culprit, I may as well share my suspicions with you." He paused. "There is one person here who knows everything about our day-to-day operations. That person also had access to the Jazz formula."

Guy spoke up. "But *no one* has seen the Jazz formula! It is kept in a locked safe at the DeHavilland laboratory. Even I do not know the combination to the safe."

Shaw pointed his finger at Guy. "But you know the formula, because you invented it. And . . . it's no secret that you and Tyger Hayes are very good friends."

"Mais oui, but I do not see what that has to do with it."

"Don't you?" Shaw spit out the words vindictively. "Tyger is the only person here who could have gotten hold of the formula."

Connie gasped. The rest of the room was silent.

Tyger was amazed. How could Shaw possibly suspect her?

Hugh Marshall was the first to speak. "Sheldon, I don't believe you. Tyger's not responsible for the sabotage. I won't countenance such accusations from anyone, not even you. I think you owe Tyger an apology."

Shaw sneered. "What do you really know? How can you be so sure that Tyger didn't do it? Look at the evidence."

Hugh Marshall's face turned red with anger. "Dammit, Sheldon! I know that Tyger couldn't do such a thing. Let's not discuss it now. I'd like to talk to you after the meeting."

Matt Phillips spoke up. "Enough mud-slinging. The question is . . . what are we going to do now? We can't come out with the same scent as Tasha."

"Theirs is not exactly the same," Guy explained. "They have used inferior raw materials. Their fragrance is not comparable to mine, in either quality or lasting power."

"A moot point," Matt said. "People are going to say I copied Tasha, because our perfume's coming out after hers."

"What if we call a press conference right away? Tell the world that Powers Perfumes stole our fragrance and duplicated it?" David Chipps said. "We could get a lot of publicity. . . ."

"No . . ." Connie said. "A big scandal will be bad for our image. Everyone will become caught up in the controversy. Even if it boosts sales, in the long run it will be bad for business." Connie was still trying to recover from Shaw's accusations of Tyger. It was an appalling thing for him to do.

"She's right," Tom Sullivan said. "I know all the buyers. They shy away from dirty politics."

"It would be hard to convince a court of law that the formula was stolen, without proof," Tim Yates said.

"You are *all* missing the point!" Matt Phillips raised his voice. "What are we going to *do?* Jazz is supposed to be unveiled in fifteen days." He poured himself a glass of water from the pitcher on the table and took a pill.

"Anyone have any suggestions?" Hugh Marshall asked.

Connie snapped her fingers. "Hot damn, I've got it! We'll use the other fragrance . . . the one Guy created for Tyger. I thought it was terrific, and so did Tyger . . . but we were voted down."

Hugh Marshall sat forward, and looked at Guy. "You've created another fragrance?"

Guy nodded. "As a gift for Tyger. She wanted to have it approved for Jazz, but Monsieur Shaw said that it was confusing to have to decide between two scents."

Tyger finally spoke. "It's a great fragrance, Hugh. Here, I have it with me, in my handbag." She handed a small bottle to Marshall. He smelled it, closed his eyes, and inhaled again. Everyone waited for his reaction.

"This is sensational! Guy, can we use this and still make our launch date?"

"If we work night and day, we can," Guy said.

"Then do it! Time is of the essence," Hugh said.

Connie laughed. "I've heard that word enough to last a lifetime."

"All right. It's late. We'll meet here in the morning and iron out details," Hugh Marshall said. "You all go home and get some sleep."

After the meeting, Connie whispered to Sheldon, "I'll wait for you outside. I want to talk to you."

"No, don't bother." Shaw was sober now. "We'll talk tomorrow. It's late. You left Tina alone in the apartment."

"I want to talk to you, Sheldon. Now!"

"No, Connie. I'll see you tomorrow," he whispered. "I love you."

Hugh Marshall closed the door. "Sheldon, those were pretty heavy accusations you hurled at Tyger."

"Look at the facts! She's the only one who could have done it."

"As far as I'm concerned, Tyger is the only one who *couldn't* have done it. I am convinced of her loyalty to Keller Perfumes."

"Well, you're wrong. I have proof that she was responsible for the fire at Novlab, and that she sold the formula to Billy Youngblood."

Hugh Marshall could hardly contain his loathing for Shaw. "Proof?"

"Yes. Call Billy Youngblood, and ask him. I'll bet he'll verify my suspicions."

"Hmmm. Do you think he will?" Hugh sat back and stared at Shaw.

"Tyger is the *only* one who could have done all those things. You're blind to that fact because she's beautiful," Shaw said spitefully.

"I would hardly call Youngblood. I'd be highly suspicious of any information that came from him . . . or for that matter of how you came to hear it from him in the first place." He stood up. "You're fired. I want you out of Keller Perfumes by morning."

"Out? Aren't you forgetting Nelson Bachrach? *He* wanted me in this job. He's not going to be pleased. . . ."

Hugh Marshall could contain his anger no longer. He shouted at Shaw, "Get out, Shaw. I don't want to be forced to say what I think of you. . . ."

Shaw stood there, hating Marshall as much as the president of Kellerco hated him. "Well I'll say what I think of you! You're an egotistical son of a bitch . . . and your time at Kellerco is running out. You know, I'll bet the reason you don't believe me about Tyger is that you're sleeping with her. That slut—she . . ."

Hugh Marshall had never punched anyone in his life. He swung his right fist at Sheldon Shaw and made crunching contact with the older man's jaw. Shaw was thrown off balance, back against the conference table. He coughed.

Hugh Marshall was breathing hard, staring at Shaw with loathing. Shaw regained his footing, and stood straight. His jaw hurt. He was anxious to look in a mirror to see if his lip was bleeding, and how badly he was bruised.

"I'll sue you for this," Shaw hissed. "And I'll get you. I almost did . . ." He stopped short, and retreated quickly from the room.

Shaw went to his office and locked the door. He headed straight for his top right-hand drawer and the bottle of vodka he kept there. He unscrewed the top and drank four or five gulps without a breath, although it hurt his jaw to swallow. He picked up the telephone and dialed Billy Youngblood's unlisted number.

"I have to talk to you," Shaw said.

"Well . . . this isn't a good time. There's a bunch of people here," Youngblood said.

"They know. About Disco," Shaw blurted out.

"Already?" Youngblood paused. "Do they suspect you?"

"No . . . I've covered my tracks."

"Good boy." Youngblood was relieved. "Now . . . what're they goin' to do about it? Are they suing us?"

"No. They don't have the proof, and they don't want the publicity. They had another perfume waiting in the wings, so they're using that one instead. . . ."

"Goddammit, Shaw," Youngblood yelled into the receiver. "Why the fuck didn't you *tell* me they had another one?"

Shaw took another swig of vodka. "Well, I didn't think it was important. I mean, they weren't using it. . . ."

"Shit, man, you should've told me." Youngblood tried to conceal his annoyance with Shaw. He assumed a reasonable tone of voice. "Look, are they goin' to make their target launch date?"

"Yeah . . . if everyone works overtime."

"Well," Billy demanded gently, "you've got to think of somethin' to screw up the works. . . ."

"Well, ah, I had a fight with Hugh Marshall. About Tyger Hayes. And I've quit . . . as of fifteen minutes ago."

"Quit?"

Shaw took another sip of vodka, a large one that spilled out of the corners of his mouth and down his chin. "Yes. So I'm free to start working at Powers right away."

There was silence on the other end of the phone. "Well, now, that's good news." Billy Youngblood's voice sounded cordial. "But under the circumstances, don't you think it would look better if you waited for a while? I mean, you don't want them to suspect *you* of stealin' the formula, do you?"

"No . . . but since I'm at liberty, it would be natural for me to get another job, in the same field. . . ."

"Shelley, trust me." Youngblood's voice took on a note of sincerity. "It won't look good—for either of us—if you come over to us so fast. No, Shelley, relax. Take a long trip with your wife. You've got the money I paid you. Then . . . in a year or two, when things have cooled down . . ."

Shaw began to realize what was happening. "A year . . . or two?"

"Sure," said Billy. "It'd look bad if you started workin' at Powers any sooner than that. So, listen . . . contact me then. Okay? Good talkin' to you. I've got to get back to my guests. . . ." Youngblood hung up.

Shaw was stunned. He realized that he had walked into that one with his eyes open. They were all bastards. He thought about Hugh Marshall and Billy Youngblood, and tried to figure out which one he hated more. Egotistical bigshots. Big honchos, drunk on power. They sucked the blood right out of you, Shaw decided. But he didn't need them any more. He had the money, the two hundred thousand. Youngblood had given him a cashier's check. With that kind of money he was free of them all. He dialed Connie's number.

"Listen, Connie, I've handed in my resignation here. I've got it all figured out. You quit, too, and we'll take off together. Go on a long trip . . . around the world, if you want."

The voice at the other end was flat and bitter.

"Sheldon, I wouldn't go around the corner with you. Not after tonight. The way you behaved . . . the things you said about Tyger. I know you never liked her." Connie had been crying, but her voice did not betray her. "But to accuse Tyger of committing crimes! I thought you were a bigger person than that. I guess I didn't know you . . . or I was fooling myself. Anyway, it's over, and I never want to see you again."

"But, Connie . . ." Shaw couldn't believe it.

"No, I mean it. I'm not changing my mind. Goodbye, Sheldon. Good luck." She put the receiver down gently.

Sheldon Shaw kept the dead phone to his ear for a long moment. He grabbed the vodka, finished it off, and tried to figure out what to do next. He remembered seeing an almost-full crystal decanter of sherry that Tyger kept on a shelf behind her desk, along with little crystal sherry glasses from Tiffany's. Well, he decided, he would take her prissy decanter and drink up all its contents. He laughed, and swaggered into Tyger's office.

When he had finished the sherry he took off his coat, loosened his tie and unbuttoned the top button of his shirt. It was hot. He cursed modern buildings with their windows that didn't open.

He was still thirsty. Tyger must have something stronger than sherry. He went over to the desk and looked through her drawers, but there was nothing. Then he focused on the Early American armoire she had bought for her office. He opened the door, and saw a multicolored Missoni knit suit hanging there. *She sleeps around so much,* he thought, *she needs to keep a change of clothes at the office.* He pulled the suit from the hanger, threw it on the floor, and rummaged around the shelves. His hand discovered a brassiere, panty hose, and a pair of beige lace bikini panties. He tossed them in the air behind him and continued his search for something to drink. He knew that Connie didn't keep liquor in her office; Jess certainly wouldn't.

Shaw was sweating. He took off his tie and unbuttoned his shirt all the way down. His head was foggy; he had to rest. He felt Tyger's crumpled suit under his foot.

He kneeled on the floor and picked up the skirt. He laid it out flat, very carefully, as if he were getting ready to iron it. He did the same with the cream-colored silk blouse, placing it carefully above the skirt. Next, he took the panty hose, and placed them on top of the skirt, with the legs extending below it. He picked up the sheer flesh-toned bra, and gently laid it over the silk blouse. Methodically, he placed Tyger's panties on top of the panty hose. He debated about the suit jacket, and rejected it, throwing it on top of Tyger's desk.

He stood and looked at his creation. The scent of the perfume that Guy Saint Denis had created for Tyger emanated from the clothes. Sniffing the air, he could almost feel Tyger in the room with him. He thought about her. If he had been younger, he decided, he could have had her. Tyger Hayes. He could have screwed the daylights out of her. She would have moaned and screamed out for more, no longer high and mighty, but desperate to feel him inside of her. She would have done anything he asked her to.

He gazed at the clothes all spread out on the thick yellow carpet. They seemed more inviting than the woman herself. Damn rich bitch; the kind of woman who never looked twice at Shaw. He was sure that Tyger never focused on him, only through him. He could show her a thing or two.

The heat in the room was unbearable. Shaw took off his

shirt and socks and shoes, then slowly unzipped his fly and slipped his pants down, and his boxer shorts. He stepped out of them, and raised his arms high above his head. He stretched; his body felt good.

Then he lowered his naked body down over Tyger's neatly arranged garments, and lay down on top of them. The carpet underneath was soft, like a cushion, a mattress, a woman's body. He closed his eyes: he and Tyger were in bed together. He smelled her perfume. His hips began grinding slowly over her lace bikini. He writhed faster, smelling her smell, humping her, harder, violently. The world was spinning with just the two of them.

He came quickly, jerkily, with a loud, ecstatic, soulful moan.

Shaw lay there for a while, smelling the mixed aroma of perfume and sweat. He dozed off. When he woke up, he remembered Tom Sullivan. An Irishman would certainly have a bottle of whiskey.

Tom Sullivan did, in fact, keep a bottle on the bookshelf above his desk. Shaw snatched it and, drinking from the bottle, walked naked through the silent corridors of Keller Perfumes. Perspiration beaded on his forehead. He wandered past the exit stairs to the roof, and doubled back. He felt so hot. He opened the door and went barefoot up the stairs. When he reached the top of the landing, he pushed open the heavy metal door. It closed before he could check to see whether it locked automatically from the inside. He tugged on it. The door didn't budge. He was stark naked on the roof, and couldn't get back inside. On March 1, at four in the morning, the weather was thirty-two degrees Fahrenheit; zero, Celsius.

Shaw didn't care at that moment. He was free. No one was watching him, for the first time in his life, it seemed. All at once, he knew what he was doing on the roof. He would still have the last laugh over Hugh Marshall. How could his precious Keller Perfumes withstand another scandal now, when the countdown for the launch had already begun? Sheldon Shaw knew what he had to do. He lifted Tom Sullivan's bottle of J&B to his lips, and drank most of it down. He climbed the metal ladder to the upper roof and crawled along a short catwalk to the larger solid expanse. The metal was cold, the gravel rough. He felt it cut into his bare knees, but he was becoming numbed to the freezing air. He walked over to the edge. There was a three-and-a-half-foot ledge. He pulled himself up and sat straddling it. The view was fantastic, the best panorama of New York he had ever seen. He looked up into the clear night and watched a plane soar slowly overhead, its red and white lights flashing. The sky was mottled with stars. He squinted and saw the Milky Way. Shaw searched for the Big Dipper, but his neck began to hurt from looking up.

Down below, the early-morning traffic was sparse. The wind came up, and Shaw started to realize that he was getting cold. The bottle of scotch was still in his hand. He finished it slowly, feeling the warmth of the alcohol burn down his throat and into his gut. Shaw hurled the bottle out into the air, and watched it fall fifty stories, onto Fifty-seventh Street. He was so far up he couldn't hear the sound of the glass smashing against the pavement, but it seemed to be right on target, in the middle of the street between the two lanes of traffic.

Sheldon Shaw stood up on the ledge and let himself feel the sharpness of the wind whipping against his naked body. He wobbled a bit unsteadily, regained his balance, and raised his arms into a V above his head, the tips of his fingers touching. He stood on tiptoe, and stretched as tall as he could. When he felt that his form was perfect, he jumped. He was in Acapulco, diving from a high cliff into the sparkling aquamarine sea.

His body landed on the trunk of a Lincoln Continental belonging to a Mr. Gerald Laird, of Oyster Bay, and driven by his son, Kent. Police car number thirty-six of the Midtown Precinct North called the ambulance. It arrived forty-five minutes later and took the unidentifiable mass to the morgue.

CHAPTER TWENTY-NINE

TYGER hadn't been able to sleep. Finally, at seven-thirty, she got dressed and took a cab to the office.

"Morning, Miss Hayes," the lobby guard, James Otis, said. "You're early today."

"A lot of work to do, James." She pushed the elevator button.

"We had some excitement a while ago. Out on the street. Somebody jumped, naked. They're pretty sure it was from this building, but they don't know who it was."

Tyger shuddered. "How awful."

"Yeah," James said. "It's the first time anything exciting's happened while I was on duty. Things are usually quiet around here."

When Tyger walked into her office the first thing she saw was her clothes spread out on the floor. There were stains on her panties. She spotted the empty sherry decanter on her desk, and her mind began racing. It didn't take her long to figure out what must have happened. But who could have done such a thing? The night watchman? Someone from the cleaning crew?

She stumbled over something and looked down. Her eyes rested on the man's clothing piled in a heap. She recognized the suit. Sheldon Shaw had been wearing it at the meeting the night before. And the shirt, and the tie.

"Oh, God," she said out loud, and dashed into Shaw's office.

It was empty. There was the drained bottle of vodka on the floor near his desk.

Tyger felt queasy. She hurried to the women's room and threw up. Afterward she put the lid down on the toilet, and sat, trying to recover and figure out what she was going to do next. She rinsed her mouth with water, splashed her face, and went back into her office. She rummaged through her armoire for a shopping bag and stuffed her clothes into it. Then she shoved the bag into the back of the closet, out of sight. Next she picked up Shaw's things and dumped them on the floor of his office.

Hugh, she thought. *He's got to know.* She hurried back to her office, flipped through her directory, and dialed Hugh Marshall's home number. The housekeeper informed her that Mr. Marshall had already left for the office.

It was Tim Yates's voice that answered the office phone.

"Tim, it's Tyger. Something awful's happened. Is Hugh there?"

"Not yet. He should be here any minute. We have an early meeting. What is it, Tyger? You sound terrible."

"It's Sheldon Shaw. He's killed himself."

"What?"

"He's dead. Sometime last night. He jumped off the roof."

"Good God . . ." Tim's voice was a shaken whisper. "I never thought this would happen. ... ."

"You'll tell Hugh, won't you? As soon as he gets in?"

"What? Yes, yes, of course."

As Tyger hung up the phone she heard the elevator door open and close, and footsteps coming down the hall. She went to see who it was.

"Tyger! What's the matter? You look paler than a ghost." Connie held up a small green bag. "I have some fresh orange juice here. Come into my office and have some. You'll feel better."

"No," Tyger stammered, "I'm . . . not . . ."

Connie handed her the paper cup of juice. "Did you hear about Sheldon?"

Tyger looked at her, startled.

Connie sighed. "He called me last night after his meeting with Hugh, and told me that he'd resigned."

"Resigned?" Tyger still felt numb.

"Yes. Then he asked *me* to quit. Said he had a lot of money and wanted me to go around the world with him." Connie unhappily bit into her bagel.

"What?" Tyger realized that she and Connie were talking about two different events.

"I'm furious at him over the way he accused you of sabotage," Connie said vehemently. "I called it quits with him. The bastard. You know, I was really crazy to get involved in the first place. . . ."

"Connie," Tyger said slowly, "did you see James on your way up just now?"

"Sure. He told me somebody jumped off the roof last night."

"Naked."

"That's right," Connie remembered. "It makes me sick to think about it."

Tyger took a deep breath. "Connie . . . there's an empty bottle of vodka in Sheldon's office. And . . . his clothes are in a pile on the floor. . . ."

It took a few seconds for it to sink in. Connie stood up, then slumped into a heap on the floor.

The rest of the morning was a grisly blur. After the police had been contacted and it was established that the unidentified man at the morgue was Sheldon Shaw, president of Keller Perfumes, the news media scrambled to get the story. Connie, in shock, was rushed to Roosevelt Hospital for observation. The rest of the office crew wandered around like zombies.

At lunchtime, Tyger took the shopping bag she had stashed in the back of her armoire and shoved it down the hall chute to the incinerator in the basement of the building. Sheldon Shaw must have been very troubled, she reasoned. She didn't want to make the story worse by telling anybody that he had masturbated on her lace bikini shortly before he took his life.

Matt Phillips put down his newspaper and sipped his morning coffee. He had not yet heard the news about Shaw, and he was feeling reasonably good, under the circumstances. The word was out that Disco was disappointing; the scent was "shallow," according to *Women's Wear Daily*. He could not resist the urge to call Tasha Powers.

"Tasha, darling! I just read what the dailies had to say about Disco. Too bad. It's just like you to take a perfectly splendid fragrance and ruin it."

"Matt, what an unpleasant surprise to hear from you." She paused. "What are you talking about, anyway?"

"About the fact that even after stealing my formula you couldn't duplicate its quality," Matt gloated.

"Stealing *your* formula? What the hell are you talking about?"

"Oh, that's a very good reading. Injured innocence. Nice."

Tasha was still confused. "I'm about to hang up. You have ten seconds to explain yourself."

"Is it possible you don't know? Oh, surely not. I'm talking about our formula for Jazz," he explained patronizingly, "which you stole and copied for Disco."

"What?" There was silence. "I don't believe you. . . ." Matt could tell by her voice that she was rocked by this news, whether she believed it or not.

"Have lunch with me, and I'll tell you the details." Matt decided that he would relish the scene more by seeing Tasha in person.

"Lunch? With you?"

"What's the matter? Afraid to be seen in public with me?"

"No," Tasha said. "It isn't that, it's . . . oh, all right. Where?"

"Do you still like Indian food?"

"Yes."

"Then Shezan . . . at one."

They sat awkwardly on the sand-colored suede banquette in the modern monochromatic dining room at Shezan. Tasha Powers gazed at the gray-carpeted walls, and Matt Phillips stared at the candlelight reflections in the metallic ceiling. The waiter brought their wine, uncorked it slowly and ceremoniously, and they placed their orders: Matt, the Tandoor chicken; Tasha, the vegetarian thali.

"I still can't believe all this," Tasha said.

"See for yourself." Matt took a sample bottle of the original Jazz fragrance and put it down on the table in front of her. "*Smell* for yourself."

Tasha skeptically raised the bottle to her nose, and sniffed it slowly. "You're right, Matt. This is the fragrance Billy brought home to me. He told me it was created by a freelance perfumer."

Matt laughed. "That Billy. Always a good imagination. But why didn't he have it copied exactly?"

"He said one of the ingredients was scarce, and that the lab was forced to use more synthetics. He assured me it would smell the same." She took another sip of wine and began to relax. "When I realized it wasn't nearly as good, it was too late. The invitations had already gone out for the Disco party. There was nothing I could do." There were tears in her eyes. "Oh, Matt, I was out to get you, but you ought to know that I'd never stoop to anything like this. I don't know what the story is, but I intend to find out as soon as I leave here."

Tasha's humility made Matt expansive. "It's all right, Tasha. I've been wanting to talk to you for a long time. To apologize for what happened . . . to us."

Tasha smiled wryly. "I guess it wasn't your fault . . . or mine. It sure messed up my life, though."

"What do you mean?"

"Billy. I never would have married him if I hadn't hated you so much. Or wanted my own design house so badly." She sighed. "I guess I got what I asked for."

There was genuine concern in Matt's eyes. "Are you unhappy, Tasha?"

"Unhappy isn't the word for it. . . ."

"But your company's doing well. You can afford to leave him."

"That's a laugh," Tasha said. "Turns out he owns everything but my tits. If I leave him, I'm flat broke and back where I started."

"No, Tasha. Remember where we started? We'll never be back there again. Listen," he said, "if you leave Billy I'll finance you until you get back on your feet. I've got enough money now."

Tasha's face colored and tears poured out of her eyes. "Oh, Matt, I can't believe it. You'd really help me?"

"Of course, Tasha." He grinned. "I still have a soft spot in my heart for you. . . ."

"In your heart? I thought it was somewhere else." Tasha smiled and wiped her eyes. "Well! We've certainly come a long way, haven't we?"

Hugh Marshall and Tyger were sitting in her office. He had come to Keller Perfumes to make a statement to the press. The news media were squeezing every bit of drama out of the shocking story. The president of a large company jumping nude from a skyscraper was big news.

"I never liked Sheldon," Hugh said quietly to Tyger. "But I never realized he was insane. I certainly didn't want to see him dead." He shook his head. "And it's my fault, too."

"No, Hugh . . ."

"I fired him just before . . ."

"What? I thought he'd resigned."

"Why would you think that?" Hugh asked.

"Connie. She said he called her last night and told her he'd quit. He said he had a lot of money and wanted her to quit, too, so they could go around the world together."

Hugh looked at her. "A lot of money? That's an odd thing to say. His salary here was good, but he had a wife, and kids in college. . . ."

Tyger was silent. So much had happened in such a short time.

"Tyger, I punched Shaw last night, because I was so angry that he'd pointed the finger at you. Now I'm wondering *why* he accused you. . . ."

"You think he did it?"

"Why else would he be so quick to cast the blame on someone else?" Hugh said.

Tyger frowned. "We can't prove it."

"No. But he told Connie he had money to spend. That could mean a payoff. I mean," Hugh said, "if he sold secrets to Youngblood then he would have been paid well."

Tyger shook her head. "I can't believe it. I never thought Shaw had the imagination for corporate intrigue."

Hugh shrugged. "Who knows what a person will do if he's desperate? We know he was unbalanced. . . ."

"I guess you're right." Tyger handed him a peppermint lifesaver and took one for herself. "What are you going to do? I mean, couldn't we sue Powers Perfumes?"

Hugh thought for a minute. "I'll have to discuss it with our lawyers. I'm inclined to let the matter drop. With Sheldon's death, it would be ugly to dredge it all up. . . ."

"Hmm, I agree. . . ." She paused. "Hugh, did you really *punch* Sheldon?"

Hugh nodded. "The first time I ever did anything like that."

"Thank you, Hugh." Tyger went over and gave him a kiss. "It's also the first time that anyone's protected my honor quite like that. . . ."

"Oh, *there* you are! I'm glad you're still here, Hugh. . . ." Jess Leibowitz strode into Tyger's office. There were problems to be solved: they still had only fourteen days to get out an entirely new perfume.

Tasha flung open the door to Billy Youngblood's office. Youngblood was going over some papers with his assistant.

"Get out, Stanley," she shrieked. "I want to talk to my husband alone."

"Of course, Ms. Powers." The embarrassed assistant scurried out the door.

"Billy, we have something to discuss."

Youngblood lit a cigar. "Of course, honey. But you were rude to poor Stan. I mean . . ."

"Billy, did you steal Matt Phillips's formula?"

Youngblood studied her face for a moment. "Of course I didn't steal it, sweetie."

"Then how come Disco turns out to be a replica of Matt Phillips's Jazz?"

"Where'd you hear that?" Youngblood knew Shaw was dead. Stanley had heard the news over the radio during his lunch break.

"Never mind." She raised her voice. "Is it true?"

Billy poured Tasha a glass of ginger ale, and himself a neat bourbon. "Sit down, Tasha." He handed her the ginger ale.

Tasha knocked the glass out of his hand. The sticky liquid splattered down the front of his jacket. "I want the truth, Billy!"

"If you get nasty like that," Youngblood sneered, "I'm not telling you anything. I don't like you in this mood."

"Billy!" Tasha yelled. "You tell me or . . ."

"Or what?" Youngblood spit the words out.

"Or . . ." Tasha burst into tears. "Oh, Billy, I have to know. . . ."

"Okay . . . okay." He couldn't stand her to cry. "I didn't steal the formula. I *bought* it. For a big hunk of money, too. The president of Keller, that fellow Shaw, came to me. He told me he hated Hugh Marshall and wanted to get even with him. He offered me the perfume formula. I vetoed the idea. . . ." Youngblood downed his bourbon in one swig, and poured another. "But you wouldn't approve any of the perfume submissions, and I was goin' crazy. Shaw stopped by again and gave me a bottle of their fragrance. I showed it to you, and you loved it. We were runnin' out of time . . . so I bought it from him after all."

Tasha shook her head slowly, with disbelief. "But *Matt's* perfume? You knew how much I hated him. I'd have settled for *anything* rather than steal from him. . . ."

"I didn't *steal* it. I paid a big chunk of money for it. For you. . . ."

"For *me?* Come off it, Billy."

"Look, I spent a fortune buying Keller people and tryin' to

gum up the works over there so your perfume would be a big success. . . ."

"Why? Didn't you think we could make it on our own?"

Youngblood was bored with the conversation, and growing annoyed. "For one thing, you wouldn't decide on a goddam fragrance. I had a bundle ridin' on this company. I wanted to ensure our success. Remember, I launched it for *you*. Because you were stormin' around over the fact that Kellerco chose Matt Phillips."

Tasha took a deep breath. She narrowed her eyes and looked at her husband with hatred. "You didn't do it for me. You discovered that there's a lot of profit in perfume. Besides . . . *you* own the company. I'm doing all the work, and you're getting all the money. . . ."

"My money is your money. Have I ever denied you anything you wanted?" Youngblood asked.

"You've taken advantage of me! And now you've made me a criminal. People won't say *you* stole the Jazz formula, they'll say *I* did. The company has *my* name!"

"No one's goin' to say anything," Youngblood said glumly. "Keller doesn't need the scandal. Not after what Shaw did. Anyway, you saw what the morning papers said about Disco. We're in trouble as it is."

"People on Seventh Avenue will find out! Look how they gossip. My pride can't stand it." Tasha walked over to the bar and poured herself a straight bourbon. Then she tossed it in Billy Youngblood's face. It ran down his forehead to his cheeks and jumped off his chin to his shirt.

Youngblood's eyes stung from the alcohol. "You're askin' for it, my dear. I've had enough!" Youngblood lunged forward and slapped Tasha's cheek as hard as he could. She stood still for a stunned minute, and then came flying at him. She punched him in the stomach with all her strength, and began beating his chest with her fists. He was dazed from the blow to his gut.

"I'm leaving you, Billy. I hate you!" She turned to go.

Youngblood grabbed her by the shoulders and shook her with such force that she began coughing. He picked her up and flung her tiny frame with enormous force against the wall. There was a loud crunch as she hit. She sank to the floor, unconscious.

Youngblood's secretary opened the door. "I heard a loud noise. Are you . . . oh, no!" She rushed to Tasha.

"Miss Epstein, call an ambulance," Billy said weakly. "There's been an accident."

The secretary rushed out of the room to summon help.

Youngblood closed the door and washed his face with a bar towel, to get rid of the stink of bourbon. He changed into a clean shirt and sports jacket from his closet. He went through his desk drawers quickly, and put a stack of papers in his Neiman-Marcus briefcase. Finally, he opened the wall safe and took out the contents—documents and some jewelry he had given Tasha—and stuffed it into his briefcase and coat pockets. He ignored Tasha, lying on the floor, still unconscious.

Billy Youngblood picked up his overcoat and walked out the door. "I'll be out of town for the next few weeks, Miss Epstein," he said calmly, and headed for the airport, for Houston, to get away from it all.

CHAPTER THIRTY

TYGER opened the bottle of Château Léoville-Poyferré. "Are you ready for me to toss the salad?"

"*Oui, ma chère.* The rabbit is ready," Guy called from the kitchen of his suite at the Carlyle. He brought it in on a silver platter. "Here is chopped parsley to put on top . . . and the green peppercorn sauce. *Voilà!*" He arranged the table. "*La nouvelle cuisine française!*"

Tyger turned down the lights. "It looks fabulous. I meant to buy candles on the way here. . . ."

"That's all right. You don't need candlelight to look beautiful."

Tyger poured the wine. "To you, your meal . . . and the new Jazz." They clinked glasses and drank.

"And now, Tyger, to us."

"To us." She looked into his extraordinary brown eyes and smiled.

Guy carved the rabbit. "I'm exhausted from the past two weeks. I'll be ready for a vacation after Jazz is introduced."

"Me, too. Unfortunately after things get underway in New York, I still have to deal with the rest of the country."

"That's not your problem." Guy handed Tyger her plate.

"It is now. Connie was supposed to handle it, but she's handed in her resignation."

Guy put down his fork. "What?"

"It just happened," Tyger said. "Connie blames herself for what happened to Sheldon. She's leaving Kellerco. She and her daughter are moving to San Francisco."

"Poor Tyger," Guy said sympathetically. "Now you have to do her job."

"Well, we're splitting her duties—Jess, Davis and I. I'll have to travel around the country overseeing the local introductions. Plus there's Sheldon's work to cover, until a new president is named." Tyger looked up and paused. "What's the matter, Guy?"

Guy had stopped eating and pushed his plate away. "I thought you would come back to the Riviera with me."

"You know I want to spend time with you there. But it'll have to be later this year."

"I *mean* I want you to come back to France with me for good. I want to marry you."

Tyger was silent. Things between them were perfect, as long as Guy stayed in New York. Tyger had thought about it, and she knew she could not live in Grasse. "Guy . . . I don't know what to say. I love you. I'd want to marry you . . . if I ever get married again. But I'm not ready." Tyger knew she was hurting him; she wanted him to understand. "Guy, I want to be with you. Why don't you stay in New York? We could spend holidays in France. . . ."

"No, Tyger," Guy said stubbornly, "you miss the point. I am a man. I love my country. I miss Grasse. I was raised there and that's where I want to live. With you. Tyger, I've never loved a woman as much as you. . . ."

Tyger felt wretched. She went over to Guy, kneeling beside him, and hugged him close. "I love you, too. I don't want to be away from you, but I can't leave my job. Not now. It took me so long to find what I wanted to do. I can't give it up now."

Guy turned away from her. "Then you don't love me."

"That's not true! Oh, darling, don't make it more difficult. I can't give up everything and move to Grasse."

"If you loved me, you would."

"But, Guy, lovers make compromises. . . ."

"And your idea of a compromise," Guy said, "is for *me* to stay in New York and visit Grasse for two weeks every summer."

"I didn't say that!" Tyger snapped.

"Oh, didn't you?" He got up and took the plates into the kitchen. Tyger followed him, carrying the uneaten salad.

"Guy, please, I don't want to fight."

"Neither do I. We won't discuss it any more." He scraped the plates into the garbage and began loading the dishwasher.

"The problem's not going to disappear by not talking about it. There has to be a solution." Tyger sat on the kitchen stool.

Guy's eyes were watering. "I have never been more unhappy. I have finally found the woman I want to marry . . . and she has turned me down."

Tyger teared up, with sadness and frustration. "I'm not exactly turning you down. There *has* to be some way we can work it out. . . ."

Guy shook his head. "I don't see any solution."

"I do!" She went over to him and put her arms around his shoulders. "You can work in Grasse, and I'll be in New York. We'll get together as often as possible. I'll come to France whenever I can get away . . . and we'll take vacations together and . . ."

"And what am I supposed to do in the evenings, when I am tired from work? When I want to have dinner and talk to you? Tyger, to me being in love means being together. Not a few days every month or so, but all the time." He busied himself by scouring down the counter with a sponge. "I would rather not make love to you at all than once a month!"

"Guy! Be reasonable. Sooner or later it would all work out. For the time being, why can't we do it that way? Vacations together."

"It's *not* what I want, Tyger." He walked out of the room. Tyger followed him into the bedroom and watched him sullenly stretch out on the bed. He reached for a magazine, ignoring her.

"I'm not giving in!" she screamed. "Men always expect women to do what they want, but I won't . . . I can't. I love my job. I love my life! I'm not changing it, for you or anybody. I'd go crazy living in Grasse. What would I do all day?"

"There are jobs for women in France, too, you know."

"I don't want any job. I want *my* job!"

Tyger stalked out of the bedroom, grabbed her coat and purse and left.

For the next hour, she sat in the bar of the Carlyle, toying with a gimlet, listening to Bobby Short, and feeling miserable. She did not want it to end like this. If it was to be over between her and Guy, it should not end in squabbling and anger.

Tyger let herself back into the suite with her key. The living-room light was on, but Guy was not there. She walked back to the bedroom. He was in bed, under the covers. Tyger stood in the doorway, looking at him. Suddenly she realized with a start that his eyes were open.

"Oh, you're awake!"

"I haven't been able to sleep."

She slipped her clothes off, letting each garment fall to the floor. Guy watched her from the bed. She couldn't see his face well in the darkened room, but she knew that his eyes, like hers, were filling with tears.

Tyger climbed onto the bed beside him and pulled the covers back from his body. His arms remained at his sides. She touched his face, and his shoulders, and his chest, moving her hands down along the body she had come to know so well, memorizing it.

When she reached his loins, she felt him beginning to stir, and she wound her fingers around him, and felt him stiffen, almost reluctantly, beneath her touch. She bent down and very gently placed a kiss on the hardened tip.

"Tyger . . ."

With a little sob, she threw her arms about his neck and kissed him desperately, deeply in the mouth, and he stroked her hair and her breasts and her buttocks, and murmured, *"Tout sera bien, ma chérie.* Everything will be all right." And when he shifted his body and came into her, it was exquisite and perfect, like a brilliant comet that would not come again in this lifetime, but would live in the memory and heart forever.

Charles Allingwood was a short, ruddy man who had done all he could with meager physical attributes. His body, which tended genetically to stoutness, was firm and toned. His custom-tailored English suits were flawless, his hands perfectly manicured, his shoes hand-lasted and gleaming, his hair expertly woven. Until two days earlier he had been the president of a small Keller subsidiary in Palm Beach, Florida. Today, he was being briefed by his new staff in the office recently vacated by Sheldon Shaw in the Solow Building at Nine West Fifty-seventh Street in New York City.

"That's about the way it all stacks up, Mr. Allingwood," Jess Leibowitz was saying. "It's a hell of a stewpot to land in on such short notice."

"Call me Charlie, please. We're going to be working too closely together to stand on that kind of formality. Well, thank you, Jess. I know I can count on you and the rest of the team here to keep me floating until I can get my bearings."

"Absolutely," Tyger agreed with a smile. "Just as soon as we get ours."

"Well, what do you think?" Jess asked Tyger as they left the briefing.

"Who knows? He seems sharp enough. I'm surprised, though. I was sure Tim Yates would get the job."

"So was Tim. You know he's quit, don't you?"

"No! Are you sure?"

"Absolutely. Handed in his resignation to Hugh yesterday afternoon, right after Allingwood's appointment was confirmed."

"I can't believe it! Tim was Hugh's right hand."

"I guess with this Allingwood business, he got to feeling he didn't know what the left hand was doing. Anyway, it's just another of those wonderful little disasters that's made Keller Perfumes such an exciting place to work."

"Tim . . . he's always been in such a hurry." Tyger shook her head. "What's he going to do, Jess? Do you know?"

"Not for sure. But the rumor is that he's going over as president of Powers Perfumes."

On the fifteenth, the day of the launch concert and party, Tyger felt dead on her feet from all of the past weeks' details and disasters. She was going down her checklist, thinking about Matt Phillips and his cocaine and Dexedrines when Matt walked into her office.

"Good morning, darling." Matt smiled.

"Hi. Don't you look terrific . . . that's a great suit." He was wearing a soft wool tweed loose-fitting jacket and baggy trousers.

"For my new show. I just finished having it made for myself. Anyway, I came by to see how things are going. Do you need any last-minute help?"

Tyger was exhausted and her mind was foggy. "At this point, I don't know. Everything we've done for this party has alternatives. I'm telling myself there's nothing to worry about . . . but I know that dozens of things can and do go wrong at the last minute."

Matt helped himself to a cup of coffee from Tyger's filter pot. "I think we've had all the bad luck we're destined for. My clairvoyant says it'll be smooth sailing from now on."

Ginger buzzed Tyger on the intercom. "Marge Francisco called from Bloomingdale's. The shipment's arrived, but there's no toilet water, only perfume. Jess is out of the office. Can you handle it?"

Tyger smiled at Matt. "You were saying?" She made a few phone calls and got the matter straightened out. She poured herself a cup of coffee and tried to relax. "Have you seen Tasha?"

"Every day. She still has headaches, but she's okay. She'll have to wear one of those ugly neck braces for a while." Matt took off his shoes and massaged his toes. "She's suing Youngblood for divorce and damages. I hope she takes him to the cleaners. Her whole company was in his name, you know. Right now poor Tasha's got nothing."

Tyger's extension rang. She talked for a minute, then put down the phone with a sigh. "Only ten o'clock, and our second crisis. . . ."

"What?"

"An enormous blizzard in Vancouver, and Herbie Hancock's plane is grounded. The airport's closed and the meteorologist predicts snow till evening. There's no way he can get here for the concert." She sighed. "Matt, do you have any speed to carry me through the day?"

"No. . . . I've sworn off drugs."

Tyger shrugged. "Just as well."

Matt left the room and returned with a large flat box. "This is the main purpose of my visit. A dress for you to wear to the concert." He held up a strapless jet silk dress with a tiny neon-purple-and-pink print, and a black velvet jacket emblazoned with tiny ruby-and-amethyst-colored stones. "You whip off the jacket, and you're ready to boogie."

"Oh!" Tyger kissed his cheek. "It's fabulous, Matt. Thank you."

"And I think you should do your hair up, with some black feathers. . . ."

The intercom buzzed again. It was Ginger with news of another calamity: the press booklets, *The History of Jazz*, had arrived from the printers with several blurred and unreadable pages. Tyger looked at Matt. "It's one of those days. Better fire your clairvoyant, Matt. It's *not* going to be smooth sailing."

At a quarter to five Davis Chipps came in with the early edition of the Sunday *New York Times Magazine*. He laid it down on Tyger's desk, open to the two-page ad spread that was kicking off the nationwide Jazz campaign.

Tyger was already dressed in her new Matt Phillips creation.

"Whew!" Chipps whistled. "You look sensational! A little dressy for the office, maybe. . . ."

"Do you think so? All the secretaries are wearing them."

He laughed. "Here's the ad. Kate looks fabulous—but not as good as you."

"Why, Davis!" Tyger favored him with her brightest smile. "What a lovely thing to say."

"I've got to rush home and change. See you at the wingding tonight."

Alone, Tyger studied the ad. Jake's photograph had printed up beautifully. Kate Cassell, in a fire-engine-red satin dress slit high up the thigh, reclined along the top of an upright piano. Glitter sparkled in her tousled ebony hair. A derby-hatted piano player with gartered sleeves and soot-black skin sat at the keyboard, a cigarette dangling from his lips. In the smoky background a bassist and a drummer played. Martine F 'nier's sleek crystal flacon was superimposed on the foreground, and Kate looked out, smiling mysteriously, as if she knew the secret of the Sphinx. The copy headline read: "Jazz—the bare essence." Other ads were to feature Kate in different outfits and settings, with tag lines such as "Jazz—the bare essence of love," "Jazz—the bare essence of life," and so forth.

Tyger put the magazine down with a mixture of satisfaction and relief. Something had finally gone right. It was a good sign. Maybe the tide was turning. Maybe it was a harbinger of good things to come.

In the day's spate of disasters, the defection of Tim Yates troubled her the most. He had in fact gone to Youngblood's company. Confirmation came when an envelope had arrived by messenger shortly after noon. Inside was a printed business card. It bore the Powers Perfumes logo, and the inscription "Timothy Yates, President." On the back was scrawled a message: "I want to talk to you. Let's have one of our famous lunches. I'll call you. Tim."

Tyger took the card out again and looked at it. What seemed so wrong about it? Was it just the disloyalty to Hugh? Executives jumped to rival companies all the time, and Tim was a bright man who had set himself a tight schedule. It was reasonable to expect that he would do everything he could to keep to that schedule.

Then what was so chilling about this card?

For one thing, Tyger realized, it was the card itself. Tim

could not have accepted the Powers job before yesterday afternoon. Where had he had a card printed up so quickly? Or had this move been planned much farther in advance?

Suddenly a phrase popped into her head, as suddenly and as clearly as a needle dropping down on a phonograph record. It was something Tim had said when she called about Sheldon's suicide, something she had passed over in the shock of the moment.

Good God, Tim had said, *I never thought this would happen.*

What had he meant by that? What *had* Tim expected to happen? What had he known?

Something else came into focus. It was a scene at the party at "21" back in September, the party that had announced the association of Kellerco with Matt Phillips, and the birth of Keller Perfumes. It was a small tableau, one she had scarcely registered at the time: Tim Yates introducing Sheldon Shaw to Billy Youngblood. It was an unremarkable scene, and one that would hardly have stuck in her memory—except that Tim had mentioned at lunch a few weeks later that he did not know Billy Youngblood.

And it was after that that the trouble had begun.

No. It was earlier. At the party for Page Cutler, after Tyger's first interview with Hugh Marshall, before she even got the job. Billy Youngblood draping his sloppy arm about her shoulders, smirking that he knew Kellerco was launching a designer perfume, when the project was still top-secret. Nobody knew about it then, except a handful of top executives. Including Tim Yates.

And Sheldon Shaw had not yet arrived on the scene.

The intercom on her desk buzzed. Tyger jumped.

"Yes, Ginger?"

"Tyger, it's Tim Yates. Do you want to . . ."

"Yes, put him on."

Tim's voice was ebullient. "Well, Tyger. What do you think of the young man on the move?"

"I don't think you want to know."

"Oh, come on, don't be like that. I say, why don't we meet for a drink? I want to talk to you."

"For God's sake, Tim, don't be ridiculous. You haven't been gone from Kellerco for so long that you've forgotten what's going on tonight."

"Look here, Tyger, I have a proposal for you. I'm in a position now to make you a rather attractive offer."

"You're out of your mind, Tim," Tyger said coldly. "I wouldn't even consider such a thing. And I can't believe what you've done to Hugh."

"To Hugh?" Tim's voice dripped with bitter amazement. "What about what Hugh's done to me? Shaw's job was mine, you know it was. But Marshall doesn't want a strong man at that desk. Shaw! Allingwood! Bloody puppets, incompetents! I know Hugh Marshall, Tyger. He's an egomaniac. He'd have kept me down forever if he could. I've seen it coming a long time, and this was the last test, the last straw. I knew how it was going to turn out, but I gave him the chance to prove it. You mark me, he'll do the same to you just as long as you'll let him. I know the man, Tyger. You don't."

"It's you I wonder whether I know, Tim," Tyger snapped. "What was your role in the Shaw-Youngblood connection? What did you do to Sheldon?"

There was a heavy silence at the other end of the wire.

"I don't know what you're talking about, Tyger," Tim said at last. "I'm sure you don't, either."

"Maybe not, Tim. But how did you happen to have a business card all printed up and ready to go?"

"Youngblood had them done. It was one of his little ploys, a sort of a psychological bait, I suppose you could say. Really, Tyger, if that's your idea of . . ."

"And what did you mean when you said, 'I never thought *this* would happen,' when I told you Sheldon had jumped off the roof?"

"I . . . well, naturally—I mean, who thought it *would?*"

"Who thought about it at all?"

"Tyger, don't be an ass! We all knew that Shaw drank, that he was unstable. That's all I meant."

"I'll tell you what I think, Tim. I think you've been in Billy Youngblood's camp from the beginning. I think you've been playing both sides, waiting to see where your best chance would come. And I think as soon as you pegged Sheldon for a weakling, you set him up with Youngblood and told Youngblood it would be a safer cover with someone like Sheldon out front taking all the risks."

"O ho!" Yates snarled. "Hayes of the New Scotland Yard. Listen, Tyger, you can think what you bloody well like. But you'd better come up with some evidence before you go around shooting your mouth off about me. Oh, by the way— shall we forget about the job offer?"

"What offer?" Tyger slammed down the phone.

The concert at Madison Square Garden was sold out, as expected. Herbie Hancock did not make it from Canada, but there was enough stellar talent on hand to thrill the most exacting jazz buff. The press coverage was phenomenal: reporters showed up from all the local papers and TV stations, as well as *Time, Newsweek, Life, Rolling Stone, People,* and a dozen other publications. Of the 800 invited guests, a record 650 flashed their invitations at the gate. A special crew recorded the event, and the live-in-concert album would be offered before Christmas as a promotional gift with a purchase of Jazz. Another crew filmed the concert, for a possible TV special and showings around the country at the Kellerco subsidiary Christmas parties.

The huge loft in SoHo that Tyger had rented for the Jazz party after the concert had been transformed into a Twenties speakeasy. A small square peephole door opened to admit everyone who uttered the password, "Jazz."

Inside, round wooden tables and chairs encircled the ultra-polished dance floor, and electric-blue velour-covered booths were lined up against the walls. The walls themselves had been stenciled meticulously by a team of artists with music notes and black silhouette murals of jazz musicians playing horns.

Bartenders dressed as members of a 1920s jazz band administered drinks from a long mahogany bar, authentically battered and scratched from service in the Jazz Age. Behind the bar hung a series of large etched Art Deco mirrors, and large patchwork mirrored balls glittered from the ceiling. Specially installed paddle fans also descended from the ceiling and whirred lazily, dispersing the heat from the hundreds of bodies that packed the large loft.

In the back room—a space nearly as large as the front—there were pool tables as well as a full gambling casino with tables for roulette, blackjack, poker, and backgammon. A special permit had been obtained, and the proceeds from the gaming tables were to go to charity.

Three jazz bands played continuously through the night. Waiters in white shirts and black satin sequined vests passed around New Orleans-inspired hot and cold hors d'oeuvre—Creole shrimp, Bayou meatballs, barbecued chicken wings, oysters Rockefeller—and brass trays with glasses of champagne or bourbon punch.

The guests included the famous from all walks of celebrated life. The pens of the columnists were kept busy recording the presence and *bons mots* of such luminaries as Oscar and Françoise de la Renta, John and Elizabeth Taylor Warner, Geraldine Stutz, Kitty Carlisle Hart, Loulou de la Falaise Klossowski, Dustin Hoffman, and George Plimpton. Dress ranged from conservative black evening suits and tuxedos to extremes of glitter and undress: embroidered evening gowns, taffeta and velvet strapless ballerina-length gowns, tight-tight purple, fuchsia or black satin pants, gold and black mesh body suits, suede and snakeskin jackets, see-through chiffon tops, sheer red bosom-to-toe body stockings, ruffled can-can skirts, short-net tutus, beaded leotards, multicolored dance skirts with camisole tops, and one leopardskin bikini. A woman with short purple-and-green hair and an outfit to match walked in with a man in leather and feathers and spiky blue hair. There were elaborately ornamented head-dresses and high-high heels. The room was a fantasy of fashion, with many of the men as ornate as the women.

Jazz and Matt Phillips for Men were word-of-mouth successes. Samples had been passed out at the concert as well as the party, and the loft exuded the sultry Jazz fragrance. For the first half hour of the party Tyger was so busy tending to minor catastrophes that she hardly had time to talk to anyone. By midnight, the party was in full swing, and the liquor and food and music flowed sweetly.

Lady Bobbie had returned from Australia that day, and Tyger had had an invitation hand-delivered to her. In spite of jet lag she made a dazzling entrance, looking younger than ever in a black silk shantung evening dress with a sweeping skirt and a tightly fitted bodice embroidered with jet beads and passementerie. Heads turned as she entered, on the arm of John Garrison, the Australian newspaper tycoon.

"Tyger!" she called out to her daughter breathily. "Is this all your doing? I'm terribly impressed." Bobbie gave her daughter a kiss. "I want you to meet John Garrison. Soon to become your new stepfather."

Tyger was elated. "Oh, Mother! Why didn't you tell me on the phone?" She turned to her mother's fiancé. "So you're going to be my new dad?"

Garrison laughed. "Your mother's so young I'd rather fancy myself your brother, if you don't mind."

Bobbie laughed. She was relaxed when she had a man. "Remember, John, it's incest no matter whether you're father or brother!"

"Not if you're only related by marriage." His eyes crinkled and he winked at Tyger. "Come visit us in Sydney. Lots of eligible young men to squire you around . . . although your mother tells me you're not in the market for another marriage."

Tyger shook her head. "Not now, at least." She looked around and saw Guy in conversation with Jake and Astrid. She also spotted Hugh Marshall standing alone, surveying the event with a businessman's eye to its success.

John Garrison stepped away, and Bobbie put her arm around Tyger's waist. "Well? What do you think? Isn't John charming?"

"Yes. Much nicer than I expected. He has a reputation as a ruthless . . ."

Garrison reappeared, having overheard Tyger. He smiled. "Well, now, Tyger . . . you can't believe everything you read in the papers, now can you?"

Tyger made her way through the smoky maze of dancers to Hugh Marshall.

Hugh kissed her cheek. "Tyger, you've really done it."

"Thanks. Things are going well, aren't they? Matt Phillips seems as happy as I've ever seen him."

Hugh tenderly brushed a sequin off Tyger's shoulder. "You've come a long way from the slightly dizzyheaded beauty I interviewed last summer because Andy Parrish asked me to do him a favor."

Tyger bridled. "I was never dizzyheaded. . . ."

Hugh laughed. "I know. You'd never have been able to do all this without at least one foot on the ground." His face grew serious. "Tyger, I want to talk to you. Could we . . ."

"Hugh, love! *Here* you are! I've been looking all over for you." It was Bobbie. She turned to Tyger and smiled. "You don't mind if I borrow him, do you darling? After all, you get to see him all the time."

Tyger grabbed a glass of champagne from a passing tray and took a long swallow. *Damn!* she thought. Even engaged, Bobbie had an instinct for upsetting her timing with Hugh. Tyger shrugged, and smiled. She supposed that there would always be competition between her and her mother, and she was beginning to learn to live with it. In the past eight months she had learned a lot.

Tyger stood alone for a few minutes. Her eyes scrutinized the assembled group, and for the first time in her life she felt proud of herself. She was her own person now, no longer the "daughter of" or "wife of." She had a sense of her own worth; she finally knew where she was going.

"Tyger, you look so forlorn standing here by yourself." Guy put his arm around her. "Have you heard Jake's news?"

Jake and Astrid joined them. "We tied the knot at City Hall today. This party's our reception . . . hope you don't mind."

"Congratulations!" Tyger kissed them both. "When you're ready to leave we'll have to throw glitter . . . there's no rice." She paused. "It's amazing—my mother and John Garrison, now you two. Everyone's getting married." Tyger stopped. She had put her foot in her mouth. Guy removed his arm from her waist. She couldn't say anything to him now, with Jake and Astrid there.

Guy looked at her sadly. "Excuse me, I see some friends from Paris over by the bar. I have been wanting to speak to them all evening. . . ." He headed off through the crowd.

Tyger and Guy were met with a blast of cold air as they left the Spring Street loft. Guy had been brooding for the past couple of hours, and although Tyger was having a wonderful time, she wanted to be someplace quiet with him. Since the party was still in full gear, they decided to take a walk.

Even at five in the morning the streets of SoHo were not completely empty. "Look, Guy! Those people are wearing Jazz T-shirts. They must have been at the concert." Several women and a man passed by. "Oh, aren't you happy? Jazz is a hit. I overheard two editors from *Women's Wear* . . . one said the fragrance was 'inspired,' the other predicted that it would become a classic. And one of the *Times* reporters was grabbing handfuls of samples to take to the office. . . ."

"Yes, Tyger," Guy said quietly. "I am happy that Jazz is a success. It is good for my career. Pierre DeHavilland will be pleased. You know, he is like a father to me. . . ." Guy trailed off and they walked half a block in silence.

In front of the Spring Street Bar, Guy turned and put his hands on Tyger's shoulders. "Aren't you freezing? Your velvet jacket can't be very warm." He folded his arms completely around her and squeezed her hard. She closed her eyes and hugged him back. They clung to each other, then kissed. Their bodies and lips were close, touching, but their minds were standing back.

Guy pulled away slowly. He planted a gentle kiss on the top of Tyger's head. "I'm leaving, Tyger. For Grasse. Tomorrow . . . no, I mean *this* morning. I have my reservation."

"No, Guy, no!" Tyger said. "Not so soon. Wait a while, and we'll figure it out. . . ."

"There is nothing to figure out, Tyger. I guess we were not meant to be." He turned and headed down the street. Tyger ran to catch up with him.

"Guy, please! I'll have some free time after next month. I'll come over and we'll drive around. You can show me the *roses de mai,* and . . ."

"No, Tyger. You know how much I love you. I am in great pain . . . but I do not want you to come to France. Unless you change your mind about marrying me, I cannot bear to see you again. There is just no point. I do not want to have you with me one day and back in New York the next." He kicked an empty Pepsi can into the street. "I know that some people can live their lives that way, but I cannot."

"We could try, Guy. Please . . ." Her teeth were chattering. She wished they were home in bed together, snuggled under the down comforter.

A vacant Checker cab rounded the corner toward them. Guy stepped to the curb and raised his arm to hail it. The taxi screeched to a halt and backed up to them. "Tyger, there is no choice. If you change your mind, you know where to find me." He kissed her lips quickly. "Goodbye."

"Guy . . . at least let me go to the airport."

"No, that would be too difficult . . . for both of us." He touched her shivering shoulder and squeezed it gently. "You will always be with me, Tyger." Guy closed the door to the cab, and the large car drove off down the dark street.

Tyger watched as the cab turned right onto Houston and headed east. She stood under the streetlight at the corner of Spring and West Broadway for a long time. She did not know how long. She no longer felt the cold. She did not feel like returning to the Jazz party. Slowly, she became aware that she was alone in the street and she began to feel nervous. As she started toward Houston hoping to find a cab, she heard footsteps behind her. She quickened her pace. A familiar voice called out.

"Tyger! Wait!" It was Matt Phillips. "What on earth are you doing wandering the streets alone?" Matt was with his new lover, Eric Nebelthau. "We were just heading to the Empire Diner for breakfast. Want to join us?" He handed her an open bottle of Taittinger champagne. "Have a swig. You look nearly frozen."

CHAPTER THIRTY-ONE

THE newspaper reviews of Jazz, both the fragrance and the party, were raves. *The New York Times* had devoted half a page in the style section to the extravaganza, and *Women's Wear Daily* called Jazz and Matt Phillips for Men the season's "scent-sations."

Tyger arrived at the office at nine, still wearing her Jazz party outfit, makeup and hairdo. She wished she had gotten around to bringing in another change of clothes. She had been meaning to for the past two weeks.

Ginger was already there. "Did you just come from the party? Gosh, I was so tired I left at three. . . ."

"I'm going home to sleep. I just came in to make a few calls. I'll give you a list of things to take care of for me, if you don't mind. I'm completely wiped out."

"There are some flowers for you. Just delivered. I sat them on your desk."

Tyger went into her office. Red roses. The card said: "I will always remember you. Love, Guy." Tyger sat and stared at the flowers for a long time. "I'll always remember you, too, Guy," she said. After a while, she got up and started making coffee.

The phone rang. "I'll get it, Ginger," Tyger called out.

"Good morning, Tyger. I'm surprised you're not home sleeping." Hugh Marshall's voice showed no signs of weariness.

"I'm heading home for a nap in a little while."

"Stop by my office on your way, would you? I have some news." Hugh sounded chipper.

When Tyger walked into Hugh Marshall's office an hour later, there was a silver champagne bucket on his desk with a bottle of Louis Roederer Cristal Rosé champagne chilling.

"What's this?" she asked.

Marshall produced two iced goblets from the freezer in his bar. "We're celebrating . . . a lot of things." He twirled the bottle and pulled it glistening from its bed of ice.

"I'm not sure that champagne is what I need right now. I'm still feeling the effects of last night."

Hugh removed the cork with a soft pop and poured two glasses. "You're going home to sleep anyway," he reminded her. He handed her a glass. "To Jazz!"

The champagne was dry and delicious. The tiny bubbles rushed through her system, lifting her spirits. She looked at Hugh and smiled. There was a broad grin on his face.

"Hugh, what else?"

"I'd like to propose another toast. . . ." He paused dramatically. His blue eyes were vibrant. "To Nelson Bachrach, who resigned as chairman of the board of Kellerco . . ." He checked his Rolex. ". . . sixty-five minutes ago!"

"Oh, Hugh, that's wonderful! Will you be the new chairman?"

"I have an excellent shot at it. Even if I don't get it, there's no one on the board who can clog the wheels any more." He smiled. "I'm free to do things my way now."

Tyger sank down in one of the oversized leather chairs. "Congratulations, Hugh. I couldn't be happier."

He refilled their glasses. "The next thing on my agenda involves you. Feel like heading up the development of a Matt Phillips cosmetics line?" He stopped and waited for her reaction.

Tyger sat, staring at him; her face was still frozen in its last expression. "What did you say, Hugh?"

"I said, congratulations. I've just made you vice president in charge of new product development of Keller Perfumes."

"Oh, Hugh . . . I'm overwhelmed. . . ."

Hugh smiled. "Say thank you."

"Thank you." She smiled back at him.

"Do you think you will be recovered by this evening? I hoped you might have dinner with me."

Tyger smiled wryly. "Does this mean I'm fired?"

"What are you talking about?"

She dropped her voice in a deft imitation of his. "Tyger, I

never mix business with pleasure . . . work with women . . ."

Hugh laughed. "Oh—no, about dinner, I just thought we could talk over some thoughts about the new cosmetics line. I . . ." Tyger was looking at him, directly into his eyes, and there was a smile twitching at her lips. Hugh Marshall shook his head. "No, that wasn't it at all, was it? I wanted to have dinner with you because I've been thinking about you more and more for so long now that I can hardly think of anything else."

Her smile played more broadly. "Yes, Hugh? What have you been thinking?"

"Dammit, Tyger, don't you know? Do I have to spell it out?"

"Yes," she said. "I'm a vice president now. I have to have the data. I can't just play hunches."

He took a deep breath. "You're not going to make this easy for me, Tyger."

"Of course not. But then, you haven't made it very easy for me."

Hugh Marshall walked slowly over to her. He looked down into her green-flecked hazel eyes, tilting her face up to him with his hands. "I'm a little out of practice. . . ."

"So far you're doing beautifully."

She felt a tremor shake his body. It was as if years of tension were falling away.

"I love you, Tyger," he said.

"Oh Hugh, I . . ." She wanted to tell Hugh she loved him too, but his lips were on hers and he was kissing her. His arms went around her and she hugged him tight. His body pressed hard against hers.

She felt his urgency, and she knew they both wanted more than the office could safely provide.

"Shall we go to dinner now, Hugh? They have wonderful room service at the Plaza."

Hugh looked at her and grinned. "Oh, Tyger, you're wonderful." He kissed her again. "Come on," he said. "I'll have Annie cancel my meetings for the rest of the day."

The early-afternoon sun coming through the windows of the Plaza Hotel cast a square of light on Tyger's naked belly. Hugh Marshall rubbed it lovingly. Tyger looked up at him and placed a kiss with her fingertips on his lips.

"Where would you be now if you weren't here with me?"

He glanced at his watch on the bedside table. "In a meeting

with the president of Keller Computers and a group of money people."

"Sounds like fun."

"*This* is fun. You know, I've never done anything like this before."

She smiled at him with lascivious amusement. "Hugh . . . I know you're not a virgin. . . ."

"I am when it comes to this sort of reckless romance. I never really believed people fell in love like this." He kissed the bright patch of warmth on her belly.

"But we can't go on meeting like this." She smiled.

"I'd like to."

"So would I. But . . . oh, Hugh, when I first met you I thought you were the only thing in the world I wanted. I've found out that's not true." She got up from the bed and walked over to the window. "There's something else that's important too. Myself. This job. It means a lot to me, Hugh. I couldn't give it up. I love you, darling, but I couldn't . . . not even for you."

She turned almost fearfully to look at him. She was afraid he might be angry. Instead, Hugh Marshall was beaming. He came over to her and put his arms around her.

"I told you I wanted to have dinner to talk about the cosmetics line, didn't I? We have to get cracking on it if we want to have it in the stores by Christmas."

"Christmas?"

"Yes. We can do it, don't you think? It'll be hard work, but . . ."

They stood together, touching. Tyger's cheek rested against Hugh's shoulder, and she felt his hand tenderly stroking her naked buttocks. Below them the view of Central Park was the same one she saw from her office window.

Tyger Hayes smiled again. "Sure, Hugh, we can do it."

GREAT ADVENTURES IN READING

THE MONA INTERCEPT   14374 $2.75
by Donald Hamilton
A story of the fight for power, life, and love on the treacherous seas.

JEMMA   14375 $2.75
by Beverly Byrne
A glittering Cinderella story set against the background of Lincoln's America, Victoria's England, and Napoleon III's France.

DEATH FIRES   14376 $1.95
by Ron Faust
The questions of art and life become a matter of life and death on a desolate stretch of the Mexican coast.

PAWN OF THE OMPHALOS   14377 $1.95
by E. C. Tubb
A lone man agrees to gamble his life to obtain the scientific data that might save a planet from destruction.

DADDY'S LITTLE HELPERS   14384 $1.50
by Bil Keane
More laughs with The Family Circus crew.

Buy them at your local bookstore or use this handy coupon for ordering.

COLUMBIA BOOK SERVICE (a CBS Publications Co.)
32275 Mally Road, P.O. Box FB, Madison Heights. MI 48071

Please send me the books I have checked above. Orders for less than 5 books must include 75¢ for the first book and 25¢ for each additional book to cover postage and handling. Orders for 5 books or more postage is FREE. Send check or money order only.

Cost $_____   Name _____

Sales tax*_____   Address _____

Postage_____   City _____

Total $_____   State _____ Zip _____

* *The government requires us to collect sales tax in all states except AK, DE, MT, NH and OR.*

This offer expires 1 September 81   8106

Get Your
Coventry Romances
Home Subscription NOW

And Get These
4 Best-Selling Novels
FREE:

LACEY
by Claudette Williams

THE ROMANTIC WIDOW
by Mollie Chappell

HELENE
by Leonora Blythe

THE HEARTBREAK TRIANGLE
by Nora Hampton

A Home Subscription! It's the easiest and most convenient way to get every one of the exciting Coventry Romance Novels! ...And you get 4 of them FREE!

You pay nothing extra for this convenience: there are no additional charges...you don't even pay for postage! Fill out and send us the handy coupon now, and we'll send you 4 exciting Coventry Romance novels absolutely FREE!

SEND NO MONEY, GET THESE
FOUR BOOKS FREE!

━━━━━━━━━━━━━━━━━━━━━━━━━━━━━

G0281

MAIL THIS COUPON TODAY TO:
COVENTRY HOME
SUBSCRIPTION SERVICE
6 COMMERCIAL STREET
HICKSVILLE, NEW YORK 11801

YES, please start a Coventry Romance Home Subscription in my name, and send me FREE and without obligation to buy, my 4 Coventry Romances. If you do not hear from me after I have examined my 4 FREE books, please send me the 6 new Coventry Romances each month as soon as they come off the presses. I understand that I will be billed only $10.50 for all 6 books. There are no shipping and handling nor any other hidden charges. There is no minimum number of monthly purchases that I have to make. In fact, I can cancel my subscription at any time. The first 4 FREE books are mine to keep as a gift, even if I do not buy any additional books.

For added convenience, your monthly subscription may be charged automatically to your credit card.

☐ Master Charge   ☐ Visa

Credit Card # _____

Expiration Date_____

Name_____
(Please Print)

Address_____

City_____ State_____ Zip _____

Signature_____

☐ Bill Me Direct Each Month

This offer expires March 31, 1981. Prices subject to change without notice. Publisher reserves the right to substitute alternate FREE books. Sales tax collected where required by law. Offer valid for new members only.